Three Broth

Three Brothers Lodge Series

Morris Fenris

Published by Morris Fenris, 2021.

THREE BROTHERS LODGE SERIES

First edition. September 12, 2021.

Copyright © 2021 Morris Fenris.

ISBN: 979-8201982072

Written by Morris Fenris.

Morris Fenris

Three Brothers Lodge Boxset is a compendium of the following three books by author Morris Fenris.

1. Justin
2. Mason
3. Kaillar

All three books can also be purchased individually.

Book 1: Justin
Chapter 1

Late October, Colorado Mountains...

Jessica Andrews clutched the steering wheel so hard, her knuckles turned white. She was currently driving her old Ford Explorer through the passes in the middle of a snowstorm that was quickly becoming a full-on blizzard. It was the end of September and she'd not even thought about checking the weather report to learn the road conditions. The leaves hadn't even finished changing color, or dropping from their summer homes!

"Why did I decide a job in Colorado was a good idea?" she muttered to herself.

She'd left sunny Arizona two days earlier, with nothing but a suitcase of clothing that she now saw was going to be completely inadequate in her new place of residence. And a small cardboard box that held the few possessions that actually meant something to her. She was running away, and while she knew it wasn't the smartest move to make, she just didn't have the strength to stay and fight.

And it was all on account of her good for nothing ex-boyfriend, Jason Walker!

Just thinking his name put a sour taste in her mouth. She'd been dating the handsome football player for just under a year, and she'd convinced herself that her future was with him. "Guess that was my first mistake!" she said aloud.

She'd taken to talking out loud to herself; occasionally she had even been known to answer her own questions. She didn't consider herself crazy, just fed up!

Jessie had been raised by her elderly grandmother in a nice Christian household where attendance at church every time the doors were open was a foregone conclusion. Her mother and father had been called to missionary work in Africa years before, and when her mother had found out she was pregnant, they had put in a request to return stateside on furlough until after their daughter's birth.

Due to tremendous civil unrest and the rise of several Islamic terror groups in the region where they normally ministered, their return to Africa was delayed by eighteen months. At that time, neither of her parents had felt comfortable taking their young toddler to such a dangerous place. Her maternal grandmother had offered her a home while her parents were overseas, and her parents had gratefully accepted. They were only supposed to be gone a year and then they would return stateside once again.

Before leaving on furlough, they had begun working on a school that would allow native South Africans to study and learn how to become missionaries to their own people. It had been the popular protocol for overseas missionaries, and while they normally supervised these schools, her parents would be returning to the States and someone else would be taking over.

Jessie had been too young to realize the sacrifice that had been made by the adults in her life, but as she grew older, she'd come to realize that without her grandmother's sacrifice, she would have most likely died right next to her parents four months after their return to missionary work. Their deaths had been brutal and designed to send terror throughout the land. The Muslims didn't want the Westerner's coming into their land with promises of hope and Christianity. Their murderers had raided the school compound, brutally murdered everyone inside, and then filmed it and placed the films on the internet. The videos had been horrific, and as a result, other American missionaries in the region had been called home.

Jessie had been told all of this when she turned sixteen and started asking questions about her parents. Her grandmother had tearfully showed her the newspaper clippings and magazine articles written in response to the brutal murder of her parents and their entire missionary team. In all, nine Americans had been murdered that day. Thirty-three South Africans had also been killed, amongst them nine children under the age of ten.

That day had been a turning point for Jessie, although she kept her thoughts to herself until she'd graduated the next year and headed off to college. She always considered her parents heroes. They'd abandoned the comforts of home to help bring hope to a desolate land and its people. But after reading the articles, and doing some of her own research, she'd come to the conclusion that only an insane person would have willingly gone back to the region.

She blamed God for not protecting the very people he had sent to such a dangerous place. Her parents had been doing His work, and He'd allowed them to die, leaving her an orphan and hurting. What good was it to follow a God who wouldn't protect you? She'd managed to hide her broken faith from her grandmother as she finished high school, but her anger had only built inside, until she'd finally found an outlet.

Once she'd arrived on the college campus, she'd done her best to partake in all the things she knew went against her Christian upbringing. Parties. Drugs. Alcohol. And then she'd met Thomas in her first classroom clinical. He'd been a bright young man of eighteen, and throughout her sophomore year, she and Thomas became great friends. And then he'd been struck down with an aggressive childhood cancer. He died three months after being diagnosed, and once again, Jessica was left trying to come to terms with a God that allowed a little boy to die in such pain, and his parents to suffer so much grief.

She'd retreated into herself, abandoning the parties and every other social activity at school. She'd been immersed in her grief, and when she met Jason Walker at the end of her junior year, she was merely going through the motions.

Jason drew her out of herself, sweeping her off her feet and bringing a smile to her face for the first time in almost a year. Her teachers all commented on the difference, and even though a little voice inside told her that she was compromising her values to be with him, she became his steady campus girlfriend. She was the eye candy and easygoing girlfriend who demanded nothing and made him look good.

He was a receiver for the football team, a senior, and a promising future as a lawyer awaiting him. He was gorgeous and sought after by lots of girls on campus. But he'd chosen to spend his time with Jessica and that had made her feel special in a way she'd never felt when dating boys before him. She'd managed to retain some of her upbringing, never quite able to abandon her ideas about morality because of her grandmother. Jason had encouraged her to give up the few friends she'd made, telling her they were holding her back and asking too many questions. She'd done so readily, not really needing them, just needing an escape from her reality that Jason constantly provided. He created a fantasy world for her, and she lived there happily.

They'd both graduated and while he'd started law school, she'd begun working on her Master of Education. She'd been convinced that the lack of true emotion she felt for Jason was a good thing and her problem, not his. She'd talked herself into believing that a true emotional connection led only to heartache, and if she could just keep her distance, and still enjoy the benefits of being in a relationship, everything would be fine. The fact that Jason had been willing to keep his emotional distance as well had been seen as a bonus, not a warning sign!

But then she'd received a phone call in March just before completing her master's degree. The call had been the pastor of her grandmother's church, notifying her that her grandmother had passed away. Jessie had gone home a week early for Spring Break, packed up the few things she held dear, and given the rest to charity. The house had been sold and she'd used it to pay off her student loans, and stuck the rest of it in the bank.

Something had shifted in her thinking through that experience. Once again, she blamed God for taking someone she loved, the only family she had left in this world, away from her. She'd returned to school, determined to show Him what she thought about His kind of love. She'd ignored the doubts and inner voice that cautioned her she was going down a slippery slope, and forged ahead. She'd been determined to prove to herself and God that she didn't need His brand of help or guidance in her life.

She'd shoved her inner voice to the side, and even when it had been screaming at her that Jason was playing her, she'd ignored it. She'd convinced herself she was happy, and that Jason's recent inattention was just a phase their relationship was going through. She'd been so wrong!

The car's tires slipped on a patch of ice as she drove across one of the many bridges on this strip of road and she yanked the wheel into the slide, gritting her teeth as she brought the car back under control. *Guess that chapter in the driver's ed book wasn't a waste after all! I certainly would never have put it to good use living in Arizona!*

The car slipped again, this time careening towards the metal guardrail and she gripped the steering wheel so tightly her hands hurt. She took her foot off the gas pedal and looked steadily ahead. She could barely see the white line at the right side of the road now, and the way the snow was falling, she figured that wouldn't last much longer.

"I should have pulled off at the last town!" She'd filled up on gas at a small station and she'd ignored the conversations going on around her about the potential road closure coming. She'd hurried back into her car, pressing hard on the accelerator as she climbed in elevation and headed for the next mountain pass. The snow had been falling steadily for over an hour when she approached the bottom of Vail Pass. Two State Patrol cars had been parked there, the men unlocking the gate that would effectively shut down that stretch of highway until the storm passed. She drove straight through, pretending she didn't see them try to wave her down and stop her. "Dumb, Jess. Really dumb!"

An hour later and the highway was completely snow packed, and large flakes were coming down so fast, she was hard pressed to tell where the road began and ended. The white line was nonexistent, and she only prayed she was actually still driving on pavement and not the shoulder of the highway. She had her headlights on, even though it was still early afternoon, wanting to make sure she could be seen by any other vehicles on the road. *Not that there were any still moving!*

She passed several passenger cars that had pulled off the road, but there didn't seem to be any people in them. She guessed they had hitched a ride with other vehicles that were more suited to the snowy conditions, rather than be trapped on the mountain when night fell.

That thought was terrifying to Jessica so she kept moving forward. She reached the top of a big hill and briefly glimpsed a sign proclaiming it the "summit". It listed the elevation, but the numbers were already obscured by blowing snow that had partially covered the sign.

The highway seemed to be headed downward now, but it had also gotten icier as well. She found herself switching the aging SUV into low gear, thankful she wasn't having to apply her brakes quite as often, but wondering how long they would keep working before they overheated and gave out.

Her vehicle was in serious need of some maintenance, but as a struggling college student, she hadn't had the money in her budget for car repairs. Her grandmother had offered to help out however she could, but Jessica also knew her grandmother lived on a fixed income that was barely enough to keep one human being alive. She'd not wanted to burden her, and so she'd developed a policy of only telling her grandmother what she needed to know. The fact that her car had been in danger of falling into pieces was not on that list! Then her grandmother had died...

She looked at the gauges on her dashboard and bit her bottom lip. "Oh man! That is so not what I need right now." The thermostat was showing on the hot side! She rolled down the windows and turned the heater up to full blast, hoping to pull the extra heat away from the engine so she could keep making her way to the next town.

She'd missed the green sign informing travelers of that distance, and she only hoped it wasn't very far. A little voice inside her urged her to pray for help, but she ignored it. As she had been ignoring it for the last six years. She could do this, if she just kept inching forward. She would do this!

She might have made it too, if she'd kept her eyes glued to the road. But while she'd been fiddling with the heater, she'd failed to notice the large white truck parked off the road. She also hadn't been aware that she was driving more off to the side of the road than in her lane.

When she slammed into the back of the vehicle, both facts were made known to her as she hit the steering wheel with her forehead. She felt her car come to an abrupt stop; the sound of metal hitting metal ringing in her ears just before everything went black.

Chapter 2

T*hree Brothers Lodge, just above Silver Springs, Colorado...*
Justin Donnelly lifted the pan of lasagna from the oven and sat it on the stove. "Grub's ready," he called out to the two men he felt privileged to call brothers. They all worked together in the outfitting and guide business they'd inherited from their uncle. They also volunteered as firemen in the small town at the base of the mountain where they lived, and they were the key personnel in the search and rescue team for the county.

It was a perfect combination of being outdoors, helping people, and not having to wear a suit and tie to work every day. The three brothers couldn't imagine living anywhere else or doing anything else.

As winter had come suddenly to Colorado, their lives became much less complex and all three of them were looking forward to the holidays and a slower pace around the lodge where they lived. They'd just completed one of their best tourist seasons ever, and with the exception of a few backcountry hunting trips still scheduled, they were ready to settle in for the winter and relax.

Mason and Kaillar wandered towards the kitchen table, sniffing as they took their seats. "Smells good, man."

"Thanks. I made enough for leftovers as well," Justin told them, pulling out his chair and having a seat. They always made twice as much food as they would eat in one sitting, having gotten into the habit of eating leftovers the next day; it took the burden off of everyone in the household.

The men all took turns cooking and doing the laundry, and tonight was Justin's turn. He'd made his signature dish: lasagna, garlic bread and a tossed salad. Mason and Kaillar had just returned from a three-day hiking trip and he knew the pasta dish would be welcome. "So, how did things look up there?" he asked, scooping a generous portion of the lasagna onto his plate.

"Quite a bit of bear activity still, considering how much snow's already fallen," Mason said. He was the youngest Donnelly brother, having just turned 22 a few weeks back. He was the only one to have taken any college classes, but he'd quit over a year ago, the classroom having no more appeal for him. He wanted to be out in nature, not sitting in a classroom learning about it from a book!

"There's another storm brewing out there right now. I wouldn't be surprised if we didn't get a few feet out of this one," Kaillar added. He knew the ski slopes would be rejoicing at so much new snow, and he was right there with them. He loved to ski and was looking forward to his fifth year on the ski patrol team. He'd also started a youth ski-racing program several years earlier, and was looking forward to the competition season starting up again. He had some very promising youngsters on his team, and was looking forward to seeing them reach their full potential.

"I hope everyone out there pays attention to the weather reports. It would be nice to get through this month without any major incidents." Justin's hope was echoed by his brothers. It seemed every year about this time, at least one hiker, group of college kids, or motorist decided to test their mettle against the mountains. Funny thing – the mountains almost always won! Especially with winter arriving so suddenly. The mountains were unpredictable right now, and getting caught unaware in one of the first major snowstorms of the season was never a good idea.

"This storm's going to blow over fairly quick. Couple of days at most."

"Good thing. We have hunters coming in next week. Any idea where we're going to take them?" Kaillar asked, referring to the upcoming big game rifle season that was set to begin in just a few short days.

"Yeah. I think so. I didn't have a chance to collect the game cameras this afternoon." Justin glanced at the clock hanging on the wall above the stove and nodded his head. "Maybe I should run up and collect them before it gets any worse out there." He took a look out the large picture windows in the front of the lodge and then changed his mind. "On second thought, maybe not. It's really starting to come down."

"We can go get them when the storm's over. The hunters aren't due in until Sunday night," Mason reminded him.

"Good." Justin sat back down and dug into his own meal.

The three brothers knew the mountains around their lodge like the back of their hands. They'd been guiding hunters for the last five years now, and found the additional income came in handy during the long months of winter. They occasionally hunted themselves, having first learned with their uncle when they were too young to get their own licenses.

They had thrived under their uncle's guidance, something that never happened while in their mother's care. Their mother, Maria Donnelly, had left Silver Springs more than thirty years earlier. The small mountain town of two hundred people was not nearly exciting enough for her. Her quest for fame and fortune had taken her first to Los Angeles, and eventually on to Las Vegas.

Unfortunately, her talents hadn't been spectacular enough to earn her a place among the stars of the movie screen and she'd quickly wound up getting involved with the wrong crowd. Drugs and alcohol had taken over her life, and then she'd gotten pregnant with Justin.

She'd come back to Colorado, but the strain of trying to live up to her parents' expectations had sent her fleeing back to Las Vegas, back to the boyfriend who'd discovered she was willing to do almost anything to score her next bag of heroin.

Her brother, Jed, had gone to Las Vegas and hauled her back several times, but nothing had been able to break her addiction to the drugs. She'd tried two more times to get her life together, coming home before Mason was born, and then again after Kaillar had entered the world, but the lure of the drugs always won over her responsibility to the three little boys she'd brought into the world.

When Justin was four, she'd run for the last time – leaving her three children behind with her brother. The Las Vegas authorities had called a few days later to say they had found her body badly beaten and abandoned in one of the seedier parts of the city.

Jed had gone down and collected her body; returning home, he'd arranged for her to be buried next to her parents. Her father had died of a heart attack shortly after Justin had been born, and her mother died of a broken heart a short time later. With no other siblings, her children had been parentless, but not without family.

Jed had applied to become their permanent guardian, and the once confirmed bachelor had become an instant father of three little boys, ages four, two and six months. His sister had neither known nor cared who the fathers of her children were. Jed had more than made up for their absence. He'd treated the three boys as his own, but rather than allowing them to call him dad, he'd made sure they kept the familial connection straight by calling him Uncle Jed.

He'd made many sacrifices for the three boys, leaving behind his preference for a solitary life on his mountain to that of regular interaction with the small town below. He'd learned to socialize with the townsfolk for his nephews' sake. Something the three brothers would never forget.

He'd passed away several years earlier. Justin had been working overseas as a helicopter pilot in the Middle East, making tons of money by putting himself into dangerous situations. When he'd received the call about his beloved Uncle Jed, he'd quit and come home. And he was still here several years later.

Mason and Kaillar had both expressed a desire to take their Uncle Jed's outfitting operation to the next level. With their uncle's life insurance money, and Justin's more than adequate savings account, they'd remodeled the lodge where they'd grown up, built several tourist cabins, and become well known as one of the best guide services in this part of Colorado.

The phone rang and Kaillar got up to answer it. A few minutes later, he replaced the receiver and frowned at his brothers. "We might have a situation."

"Might have?" Justin inquired, never having met a situation that was stuck in limbo. Either it was a situation requiring their assistance, or it wasn't. "What's up?"

"That was Shelby over at the Frisco dispatch office. She said a vehicle got through the snow gates at the west side of Vail just as the patrolmen were closing the gates. They tried to wave the driver back, but the vehicle just kept going."

"Oh, yeah?" Mason asked. "They're on the pass?"

"Shelby assumes so. That was over an hour ago and they've been monitoring the cameras along the highway for the vehicle. An older model Ford Explorer, dark blue with a rack on top. Arizona license plates."

"Maybe they missed it?" Mason offered.

Kaillar shook his head. "Shelby doesn't think so. They have the vehicle passing the summit thirty minutes ago, but it never made it to the next camera."

Justin was silent, and then he confirmed what they were all thinking. "Well, that only leaves about two miles of highway. Maybe they pulled off..."

"They never made it to the Minturn turn-off."

Justin looked at his brothers and then made a decision. "I'll take a tracker out and look for the vehicle. You two just got back and need some down time."

"Not happening. You know the cardinal rule is that we never go on a search and rescue op without backup. Since we're the only available backup, which means you're stuck with us tagging along."

"Any other vehicles up there that haven't shown up?" Justin asked, starting to put the leftover food away in the fridge. If they were going out in the weather, he wanted to make sure everyone that might be stranded was located.

"Shelby mentioned something about two other vehicles as well. There's something else you should probably know."

"Yeah?" Justin asked. The more information, the more efficient he could be. The fact that the missing vehicle had Arizona plates meant the driver might have no experience whatsoever in winter driving conditions. A sure recipe for disaster in a storm like the one currently raging outside.

"The vehicle's being driven by a woman. They have her on camera at the Edwards pullout getting gas. The attendant remembered her because she looked completely exhausted."

"And they're sure they saw her car pass the summit?" Justin asked, already thinking how nasty checking the pass was going to be tonight. Even just two miles of it.

"Yeah. Her car headed down thirty minutes ago." Kaillar looked at his brothers and then stated, "They're asking for our help to find everyone and get them to safety. At this point, the weather forecast is looking much worse than they originally thought. It's going to get cold tonight when the snow stops. Really cold. They're saying it could hit the low teens."

Justin shoved the leftover lasagna into the fridge and then headed out of the kitchen. "Well, then I guess we better get geared up and head out before it gets dark. We've only got a few hours of daylight left, and I don't want to be checking those roads in the dark."

"Me either. I'll go get the trackers out." Mason took two more bites of his dinner and then headed for the front doors of the lodge. "Might start a new pot of coffee to take with us as well."

Kaillar was already in the kitchen, his mind on the same wavelength as his brother's. "I'll meet you all in the barn."

Justin nodded and then headed for the stairs that led to the bedroom suites the brothers each occupied. He pulled his cell phone from his pocket as he climbed the stairs, placing a call to Jeremy Phillips, the pastor of the small church in Silver Springs.

"Justin?" Jeremy answered, concern evident in his voice.

"Hi, Pastor. Sorry to disturb your afternoon."

"No problem. What's up?"

Justin sighed. "We're heading out in a few minutes to check the pass. Shelby called from Frisco and they've got several vehicles on the pass that haven't reached the other side yet. We're going to try and find them before dark."

"Son, you and your brothers have my prayers. What can I do to help?"

"That's more than enough. I just wanted to let you know that I might not make practice tomorrow morning."

"Justin, don't worry about that. I'll get one of the high school boys to step in and help with basketball practice. If we even have it. This storm's looking rather fierce at the moment."

"Thanks, Pastor. Gotta go."

"May heavenly angels guide your steps this afternoon."

Amen! Justin pocketed his phone and grabbed his winter gear from the closet. His uncle had made sure his nephews went to church and had the opportunity to develop their own relationship with God while they were growing up. Each of them had taken their own path to get there, but Justin had no doubts in his mind that the Donnelly brothers were God-fearing, Christian men. He'd seen firsthand the power of prayer, and he never missed an opportunity to allow the good people of Silver Springs to put their faith into action.

He headed to the barn, seeing that his brothers were already out there and almost ready to go. Joining hands, he met their eyes, and in a tradition that had been first started by their uncle, they bowed their heads and asked for divine guidance for the next few hours.

"Amen. Mount up, boys." Justin climbed aboard his tracker, the large enclosed vehicle that was the perfect fit for snowy mountain roads. There were skis on the front, and large snow tracks on the rear. The vehicles could only go about thirty miles an hour, but that didn't worry Justin. According to Shelby, they only needed to check about two miles of highway. Under normal conditions, that would take less than an hour, but in this storm, two miles were going to feel like twenty!

Chapter 3

A half hour later, the Donnelly boys arrived at the highway and they split up. Justin and Kaillar took the eastbound lanes, with Mason taking the westbound lanes. Shelby had called back just as they were reaching the highway stating that two people had just walked in, having gotten a ride from another motorist into Frisco. The problem was of a medical nature, the man desperately needing the medication he'd forgotten in their car. They had pulled over just beyond the turnoff that led to Silver Springs.

Mason had offered to go down, retrieve the pills, and drive them into Frisco. From there, he'd spend the night with friends if it got too late, or he'd take the ridge trail home. Justin and Kaillar would locate the missing vehicles, three of them according to information they'd been given.

Within the first mile, Justin and Kaillar came across the first two vehicles. They had pulled off the highway within thirty yards of each other, making recovery of the people quick and easy. A single businessman occupied the first car, and two college boys occupied the second. All three were grateful for the rescue and Kaillar loaded them into his tracker and headed back to the highway turnoff. There was a small motel in Silver Springs, run by a native of Silver Springs and widower, Sarah Jenkins. She would be more than willing to put up the stranded travelers for a night or two.

Justin continued up the eastbound lane. He was almost at the two miles that would put him at the next camera location when he saw the bright yellow of headlights covered in snow off to the side. As he approached the vehicle, he realized there was a second vehicle, a white oversized truck parked in front of it. It wasn't until he was right up on the cars that he realized the SUV had crashed into the truck.

He quickly parked his tracker and checked the truck first. It was empty and had an orange patrol tag on the windshield indicating the vehicle had been abandoned there prior to the start of the storm.

The small SUV was a different story. It matched the description of the vehicle that had slipped through the gates just before they were closed. A woman was crumpled against the steering wheel. He tried the door, but it was locked. He rapped his knuckles on the window, but she was completely unresponsive.

A gust of wind and a new shower of snow sent him back to the tracker for something to break the window with. He used the handle of his safety axe to smash the rear passenger window. Once he had the glass cleared, he reached inside and unlocked the doors with the electric locks. He wasn't sure how long it had been since the crash, but the battery was still working and for that, he was thankful.

He hurried around to the driver's side door and eased it open. His brows lifted at the attire of the occupant. She had on a pair of thin pants made of a stretchy material, with only a thin t-shirt covering her upper torso. He glimpsed a lightweight jacket sitting on the seat next to her purse and her cell phone sitting in a holder on the dashboard.

"Ma'am? Can you hear me?" he asked her, removing his glove and placing his warm fingers along the side of her neck. Her pulse was strong, but she was out cold. And her skin was icy to the touch. There was a small trickle of blood running down past her ear, and he gently lifted the blonde locks up, seeing a large bruise on her forehead. A small cut near the edge of the bruise was the source of the blood. He reached for the box of tissues sitting in the passenger seat and dabbed at it. He reached for her purse, grabbed her wallet and discovered that her name was Jessica Andrews.

"Jessica? Can you hear me? I need you to open your eyes and tell me if you're hurt anywhere besides your head. Come on now, sugar. Open your eyes." Justin jiggled her shoulder slightly, not wanting to cause her further injury by moving her without first clearing her neck and spine. Normally, he'd wait for backup to get there and then remove her, being careful to keep her spine straight. He'd place a collar around her neck as well – everything possible to prevent aggravating any hidden spinal cord injury that might be present. He'd seen firsthand what could happen when those extra protocols weren't followed, but extreme situations called for extreme measures.

He didn't have that luxury of following all the safety protocols right now. The snow was continuing to fall, the sun was preparing to set, and it was mighty cold outside! And only going to get colder! He shivered and called to her again, placing his icy hand against her cheek. "Jessica! Open your eyes! Now!" He raised his voice, hoping to get some response from her.

She moaned and slowly her eyelids started to flutter. She opened them a few seconds later and Justin felt his heart jump inside his chest. Her eyes were the most unusual color of green he'd ever seen. He lowered his voice: "Welcome back. My name is Justin and I'd love to get you out of the cold and someplace warm, but I need to know if you're hurt anywhere besides that nasty bump on your head."

She blinked slowly and then groaned as she pushed herself back in the seat. She lifted a small hand to her forehead and then winced when she touched the large bruise forming there. "What happened?"

"Well, my guess is that you ran into the back of that truck," Justin nodded towards the large truck sitting a few feet away.

She started to nod and then winced. "Yeah. I remember it came out of nowhere. Is anyone hurt?"

"There wasn't anyone in the truck. It was abandoned before the storm started. You ran into it."

"Why didn't they pull it off the road!" she asked, her voice rising slightly. Hysteria was close to the surface and she tried to keep it at bay.

"They did. You weren't driving on the road."

Her shoulders slumped as she realized she could have just as easily ran her vehicle off the side of a cliff. She closed her eyes. "That explains it. I couldn't see..." She opened her eyes and looked outside where night was falling fast. "It's still snowing."

"It sure is and we need to get off this mountain pretty quick. Do you think you can walk if you lean on me?"

"Where would we go?" she asked, closing her eyes again in obvious distress.

"Well, as much as I'd like to get you down to the hospital tonight, I don't think that's wise now that it's getting dark. My brothers and I run a lodge about five miles from the summit. It will be warm and dry there until morning."

Jessica opened her eyes and glanced at him. "My head hurts."

"We'll get you something for that as well. Now, hand me your purse and I'll go put it into the tracker and then come back for you. Is there anything else you need out of your vehicle tonight?"

"I only have one suitcase and a cardboard box with me."

"Okay. Do you need them tonight?" he inquired, wanting to get moving soon.

"Maybe the suitcase?" she asked softly.

"Got it. Sit tight and I'll come help you in just a few minutes." Justin retrieved her suitcase and then put it and her purse in the back seating area of the tracker. The snow was making things very slippery. He grabbed her keys and then held onto her arm as she slowly swung her legs out of the car.

When she slipped on the road, he looked down and realized she was wearing tennis shoes. Her short stature was hard to miss and he placed her at 5'6" and maybe one hundred and ten pounds. She was much too thin to his way of thinking, and he found himself wanting to feed her one of his home-cooked meals.

He felt her shiver and realized he'd allowed his mind to wander. Smiling through the falling snow, he placed a guiding arm around her shoulders, urging her towards the tracker and their salvation.

The snow was already above her ankles, and he smiled when she said with a grimace, "I already hate snow!"

"Best get used to it if you plan on staying in Colorado long. Winter's not even officially here yet."

"Great!" she told him, once again regretting her decision to move here. She'd wanted a change of scenery and to get away from Arizona. "You've certainly accomplished that! What were you thinking, Jess?"

Justin looked down at her. "Excuse me?"

Jessica blushed, realizing she'd just spoken her thoughts out loud. She would definitely have to work on that bad habit. Otherwise, the people she'd yet to meet would definitely think she was missing a few screws in her head.

"Sorry. I was talking to myself."

"Ah. Well, don't worry about it. I've been known to do that a time or two myself." They reached the tracker and he opened the door, helping her get situated on the vinyl seat and then pulling the safety strap across her lap and fastening it.

"Thank you," she murmured to him just before he could shut the door. Her head hurt, but not so much that she didn't get a whiff of his aftershave. It was one of her favorites and one she'd always wanted Jason to wear, but he'd been adamant that he didn't like the way it smelled on him. *In reality, it was his fiancée who hadn't liked the way her favorite cologne smelled.* "I was such an idiot!"

He looked into her eyes and smiled. "Well, I don't know that I would agree with that. And you are very welcome. Let's get you back to the lodge and warmed up." He'd noticed she was shivering, so he slipped his jacket off and draped it across her front.

"Wait! I can't..."

"You're freezing. I'll be fine, and the tracker has a really good heater. Sit tight." Justin quickly made his way around to the driver side and climbed in. He cranked the heater up on high and slowly turned the tracker around, heading it back down the mountain.

He grabbed the radio and called Kaillar first. "Kai, you there?"

"I'm here. I just finished getting the travelers set up in Silver Springs. Did you find the other vehicle?"

"Yeah. I've got her. She's got a nasty bump on her head, but I don't want to try taking her all the way to Frisco in the dark."

"Roger that. It's really getting nasty out there. I'm looking at the Doppler radar for the mountain and this storm isn't going away anytime soon."

"Got it. Have you heard from Mason?"

"Yeah, he's good as well. Got the man his meds and he's going to head over to Jenna's for the night. She and Tyler are in Denver so their place is empty. He'll head home once the storm clears."

"That sounds good. I'm heading home with Jessica. With that bump on her head, I don't want to leave her alone tonight. You heading back up to the lodge?"

"Yeah, in a bit."

"Good. Do me a favor – stop by the clinic and see if Dr. Matthews is working this afternoon. If he is, tell him to expect a call from me in an hour."

"Will do. She going to be okay tonight?"

Justin glanced at his passenger. Her face was pale, her eyes closed with a frown between her eyes. She was in pain, but before he could do anything about that, he wanted to make sure she didn't have a concussion or any other injuries that might require immediate medical intervention.

"Justin?"

"Yeah, I'm here. I think she's gonna be fine. I'll know once I get her back to the lodge."

"Okay. I'll find the doc for you. Be careful getting home."

"I will. See you in a bit."

Chapter 4

Jessica huddled under the jacket of the man sitting next to her. Her head was throbbing in time with her heartbeat, her feet had begun to thaw out and were soaking wet, and she realized she was now headed to some isolated cabin with a man she didn't know.

But he rescued you, so doesn't he get some points for that? I mean, how many guys would come out in the middle of a blizzard to rescue people who didn't have the common sense to know they should have pulled off at the last town?

Jessica closed her eyes and wished the seat was tall enough to lean her head back on. It was growing darker by the minute, the storm having completely obliterated the waning sun. She turned her attention to the man next to her, his hands expertly steering the machine across the expanse of snow with the confidence of someone who'd done the same thing many times before.

They'd left the highway five minutes earlier, and were now making their way through the forest. She didn't see any signs to guide their way, and she only hoped he truly did know where he was going.

She tried to see where they were going, but the headlights only lit up a small area of the ground in front of them and lots of very tall trees. A sense of claustrophobia assailed her and she swallowed to try and stem a growing sense of fear.

"You hanging in there?" Justin asked, his baritone voice soft in the relative silence of the late afternoon.

"Umm...We're not lost, are we?" she asked before she could stop herself.

Justin chuckled. "No. We're not lost. In fact," he reached across her and pointed to her right. "If you keep your eyes fixed over there you should see the lights of the lodge in just...about...*now*." He slowed the tracker down as they rounded the last stand of trees and watched her face as she caught sight of the lodge for the first time.

It was a two-story log cabin, very large with a wraparound porch and rustic log furniture situated here and there. Everything was covered with a fine dusting of snow, and she looked at it with a look of wonder upon her face. "It's like something from a Christmas card."

To the right of the lodge stood a very rustic, and yet modern-looking barn. Corral fences, partially buried in the snow drifts, stretched out from either side, and the red metal roof was only visible in small patches where the snow had yet to pile up.

Justin chuckled. "Well, I don't know about that. Let's get the tracker put away and then I'll show you where you can clean up a bit. I want to check your head out as well and I'm trusting you to let me know if you have any other aches or pains."

Jessica nodded, never taking her eyes from the log cabin. There was something about it that was so comfortable and welcoming; she felt tears sting her eyes. It looked like a home! She hadn't felt that way since the last time she'd been home while her grandmother was still alive. Remembering that visit brought more tears to her eyes. *I was so horrible and secretive.*

Her grandmother had known something wasn't right, but even though she'd asked, Jessica hadn't been able to tell her grandmother how far from her values she'd fallen. Her grandmother would have been so disappointed in her. *But not as disappointed as I am in myself.*

Her grandmother had tried to get her to go and speak with the pastor of the small church she'd grown up in, and Jessica still remembered how hurt her grandmother had been as Jessica proceeded to tell her that she didn't need a pastor to diagnose what was wrong with her. And she certainly didn't need God to fight her battles for her.

In her mind, God was the reason for her troubles. He'd taken her parents, never allowing her to have a healthy relationship with the two adults who should have been a major influence in her life. And then she'd allowed her blind faith to translate from a spiritual one into a romantic one. And it had let her down. She couldn't trust herself, and she definitely didn't feel like she could trust the God who'd let her parents die. She wasn't sure she had any trust left in her when it came to her emotions.

She lost the battle to stem her tears. When they spilled over, she reached up and wiped them away, unaware that her companion had seen her.

"Hey! Why the tears?" Justin asked, concern in his voice.

Jessica shook her head and then immediately regretted the movement. "Ow! Sorry, I'm just tired." She didn't want to analyze the reason for her tears, and she definitely didn't want a stranger passing judgment on her.

Justin looked at her and she held his gaze until he nodded and looked away. He started the tracker moving forward again and drove it straight into the barn. Once he had the barn doors secured, he helped her down and then grabbed her purse and her suitcase. When he slipped the strap of her purse over his shoulder, she couldn't contain her grin.

"What?" he asked her.

Jessica bit her lip and then told him, "You put my purse over your shoulder like a pro. Do you carry your wife's purse a lot?"

Justin glanced at her purse and then laughed at himself. "No wife."

"Girlfriend, then."

Justin shook his head, escorting her out the side door and down the covered walkway. "No girlfriend. And to my knowledge this is the first purse I've ever worn on my shoulder."

"Really?" she asked as if she didn't quite believe him. *This gorgeous guy doesn't have a girlfriend or a wife? What's wrong with him?* She'd been observing him since he rescued her and right off the top of her head, she couldn't answer her own question. He seemed like a genuinely nice, straightforward guy. A rarity for sure.

"Really." He took her elbow as they climbed the four steps leading up to the porch. "Watch your step." He opened the door and then allowed her to enter first.

Jessica couldn't see enough as she stepped inside his home. An open concept allowed her to see through most of the lower level, her view only obstructed by the large staircase that led upstairs. A large fireplace took up the wall to her left, bracketed on both sides by floor-to-ceiling windows. Comfortable couches and chairs were arranged in front of the hearth, with colorful throw pillows and blankets draped here and there. The place was huge!

Polished wood floors gleamed throughout and vibrant area rugs tied everything together just so. The lighting fixtures were even a bit rustic, with a huge antler chandelier hanging over the foyer.

"This place is amazing!"

Justin looked around his home and then shrugged. "We call it home."

Jessica continued to turn her head, trying to take in everything and failing. To her right, a large pool table with dark wood and red felt occupied the space. Behind it, a wooden bar stood with stools in front and a gleaming, polished wood bar top, and a large mirrored wall behind. She sniffed the air and realized there was a wonderful smell of basil and garlic in the air.

Justin was watching her and then he smiled. "Hungry?"

Jessica bit her lip again and nodded. "I could eat."

"Good. Come on back to the kitchen with me. I made lasagna earlier this morning and we had just finished eating when we got the call to go rescue some motorists."

"Meaning me?" she asked, feeling guilty for having been the reason this man and his brothers had been out in such nasty weather.

"You were one of the reasons. But you weren't the only one. Kaillar took three people down to Silver Springs a short time before I found you. Speaking of which, come sit down and let me look at your head."

Jessica hung back. "Do you think I could clean up a bit first?"

"Sure. The second door to your right is a bathroom. There should be towels under the sink. Come back out when you're finished and I'll have some dinner heated up for you." He watched her walk away, finding himself curious about her story. She'd been travelling very light, and yet she wasn't dressed for a Colorado winter. Her driver's license had been from Arizona, and he wondered if she was just passing through.

He retrieved the lasagna from the fridge and placed a healthy portion on two plates. While they reheated in the microwave, he placed a call to Doc.

"So, how's your traveler?" Doc asked without preamble.

"Well, she's got a goose egg on her forehead with a small cut, but it had already stopped bleeding by the time I got to her. She seems to be ambulating okay and no dizziness to speak of."

"How are her pupils and color?"

"She's got good color in her cheeks and her pupils seem to be reacting normally."

"Well, she sounds fine so far. Headache?"

"Yeah, she did complain of a little headache, and my guess is she's going to have some muscle soreness by tomorrow."

"She could take a couple of over-the-counter painkillers tonight for the headache. I don't want to give her anything too strong. A good night's sleep will go a long way toward recovery."

"She looks pretty tuckered out. I figure she's been driving nonstop for the last few days. There's dark circles under her eyes and she looks a little thin to me."

Doc cleared his throat and then asked, "Do I sense more than a passing interest in your guest?"

Justin chuckled. "Trying to fix me up?"

"Sounds like you're well on the way to fixing yourself up. Can't say it would hurt my feelings to see you boys happily married and settled down."

"We'll get around to it one of these days. Don't worry."

"Oh, I'm not worried. But you're the last three bachelors in Silver Springs, and with everyone else married and already having babies, you and them brothers of yours are lagging behind."

Justin laughed. "Not every single male in Silver Springs is married."

"No, the ones that aren't are either too old to be thinking of such things, or still in need of their mommas taking care of them. All I'm saying is when a single young woman comes to town, whether by accident or not, you shouldn't pass up an opportunity to test the waters."

"Thanks for the advice," Justin told him, not taking offense since it seemed most of the older folk in town had decided the Donnelly brothers were in need of help finding their wives. The ladies' circle at church had even tossed around the idea of inviting the single adults from the neighboring towns to a Friday night get-together.

So far, Pastor Jeremy had been successful in staving them off, but with the holidays fast approaching, he'd heard the rumblings again and it seemed matchmaking was in the air. Justin made a mental note to pass the warning along to his brothers.

He heard the faucet in the bathroom turn off and opened the microwave door. He removed the plates of lasagna and then set them on the table. He added slices of crusty bread and two glasses of ice water. He was just placing the butter on the table when she reappeared in the doorway. He glanced up and asked, "Feel better?"

Jessica nodded slowly and then walked forward. "It smells delicious."

"Thanks. How's the head?"

"It's okay. Sore. Maybe I could have some ice?"

Justin shook his head, opening the freezer drawer and pulling out a frozen bag of peas, "Better than ice. It conforms to your body part."

Jessica took the bag of peas and the dishtowel he handed her, placing it on her forehead before commenting, "You speak as if from experience."

"I have two brothers, and more experience than I like to remember."

"You and your brothers fought a lot?"

"No! But like all boys, we got into lots of mischief. What about you? Any brothers or sisters?"

Chapter 5

Justin didn't expect his question to have such an effect on her. She paled and then turned away from him, returning to the dining table and sitting down. Following her, he asked, "Jessica?"

"Jess."

"What?" he queried, sitting down and watching her carefully.

"My friends call me Jess. Or Jessie."

"Okay. Jess, you never answered my question."

She sighed. "No siblings. Not even any parents I actually remember." *I would have loved to have brothers and sisters.* Growing up, she'd longed for the companionship of someone other than her grandmother. Never one to make friends easily, she'd known a few girls she called friends, but they'd never been the type of friends one hung out with at the mall, or even had sleepovers with. Those types of friends hadn't existed for Jessica while growing up.

"Wow! I'm sorry. About your parents," Justin clarified.

Jess cringed, wishing she could have held back that last statement. *Way to put how you really feel right out there, Jess!*

"Yeah, well they made a decision and it cost them their lives. At least they left me with my grandmother before they allowed themselves to get killed."

Allowed themselves to get killed? Justin reached for the butter. "Your grandmother raised you?" He steered away from the topic of her parents for the moment.

"Yes." Jessica had a smile upon her face, but it was strained.

"What's she think about you moving to the mountains of Colorado?" he asked with an easy smile on his face.

Jessica felt her heart clench, and she mumbled, "She's dead, so it doesn't matter what she thinks."

"Again, I'm sorry." Sensing that a change of subject was needed, Justin picked up his fork and then gestured towards her plate. "Eat, and then maybe we can watch a movie. It's still early."

Jessica set the bag of peas down on the table and placed her napkin in her lap. She took a bite of her food and then looked up at him in surprise, "This is really good."

"Thanks. I enjoy cooking. That was probably what I missed the most when I was over in the Middle East."

"You were in the service?" she asked in shock. He hadn't seemed like the military type. She'd met plenty of air jockeys in Arizona. It was close enough to the airbases in Nevada, and with the pleasant weather and lack of mountains, it made a great place to hold practice drills.

"No. I joined the Civil Air Patrol during high school and learned how to fly fixed-wing planes. When I graduated, I learned how to fly helicopters as well. I took all of the EMT and paramedic courses. One of my instructors took a job over in Saudi Arabia flying medical transports. When he offered to get me a job working over there as well, I jumped at it."

"How old were you?" she asked, taking another bite of her food.

Justin was pleased to see a little color coming back into her cheeks. "Twenty-one. I flew helicopters over there for just under five years. The pay was amazing, more than I could hope to make here in the States in a decade."

"What made you come home?" she asked, pushing her plate away when she was finished.

"My uncle died. Like you, we were not raised by our mother."

"What happened?" she asked.

Justin shook his head. "That's a story for another time." He stood and picked up the dirty dishes and carried them back into the kitchen. He rinsed them and then placed them with the dishes from earlier into the dishwasher. He added some soap and turned it on.

Jessica was still sitting at the table when he returned. "Feel like watching a movie?"

She lifted her head and slowly nodded. "Sure. Could I get some pain medicine first though?"

Justin nodded, "Sure." He disappeared and then came back with a small bottle in his hands. He handed it to her and then waited while she took two of the tablets. She pushed her chair back, following him back to the large couches. She settled herself into the corner of one and audibly groaned. She was beginning to feel the effects of the day and could feel her muscles cramping up in response.

"So, what kind of movies do you like to watch?" Justin asked, surveying the large collection he and his brothers had amassed over the years.

"No horror. Maybe a comedy?" she suggested. That was always a safe choice.

"Comedy it is." Justin picked out one of his favorites, a story about a family that took a road trip across the country and the various tragedies that eventually drew them closer together.

"So, you're from Arizona?"

She nodded her head slowly as the movie loaded. "Yeah. I'm starting to think I should have stayed there. Or at least found a job someplace without snow."

"Never been here in the winter?"

She laughed softly. "I've never been out of Arizona until this trip. I guess I thought it didn't snow around here until much later in the year."

"The mountains can get snow as early as Labor Day."

Labor Day? But that was in September. What was I thinking?

"Yeah, the Arizona desert is looking better all the time."

"You'll love the Colorado winters if you give them a chance."

"Maybe." She watched as the movie began and several minutes later, she asked him, "Are your brothers coming back tonight?"

"Kaillar is. Mason will spend the night in Frisco and then head home tomorrow or whenever the storm abates."

"I feel horrible that you all had to come out in that nasty storm to find us."

"Don't be. We're all part of the search and rescue team for the county. Finding people who are lost or in need of assistance is what we do."

"Well, thank you. I don't know if I'm ever going to get warm again."

Justin glanced at her T-shirt and then spied her wet socks. She'd removed her tennis shoes, but her socks were wet through. "Why don't you go put on some warmer clothes?"

Jess blushed. "I would if I had any. I figured I would have plenty of time to do some shopping once I got here."

Here? Justin was confused and asked, "Where are you headed?"

Jess looked at him and then smiled. "Here. Silver Springs. I took the job as the new elementary teacher."

Chapter 6

A few hours later, Jess asked if there was some place she could lie down and get some sleep. The stress of the day had caught up with her and she'd been yawning nonstop for the last twenty minutes of the movie. And now that she was warm again, she was having trouble keeping her eyes open.

Justin had slipped upstairs, returning with a red flannel shirt and a pair of dark grey sweatpants that were nice and soft from having been washed so many times. "I realize those are going to be way too big, but they'll be warmer than what you have on right now." He added a pair of white tube socks to the pile of clothing and then suggested she go change before they watched the movie.

She'd done so, rolling the sleeves up on the shirt, and rolling the waistband of the sweatpants down and the ankles up. She knew she probably looked silly, but with the added dryness of the too-large socks, she was warm. That's all that mattered.

"Sure, follow me. We only have two guest rooms in the main lodge."

"Main lodge?" Jess asked, following him as he carried her suitcase around the staircase and to a small hallway on the other side of the house.

"Yeah, we have six guest cabins as well. Each one is slightly different from the others." He stopped in front of a wood door. "So, you're a teacher. How old are you?"

Jess laughed. "Not as young as you think I am. I turned twenty-four last month."

"Twenty-four? Huh."

"How old are you?" Jess asked, thinking that turnabout was fair play.

"Twenty-seven. I'll be twenty-eight at the end of the month."

"Gosh, that old?" Jess teased him. It felt good to laugh, even though there'd been precious little in her life the last six months to evoke such emotion.

"Here it is, and I should probably warn you I'm known for getting even." Justin winked at her as he pushed the door open to reveal a small bedroom with a bed, dresser and night stand. The log furniture and the quilt that covered the mattress fit the space perfectly.

"Thanks. The room is gorgeous."

"Glad you like it. The women at the church make the quilts and then auction them off at the annual Christmas Bazaar. If you're going to live here, you'll hear about it soon enough. Do you sew?"

Jess shook her head. "Not a stitch."

Justin laughed at her quip. "They'll change that, just you wait and see."

"They are more than welcome to try. My grandmother tried to teach me to crochet, but it never quite caught on." They were now standing inside the small bedroom. She couldn't help but admire how big and strong this man looked next to her. She was 5'6" in height, a nice normal height in her opinion. Not too short to reach things on the top shelf. And not so tall that she couldn't get away with wearing heels.

But compared to him, she was a dwarf. Justin was easily 6'4", maybe even 6'5" in height. He had broad shoulders, but a trim waist. He had removed his outer winter gear while she'd been cleaning up and now wore well-worn blue jeans with a navy blue flannel shirt.

The sound of a door shutting had Justin turning his head towards the sound. "That must be Kaillar. Want to come meet him?"

Jess was so tired and she could feel her energy slipping away. "Maybe tomorrow?"

Justin searched her eyes, seeing that the day had taken its toll on her. "Of course. Get some sleep, alright?"

"I will." She watched him turn to leave, stopping him at the doorway. "Justin...?"

"Yes?" He turned back into the room.

"Thank you."

He searched her eyes, looking to see what might be going through her lovely mind. "For what? We've already talked about me finding you."

"I know," she nodded. "Thank you for restoring my faith in humanity. It's been a while since someone did something nice for me without wanting something in return."

"That's too bad. You'll find the people of Silver Springs live to do nice things for people. We're like one big family here."

Jessica smiled tiredly. "Family sounds nice."

Justin looked like he wanted to say something, but then he cleared his throat and nodded in her direction. "You're more than welcome. See you in the morning."

Jess watched the door close behind him and then sprawled onto the quilt on the bed. Justin had offered her kindness because it was the right thing to do. And he hadn't expected anything in return.

She lay there in the dark, trying to turn her mind off. Her forehead hurt, her shoulders were achy, and her heart was in a state of confusion. Over the last few hours, she'd been on a mental rollercoaster: thoughts of Jason and his betrayal. Of little Thomas and how short his life had been. Of her grandmother and everything she'd done for her granddaughter; but the happy thoughts were overshadowed by the knowledge that she would never talk with her grandmother again.

And then there were the various emotions associated with being here in Silver Springs. Thankfulness that she'd been rescued from the mountain road. Excitement and trepidation over her new job. And a sense of curiosity about the man who'd taken her into his home and made her feel important. As if she mattered in this world. That feeling alone was addictive to her, and as she closed her eyes and drifted to sleep, she lectured herself about not falling back into her destructive patterns. It was time to stand on her own two feet; time to try and figure out what kind of person she wanted to be.

She wondered what advice her grandmother would have given her in dealing with Jason and her future. No doubt, it would have included reading her Bible, spending time in prayer, and finding a church to attend – all things she'd grown up doing regularly, but what had that ever gotten her?

She'd spent years trying to follow the rules. She'd been the recipient of more judgments from well-meaning parishioners than most kids her age. They'd either pitied her for having grown up without her parents, or they had summarily judged her unworthy and lacking in some way. She'd heard more than once that she wasn't living up to her parents' memory. What those self-righteous women didn't know, is that they had more memories of her parents than she did!

She removed the borrowed shirt and sweatpants, slipping beneath the covers and feeling her exhausted body sink down into the soft mattress. She immediately closed her eyes and a sigh of relief leaving her mouth. She was warm, safe, and that was all that mattered in that moment. Everything else could wait until the morning.

Chapter 7

Justin closed the door to the guest bedroom and leaned against the wall in the hallway. Jessica's words had gripped his heart and he'd had the strongest urge to pull her into his arms and offer her the comfort of a hug.

It's been a long time since someone has done something nice for me without wanting something in return.

How could that be? From what he could tell, she was a beautiful young woman who had chosen one of the most noble of professions – teaching. And yet, he sensed a sadness and anger in her that didn't make any sense. He had a strong urge to help her. He tried to convince himself it was purely platonic, but he couldn't get the smell of her perfume out of his head. Or how her hair looked so soft. He'd wanted to reach out and touch it.

But all of that he pushed aside as he replayed their conversations. There had been something in her voice when she'd mentioned her parents.

"Hey, where's she at?" Kaillar asked, coming around the corner to where Justin was.

Justin pushed away from the wall. "Calling it a night. She's exhausted. Dark circles under her eyes that go beyond the stress of today."

"How's her head?"

"She's gonna be bruised for a while. Her eye will probably be black and blue by tomorrow morning. She hit the back of that truck pretty hard, and the airbags in the steering wheel didn't deploy."

Kaillar raised a brow. "She's lucky she's alive!"

"Yeah. So..." Justin rolled his shoulders. "Is it still snowing?"

Kaillar nodded his head. "I almost stayed in town myself. That second hairpin curve was downright scary tonight."

Justin looked at him. "You okay?"

"Fine. The tracker's fine as well."

"Good. I better call Jeremy and let him know everything's okay. I also think I'll suggest they cancel basketball practice tomorrow morning."

"That'd be a good idea. No sense in people getting out if they don't have to."

Justin nodded. "I'll suggest he make phone calls tonight. It's only 8:30 p.m., most people will still be awake." He pulled his cell phone from his pocket and dialed the pastor's number, walking to the large picture windows and watching the snow fall as he waited for the call to connect.

"Justin?"

"Yeah, it's me. Just wanted to let you know everyone's safe and sound."

"Very good."

"I also think it might be wise to cancel practice tomorrow morning," Justin suggested.

"Already ahead of you. I made the calls about two hours ago."

Justin smiled and then sobered. "Did you know the school board hired a new elementary teacher?"

"I did. A young woman from somewhere out West, I believe."

"That's who I rescued this evening."

"Really? Well, I look forward to meeting her. Is she staying at Sarah's?"

"No, she bumped her forehead pretty good and I didn't want her spending the night alone. I brought her back to the lodge with me. Between Kaillar and me, we'll check on her through the night just to make sure she doesn't have any negative side effects."

"Why do I sense there is something else you want to say?" Pastor Jeremy told him.

"I had a chance to talk with her for a bit tonight. I sense she is very troubled, angry even, about events that happened in her past."

"And this bothers you?" Jeremy asked, intuitive as always.

"Yeah. I guess it does. She seems kind of alone and maybe a bit lost. I was wondering if you might talk to her?"

The pastor was quiet for a moment and then he offered some advice: "Justin, I am always available to talk to those in need. But might I suggest you stop trying to figure out what is wrong with her, and just be her friend? You've only just met her, and while I'm not discounting what you're sensing about her, she's new to town and a friend will mean much more than a counselor."

Justin smiled. "Point taken. I just don't like seeing her hurting. There's more to her than meets the eye."

"Justin, you are one of the best men I know. I cannot think of a man better suited to befriending a new member of our community. Just be careful that your motivation is in the right place."

"I get where you're going with this. I would never want to do anything that might make it harder for her to be here in Silver Springs. I'm just concerned that she needs help."

"So, no romantic interest there at all?" Jeremy asked. He was about the same age as Justin, having graduated from the high school in Silver Springs the same year. But while Justin had been busy flying around the skies, Jeremy had attended Bible school in the Midwest and married the love of his life. Lacy was a sweet girl and had fit into their little community without even trying.

Justin paused before answering. *Had he noticed how beautiful Jessica was? Yes! Most definitely. Especially after bringing her back to the lodge and getting to know her a bit.* "She's gorgeous. And I enjoyed talking with her, but she's troubled. I don't know that I can help her with whatever's bothering her, but I can't seem to let it go either. I feel compelled to try and help her, while she's here."

"Don't worry about that being a short amount of time. Paul Sherman told me she signed a two-year contract, so she's going to be here for a while. Why don't you bring her into town tomorrow afternoon and introduce her around? I'm sure Lacy will want to have her over for dinner, and you and your brothers are welcome to join us as well."

Justin smiled. "I never turn down Lacy's cooking, but I would imagine Kai and Mason will have other things to do. How about I bring her in after breakfast in the morning? I can drive her down in one of the trackers and that will give her time to figure out where she's going to stay."

"Didn't you hear? Part of her contract is a lease on the old Williams place. Jeff was back here a few weeks ago and has decided to stay in New York. His wife's doing well and he told Shirley down at the real estate office to start renting the place out. They left all of their furniture here as well."

Chapter 8

In fact, Justin hadn't been made aware of that information. "I hadn't heard that Jeff was back in Silver Springs."

"Yes, I believe that's when you and your brothers were escorting that group of archery hunters around in September."

"Not that it did any good. I am constantly amazed that intelligent men would pay thousands of dollars to come hunt in Colorado, and then not do everything they could to make sure they knew how to properly and accurately shoot their weapon of choice."

"I spoke with Kaillar last Sunday, and he made it seem as if the hunter had purchased the bow from a retail shop in Denver right before driving to meet you."

"That's about what it seemed like. He had this bag of accessories, none of which had been opened. I spent two hours, opening morning, installing them before turning him loose to practice on a target Mason set up for him."

"Did the man get lucky enough to hit anything?"

"That man couldn't hit the broad side of a barn if he was standing right in front of it. He was a terrible shot, and by his own admission, hadn't ever shot a bow and arrow before coming to see us."

"Makes a good case for making out-of-state hunters pass a basic test, doesn't it?" Jeremy chuckled and then continued, "Well, to summarize: the school board agreed to provide her with adequate housing for the first two years of her contract. They leased the Williams property the day before Jeff went back to New York."

"Well, living just a block away from the school will be very convenient."

"Is her car in need of being towed? I could call Frank over at the garage in the morning and have him go get it?" Jeremy offered.

"I'm not sure how bad the damage is, but that would be neighborly."

"Consider it done. Well, I better get off the phone and go help Lacy put the little ones back to bed."

Justin smiled. "Don't spoil them too much." Jeremy was the proud papa of twin boys. They were almost six-years-old and had started kindergarten this year. They were a handful at their best, and little terrors the rest of the time. But no-one seemed to mind overly much because they were so precocious about being naughty.

Justin thought back to this summer when the church had finished the new baptismal font. It was constructed so that it could be used both indoors or in the open air. Their daddy had filled it with water the day before he was going to use it and then turned on the heater, not wanting to freeze his parishioners when they were dunked beneath the water's surface.

Peter and James had attempted to save the native population of the local pond. They'd used their granddaddy's long fishing net to capture as many frogs as possible. Then they'd released them into the baptismal font and shut the lid.

When their father had gone to check the water temperature a few hours later, he'd lifted the lid and been accosted by eight very indignant frogs. Justin briefly wondered how Jessica would handle the twins. Silver Springs was so small that the elementary classes were combined with one another.

Kindergarten through second grade met together, third through fifth met together, sixth through eighth met in the middle school building. The high schoolers had their own building and several neighboring mountain communities bused their high school students in each day.

That meant that Jessica would soon find herself teaching a very rambunctious group of youngsters, of which Peter and James would be her most challenging.

"Do us a favor and don't forewarn the new teacher about the boys?" Jeremy pleaded with a laugh.

"Oh, I wouldn't dream of doing that. In fact, I think we should let her meet the boys tomorrow and see how well they get on," Justin suggested.

Jeremy's laugh got louder. "We'll see how they're acting tomorrow. I would hate for her to turn around and go back to Arizona without even giving one day in the classroom a shot."

"Your kiddos aren't that bad?" Justin assured him.

Jeremy groaned. "You say that because you do not have to constantly deal with their mischief."

"They'll grow out of it..."

"...and into what? That has both Lacy and I scared. If they're this hard to deal with at six, what are they going to be like at fourteen?"

"My uncle always had a remedy for horsing around and juvenile hijinks, as he called them. Hard work and lots of it."

"Good, thanks for volunteering. I'll be sending them you're way when the time comes," Jeremy assured him.

"Me and my big mouth. Have a good night and we'll see you sometime tomorrow around mid-morning."

"Later."

Justin pocketed his phone and then joined Kaillar in the kitchen. "Jeremy's threatening to send his little hooligans our way when they become teenagers."

Kaillar looked at him and then smiled. "We'll probably need some ditches dug then, don't you think?"

Justin smiled, remembering the summer he'd turned fifteen. He'd gotten his driving permit and was just a bit too big for his britches. Uncle Jed had decided that all of the ditches along the fence line needed to be cleaned out, deepened and then the weeds burned out of them.

It had taken Justin and his brothers the entire summer from sunrise to sundown, with only a few days off here and there. He'd never thought to complain about the extra work, and by the time the school year started again, he was back to being his usual self. His attitude of self-importance had disappeared in the smoke of the burning ditches.

In return, his uncle had gifted him his old Chevy pickup, and Justin had proudly driven his brothers to school during his junior and senior years.

"Where'd you go?" Kaillar asked.

"Just a quick turn down memory lane." Justin's face told more than his words did, and he saw Kaillar nod his head in full agreement.

"Do you still miss him?" Kaillar asked.

Justin nodded his head. "Every day." He looked up and then smiled. "But I think he's looking down and he's proud of us."

"I hope so," Kaillar agreed. "I really do."

Chapter 9

The next morning, Justin and Kaillar were sitting at the table when Jessica emerged from the guest room. "Good morning," Justin called to her. She looked marginally better, but a large purple and green bruise marred her forehead. Her eye was beginning to blacken, and he wondered if she'd looked in the mirror this morning, and if not, what her reaction to her appearance would be.

In his experience, most women were vain on some level. There wasn't anything she could do to make her injury disappear, but he figured she would still be upset over it and bemoan the fact.

"Hi," she offered softly, eyeing Kaillar curiously.

"Hey, I'm Kaillar. You were already turned in when I got back last night. That's a nice shiner you've got going there."

Justin smacked his brother on the back of the head. "Way to go, bro. Tact and manners get left on the mountain last night?"

"Sorry," Kaillar mumbled, watching Jessica for a negative reaction.

"Don't be mad at him for speaking the truth. I imagine I'm going to look like I went three rounds in the ring before the day is out."

"It's not that bad," Justin insisted.

"Thanks for trying to help, but to tell you the truth – a bruised forehead and black eye seem pretty insignificant compared to what could have happened if you all hadn't come out and rescued me."

"Our pleasure," Kaillar told. "How about some breakfast?"

Jessica joined them at the table. "That sounds really good." She watched as Kaillar got up from the table and placed a skillet on the stovetop. "Do you all know how to cook?"

"Yes, ma'am." When she frowned, he paused to ask, "What?"

"Well, ma'am makes me feel really old, and I'm probably not much older than you are."

"She's got you there."

Kaillar acknowledged that with a grin and a nod of his head. "Says the old man."

Justin looked offended and Jessica giggled. Justin turned to look at her, and was amazed at how the happiness seemed to transform her face. She'd just gone from gorgeous to breathtaking. Her eyes were bright, the green sparkling in the morning light that shone through the windows. Her blonde hair was pulled back into a ponytail, but her bangs hung across her forehead, and he had the strangest urge to brush them aside.

He let his gaze travel over her features – the slightly upturned nose, the pink lips that were only slightly chapped, and the light blush that stained her cheeks. This morning she looked healthy and so different from the woman he'd rescued last night, he was wondering if he'd imagined the hidden pain inside of her.

Justin felt his brother's eyes on him and he looked up, seeing the knowing smirk in Kaillar's eyes. Justin ignored the look and turned back to Jessica. "After breakfast, I told Jeremy I would bring you into town."

"Jeremy?" Jessica asked.

"Jeremy is the local preacher. He and his wife have a set of twin boys..."

"You'll be getting to know them rather well. They just entered kindergarten," Kaillar told her.

"I had a set of twin girls in my last classroom. They were so sweet." When both men started laughing, trying to contain it, but failing miserably, she looked at them and asked, "What's so funny?"

Kaillar got his control back first. "Sweet is not an adjective I would ever use to describe the Phillips twins."

"Oh, I'm sure we'll get along just fine. Do you think the roads will be clear enough to go and retrieve my car today?" she asked Justin.

"Frank is going to haul it back. The front end was pretty damaged." Seeing her curious look, he explained, "Frank owns the only gas station and automobile garage in Silver Springs. He's a crack mechanic and the only one with a tow truck nearby."

"So, he's going to get my car?"

"He is. He'll take a look at the damage and then get in touch with you. I also understand that you're going to be living in the Williams house. I'll take you over there and you can get settled."

"I spoke with someone from the school board and they told me the house was completely furnished."

"Yes. It is. I think you'll probably find everything you need there, but if there's anything you don't have, I'm sure the ladies at the church will be able to help you out."

Jessica firmed her lips and nodded. "I'm sure if there's anything I need I can do without it until I have a chance to do some shopping."

"I assure you the ladies in the church will count it an honor to help..."

Jessica shook her head. "I don't really plan on having much to do with the church, so to allow them to help me would feel like I was taking advantage of their generosity."

She doesn't plan on having much to do with the church? "You didn't even ask which church I was talking about."

"Is there more than one in town?" Jessica asked.

"Well, not really, but you sounded pretty absolute about the church."

Jessica shrugged her shoulders. "Not everyone is enthralled with the idea of religion. It's not that I'm an atheist or anything, but in my experience, God doesn't always play fair."

"How can you say that?" Kaillar asked her from the other side of the kitchen.

"I can say that because I've seen firsthand how God works. My parents were a great example." *And Thomas. And Jason's betrayal.* She didn't need any more examples. Those were more than enough to her way of thinking.

"Example of what?" Kaillar asked.

"Of how God plays favorites and following him only leads to heartache and pain."

"I think maybe you're looking at your situation from the wrong perspective. If anyone has reason to be mad at God, it would be me, Kaillar and Mason. Our mother was more interested in getting her next fix than she ever was in being a mother. And for someone who didn't want the responsibilities of parenthood, she didn't do much to prevent getting pregnant either."

"Yeah, Maria Donnelly probably counts as the worst mother in the world."

Jessica looked between the two men, "And yet you don't seem to have written God off."

"No, we're thankful that He allowed our uncle to become our guardian. Without Uncle Jed's influence and teaching, none of us would have made it to where we are now. The only way to explain how all three of us are still here, and weren't born addicted to drugs, or even aborted, is God. He intervened in a miraculous way, but ultimately our mother couldn't break free from the addictions that plagued her."

"That's so sad. So, do any of you know who your father is?"

Justin looked at her. "No. So, in that way, you are much better off than we are. I imagine you have stories from family and friends about your parents, pictures, and maybe even mementos.

"The only pictures and mementos we have from our mother were of when she was a young girl. Her parents were very against her move to California and then Las Vegas. They never understood what was driving her, and later, when it became apparent that drugs were her driving force, they couldn't deal with it."

"That's so sad," Jessica told them both.

"Don't feel sorry for us," Kaillar urged her, setting a fluffy omelet in front of her. "Uncle Jed was the best father we could ever have wanted. Just like parents who adopt their children, biology is only a piece of the puzzle when it comes to parenthood. Legacy. Heritage. Beliefs and traditions. Those types of things help, but again they don't make a family. Only love can do that."

Chapter 10

Kaillar's comment, about his parents, stuck with Jessica through the rest of the day. Right after she'd finished eating a wonderful breakfast, Justin had lent her a leather and fleece-lined coat. It was rather large on her, but once they'd stepped outside and she realized how cold it really was, she was extremely grateful.

"I'm going to have to get some warmer clothing."

"Well, there's a small shop in town that sells some things, but you'll probably need to go into Silverthorne to find a better selection."

"I drove through a town called Vail just before I headed up the mountain."

Justin shook his head. "Well, I don't know about your finances, but the prices are definitely going to be much higher there."

Jessica gave a small laugh. "Where was that other place you mentioned?" In truth, she had a very nice pile of money sitting in her bank, but rather than go on a big shopping spree, she'd continued to live on what she could make, saving the money in the bank for a rainy day. Outfitting herself for life in the Colorado Mountains just might qualify as such a day!

Justin smiled. "About thirty minutes from here when the roads are cleared."

"That's not so far away. So, you're going to take me to meet..."

"Well, the preacher and his wife, and their two kids. We're having dinner with them later. Before then, I thought I'd just take you around and introduce you to whomever we meet."

"You know everyone in town?" Jessica asked, shocked at the idea.

"Well, I know most of the people who live in town. There are quite a number of people who live up in the mountains..."

"Like you?" Jessica asked, following him to the barn and watching as he climbed aboard one of the trackers.

"Yes, like me and my brothers. We've lived on this mountain since we came here to live with my uncle. He and our mother grew up here. Our great-great-grandparents were homesteaders and came here during the Colorado Gold Rush era."

"Gold? Did they ever find any?"

Justin nodded. "A bit, but never enough to open a mine."

"What do you do up here?" Jessica asked, climbing into the passenger seat.

"My brothers and I run an outfitting and guide service. During the fall, we mostly guide hunters. But as soon as the snow begins to melt, there will be a steady stream of hikers eager to conquer the 'fourteeners' of Colorado. There are five such peaks within an hours' drive from here. We also ski and make up the primary search and rescue team for these mountains."

"Wow! You guys stay busy," she commented softly.

Justin grinned at her. "We enjoy what we do so it doesn't always seem like work. Do you ski?"

Jessica laughed. "No! I don't really do anything athletic. I mean, I played a little softball when I was in school, but just for fun."

"We'll have to get you up on the slopes then. It won't be long now, not with storms like these helping out."

"I think I'll probably pass..."

"Nearly everyone around here skis. Jeff probably left both downhill and cross-country skis at the house. We'll check it out when I drop you off there later."

"Justin, I really think I'll pass. If downhill skiing is what I've seen on television, I can already tell you I will be the one rolling down the slope in a tangle of arms and legs. In fact, I would be the one setting off the avalanche."

"Firstly, you're probably referring to downhill racing, and while there are a few race courses at some of the other slopes, around here, most people just like to ski for fun. And cross-country skiing is kind of a must. Even your kindergartners will be able to move about the town on skis."

"No one said I needed to ski in order to teach..."

"You don't have to know how, but it will make getting around town much easier come January. The house the school board rented for you is only a block from the school. When there is several feet of snow on the road, skiing to school will look a whole lot more palatable than digging your car out so you can drive that one block."

"Silver Springs gets a lot of snow?" she asked in trepidation. She was definitely going to have to invest some money in her car. At the very least, she'd need to invest in some good snow tires. She grew quiet and looked around at the snow-covered trees, marveling at how crisp and clean everything looked in the light of a new day.

The skies had cleared of their storm clouds from the day before, and a brilliant blue sky could be seen through the branches of the trees. The air was crisp and clean, with no hint of smog or pollution, and a sense of peace seemed to fill her chest and expand to reach all of the dark corners.

"It's so beautiful," she murmured, mostly to herself, almost unaware of her companion.

Justin heard her soft comment and as they rounded the top of the next hill, he paused the tracker, giving her an overview of Silver Springs below and the surrounding mountains and valleys. He kept his voice low and his tone calm. "There's Silver Springs."

"It's like a picture out of some magazine. I can't believe places like this really exist."

"Believe it. Every time I see these mountains, I'm reminded of God's goodness and how magnificent his Creation truly is." Justin watched her and was shocked to see she wasn't denying either God or the concept of Creation. *So, what was it about God and church that she was so against?*

"I can't say I'm not nervous about the snow, but I'm so glad I'm here."

"Let's go see the town." Justin put the tracker in gear and slowly began their descent. The Three Brothers Lodge sat at approximately ninety-five hundred feet, with the town of Silver Springs about five hundred feet lower in elevation.

On either side of the town, magnificent mountains, their tops white with snow as they rose above the tree line, nestled the small community in their valley. As they drew closer, Jessica could begin to make out individual buildings: the school, the church, and what appeared to be Main Street. Very little movement was taking place in the small town, and she assumed that was in part due to the snow that had fallen overnight.

They passed the elementary school and she noticed the parking lot was empty. "No school today?" It was Thursday, and not a formal holiday that she was aware of. She wasn't scheduled to begin her new position until Monday, but she would have enjoyed popping in to observe her new students unawares.

"No. They cancelled it late yesterday afternoon. You'll find that happens quite often around here. The school year is built around a four-day school week, so during the months of August and September, the kids go five days a week, allowing for some extra snow days during the months of October through March."

"March! When exactly does the snow begin to melt around here?" she asked, trying to imagine living in snow for more than six months of each year.

"You look completely shocked," he commented with a soft chuckle. "It will be snowing around here until March. Maybe the first part of April. You'll get used to it, but by the time spring arrives, you'll be ready for it and summer to arrive."

"I'm not prepared for that much snow."

"How about we stop by the clothing store first then?" Justin suggested.

"I think that would be a very good idea." Jessica looked down at the borrowed, too-big coat, her one pair of jeans, her tennis shoes, and was glad that for the first time since her grandmother's death, she would have something to spend the money on that was left over from the sale of her grandmother's house. She would be able to buy whatever she needed, and for the first time ever, she wouldn't have to look at the price tags, or run a quick total in her head before approaching the checkout counter. She would be able to shop without worry, knowing that when the clerk rang up her purchases, she could simply write a check and know the funds were available.

Chapter 11

Chloe's General Store was much more than Jessica had hoped for. Justin escorted her inside the large building, waving to a dark-haired woman with glasses who stood behind the checkout counter. The woman was stunning in an almost ethereal way, and Jessica found that talking to the woman was easier than anything she'd ever done.

"Morning, Chloe."

"Hey, Justin! What brings you down the mountain this morning? Who's that with you?" The woman came out from behind the counter and Jessica watched as she waddled towards them. She was as big as a house with her pregnancy, and looked ready to deliver at any time.

"This is Jessica Andrews. Jessica, this vision is Chloe Taylor. Her husband Scott is the fire chief around here. Jessica is the new elementary teacher."

Chloe reached for Jessica's hand. "Hi! Welcome to town. We're so glad you're here. My mother has been tearing her hair out, literally. She'll be so relieved to have you here next week."

Jessica thought she was following the connection between Chloe and her mother, but she asked for clarification anyway. "Your mother is?"

"Shelly Downs. She's the school principal, and substitute teacher for the last three weeks."

Jessica nodded her head. "Do you mind me asking, what happened to the previous teacher?"

Chloe read her unspoken concern and smiled. "Nothing like you're thinking. Deidre moved to Colorado Springs to be with her husband. He's returning from Afghanistan on the thirtieth, and will be stationed there for the next two years of his life. "

"Well, I guess I'm happy that she gets to be with her husband, but I can imagine she was very sad to be leaving her small charges. I know how I felt leaving my classroom."

Chloe put her hands on her stomach and smiled. "This is our first child, but I already feel so connected to him. Do you have any children?"

"No," Jessica told her. She held up her left hand. "No husband. I'm probably a little old-fashioned in that way, but I truly believe a child needs two parents whenever possible."

"I agree with you." Chloe looked her up and down and then smiled. "You're here for some more appropriate clothing?"

"What was your first clue?" Jessica asked with a welcoming smile. The instant connection she felt to this woman was amazing. Jessica had never been able to communicate with someone she'd just met – not like she was communicating with the lovely Chloe. After Jason's betrayal, she'd distanced herself from everyone, not trusting herself to be a good judge of character any longer. *Maybe these people will be different.*

"The shoes were a dead giveaway. Come with me and we'll get you all fixed up." She looked at Justin. "She's in good hands if you have some other things to do."

Justin shook his head and held up his hands. "I get the message. I'll be over at the garage when you're through here."

"The garage?" Jessica asked, feeling a little nervous about him leaving her here by herself.

"Down the block on the corner. You can't miss it."

"Don't worry none. I'll make sure she gets there. Now, get out of here and let us get to work." Chloe shooed him away and then headed for the back of her store. "Come on back here. That's a nice coat, but a little big on you."

"Justin lent it to me. I guess I didn't really think my move through. I really didn't expect snow this soon." The more Jessica tried to defend coming to Colorado so unprepared, the more embarrassed she became.

Chloe saw that and hugged her with one arm. "Don't beat yourself up about it. It's not like they have much snow in Arizona. How about some hot chocolate?"

"To tell you the truth, before yesterday I'd never seen snow, let alone driven in it. It was really scary out there on the highway. I don't know how I'll ever repay Justin and his brothers for coming to find me. And I'd love some hot chocolate."

Chloe smiled. "That's what the Donnelly brothers do. Rescue people. Have you met the other two yet?"

Jessica shook her head as Chloe led her back to a small break room. "Just Kaillar. The other brother spent the night someplace called Frisco?"

She turned the electric tea kettle on and then handed Jessica a cup and a hot chocolate packet. "Sorry it's not homemade, but with the baby coming, and the holidays, who has time for things like that?"

"When are you due?" Jessica asked, stirring the powder into the hot water that had just been added to her cup.

"In four weeks! I can't believe it. Scott and I still have so much to do, and now with the weather getting bad, I don't know if we're going to get everything done." Chloe started pulling clothing off the hangars and dumping it into her arms.

"So, where exactly is Frisco?" Jessica, having meant to ask Justin earlier, but he wasn't around anymore.

"On the other side of the pass. Frisco's the closest place with a good-sized medical clinic and helicopter service into Denver or back to Junction. Of course there's always Vail, but most normal people avoid going there if they can. Too expensive and everyone seems to have their nose permanently fixed in the air."

"Snobs?" Jessica asked, trying to see Chloe above the mountain of clothes currently in her arms.

"The worst. Okay, that should give you a good start. If you'll just turn around, I'll open up the dressing room and you can get started. Toss out anything you want to keep, and just leave the rest on the hangar inside the cubicle."

"Chloe, how many clothes do you think I need?" Jessica asked as she dumped the pile of clothing onto the wooden bench inside the changing room.

"Well, you'll be teaching four days per week, and then there's outside activities, and church and..."

"No church. I don't attend."

Chloe looked at her. "What? But I thought I read somewhere that your parents were missionaries?" She was very confused, and didn't try to hide it.

Jessica swallowed. "Where did you read that?"

"The school board held a public meeting before they offered you the job. Your resume and bio was read by practically everyone in town."

Jessica sighed; she hadn't counted on that. She was trying to make a new start, and while she had accomplished her task of getting away from Jason, it seemed that her upbringing was now going to be the problem.

"My parents' viewpoints on religion aren't necessarily mine." Jessica pretended not to see the look of horror and then pity that crossed Chloe's face. Since becoming an adult, she'd done everything possible to ignore her heritage. Turning her thoughts to her reason for being in this store, she quickly tried on the clothing Chloe had piled into her arms and after half an hour, she'd found two pairs of jeans, some corduroy pants, three sweaters, and several turtle necks to wear beneath them.

When she emerged Chloe was beaming at her and had a selection of boots for her to try on. She had also located a sheepskin coat, very similar to the one that Justin had lent her, but this time the sleeves were just the right length, and as she tried it on, she couldn't help but enjoy the way the coat seemed to wrap her in comfort, giving her a sense of safety. *It's just a coat, Jess. Easy there.*

"So, I'll start ringing this up for you, shall I?" Chloe asked.

Jessica smiled and then nodded. "I'm not sure how to get all of this stuff..."

Chloe grinned. "Don't worry about it. We're actually going to be neighbors. We live right next to the Williams house."

"Really? That's wonderful. So, Justin told me your husband is a fireman?"

"Scott is sort of the head fireman in town. Not that we have a lot of house fires in town, but he and his crew are also trained forest fighters. With the recent beetle kill of the pine trees, the threat of a major fire disaster seems closer every year."

"It sounds like I have a lot to learn about Colorado. And here I was worried about teaching." Jessica laughed at herself and when Chloe joined in, she looked at the woman and knew they were going to be good friends.

Chapter 12

Four hours later, Jessica was getting out of Justin's tracker and looking in awe at what would be her new home for the next two years. The house was huge and magnificent, and looked so inviting and charming that Jessica couldn't believe she was going to be living there!

"Wow! How many people lived here?" Jessica asked Justin as he took her elbow and steadied her up the front walk. Someone had shoveled the snow off the concrete, and she was wearing her new snow boots, but she wasn't used to walking on icy surfaces and was still slipping around a bit.

"Easy! Jeff had four sisters and then their parents and his maternal grandmother all lived here."

"Eight people? No wonder the house is so huge. I can't possibly need this much space!"

Justin smiled at her as they reached the front door. "My suggestion is to pick out the rooms you want to use, and then close off the rest." He opened the door and gestured with his hand for her to precede him inside.

Jessica stomped the snow from her boots and stepped inside. The lights inside flared to life and she looked around at a beautifully decorated room. A large fireplace stood along the left wall and overstuffed couches sat across from each other in front of it, with several blankets and pillows tossed carelessly here and there.

Beyond that, she could see a large wooden table with benches instead of chairs, and she could already see herself cutting out bulletin board decorations on the large surface. The wooden floors showed years of wear, and the braided throw rugs reminded her of growing up with her grandmother.

"This place is lovely," she told Justin. She removed her coat and then her snow boots before venturing further into the room.

"There are three bedrooms downstairs. One of them is the suite that Jeff's grandmother used. It has a full bathroom and a walk-in closet."

"It sounds like I could easily live on the ground floor and never go upstairs."

Justin grinned. "Probably. Want to go take a look around first before you make your decision?"

Jessica smiled and nodded. She felt like a kid in a toy store. She'd never really had much choice when it came to where she was going to live. Her grandmother's house had been older with only one extra bedroom. Then she'd gone off to college and lived in the dorms.

During the two years she'd been out of college, she'd lived in a small studio walk-up a few blocks away from the college. Part of her graduate program was working part-time in a local elementary school. The extra income had enabled her to afford the extra cost, but it had been worth it to be away from the social atmosphere of the college campus.

She hadn't worried about how small the apartment had been because she'd spent so much of her time with Jason. He was actually from a town four hours away, but he'd only gone home every other week. He lived in a rented condo with plenty of room, and even though he'd tried to get her to move in with him, she'd maintained that she liked knowing she had her own space to retreat to.

That had been her best decision in the long run. One morning she'd come back from a teacher in-service to find a strange car parked outside his condo. She'd been expecting to see one of his friends from college had come to visit, or maybe his parents were visiting. She hadn't had a chance to meet them yet, but Jason had promised to make that a reality soon.

He'd not been in the living portion of the house, so she'd wrongly assumed that he'd left with his visitor. She'd headed into the master bedroom, intending to gather up the laundry and take advantage of a few hours off. But when she'd stepped inside, she'd immediately realized her mistake.

Jason had indeed been home, as had his visitor: a gorgeous redhead, with a body that models would die for, was sitting in the bed, straddling Jason's hips, and in the process of removing her clothing. A woman who had a very large diamond on her ring finger: Jason's fiancée!

She shook her head, trying to dispel the memories because they served no purpose except to remind her that she really shouldn't trust her own judgment. She'd trusted Jason and look what had happened. She been dating him for almost three years, and the entire time he'd been engaged to the redhead back home. The entire time!

She'd been humiliated more than heartbroken, and it disturbed her sense of self-confidence. In truth, getting used to being alone had been easier than dealing with the fact that Jason had lied to her and she'd believed him!

"You okay there?" a voice behind her right shoulder asked.

She turned her head and nodded. "Sorry, I guess I was daydreaming."

Justin smiled at her. "Anything you want to talk about?"

Talk about? With you? Oh, no way! There is no way I want to demonstrate how stupid I was by talking with you about Jason! That is so not going to happen! Jessica hid her disquiet behind a shake of her head. "No, thanks, but I'd rather take a look around."

"Sure thing. Let's start upstairs."

Jessica nodded and climbed the narrow staircase, reinforcing in her mind that living downstairs was going to be her preference. The upstairs rooms were lovely, but the thought of climbing that staircase multiple times a day wasn't at all appealing.

"Ready to go see the downstairs?" Justin asked.

"Yes. I think I'll close these rooms up now. I would much rather live downstairs."

"Okay," Justin agreed, helping her turn the heat down and close the doors to the hallway.

"Why did you only turn the heat down instead of off?" Jessica asked as they descended the staircase.

"You don't want the water pipes to freeze. It's okay to turn the heat down, but you need to keep all areas of the house above freezing or you'll be waking up to broken pipes."

Jessica sighed. "Wonderful. Another perk of living in Colorado."

Justin laughed and started down the hallway. "You'll get used to the way we do things here sooner or later."

They finished their perusal of the downstairs, and Jessica fell in love with the large canopy bed, which occupied the mother-in-law suite on the main floor. "This is perfect for me," she told him.

He started to say something, but the front doorbell peeled through the house. "Want me to see who that is?"

Jessica nodded and followed behind him as they went to answer the door.

Justin pulled the door open to see Pastor Jeremy standing there, a large baking dish in his hands. "Hey! We were just getting ready to head your direction."

Jeremy stepped inside as Justin stepped back. "Don't bother. Both twins had pinkeye. Lacy just got back from Doc's with them. They're under quarantine until Monday, so she sent dinner over here."

He glanced around Justin and smiled. "Hi. I'm Jeremy Phillips, the pastor of Silver Springs Community Church. And the twins I mentioned will no doubt be your biggest challenge."

Jessica smiled. "I've found that big challenges also come with big rewards."

Jeremy smiled and then turned to Justin. "I like her optimism. I almost hate for her to meet Peter and James and dispel the myth."

Jessica laughed. "I'm sure we'll get along very well. But thank you for the heads up about the pinkeye. I'll have to check with the janitor and see that the room is disinfected prior to Monday's class. I've seen it spread through an entire classroom in just a few days."

"Well, Doc already contacted Shelley and I'm sure she's already got a handle on what needs to happen. Where can I set this down?"

Jessica led the way back to the kitchen and then listened in for several minutes as Justin and Jeremy spoke about a basketball team and several other items of business. The rapport the two had was amazing, considering one of them was a pastor. He seemed so down to earth, and unlike the pastor she'd grown up knowing, he didn't come off as holier than thou or self-righteous. It was almost enough to have her second-guessing her decision to steer clear of the local church crowd. Almost.

Chapter 13

O*ne week later...*
Jessica had just sent the last of her students out the door with her parents, and she slumped into her chair and let her head fall into her hands. She was exhausted, and felt so relieved that today marked the end of her first week in Silver Springs Elementary School. She could have cried.

Handling twenty children wasn't normally a problem for her, with or without a classroom aid. But these twenty children seemed to have the energy of two hundred!

The Phillips twins were by far the instigators, even though they were some of the youngest in the classroom. Peter and James seemed to be wherever trouble was to be found, but their explanations for doing whatever it was they'd done was so well thought out and, to the mind of a six-year-old, logical, that Jessica had been hard-pressed to discipline them for most of their antics.

She'd begun to feel more comfortable in the small community, with Chloe becoming her champion. The woman had arrived each afternoon with some new place to show her. The only day she hadn't spent some time with the woman had been Sunday. Chloe had urged her to attend the morning service with her and her husband, but Jessica had remained fixed in her denial. Instead, she'd spent the morning cleaning her new home from top to bottom, at least the rooms she was using, and then walked down through the town, making note of the various businesses that existed so close to home.

Since it was Sunday she'd been able to window browse without having to deal with the owners of each business. She'd arrived back home a few minutes before noon, planned so that she wouldn't run the risk of seeing all the people filing out of the small church.

She heard her classroom door open and looked up to see Principal Shelley Downs step into the room. "Hi."

She looked at Jess and then laughed. "Oh, my dear. If you could see your face... I just came by to congratulate you on surviving week one. I promise the following weeks will be easier."

"I sure hope so. Since you're here, could you explain what's happening with the Christmas Pageant?"

Shelley pulled up another adult-sized chair. "Sure. It's kind of a big thing here in Silver Springs. The entire community comes out for it. We'll have a full Nativity scene; some of the local men made wooden cutouts of the animals years ago and the middle schoolers are going to repaint them in the next few weeks.

"Each classroom will choose several songs to sing, or maybe even a small skit. Lacy Phillips usually comes in and helps with that portion of the pageant. She has a wonderful voice and directs the children's choir at the church."

"Okay, I'll contact her..."

"You could probably just talk to her at church this Sunday," Shelley suggested.

Jessica felt uncomfortable and then shook her head. "I probably won't attend."

Shelley looked at her and then sighed. "Okay, explain to me how the daughter of missionaries doesn't want to attend church."

Jessica had come to respect Shelley over the last four days, and felt herself drawn to open up to the older woman. "Look, I realize that you and most of this town feel that God is good, and He takes care of His people. But in my experience, that's not the way it works."

"Because your parents were murdered?"

Jessica sighed. "You read my bio too?" When Shelley nodded her head, Jessica cringed. "Well, yes! I blame God for sending them back into such a dangerous place."

Shelley looked at her with compassion in her eyes. "But so much good came from that situation." When Jessica simply looked at her, Shelley pulled out her tablet and typed a few search words into it. When she found what she was looking for, she handed the tablet to Jessica and told her, "Read."

Jessica took the tablet and read a news story from more than twenty years earlier. It was a story about how the Christians in South Africa had risen up against the terror groups threatening to exterminate them.

The people being interviewed credited the missionaries and their families for showing them what true leadership was, that there was no sacrifice too great when spreading the love of Christ.

Jessica handed the tablet back, feeling her old anger issues rise to the surface. "Is that supposed to make it all better? It doesn't. And my parents aren't the only ones He's let down." She explained to Shelley about Thomas, but couldn't bring herself to admit her failure with Jason.

Shelley opened her mouth to reply, but a tap on the classroom door had both women turning to welcome Justin. Jessica hadn't seen him since Saturday when he'd brought over the box from her vehicle. She smiled at him, pleased to see him and get a reprieve from where the conversation with Shelley was headed. "Hi!"

"Hope I'm not interrupting anything?" he asked, walking inside and joining them by Jessica's desk.

Jessica shook her head, a little too eagerly. "No, in fact, we were just finishing. What are you doing here?"

"Well, Mason's cooking tonight and I thought you might like to join us. I'm interested to hear how your first week went."

Jessica knew she should decline his offer. Her mind had strayed to thoughts of the handsome man more than once this past week, but the thought of returning home with her emotions still churned up from her conversation with Shelley wasn't pleasant. "I'd love to. Let me get the classroom cleaned up and I'll be ready to go."

"Frank said to tell you he'll have the parts to fix your vehicle early next week."

"Great! Not that I'm planning to do much driving."

Shelley watched the interaction between the two and then stood up. "I'm going to get out of your hair. Think about what I said," she told Jessica, concern in her voice.

Jessica swallowed. "I will. Have a nice weekend." She turned away and began gathering up the art supplies scattered across the classroom.

"Justin, since you're here, would you mind helping me change the light in my office? It went out first thing this morning and Tim didn't have a chance to change it yet. I was hoping to get some more work done on next year's budget, but that won't happen without light."

Justin smiled. "I'd be happy to. Be right back," he told Jessica. He followed Shelley out into the hall, having picked up on the fact that she just wanted a chance to talk to him. Once they were several doors down the hallway, she stopped and faced him.

"What are you doing?"

Justin was taken aback. "What are you talking about?"

"Don't mess with my new teacher. She's really good with the kids, and I really feel that God sent her here for a reason that has nothing to do with her students."

Justin grinned. "Don't worry so much. I got to know her a bit last week and would like to know her even more. She's a nice girl..."

"With some real anger problems. Mostly directed at God."

"What were you two discussing when I arrived?" Justin wore a concerned expression, and snippets of previous conversations with Jessica flowed through his mind.

"Her parents. I think she blames God for their deaths, and has let her anger color every aspect of her life. And there was a young man who died young and she blames God for that as well."

"Yeah, I kind of picked up on that too. Want me to talk to her?"

"Only if you get the chance. She wants nothing to do with the church and I'm worried that she's denying an integral part of herself. I guess I'm playing mother here, but there's something about Jessica that makes me want to help her."

Justin knew exactly what Shelley was talking about. He'd gotten the same feeling when he'd been showing Jessica around the town on the previous Friday. Silver Springs was such a small community, and most people were involved in the church in some way. Even those who lived in the surrounding mountains tried to attend Sunday services at least once a month.

Justin had encouraged her to re-think her position on becoming involved in the church, promising that no-one was going to pressure her to do anything other than attend, but she'd been pretty adamant about wanting to keep her distance. "I'll see what I can do."

He left Shelley in the hallway and returned to Jessica's classroom. She was just picking up her coat, and he walked across and held it out for her to put her arms in. Without thinking about his actions, he scooped her hair out of the neck, lifting it up and allowing his fingertips to just barely graze the bare skin at the back of her neck.

She shivered in reaction, and he felt the strongest urge to wrap his arms around her and hold her close. He pushed the urge aside as he dropped her hair and stepped back. She spun around and looked at him, and he could see her reaction had taken her as much by surprise as his own had.

"Ready to go?"

"Sure. I need to swing by the house and change my clothes first."

"We can do that. I have the truck today since the snow has begun to melt off the roads."

They stepped out of the school and he led her to his big, black double cab truck. There were steps by the passenger door, and she knew without them she wouldn't have been able to scramble up into it without his help.

"You alright there?" he asked, smiling at her as she settled into the seat.

"What's with the monster truck?" she asked with a grin.

"Feet of snow, remember? This rig gets me just about anywhere I need to go where roads are involved. I spent many years in my late teens digging the tires of my uncle's old Chevy pickup out of the snow. With this *monster* as you called it, I just put it in gear and drive."

Jessica smiled as she watched him talk about his truck. He had such a boyish enthusiasm for the subject, and she found she really liked seeing him smile and laugh. *Had Jason ever laughed like that? Or at himself?*

As the afternoon and evening progressed, Jessica found herself comparing the two men more often than not. At every turn, Justin came out the winner. By the time he drove her back down the mountain, she was more than a little enamored of the man who seemed intent on being her friend.

It didn't help that Chloe was constantly singing Justin's praises. He was best friends with her husband Scott, and she was just sure that Jessica and Justin would make a wonderful couple. Jessica had tried to let Chloe know that she really wasn't in a position to even think about a new relationship, but without going into Jason's betrayal, her protests sounded weak.

So, you happen to like what you know about Justin. Maybe you should give romance one more try and see if you can't restore your faith in your own judgment at the same time.

Jessica wasn't quite sure what was up with her inner voices, but ever since arriving in Silver Springs they had been more vocal than ever. Her inner voices had even begun to sound a bit like her beloved grandmother, urging her not only to give herself a chance to rebuild her faith, but to give God another chance. Everything had happened for a purpose, and even though Jessica knew the words to be true deep down, on the surface she was having trouble letting go of the hurt and disappointment of the past.

Chapter 14

Saturday morning...

Jessica stretched and tried to figure out what had woken her up. It was Saturday and she had made a point of turning her alarm clock off the night before. *So what...?*

A knock sounded on the front door again and she groaned, "Go away!" Knowing they couldn't hear her, she stumbled from the bed, pulling her bathrobe on as she headed for the front door. The wooden floors were chilly, reminding her she'd forgotten her slippers.

She pulled the door open, blinking into the bright sunshine.

"Good morning! Ready to go have some fun?" Justin asked cheerfully from the porch.

"What? Do you know what time it is?" she asked, rubbing the sleep from her eyes and hoping her hair wasn't standing up all over her head.

Justin chuckled. "Someone's not a morning person, I see."

"No! Someone was sleeping in for the first time in... I can't even remember the last time I slept in. Not to be rude, but what do you want?"

Justin stepped into the house, forcing her to back up or risk getting her bare toes stepped on. "You are going to learn to cross-country ski today."

Jessica shook her head. "No way! I am going back to my nice, warm bed. But you go ahead and knock yourself out." She made to turn away, but she tripped on the belt of her robe. Her feet slid on the wooden floors, and she would have fallen backwards, had Justin not been so quick to react.

He grabbed her by the waist, lifting her off her feet and then holding her against his chest. "Whoa! You need to be more careful."

Jessica felt his arms around her waist and had the strongest urge to lay her head upon his chest and just absorb his warmth. Instead, she pushed away from him, gaining her feet beneath her and hurriedly backing away from him. "Sorry."

"Look, most of the town will be at the hill this morning."

"The hill?" Jessica questioned him with a raised brow.

"Just on the other side of town there is a moderate hill the locals use to teach their children to ski. There are also cross-country trails that begin and return there."

"I really just want to go back to bed," Jessica told him.

"Well, I have appointed myself your social director and I say you need to learn to cross-country ski. We're going to get more snow this coming week, and skiing to school will be easier than trying to walk through two feet of snow."

"We're going to get two feet of snow?" she asked, looking out the window at the sunshine currently being displayed.

"That's what they're forecasting. We'll probably get more, but it won't be a big deal if you know how to ski."

Jessica sighed. "You're not going to go away until I agree, are you?"

Justin crossed his arms over his chest and shook his head. "Nope. Might as well give in and I'll let you have the cinnamon roll from Becky's bakery, sitting in my truck along with a fresh cup of coffee."

Jessica groaned. "You don't play fair." Becky owned the small bakery in town, and Jessica had tasted her creations firsthand at the school.

"Gotcha. Go get dressed in something warm and I'll go dig the skis out of the garage."

"Fine. But I want my cinnamon roll now."

Justin laughed but went back to the truck and returned with a bag containing the cinnamon roll and a cardboard cup of coffee. "Now, will you please go and get dressed?"

Jessica took the food and wandered back down the hallway, sipping the coffee as she went. She pulled a pair of jeans from the closet, and then added a turtleneck and a sweater. She donned her snow boots, and pulled her hair back into a sloppy ponytail. She didn't worry about makeup, figuring the cold air would provide a natural blush to her cheeks in short order.

Justin was waiting for her on the front porch and she grabbed her coat before closing the door. She still had half of her cinnamon roll, and she ate it as Justin drove them out of town.

The hill became visible almost immediately, cluttered with townspeople, and Jessica immediately wished she hadn't let Justin talk her into doing this. "I don't really need to learn to ski."

"Of course you do. Look," he pointed out the window as he parked the truck. "There's Jeremy and Lacy."

Jessica turned on him. "You expect me to learn to ski where my students can see me fail?"

"You're not going to fail, and believe me, Peter and James will be too busy driving their parents crazy to notice something like their teacher falling in the snow. Besides, I'm a really good teacher, and if you just trust me, I promise to keep you from falling."

Jessica heard his words, but her mind immediately added a double meaning to them. He was watching her so intently, it was almost as if he truly meant them in more than one way. She watched him remove the skis from the back of the truck and then he came around and showed her how to adjust the buckles to fit the ski boots he'd also found hidden in the garage.

Once done, he changed into his own ski gear and then helped her out of the truck. "Okay, so the toe of each boot is attached to the ski, allowing you to lift your heel as you bend your knee." He demonstrated the movement that would allow her to push her skis forward without picking them up off the snow.

"Now, you try it."

Justin was about ten feet away, and Jessica looked around her, pleased to see that absolutely no-one was paying any attention to her. Taking a deep breath, she released it. "Okay, you can do this. How hard can it be?" She mimicked his movement, giving a short squeak of alarm when her body moved forward.

"That's it. Now repeat the motion with the other foot."

Jessica did as he requested and a moment later, she was standing by his side. She grinned up at him. "I did it!"

"Yes, you did. Let's go try one of the easier trails. We don't want to go too far today, or you'll hate me in the morning." He pushed off and she was left trying to keep up with him.

When he took a break a few moments later, she asked, "Why am I going to hate you tomorrow?"

"Well...you're using muscles that probably haven't been used like this before. You're going to be a little sore."

"Great!" she told him, her voice full of sarcasm.

"Still want to go on?"

"I'm already out here now. Might as well."

"There's that burst of enthusiasm I was waiting for," he commented with a wry grin.

Jessica laughed. "Listen, you dragged me from a warm bed, put these tiny sleds on my feet, and also expect me to be jumping for joy? That might be expecting a little too much."

Justin held out his ski pole to her. "Grab hold." When she did, he pulled her up so that she was by his side. "With you, I might expect a whole lot of things. But never too much." His tone had softened and Jessica found herself unable to look away from his eyes.

After a moment, common sense tried to intervene and she whispered, "Justin, what's going on here?"

He looked into her eyes and then smiled. "I don't know, but it could be fun finding out. Don't you think?"

Jessica returned his smile, the day too beautiful to allow memories of past disappointments to overshadow the promise of the future. "I want to believe that, I really do…"

"That's all it takes. Just a little belief. A little faith. Give whatever this is between us a chance. I've felt it since the moment I woke you up on the mountain."

"I've felt it as well, but my last relationship almost destroyed me."

Justin lifted a hand and brushed a stray piece of hair back behind her ear. "Why don't we finish the short loop and then head back to your place. I think maybe it's time we talked more about our past histories." When she tried to shake her head, he tapped her on the nose. "No pressure, only what you want to share. I want to know more about you. You said you came to Colorado to make a fresh start. I want to be part of that."

Jessica looked at him and then slowly nodded her head. "I think maybe I'd like that as well."

Justin winked at her and then used her grip on his ski pole to push her behind him. "Let's finish this track, and then go shopping. I'm cooking tonight."

Jessica giggled. "That's a really good thing since I am an absolutely horrible cook." She followed behind him, and by the time they returned to his truck her muscles were shrieking at her in protest. Something told her she was going to be more than sore come morning.

Chapter 15

Justin put the finishing touches on the steaks and then stuck them back under the broiler. "Won't be long now, do you want butter and sour cream on your potato?"

Jessica wandered into the kitchen. "Sure. Do you want to eat at the table or by the fireplace?"

"Fireplace gets my vote."

"Great. I'll go put the silverware and our drinks on the coffee table."

Justin watched her gather up forks and knives and then two glasses of ice water. She'd been acting more nervous as the day wore on. He figured it had to do with whatever had driven her from Arizona in the first place.

He didn't want her nervous, but if she couldn't learn to trust him, to listen and not pass judgment, they really didn't have much of a future together. That was not something he even wanted to consider at the present time.

They carried their plates to the living room and ate in silence for several minutes before Jessica moaned. "Justin, this is amazing! If I ate like this all the time I'd be as big as a house!"

Justin shook his head. "No, you wouldn't. And you could put on a few pounds. It wouldn't hurt at all."

Before she could respond, the lights flickered and then suddenly the house was plunged into darkness except for the light coming from the flames in the hearth.

"Whoa! Does this happen a lot?"

Justin put his fork down and told her, "Hang on for a minute." Justin went to the kitchen and returned with a flashlight. Let me go check the breaker box, and then..."

Justin paused and listened, walking to the front door and opening it before immediately shutting it. "The storm that was supposed to arrive tomorrow is here."

"What?!" Jessica went to the window and attempted to see outside. As her eyes adjusted, she saw the pine trees moving with the force of the wind. She could see snow blowing across the yard, and even more falling from the sky. "We haven't been home that long."

"Sometimes these storms come up suddenly. The combined weight of the snow and the wind becomes too much for the power lines to handle."

Jessica nodded. "How long will it be out for?"

Justin gave her a reassuring smile. "Probably until the storm abates. I can go start the generator if the dark bothers you."

Jessica shook her head. "No. I'm okay for right now."

"Good. Let's finish eating and then we can talk."

"I'm pretty much finished," Jessica told him, resuming her seat and pulling one of the afghans off the back of the couch to wrap around her shoulders.

"Are you cold?" he asked curiously.

"Not really. I just like having a blanket wrapped around me sometimes. So what did you want to talk about?"

"What brought you from Arizona?"

Jessica looked at him as he got up from the opposing couch and sat down next to her. "So? Why leave Arizona?"

"That's a really long story."

Justin looked at his wristwatch and told her, "We have plenty of time. I'll tell you what. I'll tell you something about myself, and then you can tell me something about you."

"Like twenty questions?" Jessica asked, intrigued by the man sitting in the glow of the fire. He was handsome in a rugged sort of way with wavy, dark brown hair and deep blue eyes that seemed to watch her carefully and see way too much.

"Sort of. I'll even start. I have two brothers, Mason and Kaillar."

Jessica giggled. "I already know that."

"Yes, but it's part of the complete package, so bear with me."

"Fine. Continue with your story." She waved at him.

"Well, I have no idea who my father is or was. I'm pretty sure my mother didn't know the answer to that either. My mother, in name only, was raised right here in Silver Springs, but had stars in her eyes. It seemed that her Christian upbringing was stifling her creative nature. As soon as she turned eighteen, she ran off to LA and then to Las Vegas. She wanted to see her name in bright lights and her face plastered across magazines and movie screens."

"That didn't happen?"

"Not quite. While waiting for her big break, she hooked up with the wrong people. They introduced her to drugs and alcohol. Mainly heroin. She managed to make it home each time one of us was born, but she never could make the rehab stick. The last time she left, after Kaillar was born, my Uncle Jed had to go to Las Vegas to pick up her corpse. They found her body beaten up and lying in an alley somewhere."

"How horrible!" Jessica said, covering her mouth as she tried to take in everything he was telling her. "Did they ever catch the people who did it?"

"As far as I know, they never even tried to find them. From what I've managed to piece together, the Las Vegas police considered her a junky and a lost cause."

"Wow! Just...wow!" Jessica sat there stunned. Their stories were so similar, and yet different. Telling him about her parents now seemed not so bad.

Justin looked at her and then nodded his head. "Your turn."

"How old were you when you came back to Silver Springs for good?"

"Eight. Uncle Jed had her buried next to her parents on the southern side of the mountain."

"I'm sorry, that must have been so hard on you and your brothers."

"It was." He looked up at her and then gave her a smile, wanting her to know that he'd shared something highly personal with her and lived to tell about it. "Your turn."

"How personal are we going to get here? I mean, this is your game."

Justin gave a self-deprecating laugh. "Normally my answer would be to steer clear of anything personal. But for some reason, I feel like I can talk to you. As if you might understand where others wouldn't."

"You've lost me there. I still don't understand."

"Let me ask you a question. You said you were raised by your grandmother and that your parents allowed themselves to get killed the first night we met."

"Did I?" she fired back, not sure she wanted to go down this memory lane filled with land mines.

"You did. Your exact words in fact. What did you mean by that? How did your parents allow themselves to get killed?"

Jessica sat there and shook her head. "I think it's still your turn. Tell me more about your mother."

"Fortunately, I was so young I don't remember much about her, and what I do remember isn't all that pleasant. There were times when I was growing up I wished I hadn't had any memories of her. That I could have looked at the pictures of when she was a child and listened to the stories Uncle Jed told and that would have been all I ever knew about her."

"But you have memories of her..."

"Memories of a drugged up, too skinny woman who was always promising to get herself together, and never could manage to leave the drugs and alcohol alone. I only spent a few weeks here and there with her, usually after she'd come home and dried out for a few weeks. She would then return to Las Vegas, the stars back in her eyes, and things would be good until she got tired of being turned down for some acting or modeling job."

Justin looked at her, shaking his head. "I'd rather not have had any memories of her than those. I know my uncle felt the same way. He used to say he had a hard time remembering her as a carefree young girl that would follow him and his friends around the mountains. I never saw that woman. Ever."

Chapter 16

She looked at him for a moment and tried to put herself in his position. *Would she have given up memories of her parents, even if they'd been bad?* All she'd ever wanted was a chance to know her parents, but hearing Justin's story made her somewhat glad that she didn't have any bad memories of them. No, she just didn't have any memories of them.

She looked down at her hands and then began, "My parents were missionaries to Africa. When my mother found out she was pregnant with me, they asked for furlough and came back to the states. Things would have been much different if they had stayed here."

"But they went back?" Justin filled in the rest of her story. When she nodded, he asked, "What happened?"

"Civil unrest led to the rise of a Salafist jihadist militant group with ties to the Middle East. They attacked the school where my parents conducted their work, killing all nine Americans."

"Including your parents," he added.

"Yeah."

"Were the men who murdered them ever brought to justice?"

Jessica nodded. "About three years ago. At least that's what the State Department reported. They should never have been there." She heard the anger in her voice and tried to push it down once again.

"I thought you said they were missionaries. Weren't they just going where God led them?"

Jessica huffed out a breath, her anger bright and fierce. "Yeah! Where God sent them! To die! I never have understood why he would send people who'd sacrificed everything to follow His teachings to their deaths."

She was shaking with emotion and when she dared look up, she couldn't stand the look in Justin's eyes. *Great!* "I suppose you believe in a loving God and want to offer me some empty platitudes about how my parents will have a greater reward in Heaven because they were martyrs. Well, I've heard it all my life and I don't buy it! He sent them over there to die, instead of letting them stay here and raise me. That doesn't sound like a loving God to me!"

When Justin started to speak, she shook her head and continued. "Shelley showed me some article the other day that talked about how much progress the church has made in South Africa. The writer commented that without the sacrifice of Christian missionaries like my parents, the current revival wouldn't have been possible."

"Was that a recent article?" Justin asked, turning to sit facing her on the couch.

"No. It was written several years after their deaths. But it doesn't matter."

"Of course it does. Your parents were martyred for Christ and the article was giving credit to their sacrifice."

Jessica looked up at him, tears in her eyes. "But why would God send them back over there just to die. He could have protected them. I know He could have. Growing up, I heard the stories of the miracles God performed for the children of Israel, and how blessed the disciples of the early Church were. If He could do all of those things, I know He could have spared my parents' lives!"

"So that you could have them back?" Justin asked softly.

"They were my parents!"

Justin reached for her hands, untangling her fingers and then clasping them lightly with his own. "Jessica, have you ever done wondered what drove your parents to leave their eighteen-month old baby behind? Did you ever think about how much they must have loved you to do that?"

"If they loved me they would have taken me with them." Jessica heard the words and then cringed. "But they were afraid for my safety, so they left me with my grandmother."

Justin was quiet as he let her mind sort things out. He thought maybe she was going in the right direction, and then she told him, "If God had truly cared about any of us, He would have kept them safe and prevented them from going back there!"

"But your parents had committed their lives to spreading the Good News to others. Have you ever been driven to do something? Something that others thought was stupid or crazy, but something inside of you told you to do anyway?"

Jessica shook her head "I don't think so. And I like to think that common sense would win any such conflict."

"What made you leave Arizona? You said you'd never left the state before. Why now?"

This was the part of the conversation she didn't want to have. Telling anyone about Jason's betrayal was akin to admitting how stupid she'd been. "I needed a change of scenery."

"Really? You decided to quit and move for no reason?"

Jessica looked up and realized this moment was a turning point for her. She'd not spoken about Jason to anyone. "I left Arizona because I was stupid. And tired of the past always being thrown in my face."

"I highly doubt that," he told her, holding onto her hands when she would have pulled them away.

Jessica gave a derisive laugh. "You won't say that in a few minutes."

"Try me," Justin challenged her.

"I went to college with a huge chip on my shoulder. I was finally out from under my grandmother's influence, and I was so tired of trying to live up to everyone's expectations of what I should be doing. I did all of the things I knew I shouldn't. And still, I never was truly happy. And then I met Thomas."

Justin watched the soft, sad smile form on her face and felt a stab of jealousy. *Thomas had really meant something to her.* He didn't want to ask, but a friend would do exactly that. So he did so, quietly. "Thomas broke your heart?"

Jessica cried and tears spilled over. "Yeah. He was such a cute kid. I met him during my first classroom clinical. He wasn't sick then, and he and I became cohorts in the classroom and on the playground. Then he got sick and missed a few weeks of school."

"What was wrong with him?" Justin asked, feeling guilty for having been jealous of a young boy.

"Cancer. A rare and aggressive form of cancer. He died a little while later. He had so much to live for, and yet God didn't protect him. He let that little boy die, destroying his parents and everyone who knew him."

"God didn't give him cancer. You know that right?" Justin asked her, the sight of her tears making his heart hurt.

"But He had it within His power to make it leave. Thomas hadn't done anything to deserve..."

"Whoa! Tell me you don't think bad things happen to people because they deserve it?"

Jessica didn't believe that and she hadn't meant to imply that she did. "No. I know that bad things happen to people sometimes, and I realize that people die, but why did God have to take Thomas?"

"I don't know," Justin told her, pulling her into his arms and rubbing his hand up and down her back. "I don't know, but we have to trust that God does know."

"I'm a little low in the trust department."

"Have you told Him how you feel?"

"Like He cares! I mean, my life couldn't have been worse, and then I met Jason. He swept down and made me smile again."

"Jason is?" Justin asked, not wanting to jump to conclusions again.

"My ex-boyfriend. I'm sure he doesn't even count me as that, but we were together for almost four years. The entire time he was playing me. He lived four hours away, and had gotten engaged to a very nice country club princess the week before he started college.

"At least he didn't officially ask me to marry him, just move in with him." *That would have been the ultimate humiliation!* "Luckily, I didn't do that. Something inside of me urged me to keep my own place."

"Where was your grandmother during all of this?" Justin asked, regretting the question as tears spilled out of her eyes.

Jessica took a shuddering breath and shook her head. "She died in March."

"Of this year?" Justin asked, feeling horrible if that were the case.

She nodded her head. "Yeah. I went back home and took care of her affairs, sold the house, paid off my student loans, and returned to school. I finished my Master of Education at the end of May and started working as a teacher's aide. I went by Jason's condo one day when we didn't have any students in the classroom. His fiancée had come for a visit."

Jessica stopped and pushed herself away from Justin, leaning back against the couch as she relived the humiliation she'd felt that day. "I feel so stupid," she murmured softly.

Justin was furious on her behalf. "What did you do?"

Jessica shook her head. "Nothing. I walked out, holed up in my apartment for the rest of the week and applied for about a dozen jobs out of state. When Paul Sherman called me three days later and interviewed me over the phone, I made up my mind that if he offered me the job I was going to take it. He called back an hour later, offered me the job, and I began making plans to leave Arizona."

"Didn't your ex try to explain himself?"

"I don't know. I quit answering his phone calls."

"The jerk didn't even try to talk to you?"

"That's for the best. I don't know what I would have told him."

Justin didn't believe that for a minute. "Oh, I think you could have found plenty of things to tell him. Why don't you try?"

"What?!" She looked up in shock.

"Pretend I'm the jerk and tell me what you would have told him. Let me have it. It's obvious to me that you haven't dealt with his betrayal yet, and since he's not anywhere close, pretend I'm him. Don't worry about offending me. I've got really thick skin. I can handle it."

"I couldn't do that..."

"You need to do this. I can hear the hurt and anger in your voice as if it just happened. It's been what, a few weeks?"

"Give or take a week."

"You need to heal, but before you can do that you need to get rid of some of the pain. Give it to me."

Chapter 17

Jessica could see that Justin was serious about her using him as a sounding board for her anger, pain and humiliation, but she wasn't sure letting go of her control was such a good thing.

"Jess, trust me on this. If I had a punching bag handy, I'd suggest you go beat on it for an hour or two, but I don't. I also am not going to offer myself up in that capacity. You may be little, but my guess is you can pack quite a punch in those little fists."

He tapped her fists and then kissed her knuckles before looking up at her again. "Trust me with your pain, Jess."

"I haven't told... I..." She lost control of her emotions and began to rail at him. She balled her fists up and pounded the couch. "How could he have treated me like that? How could I have been so stupid not to see what was happening? Three plus years I wasted on him. I shared my grief with him, and I thought he truly cared that I was hurting. I told him about my parents and he encouraged my anger, telling me that if God didn't care about me, why should I care about Him. I thought I had dealt with my grief, but then I found out all of it had been a lie."

She quit pounding the couch and looked at him, her breathing ragged as she sobbed. "I didn't deserve to be treated like that. I thought he cared." She collapsed against the back of the couch pressing her fists into her eyes.

Justin couldn't stand to watch her suffer and he pulled her fists away from her face, cradling her head against his chest. "Shush. Jess, I'm so sorry. He was an idiot and he's definitely not worth this much energy. You trusted the wrong person, and he let you down in a way that shouldn't have happened."

Her sobs continued, but he felt her body relax against his own and he settled back against the couch, keeping her close to him. He just sat there and let her cry. The fireplace crackled, the lights were still down, and as he sat there in the semi-dark trying to absorb her hurt, he realized that he wanted to be her rock. He wanted to help ease her hurts in the future, not just now.

He closed his eyes and his mind took a journey to a place in the future where the hurt had healed, and Jess was free to love and believe in herself and in others with joy in her heart. He wanted to be there when that happened. *But was she so damaged by the past and the hurt and anger she'd held onto that she wouldn't be able to let go of it? Only time would tell.*

When the fire began to die down and he felt the temperature of the house begin to drop, he shuffled her so that he could rise from the couch and add some more logs to the fire. She'd drifted off to sleep against his chest, and when he moved her away from him, she reached out for him and moaned in her sleep.

Well, she trusts me in her sleep. Now, if I can only get her to trust me when she's awake.

He glanced at his watch and realized it was almost 10:30 at night. He stepped into the kitchen and pulled out his cell phone. Mason answered on the second ring.

"Justin, you okay?"

"Yeah. I'm down here at Jessica's place. The power went out in town about an hour ago."

"We still have some power up here, but the way the wind is howling, I'm not sure how much longer that's going to last."

"Well, use the generator if you need to. I'm going to stay in town tonight. I don't want to risk driving the truck back up the mountain in this weather."

"Okay. Did Jeff leave the generator in place?"

"It's in the garage and there's fuel for it. I won't start it up unless I have to. We have enough wood to last until morning inside the house."

"Okay, what do you want me to tell Jeremy about the morning?"

Justin closed his eyes and groaned. "I forgot all about the morning." He'd offered to begin teaching the elementary Sunday School class several weeks ago, and tomorrow morning was his debut. "If you could bring me some clothes, I'd appreciate it. I'll be there."

"I can do that. See you in the morning."

Justin pocketed the phone and then returned to the living room. Jessica was still sleeping. He grabbed the extra blankets off the couches and made a sort of sleeping bag of sorts on the couch. When he went to lift her into the makeshift bed, she clutched at his shirt. "Don't leave me, please?"

"I'm not going anywhere. I just want you to be warm."

Jessica's eyes were puffy and her nose was stuffed up from her crying jag earlier. He could see she was having difficulty and asked, "What can I do to help?"

"Maybe a warm rag?" she murmured, trying to wipe her face off with the tissues that sat on the side table.

"Be right back." Justin returned moments later with a warm rag and a glass of water. "Here." He handed her both of them and then pulled a bottle of painkillers from his pocket. "I brought these along in case you need them."

Jessica looked at the bottle and shook her head. "No, I'm good."

He sat down next to her and felt the moment expand, and the tension between them grow. Unable to resist, he raised a hand and moved her hair behind her ear. "Feel any better?"

Jessica raised her eyes. "Maybe. I just feel raw. I haven't cried that much in a long time. Not even at my grandmother's funeral.

Everyone was watching me, looking to see what I was going to do, and all I could think about was getting out of town again."

"Well, the grief doesn't go away all at once, but it slowly does get better. You just have to keep talking about your feelings. And I promise to be around to listen."

Jessica dropped her eyes and then he watched as she fidgeted, her fingers twisting themselves in the blankets. He covered her hand with his own and asked, "What's going through that head of yours?"

She shook her head and he tipped her chin up, forcing her to meet his eyes. He wished there was more light, but the intimacy of the moment wouldn't have been the same. "Tell me."

Trust me with your thoughts. That's what he was really asking her for and Jessica found for the first time in a long while, she really wanted to do just that. She lifted a hand and cupped his strong jaw. She'd not known this man for very long, so how was it she felt so connected to him. He'd gotten her to release some of the pent-up emotions surrounding her grandmother's death and her ex's betrayal – something she'd never done before.

She did feel better. Her anger was less potent, her grief not quite so sharp. And he hadn't run away!

Her thumb brushed the corner of his lips and she wondered what he would do if she leaned forward just a few inches...

She didn't have to wonder any longer. Justin lowered his head and placed his lips tenderly against her own. He didn't press or try to take the kiss beyond the simple sharing, and his heart reveled in the connection between them. Never before had a kiss felt so right!

He broke the kiss and watched her eyes. "That was nice."

"More than nice," she agreed, licking her bottom lip before biting it.

"Want to do it again?" Justin asked softly.

Jessica didn't need another invitation. She wrapped her arms around his neck and plastered her lips against his own. She was feeling so many things for this man, and kissing him seemed so natural. She could almost believe that Silver Springs was where she was meant to be.

Chapter 18

Two weeks later...

Justin was frustrated with Jessica's continued refusal to attend church with him. She'd made great progress in dealing with her grandmother's death and Jason's betrayal, but she still felt that God had betrayed her.

Thanksgiving was a week away, and this weekend was the church potluck and Thanksgiving celebration. Chloe had been working on her, as well as Shelley, and the other people in town she routinely saw throughout the week.

Their relationship seemed to be going well, but they were quickly approaching a crossroads where Justin would have to choose between her and his convictions. He couldn't, and wouldn't, abandon his church family or his faith in God. But he also couldn't imagine letting her go. To help the situation, he had arranged to have Sarah talk to Jessica.

He stopped by the school, flowers in hand, and saw her exit her classroom. "Hey!"

"Justin, what are you doing here?" She offered him an easy smile that seemed to light up her face and his world at once.

"I stopped by to escort you home. Here, these are for you."

Jessica accepted the flowers and then sniffed them. "Thank you. What's the occasion?"

"I was hoping you could help me with something this afternoon."

"Sure."

"Okay, let's drop your things off at the house and then you can ride with me."

"Where are we going?"

"Over to the small motel and boarding house. It's owned by a woman named Sarah. "

"What are we going to be doing there?"

"We're putting together the gifting baskets this afternoon. You don't mind helping, do you?"

Jessica shook her head. "No. I don't mind at all. Gifting baskets?"

Justin grabbed her hand as they stepped out into the cold afternoon. Daylight savings time had come and gone a week earlier, and it was already getting dark by the time most people got off of work. The sidewalks were cleared of snow, but there was another major storm coming later in the week, and Justin was hoping to speak with Jessica about spending the Thanksgiving holidays with him and his brothers, up at the lodge.

Scott and Chloe had been planning to come, but with their baby so close to being born, they didn't want to leave the safety of the town. And Doc Matthews. He had delivered most of the forty and under Silver Springs population, and Justin knew it was only a matter of time before a replacement would need to be found.

He waited in the living room while Jessica changed into a pair of jeans and a soft cable-knit sweater. She and Chloe had made a trip into Silverthorne a few days earlier, the school having closed to handle the elections taking place. It was the largest building in Silver Springs and it only made sense to use it as a polling place, but with their children's safety at risk, none of the parents seemed to mind an extra day off school to keep their children and the general population separated.

In truth, there were only a handful of people living in the county, that weren't known well by the community at large. But even one person could be a threat, and Justin applauded the school board for being so proactive in protecting the town's youngsters. He never wanted to see Silver Springs spread across the news media because someone had hurt their kids.

Jessica returned and he helped her up into his truck. After he seated himself and headed for the edge of town, she asked, "So, you seem to be deep in thought. What's up?"

Justin stared at her. "Am I that obvious?"

Jessica grinned at him. "To me."

He shook his head. "And here I was trying to figure out when would be the appropriate time to ask."

"Now seems like a really good time."

"Okay. But promise to hear me out before you say 'No'?"

"You seem to think you already know my answer."

Justin smiled at her. "Here goes. I want you to spend the Thanksgiving holiday with us up at the lodge."

"You want...but..." She cleared her throat. Silver Springs was a very tight-knit community and she was afraid that if people found out, they would think badly of her. "I don't think I can do that. People will talk."

Justin sighed. "I know. Chloe and Scott were supposed to be up there as well..."

"She can't leave town! The baby could come any day."

"I know," he nodded. "That's why they're not coming. But I don't want you to be alone, and I guess I'm being a little selfish. I want to spend those four days with you."

Jessica smiled at him. "I would like that as well, but..." She broke off as a crazy idea occurred to her. "How about...?" She looked at him and then nodded. "How about you and your brothers come down to town? There are plenty of unused bedrooms in the house. Scott and Chloe could use the other bedroom on the ground floor, and..."

Justin pulled his truck over and then grabbed her, pulling her close and kissing her. She giggled against his lips and finally managed to push him away so she could speak. "I take it that idea meets your approval?"

"Yes. Now come back here and kiss me."

Jessica gave in for another moment and then they both broke apart when a passing car honked at them. She sat back, touching her lips and watching him with a soft smile on her face. "You know this thing between us is kind of crazy, right?"

Justin shook his head. "No. I don't know anything of the kind. I've been waiting all of my life to meet someone I truly liked. That would be you."

"This is moving way too fast," she commented.

"We have as much time as we like. Now, let's go pack baskets."

Chapter 19

Packing the baskets had gone smoothly. Jessica had really liked Sarah, and she'd even offered to go back Friday and Saturday to help deliver the baskets. Justin and his brothers had been slated to help as well, but a multiple-car accident on the highway had taken them out of town all day Friday.

Saturday, a group of missing skiers had taken them out of town as well. Jessica had been disappointed, but also proud that Justin and his brothers were able to do so much good.

Sarah and she had just finished delivering the last basket, and were drinking coffee at Sarah's kitchen table, when the conversation turned personal again.

"So, Justin tells me you're not sure about church and God."

"What?" Jessica sputtered. "I don't know that I'm unsure about church. Or God. I know exactly who He is. I just don't think I need Him in my life."

Sarah looked at her for the longest time and then shook her head. "Denial only leads to heartache."

"Denial? I'm not in denial..."

"Sure you are. You grew up learning about God and His love, but when you tried to apply that to your own life and circumstances, you found Him lacking. You've been focusing on the wrong things."

Jessica was hurt and angry that the friendship she'd had with this woman was going to end badly. "I don't want to talk about this."

"Good. Then listen. I've been where you are. I married my high school sweetheart, Brad Jenkins. We were so very happy, and we started this little motel and boarding house together. Things were going so well, but Brad felt strongly that he needed to join the service.

"I wasn't exactly on board with the idea, but he had it all planned out. He would join the service and then once his time was up, he'd go to college using his GI status, and we could take the motel to the next level. He wouldn't have to pay for college, and he'd have a steady income to send back home while he was active."

"So what happened?"

"He made it through basic training, and then joined a special training program. It was all very hush-hush, and he never could tell me exactly what he was being trained for. But it was also very dangerous. I found that out firsthand when two uniformed officers came knocking on the door his fifth month into their program. They regretted to inform me that there had been a training accident and Brad had been killed in the line of duty."

"Oh no! Did they ever tell you what happened?"

"No! I didn't even get his remains back. I never really got a good answer regarding that, but it didn't matter. We had a closed-casket service, and I had to deal with the knowledge that my husband was gone forever. I was so mad at God for taking him from me. Brad had been following his conscience, and we both felt at peace with the knowledge that God wanted him to do this."

"How could you be at peace after what happened?" Jessica asked, wondering how this woman got past the hurt and anger. She'd seen firsthand over the last few days how this woman felt about God. She lived her life to do His will, but why?

"Look, Jessica. God never promised any of us a walk in the park. Life is hard, and bad, horrible things happen to people who don't deserve it. Good people die. Bad people live. But we have to focus beyond all that."

"How? How do you look the other way when God allows bad things to happen?" Jessica was thinking about Thomas and how crushed his parents had been at his funeral. And yet... They'd not railed at God. She hadn't really taken time to analyze it at the time, but they'd rejoiced in the knowledge that their little boy wasn't suffering anymore and was in the arms of Jesus.

"Jess, let me ask you a question. You told me about the little boy with cancer and honestly, I think losing a child would hurt much worse than losing Brad ever did. But I haven't ever gone down that road, so I can only guess. But if you could have chosen for Thomas to live another ten years, knowing that he would be in horrible pain, and undergo medical procedure upon procedure, would you have chosen that instead of letting him die quickly and without years of torture?"

"Of course I would have. But see, you're assuming he would have been sick anyway. Why did God allow him to get sick in the first place? I've read my Bible and I've heard all the stories of great healings, both in days gone by and in other places around the world, so why not Thomas?"

"Do you believe Thomas is in Heaven? Do you believe your parents are there as well?"

"Yes. But that doesn't..."

"Think about it before you start trying to go down that road. If they are in Heaven, we will see them again. God simply took them home first. Who knows what tragedies might have awaited them here on earth if they had stayed. And yes, it is hard on those left behind. But we don't have to go through it alone."

"I've always felt alone. Even when I found Jason, my ex, and I thought he understood, he didn't. I was just an easy girlfriend at college because his fiancée was four hours away. I shared things with him, thinking he truly was sympathetic, but in reality, he was just going through the motions to humor me and keep me complacent."

"He sounds like a real piece of work and you're much better off without him."

"I know that. Until Justin..."

"Yes?" Sarah asked with a twinkle in her eyes.

"Well, I really like him and he says the same, but he doesn't understand why I can't trust God."

"Neither do I. Have you ever stopped to think about all of the blessings He's bestowed upon you?"

"Blessings? What blessings?"

"That answers my question. Thursday is Thanksgiving. Why don't you take some time over the next few days and try to answer that question. I promise you if you will, you'll start thinking about things a whole lot differently."

Jessica didn't think so, but after several more minutes, she promised to think on the issue. She even promised to share some of those blessings, provided she could come up with some, with Justin the next time she saw him.

Chapter 20

Jessica spent Saturday night alone. Justin and his brothers had found the lost hikers, but one of them needed medical attention, and all three brothers had ended up in Vail at the hospital. They decided to spend the night, but Justin had promised to come back at first light, saying his Sunday School class was counting on him.

He'd once again urged Jessica to come to church with him, but she once again refused. Not as vehemently as she had in weeks past, but she refused nonetheless. After hanging up the phone, she heated up a bowl of soup and sat in front of the fire, her mind replaying everything Sarah had told her.

Blessings? What counted as a blessing?

Her mind drifted back to her childhood when the ladies in the church were always telling her how lucky she was to have her grandmother. *Okay, that could be a blessing. Number one. Yay!*

Her grandmother had been a blessing. If she hadn't been around and willing to raise a young child, even though she was advanced in her years, Jessica might have ended up in South Africa with her parents. She could have been killed, or worse yet, taken as a hostage.

Okay, her grandmother really was a blessing.

As she thought about her life, she started adding more blessings to the list. *Grandma always had plenty of food and money to buy the things they truly needed. No, Jessica didn't get everything she'd wanted, but she had everything she needed and a little more.*

She'd been raised in a Christian household, giving her life to Jesus when she was only six. She'd known she was loved.

She'd gotten into the college of her choice. Her grades had been good enough to earn her a partial scholarship. She'd thumbed her nose at God, but still she'd never felt abandoned by Him.

That thought caused her to pause. *She'd abandoned God, but in her spirit, she'd always known He was waiting in the wings. Wow!*

That thought floored her. She'd done everything wrong and still, somehow, God had been there waiting for her to come back around. She jumped forward to Jason. That hadn't been God, that had been all her. She'd ignored the small voice inside her head, warning her he wasn't the right one. She'd set herself up for failure.

She tried to stay mad at God for taking her grandmother, but the woman was 92 when she passed away, and she'd done so in her sleep. She hadn't suffered, or had to suffer the indignities of being moved into a nursing home. She'd died peacefully in her sleep with her Bible clutched to her chest.

Tears filled her eyes as she realized how unfair she'd been to God. She'd held onto her anger, hoping to use it as a shield against the pain of loss, but had only succeeded in hurting herself in the process.

She fell to the floor, tears streaming down her face as she cried out to God to forgive her unbelief and misplaced anger. She used the entire box of tissues, and still the tears flowed.

Tears for her parents. Tears for her grandmother. Tears for the little boy and his family that would never see him grow up. She even shed some tears over Jason. For the emptiness that had to exist inside the man – otherwise, he wouldn't have been able to treat her so callously.

On a whim, she took a page from Justin's catharsis book and fired up her laptop. She pulled up Jason's email address and typed him a quick note.

Jason,

I know you will be shocked to read this, but I needed to send this for my own healing. I feel sorry for you and for your future wife. You used me for your own purposes, callously abusing my emotions, my time, and my energy, all so that you wouldn't have to face being alone while at college.

I'm here to tell you that I forgive you for doing it. I've discovered something that I hope one day you'll experience as well. Even though I turned my back on God, he never turned His back on me. I've started to make things right with Him, and part of that involved forgiving you.

So, I forgive you. I also pray that before you and your fiancée get married, you will do some soul searching and see if you aren't running from God as well.

Please don't contact me as I am putting that part of my life behind me. I'm taking the lessons I've learned with me, and I hope you do the same. I wish you a happy life. Please know that I am doing everything in my power to find a happy life for myself.

Jess

She hit send, and then closed the computer. She felt better! Amazingly, she truly did feel as if that part of her life was over. But there was still something missing. She didn't have anyone to share her transformation with.

She thought about calling Chloe, but didn't want to upset the mother-to-be. She thought about calling Sarah, but it was almost midnight, and she figured the woman would already be in bed. She turned down the lights, and then she remembered how her grandmother had always celebrated, after Jessica had gone to bed.

Her grandmother would turn on some worship music, and spend time with God. Singing. Praying. Talking. It didn't matter, but she'd spied on her grandmother more than once and been amazed at how happy she'd seemed during those moments.

She retrieved her computer and found an online Christian radio station. She turned the audio player on and just listened. Song after song talked about God as a friend, as a shelter in the midst of the storm, as a good father. She sat there in the dark and let the words soak into her spirit.

She drifted off to sleep at some point, her computer battery finally dying as well, plunging the house into peace and quiet.

She woke up as the sun peeked through the windows and sat up on the mattress. She hadn't even changed her clothes the night before, but she still felt refreshed!

She glanced at the clock and suddenly felt a sense of urgency. Church was due to start in twenty minutes, and she'd never before felt such a strong desire to be there. She didn't have any skirts, but she donned a pair of corduroys, a sweater, and her boots. The church was located three blocks away, so she grabbed her keys and was pulling into the parking lot as the church bells rang out announcing the morning service was about to begin.

She felt very uncomfortable as she got out of her car, and really wished she didn't have to walk into the church by herself. A pair of arms wrapped around her neck.

"Jessica! Welcome!"

Jessica looked up into the eyes of Shelley, and standing right behind her was Sarah. She gave the woman a hug and then walked to Sarah. "Thank you. I did what you suggested, and..." She broke off as tears filled her eyes.

"Enough of that. This is a morning of celebration. Come on. Justin's going to be so thrilled!"

The two women bracketed her, each taking an elbow and escorting her into the small church building. She saw Mason and Kaillar sitting towards the back, and gave them a small smile when they grinned at her, and Kaillar gave her a thumbs up.

Justin was down front, talking to Pastor Jeremy, but the whispers of her arrival quickly reached his ears. He looked up, and the smile that split his face was one she would never forget. It was filled with joy and...love? He came towards her, almost running down the aisle.

"Jessica! You're here!"

"I'm here. I have so much to tell you, but..."

"Later. Come, let's sit down. I want to hear about everything, but right now, I want to enjoy having you sitting beside me during the service."

Jessica allowed him to escort her back to the pew he shared with his brothers. She did her best to brush off her rusty hymn-singing skills, finally remaining silent and just allowing the moment to wash over her.

She'd come to Colorado to escape the events and her past in Arizona. She'd not only found a new beginning in her career and her love life, she'd found a new beginning with the One who had made all things possible.

As the service continued, she couldn't wait for the coming weeks and months ahead. She was where God wanted her to be, and she was determined to live every moment and make it count.

Book 2: Mason

Chapter 1

Sunday before Thanksgiving, just above Silver Springs, Colorado...

"Gracie, did anyone happen to check the weather report before we headed up here?" Becca Edwards asked, watching the ever darkening sky with a sense of trepidation. She liked nature, but her experience of being in the mountains during a storm of any kind was more than limited. It was non-existent.

The gathering black and grey clouds were alarming, and they seemed to be getting closer and lower with each passing moment. A storm was brewing, and they were fixing to get caught right in the middle of it.

"Sure I did. They were expecting maybe a few snow flurries tonight and tomorrow, but nothing big," Melanie Jenkins, now Melanie Walters, told her. "It's not supposed to get real bad until next week."

Melanie and Becca had become best friends when they'd become roommates at college four years earlier. Melanie had been a business major while Becca was a journalism major, specializing in outdoor photography. She was currently hoping to land a job as a wildlife photographer with the Division of Wildlife.

To that end, she needed some spectacular outdoor shots of the Colorado Mountains. She and Melanie had hiked in these mountains many times over the last few years, and being that Melanie was headed across the country to work in her father's company the day after Thanksgiving, they had decided to make this last minute trip.

Melanie had gotten married three months earlier to her high school sweetheart via the Internet. Her husband, Master Chief Michael Walters, had just returned from his second tour in Afghanistan, and was currently undergoing a debriefing period in Colorado Springs. He was due to get his discharge papers at the end of the month. At that point in time, Melanie and her husband would be moving to Florida, and Becca was afraid that she'd never see her best friend again.

The third member of the hiking group was Gracie Shelton. She was a seasoned hiker and climber, and up until a month ago, their third roommate. The three had been together for several years, and shared a bond and sisterhood only friends who had weathered life's storms together could appreciate.

Gracie, unlike the others who had grown up in a city environment, had grown up in Silver Springs, although she'd been gone since she was fourteen. Her parents had moved to the Denver area just before she entered high school, and while she'd never been back to visit, a part of her heart had always remained in Silver Springs, given to a teenage boy her age when they were much too young to understand that life didn't always work out the way they wanted it to.

Now she was back, and ready to check out the small town. Gracie was in a class by herself, having skipped ahead in her schooling after leaving Silver Springs; she'd graduated from high school with two years of college already accomplished at seventeen. She'd gotten accepted into medical school at nineteen, and at the age of twenty-two, was now ready to begin her career.

She'd graduated from medical school a few months back, and been prepared to work as an emergency room physician while she decided if she wanted to specialize or just practice family medicine.

She'd been having a hard time deciding just where she wanted to practice or what kind of medicine she wanted to do; nothing appeared to fit or feel right.

Then she'd seen the ad for a doctor in Silver Springs. It seemed that Doc Matthews was getting ready to retire, but hadn't told anyone in town yet. He wanted to bring in a fresh young doctor, to work alongside him over the next six months. Then he would step out of the picture, allowing the new doctor a chance at owning their own practice in the small mountain town.

It was a dream come true, and she'd immediately emailed him her resume. She had explained about having grown up in Silver Springs, and Doc had immediately inquired about both of her parents, having recognized her surname. He'd delivered her, along with half of the town, and it seemed that he never forgot a name.

She'd had several phone conversations with the man over the last two months, and it had been decided that she would start on December first. She hadn't gotten very far into her planning for the move when she had overheard Becca and Melanie talking about making a trip to Maroon Peak. Since it was directly above Silver Springs, she'd asked if she could tag along, and had laughed at the look of relief on both women's faces. They both liked the outdoors well enough, but when it came to serious hiking, they were amateurs and they knew it. Gracie did not fit into that category.

She had contacted Sarah and made arrangements for her and her two friends to stay there for a few nights. Melanie was driving to Colorado Springs on Wednesday to spend the holiday weekend with her husband, and though Gracie had asked Becca numerous times about her plans, her hurting friend had been very quiet and noncommittal. Gracie was hoping she could get Becca to open up to her during this trip.

A gust of wind drew her attention skyward, and she watched the storm clouds gather over the mountain. A sense of urgency to seek shelter assailed her, and she knew that the chances of them making it down the mountain before nightfall were slim. At least, not without some assistance. The sunlight was completely hidden by the dark clouds, and the air temperature was dropping fast. The sky had been blue when they first set out on their hike, but two hours later, it was hard to remember what it looked like. They were in trouble, and needed to get back to town. Immediately.

There were several problems with that though. It was the Sunday before Thanksgiving, and they'd passed no other hikers or campers in the area. On top of that, they were currently on the opposite side of the mountain from the closest cell tower, meaning that they had absolutely no cell phone service.

None of them had short-wave radios with them, and Gracie mentally kicked herself for not having the foresight to stick one in her camping pack. She knew better, having grown up on the mountain, but this trip had been a hurried last attempt to help Becca get some pictures, and she hadn't taken the proper precautions before leaving Denver. She only hoped they wouldn't all pay a hefty price for that mistake.

They couldn't even call for help from their present location. Deciding that it was time to speak up and try to salvage this trip, she got Becca's attention, "We need to head down."

"But I haven't gotten the shots I want yet." The park ranger had told them there was a nest of eagles at the top of the Northern Trailhead, and had described the location of their nest. That was their current goal, but not one they were going to see today.

Of the three women, Becca was the least likely of their group to handle a difficult hike down. Six months previously, she'd been attacked while walking across a parking garage late at night, and since then she'd been different. No longer confident or willing to take any sort of risk, the fact that she'd wanted to come up on this mountain had been what Gracie saw as an attempt to return to normal.

Becca had healed physically, but mentally and emotionally, she seemed to be suffering from what Gracie thought was classic PTSD. Night terrors. Jumpy in strange situations. Being stuck atop a mountain in the middle of a winter storm was not something she would handle well, or at all. She'd been prone to panic attacks since the attack, and Gracie didn't even want to think about having to talk her down from one of those while also fighting Mother Nature.

She did seem to listen to Gracie, turning to her for help and support, but Gracie knew what she had to offer wasn't enough. She had tried to get her to attend some group counseling sessions, but Becca had adamantly refused, saying she was handling everything just fine and didn't need to share her emotional meltdowns with a bunch of strangers. She was hoping to find the young woman someone to help her before she left town, but so far, that hadn't occurred. Becca was handling things on her own, and in her own way, and Gracie's biggest fear was that once she left Denver, Becca would completely shut down and isolate herself away from society. That would be detrimental to her ever recovering from the attacks and living a normal life.

She met Becca's gaze and told her, "I know that you wanted more time to shoot up here, but those clouds aren't going to go away. And if we don't get over to the other side of the mountain before nightfall, no one's even going to know we're up here. Trust me; we don't want that to happen." The park ranger would know they'd come up, and if she looked, she'd see her vehicle in the parking area, but those were pretty big ifs, and Gracie would rather save herself than depend upon a stranger to do so.

Melanie looked at the sky and nodded, "I think she's right, Becca. We really do need to retrace our steps. Maybe we can find someplace to shelter for the night, and come back and get your shots in the morning? We have enough food and water to last through the night."

Gracie shook her head at the foolish comment. It was evident that Melanie had only been in the mountains during the Summer and early Fall. This was neither, and a winter storm was on its way. "That's not going to work. We aren't prepared to survive out here overnight. Not in this type of weather."

"We have the tent and can make a fire..."

Gracie shook her head, "Melanie, we'd never keep a fire going unless it was inside the tent, and you've done enough camping to know that isn't even a possibility. On top of that, our sleeping bags are in the vehicle, which is at the base of this mountain. It's going to snow, and get much colder than it is now. We need to head down before that happens, or at least be on our way down."

Gracie wasn't going to spend any more time arguing the point. She was right, and she was prepared to do whatever she could to make sure they made it off this mountain in one piece.

"Look, I'm going to hike back down to the trailhead below. You two go around the same way we came and I'll meet you there after I get a hold of the forest service dispatch in town." They'd passed a cut wall a hundred yards back. It would lead down to the lower trail, and then she would be only a half mile or so from where she could call for help. She could easily handle the climb down. Her friends would freak when they saw the rock wall and how far down the bottom was.

Becca looked alarmed, "Is it really that dangerous for us to be up here?"

"Not right now, but in another hour or so, things are going to get pretty nasty. There was an overhang just beyond that rock slide. Wait there for me, and then we'll hike down together." She tried to downplay the danger so that Becca wouldn't spin off into a panicked state, but she also didn't want them thinking they could lollygag around. They needed to get moving. Now!

"Why don't you just come with us?" Becca asked, a note a panic in her voice that Gracie immediately tried to quell.

Gracie smiled, "I grew up here, remember. I'm a much better hiker and can move faster on my own. I'll hike down, make the call, and then meet you. With any luck, they'll have a team in the area to come up and help us get back down the mountain tonight. They might even get to the overhang before you two do."

She looked once again at the gathering storm clouds, and only hoped she'd make it down to call for help before things got really bad. A few light snow flurries were already starting to fall from the sky. "You all need to head down. Now."

Gracie turned to leave and Melanie called her back, "What happens if you don't meet us?"

Gracie swallowed her sense of dread, and then smiled and told her solemnly, "Then you two continue following the trail down and make the call. Tell them I need help. You can play rescuer to my damsel in distress."

When she saw the look on Becca's face, she quickly added, "But I'm going to be fine. Don't worry about me. I've not worried. Just get to that overhang and I'll get help on the way."

She headed off, diving off the edge of the cliff fifty yards back and scrambling her way down until she reached the next level area. She was breaking all of the rules of outdoor survival by taking off on her own, but Becca and Melanie were both amateur hikers, and there was no way they could have handled her current hike down. That would have been asking for disaster.

She paused at the top of the wall and pulled on her gloves. They were fingerless and would help her grip the rock crevices and hold her weight as she looked for footholds and such, but would still protect her tender palms from being cut. The first ten feet were easy, nicely weathered, and she had no trouble finding a place to put her toes or her fingers. But hallway down, she found herself having to use all of her skills to negotiate her way down the last thirty feet of rock wall.

She was once again thankful for the rock climbing gym she'd joined just out of high school. She'd wanted to join earlier, but her father hadn't wanted her doing anything that was reminiscent of their time in Silver Springs. She frowned, wishing that she and her father had been able to settle their differences before his passing. It had been two years now, and she still harbored some bitterness towards the man who'd uprooted their family just because she'd gone and fallen in love with a young man he didn't think suitable. At least, that was the misconception she'd operated under, before realizing there was another issue at hand.

It had taken her several years before she'd finally gotten to the root of the problem. The ugly truth had finally come out after her father was diagnosed with a failing heart. Years earlier, he'd violated his marriage vows and slept with a young woman from Silver Springs who only occasionally came back to town. She'd been trying to get her life together, and doing a credible job, but then she'd gone and fallen for Gracie's father, Bill Shelton.

The woman had left town shortly after he'd realized what he was doing was wrong and hurting so many people. He'd never said anything to his wife, and then the woman had gone and gotten killed. He'd attended the funeral, along with the rest of the community, his sense of guilt over her death something that sat heavy on his shoulders.

He felt that the reason she'd left was due in part to their sinful dalliance. He'd been able to pretend that time in his life had never happened, watching silently from the wings as the woman's sons grew up, motherless, to become teenagers. He was viewed as an upstanding citizen in the community, and his pride had kept him from coming clean, and ridding himself of the guilt he carried around.

But when Gracie had fallen in love with one of the woman's sons, he'd been afraid of the truth coming out. He said he was trying to save his marriage, but Gracie knew he'd been trying to save himself from embarrassment. As a deacon on the church board, he'd been privy to confidential information about other church members, and many times Gracie had heard him belittle someone else's sin. Now he was the one caught, and he didn't want any of the punishment coming to him.

When he knew that his time on this Earth was short, he could no longer bear the guilt inside, and confessed all to Gracie and her mother. He'd been so afraid of his secret coming out as Gracie and Mason grew closer together, he'd run. Packing up the family, he took a position with a law firm in Denver, and moved everyone practically overnight.

Gracie had hated him for doing that. She'd had to leave all of her friends, and the only boy she'd ever truly cared about. *Mason Donnelly*. Her father hadn't even given her a chance to say goodbye. She'd simply come home from school to find a moving van in the driveway and a team of men loading the boxes they had just packed into the truck.

Her mother never complained, and after her father passed away, Gracie's mother confirmed that she'd known he been unfaithful to her, but she took her side of the wedding vows seriously and hadn't said anything because she didn't want to ruin the life they'd built together. She'd secretly forgiven him, long before he'd even confessed or asked for such. Gracie hadn't been able to understand that depth of forgiveness coming from another human. She knew that God was capable of forgiving that much, but she just couldn't see how a human could do so and not constantly be reminded of the past.

A strong gust of wind brought her attention back to the present. That sad time was over with, and she was here to make a new life for herself. She'd not dared ask Sarah about Mason or if he was still single, for fear of the answer. Mason was her other half. She'd known it when they were adolescents, and she still felt the same now.

When she'd made the decision to move to Silver Springs, she had reluctantly turned the situation over to God. She reasoned that if God hadn't allowed her feelings for Mason to dissipate over the course of eight years, that maybe God knew something she didn't. She'd prayed and asked Him to only bring Mason back into her life if they had a future together. She didn't want either of them to get hurt, and it was only recently that she'd begun to have doubts regarding her father's infidelity. Mason and his brothers didn't know, and she really didn't have any intention of telling them. Or at least, she was trying to get to that point in her thinking.

Now, here she was, scrambling down the slippery face of a rock wall, hoping to reach a point where there would be cell service to phone and call for help before the storm blowing in trapped them on the mountain. She felt a sense of panic like never before, and was just about to make her final descent, when a gust of wind rose up out of nowhere. She was about twelve feet off the ground, and her strength was dwindling fast.

She grappled for the next handhold, but water had frozen in the crevice of the rocks and her fingertips only met ice. Slippery ice. Her hand lost its purchase on the rocks and she felt her feet leave the rock wall as she fell. The ground came up to meet her fast, her head bouncing on the ground as she landed painfully with her right leg twisted at an odd angle beneath her.

Excruciating pain radiated from her body, and she moaned in agony. Her head hurt something fierce and when she tried to focus her eyes, everything seemed blurry and as if it were hidden behind a shroud.

She tried to move, but the pain was intense and she felt struggled to breathe through it. She needed to get to a place where she could phone for help, but as her vision grew dark and her hands began to register the cold, she slipped into unconsciousness. The face of a young teenage boy hovered for a moment, and she silently sent out a plea to God to send help and save her. She planned to make Silver Springs her home for the next forty years or so, but first, she had to get down off this mountain!

Chapter 2

Pastor Jeremy had just finished his sermon on being thankful, ending the morning service with a prayer over the meal the church was about to consume. It was a tradition for the church congregation to come together the Sunday before Thanksgiving and share a meal after the morning service. Everyone brought something, based upon what letter their last name began with, and it gave them all a chance to socialize with one another before the busy holiday season kicked into full swing.

Jeremy moved through the congregants, keeping an eye on Justin's tall head as he did so. He'd not gotten a chance to greet Jessica Andrews yet, and he wanted to make sure that her presence had been noted and how welcome she was in their church. He headed down the center aisle, shaking hands and nodding his head to others as he did so.

This was the first time she'd come into the church, and from the look on Justin Donnelly's face, it was the perfect way to kick off the holidays. *Could Jessica finally be ready to admit what was in her heart?* He hoped so for Justin and her sakes.

He finally reached them and reached for her hand, "Jessica! It was so good to have you in service this morning."

"Thank, Pastor. It felt good to be here." She was smiling and looked completely at ease.

Jeremy looked at Justin and smiled, "You two look good together."

"Thanks." Justin looked at Jessica and then back to the pastor. Lowering his voice so that his words wouldn't carry far, he said, "I imagine we'll be coming to see you sometime in the near future. Just as soon as we work out a few more details."

Jeremy raised a brow, "Does that mean..."

Justin shook his head, "Not yet, but that's where this is going. Just thought I'd give you fair warning."

"Consider me duly warned." Jeremy turned back to Jessica, who was having a spirited conversation with some of his younger members of the congregation. Students from her classroom. He watched for a moment, pleased to see the rapport she had already developed with the next generation.

He tapped her on the shoulder and when she turned, he smiled, "Jessica, again, it was a pleasure. Enjoy lunch you two."

Mason and Kaillar had been standing off to the side and heard their brother's veiled remarks. Pulling Justin to the side, Kaillar asked, "Are you seriously considering marrying Jessica?"

Justin nodded his head, "Yes. I know it's too soon to ask her right now, but that won't always be the case."

Mason slapped him on the shoulder, "Well, just so you know, I'm fully on board with that idea. Jessica is great and she makes you smile."

"Thanks, brother. Now, let's go grab some food. I saw Mrs. Hathaway earlier walking into the kitchen with three different pies."

Kaillar rubbed his stomach and laughed, "I hope one of them is pecan. She makes it like nobody else I know."

Mason started to agree, but then the face of an angel from his past filled his vision. *Gracie Shelton.* The girl who'd stolen his heart at the beginning of high school and then left town without a word. Her mother had made the best pecan pie, and more than once, Gracie had snuck an extra piece out of the house and they'd had it with their lunch

He didn't know why he was thinking about her now, as he hadn't done so for a while. She'd been gone for more than eight years, but he smiled at the memory, and then pushed the hurt it left behind away. His Uncle Jed had spent many nights talking to him after she'd left. He'd finally come to terms with the fact that at the tender age of fourteen, Gracie was at the whimsy of her parents. She'd had no choice but to leave town when they did, and deep inside Mason had always hoped she'd come back. When she was an adult. That hope was still there, but he'd managed to bury it deep beneath the chores and responsibilities of day-to-day life.

Inwardly sighing, he pushed those memories aside. Today was a day for celebrating, not reminiscing about a past you couldn't change. A time to be thankful for the things you did have, not the things you didn't.

They all headed over to the kitchen area and Mason was just about to sit down and start eating when Sarah joined them with a worried look up on her face. The forty something widow owned and operated the only motel and boarding house in Silver Springs. She was as level-headed as they come, and seeing her so worried had all three men standing up and taking notice.

Kai was the first to speak up, "Hey Sarah. What's up? You look awfully worried for such a nice afternoon."

"I am worried. I have three young women who are supposed to be staying tonight, but they haven't called or shown up yet."

"They're probably just taking their time. Where were they coming in from?"

"Denver."

"Well, I wouldn't get too worried yet. Why were they coming up here?"

"Something about taking some pictures from the top of Maroon Peak."

"What?!" Mason exclaimed. "It's pure stupidity to think that you can climb Maroon Peak this time of year. Especially with a storm about to arrive."

"I know. I have a feeling that something is terribly wrong."

Mason wasn't one for believing in women's intuition, but in this instance, he felt a sense of urgency to locate the women and ensure that they were someplace safe and warm. Stepping to the side, he placed a quick phone call, and the sense of dread he felt magnified a hundredfold.

"Hey Kai! I just got off the phone with the ranger at the station. She said three women headed up to the top of Maroon Peak around ten o'clock this morning."

"What?! Why would they do that? Didn't they check the weather?" Kaillar, otherwise known as Kai to his family and friends, shook his head in disbelief. He and his brothers operated the only guide service and tourist lodge in the area. Maroon Peak was their stomping grounds.

The mountain was not an easy climb in good weather, and with a major winter storm due to roll in, no one should be up on the side of that mountain. Not intentionally, or even deliberately. The mountains could get nasty in a hurry, and even seasoned climbers knew better than to hike in this weather.

Kaillar, the middle of the three brothers, headed for the door to the outside, stepping back in a few seconds later, shaking the snowflakes from his hair. "It's getting pretty nasty out there already. Visibility on the mountain has got to be nil."

Mason raised a brow and then shook his head, muttering about stupid tourists and foolish women. Mason was twenty-two, with dark hair and deep blue eyes. He was also in charge of the local search and rescue team, and if there were two women lost on the mountain, it would fall to him and his brothers to find them.

"I hope they took shelter," he murmured, looking out the large picture window that overlooked the mountain beyond.

"What do you think?" Kaillar asked, taking a seat at a nearby table.

"Did the ranger happen to say which way they were going to ascend?"

"The Northern Trailhead. One of the women is a photographer and the park ranger told them about the eagle's nest at the top."

Mason nodded, "Wonderful." His voice laced with sarcasm that belied his words. "Well, at least that way has some flat ground about midway up. Hopefully they saw the storm clouds gathering and took shelter."

Justin nodded his head as well, "Think we should try to go find them before we lose the daylight?"

Mason and Kaillar looked at each other and then sighed. "Yeah. We'll go. You stay here and man the radio, just in case we find the worst."

Mason grabbed a plate and headed for the food tables, "Let me grab a piece of pie and we can head up to the cabin. We'll need our gear."

Kaillar joined him and a few minutes later, they were ready to head out. Sarah followed them out, and then pulled Mason aside.

"Mason, I think you should know that one of the women is Gracie Shelton."

Mason's eyebrows disappeared beneath his too-long hair, "What?"

Sarah nodded solemnly, "I just didn't want you to be surprised when you saw her." It was common knowledge that a much younger Mason had been enthralled with Gracie Shelton. It also hadn't escaped anyone's notice that he seemed to have changed once she left town. No longer the carefree teenager, getting into trouble and raising a ruckus. He'd become quieter, and more withdrawn. He'd also isolated himself from the rest of the female population. At least the single ones.

Even years later, his only female friends were either widows, cousins, or married. A fact the single women in the surrounding towns and Silver Springs lamented for far too often.

Sarah was sure it was because Gracie had taken his heart with her when she'd left, and she'd secretly prayed for the day when Gracie would be out from under her father's thumb and come back to Silver Springs where she belonged.

"What is Gracie doing back here?" Mason asked, keeping his voice level and without the emotion racing through him.

"Doc put an ad out to find a replacement physician. He says he's ready to retire. I understand Gracie just finished medical school a few months ago."

Mason said nothing, his mind still reeling from the fact that Gracie was back in Silver Springs. On Maroon Peak. In the way of a dangerous winter storm!

"Thanks for the warning. Kai, let's roll." Mason's desire to reach the women before the storm became too overwhelming had just raised ten notches.

The two men made short work of getting back to the cabin. Kaillar grabbed them some protein bars and water while Mason packed up the first aid kit, extra batteries for their flashlights, and some climbing gear. A short wave radio, rope, several thermal blankets, matches to start a fire with, and several C-rations completed their kits. They had no intention of being out on the mountain all night, but the first rule of survival in the mountains was to always be prepared for the worst, hope for the best, and deal with the hand you got to the best of your ability.

By 2:30 p.m., they were back in the truck and headed for the Northern Trailhead. The ranger was still waiting for them, and she described the vehicle and the three women in great detail. They'd passed the vehicle in the parking area, confirming the three women had not hiked down yet. They got detailed descriptions of each woman from the park ranger, and Mason knew. There was no doubt in Mason's mind that the blond woman described to him was Gracie. No doubt at all.

As a teenager, he'd begged God to bring Gracie back to him. Now that it appeared to have occurred, he found himself alternating between fear and jubilation. Kaillar was driving, having found the ATV trail that would take them partway up the mountain and save some much needed time. While he drove, Mason kept his gaze on the approaching mountain peak. If Gracie were up on the mountain, he would find her, hopefully before any harm could come to her. That was his mission; he only hoped that he'd be successful in making it a reality.

Chapter 3

Gracie felt icy water on her face and slowly opened her eyes, taking in the ominous clouds right overhead. Snow was already beginning to fall from them, in great big flakes that were full of moisture. Looking at the surrounding ground covered in the white stuff already, she knew it had been snowing for quite a while, a period of time where she'd lain unconscious on the hard ground.

She started to move, but pain radiated through her body, and she recalled falling from the rock face. She lay still and tried to take stock of the injuries to her body. Her ribs were achy, but not so much so that she worried about cracks or breaks. Just bruises were bad enough. Her head hurt, and when she lifted a hand to her temple, it came away with blood on it.

Moving down her body, she was freezing, her teeth chattering, and her arms feeling sluggish and heavy. Her mind felt slow, and she wondered how long she'd been lying there. It was starting to grow dark, but she couldn't tell if it was from the gathering storm clouds, or if the sun had already gone down behind the mountains.

Her back felt fine, and she gingerly tried to turn her head, relieved when she was able to do so without causing pain in her neck. Her head ached, but that was to be expected since she' hit it hard enough to lacerate it. She carefully took inventory as she moved from her neck down, grimacing in pain when she reached her legs. Her left ankle was throbbing in time with her heartbeat. It was crumpled beneath her, and the pain centered around her knee for the moment. She gingerly rolled herself over to her right side, slowly untangling her left leg until it was mostly straight. It didn't want to cooperate, almost as if the top and bottom halves were no longer connected. Stabbing pain in her knee told her she wasn't walking out of here on her own.

She could still wiggle her toes, and based upon the location of the pain, she guessed she'd done significant damage to the ligaments holding her knee together. She gritted her teeth, and pushed herself up to a sitting position. She was about half a mile from the overhang where she was supposed to meet her hiking partners, and she hoped they had listened to her instructions and headed down the mountain when she hadn't shown up.

Her pack had come off, and she scooted along the wet ground until she could reach it. She pulled her cell phone out, hoping for at least one bar of service. "Please, God." She pointed it in all directions, but still came up with nothing. She wasn't far enough around the side of the mountain yet.

It was snowing harder now, and for the first time in her life, Gracie began to panic. *Pull it together, Grace. You know these mountains. Think. There has to be someplace you can hole up until morning.*

The thought of spending the night, alone and cold, on the face of the mountain was daunting, but Gracie was a fighter. She unzipped her pack, and pulled the thermal blanket from its zipper pouch. She wrapped it around her shoulders, hoping to stave off getting any wetter while she examined her options.

She was sitting at the base of the rock wall, no shelter in site. If she could make it down the mountain another twenty yards or so, she could at least take shelter in the trees and the pine needles. She'd never had a chance to use the survival skills they'd learned in seventh grade science, but suddenly pieces of information popped into her head.

Find shelter from the wind and moisture. The trees would have to do.

Stay someplace where you could be seen from the air by a search and rescue plane. That one was a little more difficult. There was no open space close, but Gracie's jacket was bright red and purple. That should count for something.

Snow caves can save your life. Okay, there wasn't enough snow to build a snow cave, but the idea was that one could use nature to conserve body heat. There was a deep bed of pine needles beneath the trees. She only hoped that it was cold enough that any bugs who'd inhabited the needles during the warmer months had died or were in hibernation. She wasn't a prissy girl who screamed at the sight of a spider, but she also didn't feel up to sharing her makeshift bed with them.

She put her pack on her front, slipping her arms through the straps and tightening them so she wouldn't have to worry about it falling off. She needed all of her concentration for what was to come. She scooted over to the rock wall so that she could try to pull herself to a standing position. It took her several attempts, but she finally was able to use her good leg to push her body up along the rock surface. She was panting with her efforts afterwards, and she stayed there for several minutes to let her head stop spinning and the nausea in her stomach ease. Her knee was protesting the slightest movement vehemently, but she pressed onward.

Ten minutes later, she felt able to continue. She brushed the snow off her hair, and took a look at her goal. The trees to be more specific. She had all of her weight resting on her good leg, and she was trying to ignore the pulsing pain in her injured knee. She just needed to reach the trees. She edged her way along the rock wall, using it as a support beam for as long as possible. When it was time to step out and head for the trees, she gingerly placed some weight on her left leg, screaming in pain as it buckled and she fell forward to the ground. She lay there panting, trying to control the pain, all while refusing to give in to the tears of despair and frustration that were stinging her eyes. "Come on, Grace! You have to do this!"

She pushed her torso up, and slowly began to crawl across the now snow-covered ground, using her good leg to push herself up while her injured leg simply dragged along. Her injured leg felt every stick, rock, and bump along the way, but Gracie gritted her teeth and pressed on.

She felt rocks and debris poke through her gloves, but she didn't stop. If she stayed out in the open, it would possibly be the last thing she ever did. If she reached the trees, hopefully someone would come looking for her soon. If not tonight, then at first light. Her vision was blurry, and her arms felt leaden, but still she moved forward.

It was small comfort given her present predicament, but it was all she had. Determination had gotten her far, and it would see her through this situation as well. It took her twenty minutes before she reached the dense trees. Tears were streaming down her face, freezing before they could drop to the ground and mud and debris covered most of her body.

She lay there, panting with her efforts, trying to take shallow breaths so the nausea would abate. She rolled to her back, and then leveraged herself up under the first tree she came to that was still relatively dry underneath. Her thermal blanket was now covered in mud and melting snow, but she wrapped it around herself anyway. She tried to bend her knee to keep her body heat in close, but the muscles had finally stiffened up to the point that she couldn't even bend it the slightest bit.

She scooped pine needles over her leg, hoping the survivalist who had taught their class actually had known what he was talking about. She wrapped the thin thermal blanket tighter around herself, covering her head and praying for morning to come quickly.

The wind howled, the snow continued to fall, and Gracie finally allowed the exhaustion and pain to overtake her, forcing her body into a deep sleep as her body temperature started to drop.

. . ⚓ . .

MASON WAS SICK WITH worry.

He and Kaillar had found two of the women an hour and a half ago, huddled beneath a rocky overhang, just where Gracie had told them to seek shelter. They were scared and cold, but otherwise in good health. They'd been relieved to see the two men, and then expressed feelings of guilt for not having attempted to make it down the trail on their own.

Neither woman seemed to have enough hiking experience to be up on the mountain in bad weather. Mason had assured them that staying put was actually the best choice they could have made. But they'd been worried sick about their friend. Gracie Shelton.

She was missing, and Mason and Kaillar felt horrible confirming that she had never made a phone call to the ranger station for help. Mason sent Kaillar back down to the station with the other two women, and he pulled a map from his pocket.

The women had described the location where Gracie tried to climb down, and he decided to take an approach from the bottom up. The snow was already an inch thick in most places, and more was accumulating by the minute. Even with ropes and anchors, trying to scale a rock wall in this weather was suicide.

He carefully made his way around the western side of the mountain, using the known trails and avoiding the rockslide areas, as they were too slippery and dangerous in this weather.

He finally reached the rock wall that he assumed Gracie had attempted to climb down, looked up, and shook his head. In this weather, he would have trouble descending this particular wall, and he was an expert climber. *I wonder if she actually scaled the wall, and where she learned to do something this difficult.*

He looked around the ground, and would have missed the signs that someone had been there if he hadn't started to slip and reached out to catch himself. His hand came away from the rock with fresh blood smeared across it.

He looked around frantically trying to see through the falling snow. Cupping his hands around his mouth, he called out, "Gracie!" He sent up a silent prayer, hoping the blood was hers and at the same time, hoping it wasn't. "Gracie! If you can hear me, call out."

He listened carefully, the wind making it difficult to hear. He searched the ground for further evidence, and took his eyes in an ever increasingly wide circle out from the rock wall. When he was almost thirty yards out, he found what he'd been looking for. Drag marks!

He went in that direction, cupping his hands to concentrate his voice, "Gracie!"

He followed the drag marks, and then he saw the shiny silver blanket, partially covered in snow, but covering what appeared to be a very still form.

He slid down the remaining feet, and then quickly brushed the snow off the huddled figure. He pulled the thermal blanket open to reveal a mud covered female he could only assume was the girl of his dreams? *This can't be right. In my dreams, Gracie and I were always re-united in prom attire! Crazy dreams of a teenager, and this is most definitely a full grown woman.*

Shaking his head at the fanciful ideas racing through it, he pulled off one glove and searched for a pulse. It was faint, and her skin was cool to the touch. Too cool. He immediately began to worry about hypothermia.

He shook her shoulder, "Gracie!" He didn't even consider that the woman wasn't Gracie. She bore the same half-moon scar over her right eyebrow as Gracie. A scar she'd received when they'd slipped past the safety gates and gone exploring inside the Silver Springs Mine. They'd been foolish, but at the age of twelve, they'd thought themselves invincible. With the images from the most recent *Raiders of the Lost Ark* playing in their heads, they been searching for buried treasure and adventure.

When Justin had realized where they were, they'd hurried to exit the mine before he reached them and had proof of their foolishness, but Gracie hadn't ducked far enough and the metal bolt sticking out of the safety gate had caught her just above the eye.

Doc had taken one looked at her and silently stitched her up before asking how she'd hurt herself. When a tearful Mason had tried to explain, Doc had given both of them a lecture on the dangers of closed up mines, and threatened to tell his uncle and her father if they ever did anything so stupid again.

A gust of wind forced his mind back to the present. He moved her hair back, and that's when he saw the cut and large bump on her forehead. Blood had dripped down the other side of her forehead, but seemed to have mostly stopped now. "Sugar, what did you do to yourself?" He was stunned at the depth of feeling that pulsed through him. He wanted to gather her close to his chest and protect her from all harm. But first, he needed to figure out how she was hurt and find them some shelter.

She wasn't responding to him, and he didn't feel that they had time to waste. He pulled his radio from his pocket and waited until Justin came on. "Mason's on his way to the ranger station with two of the women. The other one tried to climb down the cut wall to call for help. It looks like she fell and cracked her head pretty good."

While speaking, Mason had been moving the leaves she'd piled up around her, pausing when he saw the angle of her extended leg. "She's got some sort of leg injury and a small cut on her head. How about sending the chopper up here?"

"Mason, I wish I could. Visibility is awful, and they just shut down the closest airports."

"Chopper?" Mason asked, already knowing the answer.

"Not until the visibility clears up. How far up are you?" Justin asked.

"About ten thousand feet would be my guess. It's already dumped a few inches in the last half hour. She can't walk down, and I can't carry her that far. Too steep."

"Can you get her down to one of the line shacks?"

Mason thought for a moment and then smiled, "I'd forgotten about those. Yeah, I think I can get her down that far. We should be directly above the closest one."

"That's what I would do. If you can get her some place dry for the night, I'll send someone up to get you just as soon as the storm clears."

"Will do. I'll check in once we reach the shack." Mason pocketed the radio, and then stuffed her thermal blanket back into her pack. They had about a half hour of sunlight, and they needed to be close to the shack before night fell. It was time to put himself to the test. Both of their lives depended upon it.

Chapter 4

Mason made it to the line shack and kicked the door open. Gracie hadn't stirred during their slippery walk down the side of the mountain. He was grateful for that fact, as he'd not been able to carry her through the trees without adding some bumps and bruises to her body.

He laid her down on the floor, and quickly shut the door. It appeared that this shack had been used during the summer as a fresh supply of firewood was in the carrier and someone had taken the liberty of stacking some in the hearth. A stack of old newspapers lay nearby, and he wadded some up and stuffed then beneath the logs before lighting them.

Once he was sure that the fire was going, he took a survey of their surroundings, finding several wind-up lamps and two oil ones. He lit them all, placing them around the single room shack to provide as much light as possible.

Turning back to Gracie, he could see her body shivering as it attempted to maintain her body temperature. He removed her boots, pulled her jacket from her body, and then her jeans, being careful not to disturb her injured leg any more than necessary. She had full thermal underwear on beneath, and he tried to ignore the way his body appreciated her lithe form. She was beautiful, but right now, she was out cold and Mason was growing more worried with each passing minute.

He pulled out a gallon of water from one of the shelves, and used it to wet some paper towels. He carefully wiped her hands and face off, carefully cleansing around the cut on her forehead and wishing they had the benefit of a medical exam. The purplish bruising and swelling was significant, but it was the fact that she was unconscious which worried him most.

He located the sleeping bags, and after shaking them out to make sure they didn't have any uninvited guests, he spread two of them out on the floor in front of the fire. He picked her up, laid her on the sleeping bag, and then opened up another one and covered her with it. He removed his own boots and outerwear, and then sat down next to her.

He let his eyes travel over her still face, seeing the girl she'd been in the woman she'd become. She was gorgeous, her hair was tangled with dirt, leaves, and he thought about trying to comb it out, but just then she started to stir.

Gracie came awake to the feeling of warmth on her face, but her back was freezing cold. She attempted to switch positions, but her leg wouldn't move and the more she struggled, the more pain she felt.

"Easy there, Grace," Mason called to her, laying a gentle hand on her shoulder to keep her in place. "You've injured your knee, but I can't tell how badly..."

"The ACL is tore," she murmured, opening her eyes and gazing up into the face of the man who was both familiar and a stranger to her. She opened her eyes more fully, and took in her surroundings. They were in some sort of cabin, and while it didn't look very sophisticated, it was dry and the heat from the fire was miraculous, considering she'd thought she was going to freeze to death.

"Mason?" she murmured, wanting to make sure she wasn't just imagining him.

"Yeah, sugar. It's me. I almost didn't recognize you. You've changed quite a bit since I last saw you."

Gracie gave him a half smile, "You haven't seen me for eight years. You've changed as well." *But not so much that I didn't immediately recognize you. Still the same little scar on his chin from pretend sword fighting with Kaillar when you were eight. The same dark blue eyes that seemed to see right into her very soul. The hair that always looked like it needed a good combing.*

"You cut your hair," Mason murmured.

Gracie reached up a hand and touched her short strands, "Medical school was tough enough without having to take care of my hair thirty minutes a day."

Growing up, Gracie had never cut her hair. When she'd left Silver Springs, it had reached to just below her waist. She'd loved her long hair, but after getting into medical school, it became a hindrance she didn't need. She'd donated the long locks to a local cancer society that used donated human hair to make wigs for cancer patients.

"Medical school? I heard a rumor that you were talking to Doc Matthews." He watched her carefully, wanting the rumor to be true.

Gracie nodded her head and then winced, "Ouch!"

"You bumped your head pretty good back there. What were you thinking, trying to scale down the cut wall in a snow storm?" Mason allowed just a hint of anger to creep into his voice.

Gracie blushed, "Firstly, it wasn't snowing when I started down. Secondly, I'm an experienced climber. That wall should have been a piece of cake, but I didn't think about there being ice in the crevices. Free climbing isn't my forte, I'll admit, but if I hadn't lost my grip on a crevice full of ice, I would have been fine."

"You're lucky I found you."

"I know that. My friends..."

"Your friends are fine. Kaillar took them back down to the ranger station, and then was going to make sure they arrived at Sarah's safe and sound."

Gracie relaxed and shut her eyes for a moment, the effort of staying awake causing her head to throb painfully. "Thank God. I really was trying to help. They didn't understand the danger of getting caught on the mountain in a snowstorm, and I was hoping to call for help while they took the easier route down. I thought if I could get someone to come up and help us, we could all get down before the storm descended on the mountain."

"That didn't quite work out like you planned it. Did it?" Mason asked, no judgment in his voice.

Gracie looked at him, "What were you doing up on the mountain?"

"My brothers and I are the search and rescue first responders for the county."

"Your brothers are all still in Silver Springs?" she asked in surprise.

"Yeah."

"What about your uncle?" she asked. She'd always liked their Uncle Jed, and he'd always treated her with the utmost respect, and had expected his nephews to do the same. It was one of the first differences between Mason and other boys she'd noticed upon leaving Silver Springs. Mason had always treated her as a lady, and never did anything that could be considered rude or vulgar around her. At med school, she'd met plenty of guys who didn't care that she was a female. They'd engaged in vulgarity just to see her reaction, something she'd been hoping would go away once she got out of high school. It had been her experience that many boys never grew out of that particular character defect.

"My uncle passed away a few years ago," he told her softly.

Gracie felt tears spring to her eyes, "I'm sorry. I know he was very close to all of you."

Mason nodded and then he asked, "What about your parents?"

Gracie swallowed and looked away for a moment. *How do I tell him about my dad and his mom?* She knew that no one in Silver Springs was aware of what had transpired. Part of her wanted to tell him what she knew so that there would be no secrets between them going forward. Another part of her wanted to forget that she knew anything – but ignorance wasn't bliss. As she'd so clearly found out in her own life.

"My dad died a little while ago. My mom is travelling with a group of her friends on a cruise around the world."

"Wow! I'm sorry to hear about your dad. He never did seem to like me much."

Gracie chose to say nothing, not wanting to lie to him. Her father hadn't really liked any of the teenagers in the area. The Donnelly boys had just had the misfortune of being their mother's children, making them even less likable to her father.

Changing the subject, she looked at her surroundings and asked, "So, where are we?"

Mason gave her a look. He appeared to be watching her for panic or something else. She wasn't sure, but before she could ask, he told her, "One of the line shacks on the mountain. They're mostly used by the sheep herders during the summer months, but also by hikers and others who miscalculate and get stuck on the mountain overnight."

"Does anyone know where we are?" she asked, just starting to realize the peril she'd been in.

"I spoke to Justin a bit ago. He knows where we are, and he'll send a chopper for us as soon as the storm clears out."

"Tomorrow?" Gracie asked, her knee starting to talk to her quite loudly. Her head was pounding and the nausea had returned. She didn't want to complain, but she felt horrible.

Mason watched her and then shrugged, "I'm not going to lie to you. Maybe. How's the leg?"

Gracie gave a rough laugh, "To be honest, it hurts. Bad."

"I brought along a first aid kit. Want to take a look, and see if there's anything in there you can use?"

Gracie nodded her head, "Please." Even some over-the-counter pain medication would give her a small amount of relief. "I hate to ask, and actually, can't believe I'm saying this, but is there something around here that could be used as an ice pack?"

Mason chuckled, "Yeah, I can't believe you asked that either. I'll find you something, and there's more than enough snow out there to keep you in ice packs all night long."

Chapter 5

Mason found an empty plastic bag, and stepped outside to fill it with fresh snow. He also grabbed the first aid kit from his pack by the door. He took an extra moment, and looked up at the cloudy sky. "Thank you for helping me to find her."

Mason had gotten them down to the line shack in record time, and then called Justin to give him an update. It was the best he could do for her at the moment, and he was more relieved than he cared to admit that she'd regained consciousness.

Filling the bag with fresh snow, he stepped back inside the shack and shut the door, barring the wind from coming inside.

He walked over to her, gently moved the blanket lying over her legs, and laid the makeshift ice bag on her knee, "That should help some."

"Thanks." Gracie blushed, having just realized that someone had removed her outer clothing. Since there was no one else around, she knew that someone had to be Mason. She'd taken a closer look at her surroundings while he'd been getting the snow, and she'd easily identified her clothing lying in a pile a short distance away. It was caked with mud and very wet.

"I've got some over-the-counter painkillers if you think they might help?" he offered, opening up the first aid kit and pulling out two different bottles. He handed them to her and after she made her choice, he pulled his pack over and pulled out a canteen of water. "Here, this should help wash those down."

"You're a regular Boy Scout, aren't you?" Gracie asked, thankful for everything he did have.

"That's me. I even have a few protein bars and some freeze-dried soup." He didn't have to tell her that Silver Springs had never had a Boy Scout Troop while they were growing up; she knew that.

"Freeze-dried soup?" Gracie asked. "Explain to me how that is supposed to work."

Mason smiled, "I'll go one better and fix us both some." He rummaged through his pack again and came out with a small tin container, two foil packages, and his water canteen. He poured some water into the tin and then set it near the fire. He kept an eye on Gracie as he got the packages ready for the water, not liking how pale her face was; or the fact that she seemed to be having trouble keeping her eyes open.

"Hey, you still with me?" he asked softly, watching her eyes flutter open as she turned her head to look at him. She gave him a small smile, and he grinned back, "You wouldn't want to miss this culinary delight I'm cooking up."

Gracie pushed herself up a bit, so that she was sitting, rather than lying down, grimacing at the new pains that made themselves known. "Did you ever learn to cook?"

Mason grinned, "You still remember Home Ec, huh?"

Gracie grinned, "I don't think any of us will ever forget how you almost burned down the school. Mrs. Peterson even retired at the end of the school year."

"Not because of me," Mason reminded her, remembering how everyone had teased him about being the reason the matriarch of the middle school had decided to move to Florida and play golf, rather than try to teach pre-adolescent boys how to work an oven.

Gracie nodded, "I'm just teasing you. So, I imagine lots of things have changed in Silver Springs?"

Mason grabbed a glove and added some of the hot water to each foil package, using a plastic spoon to stir them up before folding over the tops. "They just need to sit for five or so minutes, and they'll be ready to eat. And, some things have changed, but not as many as you might think."

Mason watched her face and then stated, "Are you seriously considering taking over Doc's practice?"

Gracie nodded, "Yeah, I am. I've always wanted to return, and now that I don't have to fight my dad, I'm really thinking about doing what I want to do."

Fight her dad? What's that mean? Mason didn't ask the question, but echoed her statement, "Coming to live in Silver Springs is what you want to do?"

Gracie nodded, "It is." There were so many things she wanted to ask. And say, but the version of Mason sitting across from her was one she didn't really know. She didn't want to assume he was still the same as the fourteen year old boy who'd given her the first romantic kiss of her life. The same boy she'd swore she loved, and that they would be together forever. They'd been young, and after her father had uprooted his family and moved them away from Silver Springs, everyone had assumed she would forget all about him. But she hadn't.

All through high school and then college, she'd compared every boy who asked her out to Mason. None of them were ever able to measure up, so she'd finally just given up on having a social life that included dating a member of the opposite sex.

She'd thrown herself into her studies, joined a few service organizations, and put finding love on the back burner. Her heart had been given to Mason, and when she'd first thought about returning to Silver Springs, she'd found a hope that somewhere, she might find her heart there as well as her future.

· · ⚓ · ·

"I'M HEADING DOWN TO Sarah's, do you want to come along?" Justin asked Jessica. Kaillar had called in a few minutes earlier to say that the two women hikers were safely ensconced at Sarah's and seemed to be suffering no lasting effects. At least, not physical ones.

"No, I'm good right here where it's warm. Want me to make dinner while you're gone?" Jessica asked.

Justin smiled and then quickly shook his head, "No, I'll throw a pot of chili together when I get back. Won't take that long to heat through and dinner will be ready." By Jessica's own admission, she couldn't boil water without burning it. There was no way Justin wanted her using the lodge's gas stove with nobody around to put out the fire.

"Are you sure?" She gave him a look that was part teasing and part relief.

"Positive. I'll be back with Kai in a bit." He kissed her on the forehead, feeling blessed to have her in his life. He knew that she still had things to work out, most of them between God and herself, but for the first time, he really felt positive that they had a future together.

Justin headed down the mountain, using the alone time to thank God for helping Jessica deal with her lack of faith. Seeing her walk into the church this morning had been like Christmas come early. "Guess I have a lot of things to be thankful for this week."

He arrived at Sarah's, and found Kaillar speaking with one of the women named Melanie. The other woman was sitting near a window, her arms wrapped around herself in a self-protective gesture, as she watched the snow fall outside.

"She okay?" he asked Sarah quietly.

"Don't know the answer to that one yet. The friend said she's doing okay now, but I guess she started to slip on their way down, and Kaillar caught her. She freaked out; acting completely terrified, and has been withdrawn and quiet since they got here."

Justin watched her for another moment, and then joined Kaillar and Melanie. After the introductions were made, Justin asked Melanie, "What's up with your friend?"

Melanie looked at Becca with compassion in her eyes and smiled sadly, "She was attacked a while back, and I think when your brother grabbed her to stop her fall, it was just similar enough to her attack that it caused all of those old feelings of terror to rise to the surface. She's never dealt with them in my opinion, and it was just a matter of time before something like this triggered a bad reaction."

Seeing how concerned the brothers were, she hurried to assure them, "Don't worry. When Gracie gets here, she'll know what to do, and can medicate her if necessary. She's had to talk her down before."

"Talk her down?" he queried, his eyes on the young woman who seemed to be trying to make herself as small as possible.

"She gets panic attacks sometimes. I think she'd get caught up in her head. Starts making things out to be more than they are, and then they spiral out of control."

Justin shared a look with Kaillar and then turned to address Melanie. "What happens if Gracie doesn't talk her down?"

Melanie's face stiffened, "The last time she had an attack, they had to take her to the ER and put her under. She woke up, tied to the rails of the bed, and under a seventy-two hour psychiatric hold. She's not crazy, just hurting. Gracie will make it all better, though."

Justin cleared his throat and told her quietly, "She's not coming down off the mountain tonight."

Chapter 6

Justin wished he had better news, but he didn't. Plunging ahead, he told her, "Gracie injured her knee, and is going to need a chopper or medivac whenever this storm clears."

"Rats!" Melanie looked at her friend and then asked, "Is there a way for her to talk to Gracie tonight? Maybe that would be enough to keep her from imploding."

Justin looked at Kaillar and shrugged, "We could try the radio from down here. Not sure if the signal is strong enough, but it couldn't hurt."

Kaillar nodded and then grabbed the radio from Justin, "Let me, since it seems I'm the reason she's shut down. I was only trying to help."

Kaillar slowly approached the young woman, trying not to notice her strawberry blonde hair, or the little pixie face that looked so sad and alone. He had the strangest urge to wrap her in his arms and protect her, but he pushed it away. Touching her was the last thing she needed.

"Hey, Becca? I was wondering if you might want to talk to your friend for a minute or two. It seems that Gracie hurt her knee in a fall, and isn't going to make it back down the mountain tonight."

"What?! But she has to come back down. It's too dangerous up there, she'll freeze to death and then..."

"Whoa!" Kaillar held up his hands, stalling her from rising from the chair. "Becca, my brother's with her and they're inside one of the line shacks. They're warm and dry and out of the elements. When the storm clears, we'll fly up and get them. Now, would you like to talk to her?"

Becca slowly nodded her head, and then watched with wide eyes as Kaillar turned the radio on, "Hey, Mason! You copy?"

"Kaillar? Your signal's not very strong. What's up?"

"One of Gracie's friends needs to speak to her for a minute. Is she able to talk?"

"Sure. Just a minute."

"Becca?" Gracie's voice came through the radio loud and clear a few seconds later.

Silent tears streamed down Becca's face, "Gracie, are you all right?"

"Hey, you're crying. I can tell. I twisted my knee a bit, but I'm fine. Mason found me."

"Mason? Isn't he the boy you..."

"Yes, that's the one. Are you and Melanie doing okay?"

"We're at Sarah's. She's really nice. Melanie's husband is coming to get her tomorrow morning."

"I'm sure she's happy about that. What did you think about Kaillar? Have you met Justin yet?"

"Is he the other brother?"

"Yeah. You'll like them all once you get to know them."

Mason listened to the conversation, his eyes never leaving Becca's face. She wasn't arguing with Gracie, but her expression said that getting to know him or his brother was the last thing on her list of things to do.

"What about you? Are you going to be okay until I get back there? I may have to have surgery on my knee to fix it. I think it's torn."

"Uhm...I need to get back home...Surgery...what..."

"Becca, slow down now and breathe with me. Come on. One, in. Two, out. Keep going. One, in. Two, out."

The sounds of Becca breathing and Gracie counting ensued for several more minutes before Gracie lowered her voice, "Better?"

"Yes. Thanks."

"Good. Look, I don't want you trying to get back by yourself. I'd say borrow my car, but the keys are up here with me. Can you stick it out until I can get them to you? You can take my car back to Denver. I won't be driving it until my knee heels."

"Gracie...are you really going to be okay?"

"Yeah. I am." There was a brief pause and then Gracie asked, "Can I talk to Melanie for a minute?"

Becca silently nodded and handed the radio back to Kaillar. She made sure their hands didn't touch, and she refused to meet his eyes. Kaillar was more worried about her now than before. She seemed to have shut down before his eyes while talking to her friend. The exact opposite reaction the phone call was to have had.

"Gracie wants to talk to you," he told Melanie, handing her the radio.

"Gracie?"

"Hey, Mel. What's up with Becca?"

Melanie briefly explained what had happened on the way down the mountain. "She's losing it, Grace. Completely shutting everyone and everything out."

"I wish I was there to help. You need to get her to sleep. Can Michael stick around until I get off this mountain? I don't want her left alone."

Melanie smiled, "Your compassion is what makes you the perfect person to be a doctor. Yeah, Michael's debriefing ended early. He's officially out as of today. He was going to drive over and surprise us anyway. Now he's just coming in without the element of surprise."

"I'm happy for you. See if you can get Becca to get some sleep tonight."

"I will. Justin offered to call the doctor if you think it would help?"

"Only if he'll give her some sleeping medication. She needs to break the cycle of terror her mind is caught up in right now. But just going to sleep might only make it worse. She needs to sleep so deeply that her mind has to turn off for a bit."

Justin gestured for the radio and Melanie handed it to him, "Gracie, its Justin."

"Hi Justin."

"Hey, I'll call Doc myself. Do you have a recommendation for what might help her?"

Gracie rattled off two different sleeping medications she'd used on Becca before when she was like this, and she even gave him the dosages she would recommend if she were there. "Don't forget that Doc has a lot more experience than I do. If he suggests something else or a different dosage, follow his instructions, not mine."

"Are you sure? I mean, you know Becca better than he will."

"I'm sure. I trust Doc to make the right decisions." Gracie sounded confident, and that was good enough for Justin.

"Okay. I'm on it. You and Mason doing okay up there?"

"Just dandy .He just made me freeze-dried soup, and I can't believe I'm saying this, but it wasn't half bad. Not something I'd want to eat on a regular basis, but not bad."

"Good to hear it. Tell Mason we'll be up as soon as we can. Right now, the storm seems to have stalled over the mountains, and doesn't look like it's going to be moving on anytime soon."

"He's right here and heard you. Thanks for taking care of my friends."

"No problem. Talk to you guys soon. Be safe."

Justin turned the radio off, and called the doctor. After explaining to him about the incident on the hike down and Becca's reaction, he also told Doc about Gracie's recommendations. Doctor

Matthews seemed impressed with her recommended treatment, and promised to get the prescription filled and bring it by Sarah's in the next half hour.

Meanwhile, Justin and Kaillar could head on up the mountain. He'd check on her when he delivered the sleeping medication, and then Sarah and Melanie could take turns sitting with Becca until she fell asleep.

With a plan in place, Justin and Kaillar headed home, with Sarah promising to call if she needed help of any kind. Melanie's husband was en route, but with the storm, it would be hours before he arrived.

Sarah promised, and Melanie thanked Kaillar again for coming to their rescue. The two brothers headed out, making their way back up the mountain through the ever deepening snow. Justin could tell that Kaillar's mind was still on the frightened woman, and he hoped that they'd have a chance to meet one another when she wasn't quite so terrified. She seemed like a sweet kid, and Justin had seen the look on Kaillar's face. There was more than a passing interest there.

Justin wasn't sure if it was her vulnerability, or how fragile she seemed, that had sparked Kaillar's interest. Growing up, Kaillar had always had a soft spot for those in need. He always championed the underdog, and he tended to be the good looking guy who asked the mousy secretary type out because no one else would.

He'd had plenty of chances to find a girlfriend while working at the local ski resorts. Justin had seen him flirt with the snow bunnies, and yet, he never let the interaction go beyond the ski slopes. It had been the same way in high school. Kaillar had been more interested in playing football than girls, and Uncle Jed had fostered that situation as much as possible.

Now that Kaillar was an adult, Justin knew that he'd been feeling the same pull to settle down and find a wife. To raise some kids. But so far, Kaillar hadn't shown more than a passing interest in anyone he'd met. Until now.

Something about the woman with the pixie face and sad, bruised eyes had gotten to him.

Chapter 7

Monday morning....

Gracie woke up, stretching inside her sleeping bag as she listened for signs of the storm outside. The wind had continued throughout the night, and she and Mason had done their best to stay warm and not worry about how they were going to get back down the mountain in the morning. Mason had continued to feed the fire throughout the night, and she made a mental note to thank him.

They didn't have any cell phone service on this side of the mountain, but they still had the radio, and Mason confirmed that they were only about a mile from the position where he and Kaillar had found her friends.

Gracie tried to shift around, her body clamoring for her to get up and take care of nature's call, but each time she tried to move her leg, the pain in her knee stole her breath away.

"Hey! You doing okay?" Mason asked softly, wanting to let her know he was awake and yet not startle her.

Gracie turned her head and looked at him with a half-smile. "Morning. Did the storm stop?"

"I think so. To tell you the truth, I'm almost afraid to look outside. You girls sure didn't plan this trip out very well, did you?"

"That's my fault, I guess. Although Melanie and Becca were already planning to come up here regardless. I simply asked to tag along, and then ended up driving us here. I should have checked the weather myself instead of relying on one of them to do it."

"Well, don't beat yourself up about it. The mountain seems to have already done a credible job of that." Mason slipped from his sleeping bag, the ultra-low-temperature bags having been part of the accommodations they found in the line shack.

He squatted down next to her, and then checked her forehead, "Hurt?"

"Just a bit. Uhm...well, I hate to ask, but is there any way you could..."

"Don't say another word." Mason scooped her up from the sleeping bag, after unzipping it and assuring himself she wouldn't freeze by spending a few minutes outside in the cold.

He carried her to the door of the shack and then nodded, "Open that, will you? My hands are full at the moment."

Gracie couldn't help but smile in the face of his silliness. She tried not to notice how right it felt to be in his arms. Or how little tingles of reaction shivered up and down her spine. Or how nice he smelled...*Girl, get your head back in the game here. Survival. That's where your brain should be. Oh, and ...*

Mason carried her a short distance away from the shack and then propped her up against a tree. "Hang on a second," he urged her, using his booted feet to scrape the majority of the snow away from the base of the tree.

"Just hold onto the tree for balance. When you're finished, holler out and I'll come get you. Do you need anything else?" he asked, shoving some tissues into her hand.

Gracie blushed and shook her head, embarrassed beyond imagination. Mason took himself back towards the shack, and Gracie answered nature's call as quickly as possible.

She tried to reason with herself that this was a simple bodily function, but her modesty and sense of propriety wasn't buying it. *Come on, you dealt with more embarrassing situations in med school. This is nothing. Only what you make of it.*

She finished her business, and then righted her clothing once more. "Mason?" she called out more softly than she intended.

"Right here, sugar. Ready to get back inside and out of the cold?"

She tried not to think about how much she liked his use of the endearments. They made her feel special. Cared for. Dare she say loved?

Gracie nodded and tried to take a step towards him, but the pain in her knee when she put the faintest amount of pressure on it was staggering and swift.

"Ow!"

"Hang on, there girl. Let me carry you back inside." He scooped her up for the second time that day, and Gracie felt her heart speed up at his closeness.

Mason was a gorgeous man, both inside and out. She hadn't seen him in eight years, and had only been reacquainted with him for twelve hours, but his goodness shone like a beacon in the dark. The Mason she'd fallen in love with as a young teenager still existed. And from what she could see, he'd only perfected with age.

As he carried her back into the shack and settled her on top of the sleeping bag spread out before the fire, she couldn't help but let her eyes wander over his face and shoulders.

"How come you're not married?" she murmured, wishing now that she'd had the guts to ask Sarah about Mason and his brothers.

"Never found anyone I wanted to spend the rest of my life with. No sense in dating someone you know isn't the one. I didn't want to waste my time or my affections. My heart was given away a lot of years ago."

His heart was given away a long time ago? How long ago? Could he mean... Gracie watched him, and then searched his eyes, "How old were you?"

Mason met her eyes and then gave her the only answer he could. The truth. "Fourteen."

Gracie sucked in a breath, unwilling to dare to believe that Mason had felt as strongly about her as she had him. True, they'd promised to be there for each other for the rest of their lives, but they'd been so young. No one had really thought they knew their own minds back then.

Now, eight years later, Gracie found herself trying to adjust to the knowledge that Mason might still have feelings for her. Feelings that might mirror the ones she still held for him? Was it even possible? She had no problem reminding herself how much Mason had meant to her back then, but she'd never in a million years figured that Mason would care the same way still.

Realizing things were headed into waters that she wasn't ready to swim in yet, she looked around and changed the subject. "It looks like something one would find on a Christmas card."

Mason gave her a sidelong look, but then allowed the change of topic. "We got at least a foot of snow last night. And it's mighty wet snow at that. Avalanche danger is going to be high in the backcountry for the next several days."

Gracie nodded, having forgotten how risky wet snow this early in the season could be. "You and your brothers don't..."

Mason shook his head, "No. Not anymore. We did for a while, but there was an accident a few years back where a park ranger guessed incorrectly about the safe zone. He shot the charges to trigger the avalanche, and ended up dying in it. Now, they contract out with professionals."

Gracie felt relieved at that knowledge. She felt a chill as the wind picked up and changed direction. Rubbing her arms for warmth she inquired, "Do you think the chopper is coming sometime today?"

"Justin radioed a few minutes ago. It's already scheduled to be here in a few hours. There's just one little problem. The wind on this side of the mountain is too dangerous and unpredictable for him to land here."

"What does that mean?" Gracie asked, sure she wasn't going to like the answer.

"It means we need to get to a clearing about half a mile from here before he can pick us up safely."

Half a mile? It seemed like an impossible feat in her current condition. "Mason, there's no way I can walk half a mile."

"You won't have to. I have a plan." He looked almost excited at the prospect of putting his plan into action.

"This is really not going to be much fun," she murmured more to herself than the man watching her.

"Are you doubting my ability to get us to our pickup location?"

Gracie looked at him and shook her head, "Not really, just stating the obvious."

Mason grinned at her and then asked, "Remember what we used to do on days right after a big snow?"

Gracie looked at him, realizing where his thoughts were going and immediately started shaking her head with an incredulous laugh. "No! You can't be serious!"

Mason nodded his head, grinning broadly, "Oh yeah! I'm serious. Rest up. I'll be back in a bit."

Chapter 8

"Okay, mademoiselle. Your chariot awaits," Mason told her as he stepped back into the shack almost an hour later. He gave her a bow, and pretended to remove his hat as well.

Gracie chuckled, smiling as pure happiness filled her soul. It seemed like forever since she'd felt this happy inside, and it was all because of the man standing in front of her. "Mason..."

She searched his eyes, wanting to tell him how she was feeling, and yet afraid that she'd misread him and the entire situation. *Maybe it's just being in this place that feels so good.*

"Hey! Don't think so hard. This is going to be fun, and I promise not to go too fast."

Gracie rolled her eyes, "That is so very encouraging, Mario." She used the nickname his brothers had given him one winter when they were ten, borrowed from a famous race car driver known for his speed – Mario Andretti. Mason loved speed and whether it was a toboggan, an inner tube, or skis – he was reckless and fearless. And Gracie really wasn't sure he'd changed much. The laughter in his eyes was so much like the younger version she remembered, she wouldn't be surprised if they both came to regret what was about to happen.

"Hey!" Mason evidently had seen her doubt and the concern in her eyes. He squatted down and cupped her chin, "I promise to go nice and easy. Slow even." He said the word as if it was something horrible but nodded his head to back up his promise.

Gracie laughed, "Okay, let's go see this chariot you constructed."

Mason stood up, and then scooped her up into his arms. Striding to the open shack door, he stepped out into the morning sunshine, "Tada!"

Gracie looked at the rough litter he'd constructed from fallen limbs he'd scavenged and what looked like a...door? He'd laced the boughs together with a length of rope she assumed he had in his pack, and then padded it with fresh pine boughs. "Wow!"

"Cool, huh?"

"Like I said, a regular Boy Scout." She looked at his creation once more, and then looked at his face, "Just one question, where did you find a door?"

Mason pointed towards the outhouse she hadn't even noticed sitting behind the shack. "I borrowed the door. No one will be using this area until Spring, and I'll personally make sure that the door is returned, or another one is installed before then."

"You made a survival sled out of an outhouse door?" Gracie asked in wonderment as her eyes took in the contraption he'd pieced together.

"Right? I'm a genius, I know. Now, let's see how well it works." He sat her down on top of the pine boughs, and then retrieved both of their packs. He handed hers into her hands and then fiddled around with his much larger one until he produced a pair of snowshoes.

"What are you going to do with those?" she asked, not seeing how they were going to help them sled...she broke off when he also produced two nice smooth pieces of wood which he clipped onto the bottom of the snowshoes. "Ah!"

"Clever, huh? I haven't had the opportunity to play with these as of yet. This should be fun!"

"Mason, I don't know..."

"Trust me."

Trust him? "Well, I would love to, but Doc is really counting on me being alive to take over his practice. Maybe you should go meet the chopper, and bring one of the snow machines back up here, or something..."

Mason had finished strapping the shoes to his feet, and slipped his pack over his shoulders. Taking a few small experimental steps, he grinned when he didn't fall over, but smoothly slid over to where she sat.

"Ready?"

"To die? Sure," Gracie told him, both teasing and silently praying that in this area, Mason had most definitely changed. Rushing headlong down the side of Maroon Peak on top of a makeshift litter was not her idea of a pleasant way to die. Not today anyway.

"Oh ye of little faith!"

Gracie laughed, "Quoting Scripture? Really? Well how about 'Forsake foolishness and live!' That's seems to fit quite nicely."

Mason chuckled, "Proverbs?"

"Words to live by," she added with a smile.

Mason chuckled and then told her with confidence, "This is not foolishness. This is ingenuity at its finest." Without further ado, Mason slipped on his gloves, picked up the long poles on the litter and suggested, "Hang on!"

Gracie grabbed the sides of the litter, emitting a little scream mixed with both joy and fear as the litter began to move forward. She did her best to keep her weight in the middle of the litter so that they wouldn't accidentally tip over. Mason guided the litter over the fresh powdery snow, and as they exited the trees and entered a nice open space, she tipped her head back and met his laughing eyes.

"Okay! This is awesome!"

"Told you so." He made sure to keep their speed down, and soon he could see the chopper circling overhead. "There's our ride!"

Gracie looked up, shielding her eyes from the sun. The chopper circled overhead once, and then it slowly descended to land on the snow a short distance away. Mason stopped their litter, and quickly removed his snowshoes before reaching down for her.

"Ready to go get that knee looked at?" he asked, knowing that she'd been in pain all morning and doing her best to ignore it.

Gracie groaned, "A shower sounds better, but I guess I better go get it checked out."

"Okay. Let's hit Vail first and then if they release you to go today, I'll have Justin or Kaillar drive over and pick us up."

"I don't want to put you guys out any more. You don't have to stay at the hospital with me." *But I really hope you will.*

Her wish seemed to be his as well. Just before they reached the chopper, he stopped and whispered into her ear, "Tell me I'm not the only one who feels like you never left eight years ago."

Gracie searched his eyes and shook her head, "I can't. I feel the same way. This morning..."

Mason kissed her forehead tenderly, "Was just the beginning. Let's get your knee fixed up and then go from there. I'm really glad you came back to Silver Springs."

"So am I." *I wish I'd never had to leave.* She tried not to think about the reasons she'd been forced to leave in the first place. She didn't want to dredge up the past, knowing that nothing other than pain would result. For her. And for the Donnelly brothers. Her father was the impetus that had caused their mother to take off, and the reason she'd never been able to come home again.

Would Mason still have feelings for her once he knew the truth? That was one question that she was in no hurry to get answered.

Chapter 9

V*ail Hospital facility, Monday afternoon...*
    Gracie gave the orthopedic surgeon a small smile as he left the exam room, and then she leaned her head back against the gurney and closed her eyes. *Guess you're going to get a chance to see what being a patient is like, up close and personal.*

She'd been right in her initial assessment that she'd done a number on her ACL- her anterior cruciate ligament. Just a little piece of fibrous tissue, but one that performed the job of connecting the major bones in her leg together. She hadn't torn it completely apart, but the tear was significant enough that without surgical intervention, it most likely would never heal properly.

Dr. Geske was a very well-known orthopedist who just happened to be available to immediately perform the surgery. Since she'd not eaten anything for breakfast due to some nausea, and her head CT had come back clean, she was good to be put under anesthesia right away.

Mason stuck his head around the exam curtain and moments later asked "Hey! Can I come in?"

Gracie scooted herself back up on the bed, her leg completely immobilized by the leg brace a nurse had applied to it upon her arrival. She smiled and waved him forward, "Sure, come on in."

"So I passed Dr. Geske in the hallway, and he said you're headed up to surgery in a few minutes?"

"Yeah." Gracie cleared her throat, and then nodded her head, "The ACL is torn pretty badly. But the good news is that Dr. Geske is here and can fix it today. I'll be in a leg brace for six weeks or so, which will make getting around in the snow interesting, but after that and some therapy, I should be good as new."

"That is good news. Not the surgery or the rehab part, but I'm glad Stan's here to fix things up."

"Stan?" Gracie asked.

"Dr. Geske. He's been courting Sarah for the last several months, but she's pretty adamant about not giving up her place in Silver Springs, and he can't really move too far away from the hospital."

"Do they..."

"Love each other?" When she nodded, he grinned, "Yeah. But Sarah has some misguided notion that if she leaves town, no one will take over the motel and travelers and visitors alike won't have any place to stay. Not everyone wants to drive up the mountain for a night's stay."

Gracie's brain took off running. *Becca would be perfect taking over for Sarah!*

Gracie knew that moving to a small town would be a perfect place for her damaged friend to heal, and Becca knew firsthand how to run a hospitality business. She'd grown up on the Big Island of Hawaii, her parents owning and operating a tourist resort there. Gracie had never understood why a beach girl would leave and move to the mountains of Colorado, and Becca had never gone back home to her knowledge. At least, not in the last four years they'd known one another.

"Hey, where'd you go?" Mason asked, reaching over and clasping her cold hand in his big warm ones.

"I was thinking about Sarah's problem and a solution to it."

"Really? Well, I'm sure Stan would love to hear about it."

Gracie nodded her head, "Once I get out of here, I'll see what I can do. Not sure it will work, but I think I know of just the person to take over Sarah's place so that she can move here."

"Well, why don't you worry about getting yourself better before you try to solve everyone else's problems? I called Justin, and Kaillar's going to drive over tonight. He'll drive us both home in the morning."

"Home?" Gracie murmured, not having given much thought to the logistics once she left the hospital. The surgery would only require an overnight stay, and then only because it was happening so late in the day. They wouldn't let her leave until they were sure that she wasn't going to experience any negative side effects from being put out. They would also want to make sure she had good control of her pain level. Being a physician herself, she would be given more leeway than other patients, but only as much as she could convince Dr. Geske she was going to be a good patient.

"I also spoke with Doc. Now, don't be upset; but I thought he would want an update on your condition. He wasn't expecting you to start until after this week."

"I wasn't planning on it. My trip up here was designed to lock down a place to stay and get the paperwork figured out."

"Well, is there any reason you need to go back to Denver before the weekend?" Mason asked, hoping she would say no.

Gracie thought for a moment and then shook her head, "Not really. My lease on my apartment is up at the end of the month, and Melanie is good to go with her husband now since his discharge is complete."

"What about the other girl? Becca?"

Gracie shook her head, "Becca moved out last month. She's hoping to land a job with the Division of Wildlife as a photographer, and she didn't want to hold Melanie or me up. She's renting on a month to month basis right now."

"So, what about your stuff?"

"Well, I do need to go back and finish packing things up, but with my knee...I don't know how that's going to happen. I might just have to hire some movers..."

"Nonsense. How about you spend Thanksgiving with us at the lodge, and Friday we'll head back to Denver with the truck and the trailer and move you back here?"

Gracie looked up at him and shook her head, "Mason, you don't have to take care of me. I know you must have other things to do..."

Mason sat down on the edge of the bed, keeping her hand in his. He met her eyes and lowered his voice, "Gracie, I feel like the last eight years I've been in a holding pattern. I never forgot you, and while I admit there were days I didn't think about you, I never much looked at another girl. I couldn't. When you left Silver Springs, you took my heart with you. And now you've brought it back."

He stood up and shoved a hand through his hair, "I know this sounds crazy. And I can't explain it, but seeing you again...being with you...I feel like my life can finally start moving forward once again."

Gracie felt tears sting her eyes. No one, not her parents, or even the few friends she'd made in med school, had been able to understand how a boy she'd grown up with and given her heart to as a young teenager could affect her so strongly. They had all accused her of being overdramatic, and living a childhood fantasy.

But Gracie had known, deep in her soul that Mason was the one God had set aside for her. She'd known it then, and she knew it now.

"Mason, you don't have to try and explain it to me. I feel the same way."

"Then it's settled." Mason stopped speaking when a nurse and the anesthesiologist entered the room. "I'll see you on the other side." He winked at her, and then slipped back out of the curtained area.

"So, Miss Shelton. I hear you're going to be our guest for the next few hours. Just a few questions, and then we'll head upstairs..."

Mason headed for the surgery waiting room, praying silently that God would watch over her, and offering up prayers of thankfulness for keeping them safe thus far. Gracie would get her knee fixed and for the first time in years, Mason was actually looking forward to the upcoming holidays. He had much to be thankful for this year.

Chapter 10

M onday evening, Vail Hospital...
Gracie was having the most horrible dream. She was standing on the top of Maroon Peak, the snow was blowing around her, and she was pleading with someone. She looked around her, and there in the distance was her father. She was pleading with her father to undo it. To take back the wrong he'd done, and not destroy all of their lives.

Her mother stood a short distance away, a blank expression on her face as she watched the interaction between her husband and her daughter without emotion.

"Mom! Make him undo it!"

"Dad! Why can't you undo it? Please! At least tell the truth!"

Her father wasn't saying anything. He just stood there, looking resolute. Determined to hide his sin for as long as possible, no matter what the cost to his wife and daughter.

Gracie wasn't a young girl in her dream; she was a grown woman. A grown woman who had allowed his father's actions to destroy her life.

And then her dream shifted, and she was standing at the edge of canyon. Mason stood on the other side, and she walked up and down, trying to find a way across to him. There was no bridge, just the remnants of rope and boards, dangling from the opposite side.

"Mason! Help me!"

Justin and Kaillar joined Mason, and handed him a picture. Mason looked at the picture and then at his brothers. Finally, he looked across the canyon to where she was standing with her arms outstretched.

"Mason! Help me! The bridge is out!"

Mason looked at her with saddened eyes, turning the picture in his hands around so she could see it. It was a picture of his mother. When he looked up at her again, she felt his abandonment clear to her soul. He knew what her father had done, and now wanted nothing to do with her. Nothing...

Gracie jerked awake, a scream of agony lodging in her sore throat. She blinked her eyes to see pale green walls, and the persistent beeping of a machine nearby. She turned her head, and could see the heart rate monitor and pulse oximeter happily running, and then she realized she was in a hospital room. In a hospital bed, to be exact.

The dream was still so vivid in her mind, that when Mason walked in a moment later, she felt tears flood her eyes as she waited for him to leave her a second time.

"Gracie? Sugar, what's wrong? Are you in pain? I can get a nurse," he seemed frantic as he pushed her call button and searched her face. "Hang in there, hon. They'll get you some more pain medications in just a minute."

Gracie shook her head, "No meds." Her voice was hoarse, and she realized it was from the ventilator tube they'd inserted during the operation. Her throat hurt almost as bad as her knee.

Mason gave her a tight smile, "Of course you need more meds. I don't like seeing you hurt."

But you're going to hurt me when you find out the truth. You won't be able to stop it.

Suddenly, Gracie knew that she'd never be able to handle his rejection when it came. *Better to go back to the way things were before she came back to Silver Springs. Better to only grieve a dream, and never know just how perfect her life could have been. If only...*

She looked up at him, and then away. She couldn't do this. Not with him standing there, looking so concerned for her. Loving her? *Heavenly Father, please give me strength...*

She waited for some measure of comfort to fill her soul and mind, but it was as if she'd just asked a brick wall for help. All she felt was helplessness as she contemplated making Mason leave. *Don't send him away. Trust him.* The little voice inside her head was trying to talk sense into the muddled mess of her emotions, still vividly entangled with her dream. Reality and fantasy seemed to blend together, until she could only feel the gaping hurt from her dream.

The nurse entered and misread the situation entirely. "Gracie, I have a stronger painkiller right here. I'm going to put it into your IV so it will kick in faster."

Gracie kept her head turned away until the nurse started to leave and then she reached out and grabbed her hand. She kept her eyes off Mason and then begged the nurse, "Please have him leave."

The nurse looked at her as if she were insane, "Hon? Surely you don't mean that."

Gracie nodded her head, more tears falling from her eyes. "I'm sure." She turned her head away, listening as the nurse, Glenda according to her name badge, explained to Mason that Gracie needed her rest, and that his presence seemed to be upsetting her.

When Mason protested vehemently being asked to leave the room, Gracie's heart broke in two pieces as the nurse told him that her patient had requested he leave.

"Gracie? Sugar, what's going on?"

"Sir, I really must adhere to my patient's wishes. You could leave your name and number at the nurses' desk, just in case she changes her mind."

Gracie could hear Mason arguing with her, begging the nurse to just let him find out what was wrong, but she was a fierce warrior and ushered him from the room with a dire warning to not come back until he was asked.

The nurse stepped back inside the room, handing her a handful of tissues and told her, "Girl, I don't know what craziness is going through your brain, but that man out there loves you. He hasn't left your side except to use the facilities since you came out of surgery. Frankly, he was starting to drive us all crazy with the questions and such."

Glenda came around and sat so that Gracie and she could see each other. "Gracie, hon, you look like your world just crashed down around you. It might help you to get things back into perspective if you could talk about them."

"Talking won't undo what's already been done. I should have never come back to Silver Springs. I just wanted to forget the past and move forward, but I guess deep down I knew that wouldn't be possible. No one can truly move forward if they don't deal with the past first, right?"

Glenda looked at her and then asked, "That depends on whether or not it's your past. Hon, do you believe in God?"

Gracie nodded her head and offered a watery smile, "He's the only reason I've made it this far."

"Good, then you know there's nothing too hard for Him to handle. Let me ask you something. This thing that can't be undone – did you do it?"

Gracie shook her head, "No. And that's what makes it so hard. I didn't even know what had happened until years later. But it robbed that man out there of the chance to grow up knowing his mother. And when he finds out why she ran off and got killed, he's going to blame me."

Glenda was quiet for a long moment and then she asked, "Would you blame you if the roles were reversed?" Glenda asked.

Gracie blinked, once and then again. "I...I guess..."

Glenda stood up and patted her shoulder, "That pain medication is starting to take effect. Do yourself and that young man out there a favor and put yourself in his shoes; figure out how you might react if the roles were reversed. I'll be back later to check on you."

Glenda exited the room to see Mason leaning up against the wall outside; a stricken and confused look on his face. She walked over and stood right in front of him, "Give her some time."

"I don't understand...what's going on here?"

"My guess is she was keeping something from you and the anesthesia caused everything to get all jumbled up in her head. She seems to think she's to blame for your mother's death."

"What?! That's preposterous. My mom died when I was an infant. How could Gracie have had anything to do with that? I need to go talk to her."

Glenda stayed him with a hand on his arm, "I can't let you do that. Look, whatever this incident in her past is, she believes you'll hate her when you find out the truth. My advice to you, stay close and pray that God will help her realize she's not responsible for the actions of another."

"What other? She feels guilty for something someone else did?"

"I believe so. Now, I need to get back to work. Don't give up on her. This may seem like a tsunami, but I've lived long enough to know that true love can weather any storm. That little girl in there wouldn't be so devastated if you didn't already own her heart."

Mason nodded, and watched the nurse walk away. He glanced at the door to her room, and wanted so badly to push it open and demand that she talk to him, but for some reason, she was shutting him out.

He'd seen the hurt in her eyes and the tears. She thought she knew what was best for them both. But he knew a thing or two about doing the right thing, and that was why he walked down to the waiting room and prepared himself for the longest night of his life. A night where he would stand in the gap for her and make sure that if she needed him, he was there for her. He wasn't going to leave. He just got her back, and unlike when they were fourteen and her parents were making all the decisions, he wasn't letting her go without a fight.

Chapter 11

Kaillar arrived at the hospital in Vail, and found a place to park. He'd heard from Mason an hour earlier, and something was definitely wrong. Gracie had made it through her surgery with flying colors, but Mason had sounded off, and his voice was strained.

He asked at the front desk, and was directed to the third floor waiting area. He pushed open the door to see Mason looking much worse for wear.

"Hey! You look awful," he told Mason, taking a seat next to him.

Mason seemed to pull himself together, and took a deep breath, "Did you just get here?"

"Yeah. Why are you sitting in here instead of in there with Gracie?"

Mason was exhausted, and his ability to control his emotions was almost gone. "She kicked me out."

"Were you making a nuisance of yourself?" Kaillar asked, remembering times when all the boys had been sick and Mason had been a pest. He seemed to always recover quickest, and had loved teasing his older brothers, with anything available. Food. Playing outside. Going to town with their uncle.

"No. I mean," he took a breath; "she said she doesn't want to see me. She had the nurse kick me out of the room."

Kai looked at him and then the door leading to the hallway. "And you don't know why?"

Mason shook his head, "I've been sitting here trying to figure out what I did that...Everything was fine before she went into surgery. She was happy. I was happy. Seeing her again...it was as if she'd never left. But now...Kai, she seems to think she's somehow to blame for mom's death."

"Mom? She never knew mom. None of us really did, except for Justin."

"The nurse seems to think she's just confused from the anesthesia, and that she'll come around once her system gets rid of the drug."

"Is that normal? Or even possible?" Kai asked.

"I don't know. How could she think she's responsible for our mother's death? We hardly ever talked about our mother growing up."

Kai nodded his head. The subject of Maria Donnelly rarely came up between the boys. They had all managed to forgive her early on in their lives, and saw no reason to bring her up, or let her have any control whatsoever over their lives. He wasn't about to let the status quo change now. "Let me go try to talk to her," Kai offered.

"Be my guest." Mason didn't expect his brother to make any headway, but he was willing to try anything. He really needed some answers.

Kaillar nodded once, and then headed towards the nurses' station. "Glenda?"

"Yes?"

"Hi. I'm Kaillar Donnelly. I was wondering if I could see Gracie Shelton? I realize it's kind of late, but I just spoke with my brother..."

Glenda nodded, "Room 306. Please be aware that if she pushes her button and asks me to escort you from the room, I won't have any choice but to do so."

"I understand. I don't want to upset her. Gracie, and I go back to when we were kids. We all grew up together."

Glenda smiled and nodded her head towards the door, "Good luck."

Kaillar pushed open the door to Gracie's room and noticed right away that there were no lights on, no television playing, just darkness and the beeping of the machines next to her. He closed the door quietly, and then made his way to the bed.

He didn't want to wake her up, but there was just a sliver of moonlight coming through the windows and he could see her eyes were wide open. "Gracie?" he whispered.

She turned her head and then gave him a sad smile, "Kai."

"Hey, sweetie. I thought you went to medical school to become the doctor, not the patient?"

She smiled and then swallowed painfully, "Water?"

Kai looked around, and spied a pitcher of ice water sitting on the bedside table with an empty glass next to it. He poured the glass half full, and then added a flexible straw to the glass so that she could drink without wearing it.

He held the glass for her, noticing how shaky her hands were. When she was finished, he put the glass down and pulled up a chair. "You feeling any better?"

"Pain's manageable." She paused and then asked, "Where's Mason?"

"Waiting room trying to figure out what he did wrong."

Gracie's eyes filled with fresh tears. "He didn't do anything wrong. None of us did anything wrong, but that ..."

"Gracie, hon, you're not making any sense. The nurse told Mason you think you're to blame for our mother's death?"

Gracie nodded, her tears making speech impossible.

"Hon, what do you know about our mother? To my knowledge, we didn't spend any time talking about her while growing up."

"My parents knew her."

"Your parents grew up in Silver Springs, as did my mother and Uncle Jed. So did Sarah and half the town. I would expect all of them to know her. What did they tell you about her?"

"Not they. My dad."

"Your dad told you about my mom?" Kaillar asked, trying to figure out what questions he should be asking, but so far, the conversation didn't appear to be going very far very fast.

"How did your mom die?" Gracie asked in a whisper.

Kaillar sighed, "They aren't really positive, but she was found in a dark alley in Las Vegas. She had drugs and alcohol in her system, and had been beaten up pretty bad."

"I'm so sorry. So sorry." Gracie kept whispering her apology as tears dripped from her eyes.

"Gracie, why are you sorry? Our mother made her own choices. Justin, Mason and I are just thankful that she had the good sense to come home each time she got pregnant with one of us, and that Uncle Jed stepped in to raise us when she couldn't."

"She could have if she'd stayed in Silver Springs."

"She never stayed long in Silver Springs. Gracie, our mother was a druggie and all manner of other things. According to Uncle Jed, she had dreams of becoming famous, and when they fell apart, so did she. She turned to whatever would pay the bills and buy her next fix. I don't know what you think happened, but Maria Donnelly lived for herself and only herself."

Gracie shook her head, "My dad said she was trying to get her act together. After Mason was born, she was trying to stay clean..."

"Yeah, that's what Uncle Jed thought as well. When she left, she cleaned out his bank account, and left him a letter begging him not to come after her. She wanted him to raise her boys, and save them from knowing how badly she'd messed up her life."

"Why did she leave? What caused her to run away?"

"She didn't run away. Running away would mean she at one point intended to stay. Gracie, our mother never wanted to live in Silver Springs, or be a mother, or any of the other things normal people do. She left and went back to her life. Her choice. No one else's."

Gracie wanted so badly to believe what Kaillar was saying, but she'd been afraid of Mason and his brothers finding out what her father had done for so long, she couldn't just let it go. She hadn't fully appreciated how afraid she'd been, but her dream – nightmare really, had brought everything to the forefront of her mind.

The absolute loneliness and hurt she felt when the dream Mason turned away from her was not one she could, or would, soon forget. She saw and felt it each time that she closed her eyes. She knew she'd relive it each time she saw him.

"Gracie, whatever you think you're responsible for, you're not. You were an infant when our mother died. By her bad choices, not those of a baby."

She kept silent, closing her eyes as exhaustion and the pain meds pulled her under.

"Sleep now. And remember that Mason loves you. He's always loved you, and if he has to lose you again, it will destroy him. And, I think it would destroy you as well."

Kaillar left her room, his heart heavy as he tried to figure out what Gracie was so afraid of. And she was afraid. He could see it in her eyes. He stopped by the nurses' station, and met Glenda's eyes, "She's sleeping now."

"Did you get any answers?"

"No, but whatever is bothering her has to do with our mother. I'll go join my brother..."

"Look, she's probably going to be out for most of the night now. Why don't you and your brother head up to the sixth floor. There are some guest suites up there for family members to use when they're here overnight. Get some rest, and hopefully everything will look much better in the morning."

Kaillar thanked her, and went to retrieve his brother. A goodnight's sleep could be used by everyone. Most especially Gracie and Mason. He had a feeling that things were going to get more confusing before they got any better.

Chapter 12

Tuesday late morning...

"Gracie, I would like to see you in ten days to check how things are progressing. You'll need to start physical therapy, but not for at least six more weeks. I know that seems like a long time, but you will need to be your own best patient if you want a full recovery."

Gracie nodded her head, "Yeah. I'll be careful. So," she read over her discharge instructions, "Rest. Ice. Elevation. No weight for six weeks. Got it."

Stan smiled at her, and then folded her chart closed, "I understand that you might have someone in mind to help Sarah manage the motel and boarding rooms in Silver Springs?"

Gracie hadn't even given that another thought; her mind had been occupied with what she was never going to have. "Maybe. I'll have to speak to this person and then if it sounds feasible, I'll have them contact Sarah."

Stan sighed, "If this pans out, it would be an answer to prayer. Sarah has no problems moving over here and marrying me, but she says she won't do it if it's going to leave Silver Springs without proper accommodations."

"I may have been gone for eight years, but that sounds like the Sarah I once knew. After her husband died, I remember that she threw herself into helping at the schools and the church. Anywhere she could put her hands to use, and not sit around bemoaning what she didn't have any longer."

"She's an amazing woman, and I feel blessed just to know her. Even more so to know that she's in my life."

"Congratulations. I'll speak to my friend soon."

"Thanks. One more thing before I take off," Stan told her. "There are two men out there in the hallway, one of whom is hurting because you're hurting." He paused for a moment, and then looked at her with compassion and understanding, "Gracie, whatever is going on in that brain of yours can't be as bad as you think. You've no doubt read about the side effects of anesthesia. Combine those with a deep seated fear, and reality tends to get warped along the way. Talk to Mason. Remember, God didn't create us to go through this life alone."

Gracie nodded, "Thanks. Things don't seem quite so dire as they did yesterday, but that doesn't mean there isn't still going to be hurt feelings..."

"Gracie, do you have feelings for Mason? Before you answer, I know all about you leaving when you were fourteen and the two of you only becoming reacquainted again in the last two days. But Mason seems sure of his feelings. How about you?"

Gracie swallowed and looked out the window before answering, "Have you ever wished you didn't know something?"

"Yes." When she didn't say anything else, he asked, "Is this something what you're afraid of?"

She nodded, not saying anything. He gave her an encouraging smile, letting her know that silence was okay in this instance. "Is this something only you know?"

"And one other living person." *My mother who seems to have gone on living without a care in the world.*

"What have they done with the knowledge?"

Gracie gave a rueful grin, "They forgave and moved on with their life. But the people who don't know, I'm afraid they won't be able to do that. And I will be a constant reminder of what might have been."

"My best advice is to follow your heart. If you have feelings for Mason, you'd be a fool to throw them away. He's one of the good ones." Without another word, he turned and headed for the door. "Oh, and I'm letting him take you home to make sure you follow my discharge instructions."

"But...," Gracie stammered after him, but he walked out of the room and the door closed firmly behind him. She was still staring at the door long moments later, when it opened and Mason stepped in.

She averted her eyes and struggled to keep her composure. She couldn't think of a thing to say to him, but he seemed to realize her trouble, and came to her rescue.

"Stan says you're already to go. Nurse Glenda is bringing up a wheelchair right now." He walked closer to her and then sat down on the edge of the bed so that they were eye level with one another. "Gracie, I don't know what happened yesterday, or what you're not telling me. And if you never want to tell me, that's fine. I don't need to know. If whatever it is causes you this much pain, keep your secret to the grave and I won't ever ask. I just want you to know that no matter what it is, nothing could ever change the way I feel about you. Nothing."

Gracie raised damp eyes to his, "How can you say that when you don't know what it is?"

He smiled at her, "I can say that because I know that no matter what has happened in the past, I can't change a thing. I don't think you could have changed a thing either, and to penalize yourself for the rest of your life doesn't seem fair. I want a relationship with you. I want moonlit walks along the river. Camping trips under the full moon. And I want to see little images of you and me running into my arms at the end of a long day.

"I want the whole package. If you had asked me three days ago if I knew what I wanted for my future, I would have shrugged and told you I hadn't found it yet. Because I wasn't really looking. I think my soul knew that one day you and I would be in the right time and place to make this work. Please, come to the lodge with Kaillar and me for Thanksgiving. Justin is cooking, and he's much better than I am. Give us a chance."

Gracie wanted what he was offering so badly, and since she really didn't have any other options, she slowly nodded her head, "Okay. I'll come to the lodge. Justin's not making freeze-dried turkey is he?"

Mason smiled at her, and slowly shook his head. She felt her heart turn over in her chest, and little butterflies took flight in her stomach. He'd said he didn't need to know her secret. *Could it really be that easy? That she could just not ever tell him and his brothers, and she could pretend that she didn't know anything?*

Somehow, she'd never found anything in life that easy. She was still pondering that when Glenda pushed a wheelchair into the room and shooed Mason out so that she could help Gracie get dressed.

"Came to your senses?" Glenda asked, as she removed her IV and wrapped a piece of pink stretchy tape around her wrist in a pressure bandage.

"Not really, but he says he doesn't need to know what I haven't told him."

"Sounds like a prince among men if you ask me."

Gracie lifted her hips off the bed as the nurse slid a pair of scrub pants up and over the bandaging around her knee. "He's pretty special."

Glenda looked at her and placed her hands on her hips, "Maybe I should get the eye doctor up here before you leave. If you're just seeing that now, girl, maybe you don't deserve him." She fastened the leg brace in place over the scrubs, and then asked, "Too tight?"

Gracie shook her head, and took the scrub top from the nurse, slipping it over her head.

Gracie let those words play over in her head, things that Kaillar and Stan had said replaying in her mind. *Deserve.* The word seemed to be stuck in her head and try as she might, she couldn't get rid of it.

All the way across the mountain and then up to the lodge, she sat silently in the back seat of Kaillar's Range Rover, looking at the mountains and snow, and trying to figure out what she deserved.

She wasn't any closer to figuring things out when they pulled up in front of the lodge than when they'd left Vail. As she looked at the lodge, really looked at it for the first time in years, and all she saw was beauty. The log cabin looked so inviting, and she was suddenly so homesick, she felt tears spring to her eyes.

The two story structure was nestled among the trees, just like when she'd been here last, but there had been significant changes made as well. They had continued the porch all the way around the structure and poured a large patio deck off the side. Rustic log furniture was situated on the deck, and around a large fire pit that rose up from the concrete patio.

Several feet of snow covered all of the unadulterated surfaces, and larger piles of snow were evidence of some shoveling that had occurred earlier in the day. The red metal roof was barely visible beneath the snow, and the splashes of color gave the entire place a festive appearance.

Pine trees, mixed with bare-limbed quaking aspens, had been expertly left in place around the smaller cabins, making it appear as if the cabins were part of the natural order of things. Corrals stood off to the side of the large equipment barn, and horses wandered through the snow, tossing their heads to and fro in delight.

She let her eyes take it all in, and she felt an ache deep inside for the eight years she'd been away from this. Home. Her heart knew it. Now, if she could just get her head to believe...*What? What did she want her head to believe? That she truly belonged here? Yes! Most definitely. That the mistakes of the past didn't matter? That too.*

She felt more tears spring to her eyes as her heart and her mind battled for supremacy.

That was how Mason found her moments later when he opened the back door to lift her from the vehicle. Crying. Again.

Chapter 13

Mason leaned his arms against the top of the vehicle door, and watched her with careful eyes. When Kaillar opened the door on the other side, Mason shook his head and gave him a look that only brothers would understand. *Leave. Now.*

Mason waited until Kaillar had gone inside and then he sighed, "Why are you crying? Is it your leg?" His tone of voice indicated that he already knew the answer.

Gracie looked at him, and felt bad for putting that cautious look in his eyes. "The lodge is beautiful."

He watched her for a moment and then laughed softly, "You're crying because you like the way the lodge looks?"

Gracie blushed and nodded her head, "Sorry. Maybe the pain meds don't agree with me? I seem to be on this emotional rollercoaster and I can't get off."

She was openly crying now, and Mason wrapped his arms around her, pulling her tear-stained face into his chest. "Shush. You can get off anytime you want."

"Can I? I don't think so."

"Gracie...let's go inside. I know Justin is anxious to see you, and he wants you to meet Jessica. Also, just to warn you – Melanie and her husband are here as well as Becca. Let's forget everything for the rest of the day and just try to enjoy each other, our family, and friends. Okay?"

Gracie pushed away from his chest, and used her fingertips to wipe the evidence of her tears away. "Okay." She took a breath and then looked up at him, "Any idea how I'm going to get out of here?"

Mason chuckled and then nodded, "Sit tight. I'm going to pull you out and carry you inside."

"You can't keep carrying me around," she argued, wrapping an arm around his shoulders anyway.

"Gracie, I will carry you for as long as you need me to."

She heard the double entendre in his words, but she chose to ignore it. "Well, I will accept that for the next little while, seeing as how I haven't any idea of how to walk around on crutches. And frankly," she looked around at the piles of snow everywhere, "is it even possible to walk on crutches in two feet of snow?"

Mason laughed, "Do me a favor and don't try? I would rather not make another trip to the hospital until your scheduled appointment."

"Deal. So, who is Jessica?"

Justin chose that moment to exit the house, no doubt wondering what was taking them so long to come inside. When he saw Mason carrying Gracie, he hurried down the steps to shut the car door and grab her stuff. "Hey! There she is. How you doing Gracie?"

"I'm going to be fine, Justin."

"Good to hear." He looked at Mason and inquired, "Everything else okay?"

Mason nodded, "Everything's fine. Since you're here, you can answer Gracie's question."

"What question?"

"Who is Jessica?" she asked, watching Justin's face go soft, and a slight blush stain his cheeks.

"Jessica is the woman I hope to marry one day in the near future."

"Wow! How long have you two been together?"

Justin's blush increased and then he cleared his throat, "There is nothing set in stone that says a couple must know each other for years before they know they're right."

Gracie nodded in agreement, as Mason climbed the stairs with her held securely in his arms. "You're right. There isn't. So, how long?"

"About a month." He smiled at her, and then openly laughed when he realized she wasn't going to lecture him.

Gracie raised a brow and then asked, "Are you sure she's the one?"

"Absolutely positive!"

Gracie smiled and relaxed in Mason's arms, "I'm happy for you. So, can we go inside now? I'm freezing."

Justin and Mason both started, and she chuckled as Justin hurried to open the door so that Mason could carry her inside. "Careful, don't bump her sore leg."

Mason froze, and then carefully walked them through the door frame, "Sorry. I didn't hurt you did I?"

Gracie shook her head, "No. I'm fine. In fact, you could put me down. I have to learn to get around on those crutches sometime. Six weeks is a long time. And before you offer, even you can't carry me around for six weeks."

Mason started to open his mouth, and then he realized how silly his protest would be. He couldn't carry her around for six weeks. He stood her up in the foyer, and then turned and accepted the crutches from Justin. They had been adjusted to the proper height back at the hospital, so all she had to do was slip them under her arms and start moving.

Gracie took a few hesitant steps, and then she looked up and saw everyone watching her, "Hey guys! Whoever said that doctors make the worst patients must have spoken from experience. Never again will I tell someone to stay off their feet for weeks, or hand them a set of crutches and blithely send them on their way. This is horrible!"

Everyone in the room started laughing and the tension dissipated that fast. Melanie and Becca both came over and hugged her, being careful not to disrupt her fragile balance. "I'm so glad you're going to be okay."

"I'm going to be fine. How are you?" She watched Becca blush and slip a glance towards Kaillar, but then she ducked her head and answered softly.

"I think I scared him by freaking out, but I'm fine now. A good night's sleep helped."

"Good. I have something I want to talk to you about before you guys head back to Denver."

Becca nodded, "We've been invited to stay for Thanksgiving dinner, so we aren't going back until Friday morning. Justin said you and Mason might be coming back then as well to get the rest of your things?"

"That's the plan." *I have some thinking to do before then, and I really need to talk to Doc. I want this to work. Maybe he'll have some great advice for me.*

"Good."

Justin walked over with a beautiful blonde's hand in his own, "Gracie this is Jessica Andrews. Jessica, this is Gracie Shelton."

Gracie smiled at the woman, and juggled her crutches until she could shake her hand. "Nice to meet you."

"You too. Justin has lunch ready. Are you hungry?"

Gracie looked up and then asked, "You cook?" She looked at Mason and shrugged her shoulders when he raised an eyebrow. "Fine. I admit it. I thought you were joking about Justin cooking Thanksgiving dinner, and I really was expecting freeze-dried turkey and stuffing in one of those little foil bags."

Justin smiled and waggled his eyebrows at her, "I am a man of many talents. Come on. Get situated on the couch, and I'll have Mason bring you a plate."

Gracie followed his advice, and just like that, she felt the heavy burden of knowledge fall away to the back of her memory. She was going to live in the moment. At least for today.

Chapter 14

Wednesday morning...

Becca had just finished helping Gracie get dressed in a pair of borrowed sweat pants and a long sleeved t-shirt when they heard someone holler up the stairs that breakfast was ready. The two women made their way slowly into the large living area to see both Kaillar and Justin sitting at the table, along with Jessica, while Mason continued to make stacks of pancakes.

"You girls ready for breakfast?"

Gracie stopped and stared at him, "You cook?"

Mason smirked at her, "Thought you knew everything didn't you? And yes, I can cook. Have a seat."

Gracie looked at Justin, and shared a grin with him, "I kind of reminded him about his adventures in Home Ec while we were up in the shack."

Kaillar burst out laughing, "Oh man! I remember that. Uncle Jed was completely at a loss for words..."

Justin joined in and then whispered loudly, "We all started learning to cook right after that. Uncle Jed had several of the women from town come up and give us cooking lessons on the weekends and school vacations."

"I didn't know that," Gracie told him. She looked at Mason as he set a plate of pancakes in front of her, "How come I didn't know that?"

Mason tapped her on the nose, "There are lots of things you didn't get to know."

Gracie shook her head at him, "There can't be that many. From the time we were ten until I moved away, I practically lived up here."

Justin grinned, "Uncle Jed didn't seem to mind. He loved having you around. So, how is your knee this morning?"

Becca answered before she could, "She needs ice and elevation. She also needs some pain pills but after she eats."

"Are you my mother now?" Gracie asked on a laugh.

"No, but you've taken care of me enough times, I thought it was time to return the favor. I saw some board games on the bookshelf last night. Maybe we could play one after breakfast?"

"Monopoly?" Gracie asked with a twinkle in her eyes.

Becca groaned, "Sure. Why not? I like to lose."

"Do you guys have room for another player?" Jessica asked.

"Sure." Gracie looked around and then asked, "Where are Melanie and Michael?"

Justin grinned, "We set up the honeymoon suite for them. They have an entire cabin to themselves. Seemed only right to give them some quiet time together."

Gracie's heart melted and she reached across the table and covered Justin's hand with her own, "Thank you. I know that will mean the world to both of them. Before he came back to the States, Melanie did her best to stay positive, but every time there was another report of American soldiers dying, she would withdraw just a bit until the names were released. Then she would breathe easy for another few days, or weeks, and go through it all again."

Jessica shook her head, "I can't imagine how hard that must have been on her."

"But it all has a happy ending now. She's going to work for her dad in Florida, and Michael got his discharge, so they can be together now."

"More pancakes, anyone?" Mason asked, a spatula raised up above the skillet. When no one answered him, he turned the gas off and started cleaning up. Their Uncle Jed had been one smart cookie, and he'd quickly realized that boys who cleaned up after themselves in the kitchen learned the art of economy and multi-tasking with the cookware and utensils. The lodge had many modern appliances, but a dishwasher hadn't been added until Justin came home from the Middle East and the brothers decided to build their futures in Silver Springs.

Justin and Kaillar headed for the back door, grabbing jackets and gloves on their way out. "We're heading down to start the walks. Join us when you're done."

"Sure thing. I'll just make sure that the girls are set and be right out."

Becca, Jessica, and Gracie had already moved to the large couch, and were in the process of setting up the Monopoly board when he tossed the dish towel onto the hanging rack and joined them. "So, you girls need anything before I head outside?"

He'd watched Gracie shut down after she'd mentioned Melanie going to work for her dad. *Could this all have something to do with her father? She said she'd been fighting with him.*

"We're fine, thank you."

"Good. If you need anything, just let Jessica know. She's been up here enough that she knows where most things are located."

Gracie watched him from beneath her lashes as he slipped his jacket on, and then grabbed his gloves. He gave her one last searching glance before shaking his head and stepping outside.

"What was that all about?" Jessica asked once he was gone.

"What are you talking about?" Gracie asked.

"Come on. We might not know each other, but I do know some of Mason's tells. What's with all the looks? At times Mason looks completely happy, and then he watches you and looks like someone kicked his new puppy."

Gracie dropped her eyes, "It's complicated."

Jessica nodded her head and then suggested, "So uncomplicate it."

Becca took her hand, "Do you remember what you told me? After the..." She cleared her throat, glanced at Jessica, and then finished her sentence, "After I was attacked?"

Gracie shook her head, "Not really."

"Well, I do. I kept saying that it was all my fault. That I should have been more careful, and you got mad at me. You were almost yelling at me because I wouldn't listen to you. You said...you said that I didn't make the choice to be attacked. I made the choice to walk through the parking garage to get to my car. A perfectly normal activity that should have been safe.

"But the men who attacked me, they also made a decision that night. One that ended up hurting me and costing them their freedom. It didn't take right then, but over the next few days, I kept hearing you telling me that it wasn't my fault. That I didn't do anything to deserve getting attacked."

"Do you believe me now?" Gracie asked, her voice full of compassion at what Becca had gone through.

"I do. Now, I want to return the favor. Tell me what's going on between you and Mason. Please let me help you."

Gracie sighed, the board game forgotten. She looked up, and then shook her head, "Nothing's wrong." She'd enjoyed breakfast, the easy banter between her and everyone else. She wanted to continue basking in the warmth and love the Donnelly boys offered, and thoughts of the past would ruin that.

"Let's play," she said a bit too gaily. *One more day? Please God, just one more day before I have to start thinking about the future.*

Chapter 15

Mason grabbed a snow shovel, and started in on a section of the walkways that was still covered in snow. He could see Justin and Kaillar up ahead, and made it his personal goal to finish before them. Even though he'd gotten a late start.

That's how it had always been. The three boys challenging each other to be better, faster, smarter. Everything had been turned into a competition, and their Uncle Jed had been an expert at harnessing that competitive spirit and teaching them how to win and lose with grace.

Mason tossed his hands up as he finished two shovelfuls ahead of Justin, and five ahead of Kaillar. He and his brothers headed to the equipment barn, with Mason pulling out three sodas from the fridge kept there.

He popped the top, and hauled himself up to sit on a hay bale. "So, Becca seems more stable today."

Kaillar nodded, "Yeah, she slept well the first night, and seems to be handling being around me a little better."

"That's good news. Any idea of what happened to her yet?"

"Melanie kind of filled me in. She was attacked a few months ago in a parking garage. The attack stole her confidence, and Gracie diagnosed her as suffering from PTSD. She refuses to get some help, and according to Melanie, she refused to call her parents and tell them what had happened."

"That doesn't sound good."

"No. It isn't. But I'm not going to worry about it. I could see myself getting to know a girl like her, but she lives in Denver, and I already know I'm not up for a long distance relationship. Besides, she needs someone who's going to be around all the time."

Mason and Justin nodded, in agreement with his assessment. Changing the subject, Mason asked, "You up for a trip to Denver Friday morning?"

Justin nodded, "Yeah. Jessica will probably want to tag along as well."

"Good. I figured we'd take the small trailer and bring back whatever belongings she's bringing here."

"That's doable. You planning to spend the night?"

Mason shook his head, "I wasn't really planning on it."

"Well, do so. You in, Kai?"

"No. I'm scheduled to act as ski patrol all weekend. You guys go and have fun. I think Melanie and her hubby are heading out Friday morning as well. That probably means that Becca will be out of here as well."

Justin nodded and then turned to Mason, "So what happened up at the hospital?"

Mason looked up at the rafters and then shook his head, "Wish I knew. Something about mom."

"Whose mom?" Justin asked for clarification.

"Our mother. Gracie told the nurse that she is responsible for mom's death."

Justin said nothing and then he suggested, "Think she needs to talk to someone about the thoughts in her head?"

"You mean like a shrink?" Mason asked, already shaking his head, completely against the idea.

"No. Like a pastor. Or Doc. Both men could provide an unbiased ear to listen. As well as some valuable insight and good advice."

Mason thought for a moment, "That's not a bad idea. Doc was alive when mom was growing up and Jeremy wasn't. That would provide Gracie with two different viewpoints on whatever's bothering her.

"I told her she never had to tell me whatever it is. She seems to think it will change how I think about her, but I've assured her it wouldn't. I don't think she believes me."

Justin smiled, "Leave it to me. Jeremy and his family are already planning to join us for dinner tomorrow. Doc Matthews already had plans, but I could probably get him to drop by and visit his replacement later this afternoon."

Kaillar smiled, "Throw in dinner, and I can guarantee he'll be here."

Justin laughed; everyone in Silver Springs knew the best way to get around Doc Matthews was through his stomach. The man loved food, and Justin had often wondered how he stayed in such good shape, eating the way he did.

"I'm cooking steak tonight, baked potatoes with all the fixings, and some greens. I'll call Doc as soon as I get back into the house. I promised I'd take Jessica and Becca out in one of the snow machines this afternoon. Becca is a photographer, and is hoping to catch some wildlife shots for her portfolio."

Mason looked at Kaillar, who was listening to the conversation about Becca. *There's more than a passing interest there. Very interesting.*

The three men headed back into the lodge half an hour later, the sound of the girls giggling uproariously over something that eluded them immediately grabbing their attention. Stopping in the doorway, they asked, "Girls? What's so funny?"

Justin walked over and sat down behind Jessica, pulling her back against his knees, "So who is winning?"

That question caused more giggles to erupt. "Okay. Let me rephrase my question. Are you even playing?"

Again, more giggles. He stood up and then shook his head at them, "I'll let you three help each other out with the explanations then." He kissed Jessica on the top of her head, and then sauntered off, with Kaillar right behind him.

That left Mason alone with the three women, and he immediately grabbed one of their tea cups to see if they'd gotten into the cooking brandy kept in the kitchen. It was one of the few alcoholic beverages that could be found on the premises, and was only used very rarely.

Jessica sobered and trailed after Justin, "See you girls later." Becca took one look at Mason's face, and scampered after her as if she were being chased by a pack of hounds.

"Well! I guess that just leaves you to explain all of the laughter," Mason told her.

Gracie took one look at his face and then she stopped laughing, growing sober, and feeling that terrible weight from her conscience weighing her down.

"Whoa! Stop! Whatever is going through your mind, just stop it."

Gracie gave him a sad look, and then lowered her eyes to her lap. "I'm trying."

Mason moved so that he was sitting right next to her. He carefully wrapped an arm around her shoulders, "I know. Justin is inviting Doc up here for dinner. We all thought you might want a chance to talk to him, and getting around town right now is going to be more than difficult."

Gracie smiled at him and nodded, "Thank you. So, tell me about the other changes that have happened to Silver Springs. Jessica said she's the new elementary teacher?"

Mason released her shoulders, and spent the next hour trying to catch her up about the town and its inhabitants. Some minor things had changed while she'd been gone, but very few major things had. Silver Springs was still just a small Colorado mountain town.

After filling her in on the important facts, he stood up and then scooped her into his arms.

"Wait! Where are you taking me?"

"To the kitchen. I'm making lunch, and you are going to watch and be amazed," he predicted.

"Oh really? This I definitely have to see." She paused for effect, and then lowered her voice, "You're not making a cake are you?"

Mason tickled her ribs, and set her down at the large island. He handed her a cutting board, a knife, and a pile of vegetables. "Chop."

Gracie smiled and then asked, "What are we making?"

"Chicken noodle soup and cheese sandwiches."

"Yum." Gracie chopped vegetables, and watched Mason move confidently around the kitchen. She watched him add spices without measuring, and found herself smiling and relaxing in his presence.

When the soup was all put together and left to simmer on the stove, Mason covered it, and then turned to her with a smile on his face, "Want to go play in the snow?"

"Uhm...no! Not with this knee. I'm happy to watch from the window though, while you build me a snowman."

Mason grinned and scooped her back up into his arms. He deposited her in a chair facing the large picture windows, and helped her prop her knee up on the ottoman. He grabbed a bag of ice for her, and then kissed her nose, "One snowman coming up. Watch and be amazed!"

Gracie did watch, and she was amazed. Amazed that she'd managed to survive away from this place for so long. Silver Springs was home, and she just needed to find a way to deal with the past and move forward. *Like her mother had done.*

Chapter 16

Doc Matthews didn't need a second invite, and around 2 o'clock Wednesday afternoon, he arrived at the Three Brothers Lodge with a smile on his face and several questions rolling around in his brain.

"She's right in here," Justin informed the older man.

Gracie looked up from the book she'd been pretending to read to see a familiar face beaming at her from the doorway. "Doc! I'd get up to greet you, but as you can see, I've decided to find out what it's like to be on the other side of the exam table."

Doc came over to the couch and seated himself on a side chair, barely noticing when Justin slipped away from the room. "I'll tell you a little secret. When I was just out of my residency, I thought I had the world by the tail. Then I got too cocky and fell off a horse."

He laughed at himself, "I spent two weeks in the hospital with my leg in traction, and another three months hobbling around in a full leg cast. When I was finally able to start rehab, I had a much better understanding of what my patients were going through, and it changed the way I did medicine."

Gracie nodded her head, "I can already tell you I feel the same way. I will never prescribe a patient stay off their feet again without understanding how difficult a task that truly is."

Doc smiled at her and then asked a few questions about the surgery and her prognosis before inquiring, "So, how does it feel to be back in Silver Springs? You were fourteen when your parents uprooted you. A difficult time to be sure."

Gracie sighed, "To tell you the truth, all I've thought about since we left, was coming back. Part of me loves being back here. The town. The mountains."

"The men?" Doc questioned. "I seem to remember you and young Mason were inseparable. And he's the one who rescued you on the mountain, correct?" When she nodded, he looked at her and then asked, "Sparks still there?"

She closed her eyes briefly and nodded, "In some ways it's like I never left. But..."

Doc sat back and then sighed, "You can't get past what you know that he doesn't." It was a statement and not a question.

Gracie looked up at him in shock and questioned, "How...I mean,.."

Doc gave her a sad look, "Give an old man a moment to clear his conscience, will you?"

"Okay."

"Let me tell you another story. About a young woman who hated the simple living of Silver Springs. She had stars in her eyes, and a desire to be sought after for all the wrong reasons. She bolted from here just as soon as she could, seeking fame and fortune in the big city.

"But as is wont to happen in such cases, she was naïve and ripe for the picking by every user she met. Fame was elusive, and fortune just a myth. She ended up buying the snake oil that was sold as a cure all for her ills. But all it brought was further destruction and addictions that ruled her life.

"Then came the decisive moment when she had to think of someone other than herself. And she made the right choice. She came back to Silver Springs, but soon the allure of the bright lights and big city drew her back.

"This destructive cycle continued. No matter how many times she was rescued, she was never able to abandon her yearning to be somewhere else."

He paused and Gracie shook her head, "That is such a sad story. Was she someone close to you?"

Doc shook his head, "Not in the way you're thinking. When I first came to Silver Springs thirty-seven years ago, this young lady was eight. I watched her grow up, as I did so many young people in and around this town. When she came back home, I helped her parents try to deal with her addictions, but those were only physical things. Her mind was the real problem, and psychiatry is not my specialty."

"What happened to her?" Gracie asked, still not having put the pieces together.

"She died. Alone. Probably afraid. Her choices came back to seek their revenge, and she paid with her life."

"Her parents must have been so sad."

"Fortunately, God was gracious and neither of them lived to see their daughter's ultimate fall. See, she'd been raised in a good Christian household. Was a member of the youth group, and had parents who loved and cared for her. She even had a brother who would do anything to help her out. None of that made a difference."

"I don't get how someone who was raised one way can abandon everything and go so far in the opposite direction."

"Have you talked with Jessica?" he inquired.

"Just a few minutes here and there."

"Her parents were missionaries to South Africa. They were murdered, and she spent years running from God, blaming Him for taking her parents away from her. Blaming Him for leaving her all alone."

"She doesn't seem bitter."

"Not today. That's because she finally decided that the past belongs precisely there. In the past. But, I digress. There's more to my story.

"The young woman was like a bad apple. Even though she came home humbled and trying to do the right thing, she never let go of her desire for a different lifestyle. Over the years, there were people whose lives were sullied by her. By her actions.

"See, this young woman's conscience had been seared, and she no longer held to the traditional concepts of right and wrong. Black and white. And in any group of people, there are always those whose will to withstand temptation is weak and untried. It was those people that she appealed to and took down to her level."

Gracie was trying to understand, "She brought drugs to Silver Springs?" She wasn't aware there was a drug problem in the small town. It wouldn't surprise her overly much, but it would still be worrisome to her.

"No. It wasn't the drugs she brought; it was her addiction to personal pleasure. Her selfishness when it came to respecting marriage vows."

Gracie suddenly felt uncomfortable. Her father had been such a man; weak. All too willing to abandon his marriage vows for a few brief moments of pleasure. "Did these men ever get found out?"

Doc sighed, "Some. Others went to great lengths to hide their transgressions. Even going so far as to uproot their family overnight with the mistaken notion that they could leave their actions and guilt behind just as easily."

Gracie looked at the older man with wide open eyes, "You knew."

Doc nodded his head, "I suspected. When your dad took you and your mom away so suddenly, I was sure."

"My dad...it was years after we left before he finally confessed to my mom and me. He told us how he'd been consumed by guilt and called things off with her. She'd been upset and taken off for Las Vegas. Where she'd died several days later."

"Her choice. Remember that."

"My father's choice. A choice that caused Maria to rush away..."

"She would have left anyway. It wasn't in her nature to stay. Gracie, look at me." He waited until she did so, "If you are carrying any guilt around for your father's actions, you need to let it go. You can't re-write history. You don't deserve to live under that kind of shadow."

"Deserve? Did Mason or his brothers deserve to grow up motherless?"

"Even if she'd lived, those boys would have stayed with their uncle. He loved them, Maria loved herself."

Mason stood in the doorway and spoke up just then, "Doc's right, you know. My mother was the most selfish woman I've ever heard of." Mason came and sat down next to her, "Is that the secret you've been afraid to share? That your father cheated on your mother with mine? Trust me; we've heard it all before. Our mother had no morals, and even less of a conscience."

"But, my father said that she was upset when he called the dalliance off, and that's what sent her running back to Las Vegas. Where she died."

"No, sugar. Her addiction and lifestyle choices drew her back to Las Vegas. Your father was just a pawn, used by her for her own means."

Gracie stared at him, barely registering when Doc left the room, leaving her alone with Mason and her chaotic thoughts. "I was sure you'd hate me when you found out what my father had done."

"I'm hurt you didn't trust me more, but I also understand that you've lived with this knowledge for a while, and didn't truly know how messed up our mother was." Mason looked at her and then held open his arms, "Gracie, I have never allowed my mother's sins to affect my life. Can you do the same with your father's sins?"

Gracie was once again crying, sobbing actually at the sense of relief she felt. For the first time since hearing of her father's actions, she didn't feel guilty. Hearing Mason, as he continued to murmur to her, saying that he cared about her, and not about the actions of her father, was like a balm being applied to a fresh wound.

"I'm sorry," she cried against his chest. "I'm sorry I didn't have the guts to just tell you what I knew and trust you to deal with the information correctly."

"Don't be. We have eight years to make up for. We are going to make up for them, aren't we?"

"I'd like that."

Mason hugged her close, and then pushed her back to tip her eyes up to meet his own. He touched her lips with a fingertip and then asked, "I gave you your first kiss. Can I give you another one now?"

Gracie didn't wait for him to act, she lifted her mouth towards his, meeting him as he lowered his lips to take hers in a sweet kiss full of promise and love.

The door in her heart swung wide open, and she could honestly say she was now at home. Silver Springs was going to become her new place of residence, but wherever Mason was would always be home.

Chapter 17

Thanksgiving Day...

"All right everyone. Dinner's ready."

Mason scooped Gracie up and placed her in the chair that had been set at the end of the long dining table. By turning just a tad sideways, she'd be able to keep her leg elevated and still join everyone else at the table. Mason took the chair right next to her, making sure that he could easily help her if she required it.

Gracie grinned at him and whispered, "You do realize it's my knee that's hurt and not my hands. Or my arms. Or my head?"

Mason blushed, "I just have this need to take care of you. Enjoy it."

Gracie kissed him on the cheek, "I am."

Justin stood up and looked around the table. Jessica was seated to his right. Kaillar was seated to his left with Becca, Melanie and Michael rounding out that side of the table. Sarah sat next to Jessica, and Scott Taylor and his wife Chloe finished that side of the table. Their newborn baby sat on a chair between them, sleeping peacefully in a carrier.

"Shall we say grace?" Everyone bowed their head and Justin raised his voice up, "Father, on this day of Thanksgiving, we remember the many blessings You have brought our way this past year. The relationships You've restored, the new ones You've brought into our lives."

"We especially offer up thanks for bringing Gracie back home to us. Now as we eat together, we ask that Your hand would stay upon us and guide us in the coming year to do Your will and help our fellow man."

"Amen."

Everyone looked up and the feast began. Gracie watched as bowls of food were passed around, and laughter seemed to be the mode of the day. She'd missed this. After leaving Silver Springs, her home had become very tense and strained. Her mother had tried to make it like it was before, but that had been impossible.

When Gracie had been offered a full-ride scholarship with room and board, she'd jumped at the chance to get away from the oppressive atmosphere of her home. But she'd been years younger than her classmates and more of an oddity and someone to be pitied than someone to hang out with. Loneliness had become the norm.

"You okay?" Mason murmured to her, scooping potatoes onto her still empty plate.

"Just thinking how nice it is to be here with you all. I missed this."

Mason smiled at her, "You're home now and you never have to leave again."

"I don't?" she teased him.

Mason grew very serious, and then he looked down at his plate for a moment. When he looked back up, Gracie saw something in his eyes she'd never seen before. Emotion and a yearning that tugged at her heart.

"Gracie, I know this probably isn't the right time or place, but waiting around for that doesn't seem to always out so well for us. So...I don't want you to ever leave. I guess what I'm saying is, I want us to be forever."

Gracie watched him with tear-filled eyes. She reached up to wipe them away and laughed, "Why am I always crying around you?"

"I don't know, but I promise to always be there to wipe them away. What do you say? Want to stay here forever with me? Like this? Gracie, will you marry me and make it official?"

Gracie nodded her head, happier than she'd ever been in her life. Mason tipped her chin up and kissed her, right there at the dinner table.

When the hoots and hollers of the others in the room reached their ears, Gracie turned bright red and bit her bottom lip. Mason absorbed their teasing as his due, "We're getting married!"

Justin and Kaillar both got up and hugged Gracie, "Welcome to the family sweetie!"

"Welcome home, Gracie girl."

"Thanks, guys. Let's eat."

Everyone got back to the act of eating dinner, and Gracie kept a careful eye on Becca. She'd sat down before Kaillar, and Gracie had seen the momentary look of panic on her friend's face when Kaillar had accidentally brushed her shoulder as he slipped into his chair.

She seemed to be handling things okay, but it was becoming very apparent to Gracie that Becca needed some professional help. And not on her timeframe. She needed help in the here and now.

As dinner wound down, Scott and Chloe disappeared to one of the guests rooms so that mommy and baby could both take a nap. Melanie and Michael returned to their small cabin with a plate of leftovers and orders not to return until 10 o'clock the next morning when everyone would be heading either to the ski slopes, back to town, or into Denver.

Sarah convinced Becca to come spend the night with her so that they could eat popcorn and watch sappy movies, and Gracie was happy to see a smile on her friend's face. Kaillar headed to the barn to get his skis ready for his work on the slopes the next morning, leaving Jessica, Justin, Mason, and Gracie in the house to fend for themselves.

Justin and Mason migrated towards the den and whatever football game happened to be still playing, and Jessica kept Gracie company. When she produce a tablet and brought up several stores in the Denver area that catered to off-the-rack wedding dresses, Gracie looked at her with a question in her eyes.

Jessica nodded her head, a happy smile on her face, "We were going to let it be a surprise once we got to Denver, but maybe we should both look at dresses while we're there?"

Gracie started giggling, and soon Jessica had joined her. The sounds of their laughter brought their men back in and once again, they couldn't seem to explain what was so funny.

Justin finally picked Jessica up and carried her out of the room, hoping that distance would help the two women get control of themselves. His actions caused another round of giggles.

Mason sat down next to Gracie, watching as she cried through her laughter and held her ribs because they hurt. "Is it something in the water, because I know you girls didn't consume any alcohol at dinner?"

Gracie shook her head, "I'm just happy. I'm not sure if that's what does it for Jessica, but I'm happy. Deliriously happy."

Mason smiled at her, "I can see that." He noticed the tablet on the ground, and picked it up, but the picture on the screen caused him to pause and look at her curiously.

"Jessica's idea. It seems that she and your brother have agreed to get married, but were waiting to keep it a secret. That's why he wanted to spend the night. So that they can fit the gown she chooses and she can bring it back with her."

Mason looked thoughtful, "Is that something you'd be interested in doing?"

Gracie watched him, "We haven't really talked about when and..."

"Today. Tomorrow. As soon as we can."

"I might need a bit more time than that. How about next week?"

"That sounds perfect."

"Then, yes. I'd like to look at dresses while we're in Denver tomorrow."

"Consider it done. You and Jessica can go dress shopping, and Justin and I will take care of packing up the rest of your things. Pick something pretty. Like you."

Gracie blushed, and then she couldn't think because he was kissing her. Life was perfect.

Epilogue

A delaide's Wedding Shop, Friday afternoon...
"I really like this one with the full skirt," Jessica said, fingering the satin material of the ivory wedding dress. It had a sweetheart neckline, and tiny seed pearls attached in a delicate scroll pattern across the bodice and over the capped sleeves.

"That's gorgeous. You should definitely try that one on." Gracie was still trying to decide if she wanted to go traditional, or if she dared to find the dress she'd only dreamed about.

"Gracie?" Becca stood by her elbow, having decided that she would rather go dress shopping than sit at home by herself all day. Gracie was proud of her and hoped to find time today to discuss her moving to Silver Springs and taking over for Sarah.

"Hey!"

"What kind of dress are you looking for?"

Gracie sighed, "I don't know."

Becca smiled at her, "I doubt that. Tell me about the dress you wear in your dreams."

Gracie grinned, "But that is only a dream dress. And they don't really exist."

"Tell me anyway, okay?"

"Velvet. In my dreams, my wedding dress is white velvet. It had a scoop neckline and lone sleeves with those little strings that hook over your middle finger to keep them in place. And a long skirt that swirls around my ankles when I walk, but drapes along the ground behind me."

"It sound gorgeous. Tiffany, do you have anything like that?" Becca asked the store attendant Gracie hadn't known was standing behind her listening in.

Tiffany smiled, "I have the perfect dress for you. Head on back to the dressing room, and I'll bring it to you."

Gracie looked at her, hope shining in her eyes, "You really have a dress like what I described?"

"Go on back and you'll see. It must have been made just for you."

Twenty minutes later, Gracie emerged from the dressing room, and everyone stopped and gasped at the picture she presented. She was stunning in the dress, and a more perfect fit didn't exist.

"Oh, Gracie! Look at yourself!" Jessica and Becca urged her.

Gracie took a breath and turned to face the three-way mirror. She gasped, and felt tears spring to her eyes. "It's perfect! Just like in my dreams."

Becca wrapped an arm around her waist, "Who was your perfect groom in your dreams?"

"Mason," Gracie whispered.

"A match made in heaven. She'll take it."

"Perfect." The store attendant was beaming as she walked away to start the paperwork.

"Now we have to find Jessica the perfect dress," Becca said.

"Well, I don't think I'm ever going to find anything as perfect as that one, but I have several to try on."

"Then get to it," Becca told her with a laugh.

Gracie changed back into her street clothes, and handed the gown over to be pressed one last time and then hung in a garment bag. Everything seemed to be going so well, and Jessica finally settled on a dress of her own that made her look like Cinderella ready for the ball.

They headed back to Jessica's apartment, and were pleased to see the boys loading the last of the boxes into the trailer.

"All done?" Gracie asked in wonder, glancing at her watch. They'd only been at it for three hours, but what they'd accomplished would have taken her three days. "Thank you."

"How about we go get some pizza?" Kaillar suggested, making sure that Becca knew she was invited as well.

"That sounds good. I know the perfect place just a few blocks down."

"Great."

Everyone started piling into the vehicles, but Becca's phone rang, and she hung back to answer it. Gracie watched her walk away before putting the phone to her ear. Becca's back stiffened, and then Gracie watched her phone drop to the ground.

"Becca!" Gracie sought Mason out, "Help her! What's wrong? Becca! Mason, take me to her."

Kaillar was closest and reached her first, catching her just as she fainted and would have hit the ground. "She's fainted."

Gracie waited impatiently while Kaillar and Justin checked her over. Kaillar picked her up, and settled her in the back of the vehicle next to Gracie. "What's wrong with her?"

"I don't know. Becca? Sweetie, open your eyes." Gracie looked up with worried eyes, "Where's her phone?"

"She dropped it." Kaillar retrieved it and then handed it over to Gracie. The screen was shattered, but Gracie ignored that and pulled up her most recent calls.

"Who just called her?" Justin asked, Jessica hanging on his arm.

Mason looked over Gracie's shoulder, "It said 'Mom.'"

Gracie shook her head, "She doesn't talk to her parents. Not ever."

Becca moaned and began to come around. Gracie held onto her arm, and spoke softly to her, "Becca, you fainted. You're in the car with me. Who was on the phone?"

Becca stared straight ahead, "My mom."

"Your mom in Hawaii?" Gracie asked.

Becca nodded, "My dad's dead. The funeral is Sunday, and she wants me there."

Gracie's heart broke for her friend and she wrapped her in a hug, "Oh Becca. I'm so sorry. Honey, what can we do?"

Becca wasn't crying and that worried Kaillar more than the fact that she'd fainted. "She wants me to come for the funeral. I..."

"If money is a problem, I can lend you as much as you need..."

"No. I can...I just...," she looked up at Gracie with tears and fear in her eyes. "I can't go back there like this. Weak. I just can't. Not by myself. I..."

Gracie felt so helpless. With her knee, there was no way she could handle a journey to Hawaii. No way to get around on a plane, or...

She looked up and met Kaillar's eyes and saw the question there. She looked at Becca, who was unconsciously holding onto his hand. She nodded once, and Kaillar took over.

"Becca, darling. Do you want someone to go with you?"

Becca's mind was almost numb, but she nodded anyway. She raised teary eyes to him, and he felt a piece of his heart break away. "I'll take you home. Will you let me do that? Will you let me take you home to say goodbye to your dad?"

Becca shivered once, but she didn't look away from him. "Yes."

"Good. Justin, we need a ride to the airport."

"Done. We'll stop by her apartment and pack whatever she needs on the way. Jessica, would you mind finding the first flights out of here?"

"Not at all." She reached across and squeezed Becca's shoulder, "It's going to be all right. We're all here for you. It's what family does. They help each other in the good times and in the bad."

Book 3: Kaillar
Prologue

Four and half years earlier, Pe'ahi, Maui, Hawaii...

F Becca Edwards sat silently as her soon-to-be ex-boyfriend parked his Jeep at the top of the beach. Without even looking at her, he slammed the vehicle off and jumped from the driver's side. He grabbed his surfboard from the back, then stopped at the door to the vehicle, and she could feel him staring at her.

It took everything she had left in her to keep her eyes forward and not look at him. *If I look at him, I'm going to throw up. Don't look at him. Just ignore him and he'll leave, and then you can deal with it.*

"Becca, do yourself a favor and wash your face before you come down to the beach. You look awful." He waited for her acknowledgement, and when it didn't come, he slammed his fist on the side of the vehicle, the unexpected noise making her jump and emit a soft cry of fear.

"Whatever!" He grabbed his board, and headed towards the beach, and the blue water beyond.

Becca stared straight ahead, willing the tears brimming in her eyes not to fall. He'd already made her cry once; she wasn't going to let him have the satisfaction of seeing her cry a second time today.

Dagan Carlson was an up-and-coming surfer, coming in second place in the World Championships the year before. This year, he was pushing himself to take on bigger and stronger waves, determined to come out on top at the end of the season.

Becca had met him at the end of the previous season, but since she wasn't even out of high school yet, they'd done nothing more than flirt a bit. He was a star, and had gorgeous, bikini clad girls throwing themselves at him all the time. Something that had bothered Becca immensely.

They'd started emailing each other over the summer months, and then he'd announced that he was coming back to Hawai'i to train during the winter. She'd done everything in her power to persuade him to stay on the Big Island, and it seemed to have worked. He'd booked several bungalows at her parents' resort for himself and his surfing buddies. Becca had been ecstatic when she'd heard the news.

She'd done what she could to keep track of him once he arrived. Her brother, Kevin, and his best friend Kalino had helped in that regard. At the age of fourteen each, they were the reigning Island Junior Champions, and showed great promise for taking on the bigger waves once they became more mature. Getting to surf alongside someone of Dagan's caliber was every teenage surfer's dream.

Hawaii was full of great surf spots, and since Kalino's dad happened to own and operate a charter flight service, getting around the islands was cheap and easy. Today the boys were surfing at Pe'ahi. The islanders and surfers alike reverently referred to the waves that crashed upon her shores as "Jaws" because if you weren't prepared, she would chew you up, and you'd be lucky if she spit you back out.

The waves at Pe'ahi were some of the strongest and biggest in the world, and both Kevin and Kalino had been warned by their parents to stay inside on the smaller waves. The boys weren't stupid, and there was no doubt in anyone's mind that they would take great care in these more dangerous waters.

Becca had tagged along for the day after making plans to meet up with Dagan for an early lunch. He'd been island hopping for the last month, training, but also playing quite a bit. He'd taken an interest in Becca, and she'd returned it wholeheartedly, much to her parents' dismay.

Her mother had been adamantly against her spending any time with the cocky surfer who was four years older than her daughter was. But Becca had a big case of puppy love, and hadn't taken any of her mother's warnings to heart. Warnings that had come to fruition just a short while before, forever changing her life in a not so pleasant way. Innocence almost lost, and trust and a belief in happily ever after seemed very far away right now.

Realizing that she'd been sitting in the Jeep too long, she carefully wiped the tears from her cheeks, wincing when she touched the spot on her cheek that would probably show a bruise in the morning. She swallowed carefully, her throat sore from where Dagan's hands had wrapped themselves around it while he...

She took a deep breath, and then slipped from the vehicle. *I should be grateful that park ranger came along when he did, or I'd have more than a sore cheek, split lip, and sore throat.*

Dagan had been pushing her to move forward with their physical relationship for the last week, but Becca had held fast to her convictions. Convictions that Dagan hadn't even tried to honor not even an hour ago. He'd become another person, shoving her down into the soft sand, and choking her as he tried to pull her clothing off her body. *Come on Becca. I promise you'll like it if you just try it. Don't be such a prude!*

Her thin cotton shirt and cut off jean shorts over her bikini were little barrier to his searching hands. She'd struggled, and he'd slapped her across the face to keep her quiet. She'd yelled anyway, bringing her knee up in an effort to get him off her, and that's when the park ranger had called out.

Dagan had quickly risen to his feet, chuckling when the park ranger had looked at them as naughty children. Becca had been so embarrassed; she'd kept her face hidden until the ranger had left.

She'd rushed back to Dagan's rental Jeep, and demanded that he take her back to the beach.

Dagan had assured her they would have plenty of time to finish things later that evening. The surfers were planning to camp out on the beach so they could catch the early morning waves. Becca and the two boys had gained permission to do so as well, with a promise that Kalino's dad would be heading back to the Big Island around suppertime should they change their minds.

Becca didn't mention to Dagan that she was grabbing her brother and Kalino and heading straight for the airport. Even if they had to wait on Kalino's father to pick them up for hours, she wanted nothing to do with Dagan Carlson. Ever again. Whatever infatuation she'd had for him was gone, right along with her ability to trust.

As she walked down to the beach, searching for her brother, she found him, but she hadn't realized how badly bruised her face had already become. Kevin knew she'd taken off with Dagan, and he instantly jumped to the right conclusion.

"I'll kill him!" He'd turned, searching the beach, and then he'd taken off running for the water. For being her younger brother, he was fiercely protective of his sister, and with that went a lack of self-control that oftentimes scared Becca.

"Kevin! Don't! Let's just leave!" Becca chased him towards the water, "Kevin!"

He didn't listen to her. Kalino came running over to see what had upset her so much.

"Becca! What's wrong?"

When she'd turned to look at him, his eyes went wide, and his face took on a furious expression. "Kalino! Go after him!"

"No! Dagan deserves whatever he gets. Kevin's going to kill him!"

"No! Dagan's heading out to the big waves! You know Kevin can't handle waves that big. Go get him. Please!"

Kalino immediately realized that Kevin wasn't thinking with anything other than the fury consuming him. He grabbed his board, and started paddling furiously after his best friend. He reached the first break point, and then watched in horror as Kevin kept going.

Dagan was already sitting on his board, waiting for the next big wave to form, and Kevin was headed straight for him.

"Oh no! Kevin!" He cupped his hands around his mouth, and yelled until he was hoarse, and then he watched in horror as the wave formed and Dagan paddled for it. Kevin wasn't in the right position to take on the monster wave, but he still kept going after Dagan.

The wave was the largest that Kalino had ever seen, more than fifty feet in height, and with a speed that had him fearing for his own safety some hundred yards away.

He watched as the wave started to break, and Dagan expertly entered the curl, but Kevin wasn't so lucky. He made it to an upright position, but the wave was breaking too fast for his inexperience. Kalino watched as the wave crashed down upon him, quickly obliterating both the boy and the board from site.

The wave didn't stop there though. It was Dagan's match, and before he could safely exit the tube, the wave took its second victim. Kalino paddled furiously towards where his friend had gone down, but another rogue wave came out of nowhere, lifting him and his board up, and sending him flying some twenty yards away.

He was the lucky one. Several other seasoned surfers had seen what happened and had already paddled out to lend a hand. Someone managed to pull him onto their board and take him back to the beach. They took him to the hospital, where he spent more than three weeks in a coma.

What followed was the stuff nightmares were made of. Two funerals. Two grieving parents who couldn't understand how she'd let this happen. One father who mourned his only child, even though he'd raised a daughter as his own since birth. One mother who'd taken one look at her disheveled and bruised daughter and thought the worst. One sister who was so consumed with guilt over Kevin's rage, she actually contemplated taking her own life a time or two.

But killing herself wouldn't bring Kevin back. It wouldn't restore her trust in guys, and it wouldn't heal the rift between her parents that seemed bigger than the Grand Canyon. Only time and distance could do that, so she'd made preparations to leave.

Becca waited around the islands until she was sure Kalino was going to pull through, and then she packed a bag and left. She didn't tell anyone where she was going, but her parents' house was like a tomb. No one spoke to her, and the guilt and remorse she felt for her part in Kevin's death was more than she could bear on a daily basis.

The surfers left and her parents quit taking future reservations. It was as if they themselves had died along with her brother. Every time her father saw her, his eyes grew cold, and he turned his face away from her. Her mother's looks of condemnation and judgment were even worse. In order to save herself, she needed to leave.

She left Hawai'i, her parents, and everything she'd known to make a new start for herself. Running as far away as Colorado had seemed like a good idea, and when she stepped off the plane on a cold wintry day, she prayed and hoped that one day she would be able to forget and move on with her life. One day maybe she could return to Hawai'i and reconcile with her parents and herself.

Chapter 1

Friday afternoon, the day after Thanksgiving Day, Denver, Colorado...

Jessica, Gracie, and Becca were standing in Adelaide's Bridal Shop, looking at a sea of wedding dresses. So far, Gracie had suggested several dresses for Jessica to try on, but none for herself.

Jessica was marrying Justin Donnelly, and Gracie had just become engaged to his younger brother Mason. Becca was just along for the ride, but she was having fun nonetheless. After a miscalculation on their recent hike to Maroon Peak, Becca had become temporarily stranded in Silver Springs, Colorado. Gracie had been her ride from Denver, but she'd injured her knee in a fall that had required surgery. She'd also gone and fallen in love with Mason Donnelly, a beau from her childhood.

They had announced that they were getting married, and Jessica and Justin had secretly confided they were headed down the aisle of matrimony themselves. Both girls had decided that a dress shopping excursion was in order.

After enjoying Thanksgiving Day at the Three Brother's Lodge, owned and operated by the three Donnelly brothers, Becca had ridden back to Denver with them. She was dreading going home to her small apartment, knowing that on the morrow Gracie would be returning to Silver Springs. Melanie had been her other roommate prior to her moving out a month earlier, but her husband had finally gotten his discharge papers from the military, and they were already headed to Florida to be with her family.

So here she was, helping the woman who was not only her best friend, but also her savior and counselor, pick out a wedding dress. The only problem was that Gracie couldn't seem to decide on anything today.

"Gracie?" Becca stood by her friend's elbow, hoping to help her get things started.

"Hey!" Gracie smiled at her, looking overwhelmed and a little out of sorts. She was normally very organized and together, but today, she was a little scattered. Becca chalked it up to the newness of being engaged, and knowing that her life was getting ready to change for the better.

"What kind of dress are you looking for?" Becca hadn't thought about marriage for herself since leaving Hawaii, and now that she was in the store, surrounded by yards of lace, satin, and sheer fabric, she wondered if she would ever be able to trust a man enough to make this type of commitment to him. She hoped so, but only time would tell.

Gracie sighed, "I don't know. I'm a lost cause today."

Becca smiled at her, "I doubt that. Tell me about the dress you wear in your dreams."

Gracie grinned, "But that is only a dream dress. And they don't really exist."

"Tell me anyway, okay?" Becca insisted. She knew Gracie had always dreamed of a wedding to her childhood beau, and now that her dream was getting ready to come true, she might as well have the dress to go with the rest.

"Velvet. In my dreams, my wedding dress is white velvet. It has a scoop neckline and lone sleeves with those little strings than hook over your middle finger to keep them in place. And a long skirt that swirls around my ankles when I walk, but drapes along the ground behind me."

"It sounds gorgeous. Tiffany, do you have anything like that?" Becca asked the store attendant Gracie hadn't known was standing behind her listening in.

Tiffany smiled, "I have the perfect dress for you. Head on back to the dressing room and I'll bring it to you."

Gracie looked at her, hope shining in her eyes, "You really have a dress like what I described?"

"Go on back and you'll see. It must have been made just for you." Tiffany turned to Becca and grinned, "This is weird, but she could have designed the dress I have hanging in back. It was sent here, by accident, from a European designer, and is a one of a kind. The shipping to send it back was going to be astronomical, so we decided to keep it."

Twenty minutes later, Gracie emerged from the dressing room, and everyone stopped and gasped at the picture she presented. She was stunning in the dress, and a more perfect fit didn't exist.

"Oh, Gracie! Look at yourself!" Jessica and Becca urged her.

Gracie took a breath, and turned to face the three-way mirror. She gasped and felt tears spring to her eyes. "It's perfect! Just like in my dreams."

Becca wrapped an arm around her waist, "Who was your perfect groom in your dreams?"

"Mason," Gracie whispered.

"A match made in heaven. She'll take it." Becca turned to Tiffany with tears stinging her own eyes. Gracie had been her saving grace more than once, and she was so happy for her friend, and yet – she knew she was going to miss her terribly when she returned to Silver Springs tomorrow. She fought back her tears, not wanting her own neediness to overshadow the day.

"Perfect." The store attendant was beaming as she walked away to start the paperwork.

"Now we have to find Jessica the perfect dress," Becca said.

"Well, I don't think I'm ever going to find anything as perfect as that one, but I have several to try on."

"Then get to it," Becca told her with a laugh.

An hour later, both girls had found the dresses of their wedding dreams, and they were heading back to Jessica's apartment. The same one she had shared with Becca and Melanie. They arrived to see the boys loading the last of the boxes into the trailer.

"All done?" Gracie asked in wonder, glancing at her watch.

"How about we go get some pizza?" Kaillar suggested, making sure that Becca knew she was invited as well. She liked Kaillar, and part of her wished she could get rid of her distrust and give him a chance. He was the middle Donnelly brother, and the most handsome in her opinion. He also seemed to like her. *You know better, he likes you – a lot. He's also hoping for – what she didn't know.*

While she was thinking about these things, plans were made to go get pizza from a place just a few blocks from the apartment, and Becca headed for Mason's car. She was halfway across the yard when her cell phone rang, stopping her in her tracks.

Upon leaving Hawaii, she hadn't changed her cell phone number. She'd kept it, even keeping the unique cell phone tones for her family members, hoping that one day her mother or father would call her and ask her to come home. It hadn't happened in four years. Until now.

With shaky hands, she turned and walked a short distance away. She pulled the phone from her pocket, and slid her thumb across the screen to answer the call, "Hello?"

"Becca?"

"Mom?" Becca asked, her voice going soft with disbelief. Her mother was calling her after all these years. *Why?*

"Becca, something horrible has happened."

Becca felt her heart crack a little more, the brittle pieces already in ruins. "What?" she whispered, closing her eyes as she willed the bad news away.

"Your father had a heart attack this morning. He's gone."

Becca heard her mother crying over the phone, and she felt her hand tremble. "What?" she asked incredulously.

"The funeral is Sunday. I'd like you to be here for the funeral."

Becca felt the world start to spin around her, dark spots forming in front of her eyes as she dropped the phone from lifeless fingers to the ground below. She tried to keep the darkness from taking her, but it rushed at her.

She moaned, and began to come around a few minutes later. Kaillar and Gracie were both peering down into her face, looks of concern on their faces. She looked around and realized that she was in the back seat of the car. She could hear Gracie's voice coming from the front seat. *What's going on?*

"Becca, you fainted. You're in the car with me. Who was on the phone?" It was Gracie speaking to her, softly and with compassion for her friend evident in her voice.

Becca stared straight ahead, "My mom."

"Your mom in Hawaii?" Gracie asked.

Becca nodded, "My dad's dead. The funeral is Sunday and she wants me there." She heard her voice, but it really didn't sound like her. The words she was speaking couldn't be coming from her mouth, and yet – they were. Her father was dead, and her mother had called...

Gracie's wrapped her in a hug, "Oh Becca. I'm so sorry. Honey, what can we do?"

Becca wasn't crying. Not yet. "She wants me to come for the funeral. I..."

"If money is a problem, I can lend you as much as you need." Gracie was a problem solver, and she'd never met one she couldn't handle. Especially if the problem belonged to someone else. Gracie wanted everyone around her to be happy with life; it was one of the things that had originally drawn Becca to her. Gracie generally seemed happy, while Becca had been simply existing.

"No. I can...I just...," she looked up at Gracie with tears and fear in her eyes. "I can't go back there like this. Weak. I just can't. Not by myself. I..."

Becca felt horrible for even voicing her fears. She wasn't normally weak, but the recent assault had taken a greater toll on her psyche than even she wanted to admit. She saw Gracie's silent communication with Kaillar, and then he was speaking directly to her.

"Becca, darling. Do you want someone to go with you?" Kaillar had squatted down to peer into the vehicle, and she tried to meet his eyes and failed. *He deserves so much more than I can give him. But I don't want him to quit trying. I really don't.*

Becca's mind was almost numb, but she heard Kaillar talking to her and it sounded like he was offering her a lifeline. One she desperately needed right then. *Do I want someone to go with me? Yes, please!* She nodded her head, raising teary eyes to his own and watching them soften with compassion and something else she couldn't identify.

He laid a gentle hand on her shoulder and held her eyes, "I'll take you home. Will you let me do that? Will you let me take you home to say goodbye to your dad?"

Becca shivered once, but she didn't look away from him. "Yes."

"Good. Justin, we need a ride to the airport." Kaillar didn't hesitate and Becca sat there numbly, her mind replaying her mother's words over and over again. *He's gone. Her dad was dead.*

And just like that, Kaillar had stepped in and orchestrated everything. A quick trip by her apartment for clothing and toiletries.

A quick shopping trip at a local clothing mall had yielded several outfits along with a small suitcase for Kaillar.

Then it was off to the airport where they caught a flight before dinnertime was over. Kaillar had stayed right by her side in the terminal, watching her carefully as if he expected her to breakdown any minute.

Becca purposefully shut her mind off. She thought of Gracie's last words to her, and she was amazed at the comfort they provided her. *Family. Family was more than just who you were biologically related to. Family was whomever you became attached to. People you would do anything for. People who stuck by you in the good times and the bad.*

Family was what she'd found in Colorado. *So what was she to do with the family she'd left behind in Hawaii?"*

Chapter 2

Saturday, Honolulu International Airport, Oahu, Hawaii ...
Becca Edwards watched the approaching tarmac with a sense of sadness so overwhelming that she wasn't sure if she would survive this trip home. So many memories...

She'd left the islands a little over four years ago. Four years that seemed like an eternity to her. She'd moved to the mountains of Colorado, figuring they were about as different from the lush tropical landscape of the Hawaiian Islands as she could get. She hadn't been wrong.

Mountains were the norm in Colorado, but unlike Hawaii where more often than not they were covered in cooled, or cooling lava, the mountains here were covered in snow for at least six months out of every year. She still remembered the first time she'd watched it snowing outside. The large flakes falling from the sky, so silently and peaceful looking.

She'd grabbed her camera and captured the moment. The first of many over the last four years. She'd always been interested in photography, and was a hobby writer, so majoring in photojournalism had seemed to be the perfect career choice for her once she landed in Denver. Becoming roommates and friends with Gracie and Melanie had also been perfect.

She'd been looking for a place to live, close to her classes, and Gracie and Melanie had been looking for a third roommate to help share their home and pay a third of the bills. The trio had hit it off from the very first, and Becca had thanked her lucky stars for meeting the two women who had helped her through one of the toughest times in her life. Even if they hadn't known what she was going through.

Everything in her life seemed to have been coming together, so much so that she'd stopped feeling so adrift on the sea of life. She'd seen some pictures taken by the Division of Wildlife personnel, and decided right then and there that was what she wanted to be doing. Getting out into nature and taking photographs that showed the beauty of life all around.

She'd still missed her family, but she'd not received one phone call from either of her parents since leaving Hawaii. She'd left them a letter, explaining that she couldn't live in a place surrounded by memories of what might have been, and that she was going somewhere to start over. She'd promised to come home when the time was right, but so far, thoughts of returning to Hawaii left her in a cold sweat. The only concession she'd made was once a year, a week before Christmas Day, she sent a postcard to let them know that she was still alive and not ready to come home yet.

She hadn't even chosen the postcard she was going to send this year, and now it seemed that she wouldn't be following that ritual for a fifth time. She rolled her head from side to side, trying not to let the questions of the past swamp her thinking.

What if her dad still felt the same way as he had when she'd left? What if her mother still had that look of condemnation in her eyes?

Either of those would have destroyed her, so she'd stayed away.

Not even after the assault had she considered calling or going home. She knew that Gracie and Melanie were both worried about her, but when she'd been grabbed in that parking garage, and the men had held her down, one with his hands around her throat, her brain had instantly reverted to the other time that had happened. And the horrible aftermath when her brother had found out what Dagan had done.

Her attackers had grabbed her from behind, muffling her screams for help. They'd dragged her off to a waiting car, where her nightmares had taken on new meaning. There had been three of them, all Hispanic and all speaking in what she thought sounded like Spanish.

They'd ripped her clothes, pinching and slapping her body to the point that she had feared for her life. One of them had produced a knife and tormented her by dragging the blade over her exposed body. He'd cared not that he'd broken the skin in several places, seeming to take great joy in the beads of blood left behind on the welts.

Becca had been sure she was going to die that night. But then, a security car had driven through the parking garage and had spooked her attackers. They'd kicked her to the garage floor and sped off. She'd been found moments later, and transferred by ambulance to the hospital. The nurses in the emergency room had all been very kind, and after treating her physical wounds, and ascertaining that her attackers had been disrupted before they could sexually assault her, they'd called in the resident shrink.

She'd been leery of trusting him, after her last mental health fiasco, but she'd also known that she needed to release the memories so they could start to fade. She'd told him everything that had happened and that had been said to her. After she'd finished, he'd wanted to know why she hadn't taken more steps to protect herself. After all, walking through a parking garage, at night, by herself, was practically begging someone to mistreat her.

His words had been so similar to the last counselor she'd sought out, a few weeks after arriving in Colorado, she'd felt like she was in a time warp.

Becca had kicked the hospital's psychologist out of her room and demanded that someone call her roommates to come and get her. When the nurses had asked her what was wrong, she'd refused to say a thing. She was done trusting people with her feelings and emotions.

Gracie had arrived fifteen minutes later, horrified that Becca had gone through such a trying ordeal and her roommates were just hearing about it. Becca hadn't told Gracie about the counselor, afraid she would say too much and leave an opening for her friends to start asking questions about the past as well.

It had been six months since her attack, and she still felt jumpy and nervous in dark places. Physically, she'd had some bruises and cuts, but mentally, it was as if her brain had been fire-stormed. Night terrors were just one of the ways her brain had chosen to deal with her attack. Panic attacks and an aversion to being touched were others.

Gracie seemed to think that she was suffering from a sort of PTDS, but Becca was adamantly against any kind of counseling. She'd tried that briefly after arriving in Colorado. The college medical center had a mental health doctor, and she'd gone to him exactly twice. The first time had been more of a meet and greet session.

But during the second session, the counselor had told her that she'd set herself up to be attacked by Dagan. He'd insinuated that she'd basically asked for what had happened and everything that had followed was in part her responsibility. He'd affirmed her guilt over her brother's death, reminding her that she was the one who made the decision to take off with her boyfriend. Her brother had paid for her lack of judgment.

She'd never gone back to another session, believing she could heap guilt on her own shoulders and didn't need to pay someone hundreds of dollars to help. Becca had slammed out of his office, recommending he find another vocation because his ability to listen without passing judgment was deplorable.

Coupled with her experience in the emergency room, Becca had no use for the entire counseling profession. Except for Gracie.

Gracie was a medical doctor, but she seemed to know more about how Becca's brain processed things than even Becca herself did. Without Gracie, she wasn't sure how she would have survived the last six months.

And yet, here she was heading to Hawaii without her. Gracie couldn't travel because of her knee surgery, so Kaillar had stepped in to provide the companionship and support she needed. For the first time in years, Becca could honestly say that she was glad to have a man's shoulder to lean upon.

Chapter 3

The plane's wheels touched down, and she felt her companion stir in the seat next to her. *Kaillar Donnelly.*

She glanced at him from the corner of her eye, watching as his lashes fluttered several times before opening and revealing his deep blue eyes beneath a mop of unruly dark blonde hair. He'd fallen asleep somewhere over the Pacific Ocean, and Becca had spent many long moments watching him sleep.

He was the middle brother of the three Donnelly men, and had offered to escort her home to say goodbye to her father. She'd tried to figure out why all of a sudden he had seemed to be safe to her, when only days earlier he'd sent tendrils of fear rushing through her body because he had stood too close to her.

Those feelings seemed to have vaporized and as he'd slept, she'd wanted nothing more than to lay her head on his shoulder and seek the same refuge in slumber. But Becca's dreams were more often than not unpleasant; and the fear that she would have a nightmare while trapped in this seat and on the plane had kept her awake the entire trip. A feat that even now was taking a great toll on her ability to function correctly.

Becca had never been the type of person who functioned well on just a few hours of sleep. She always felt as if she was wading through muddy waters, and that everyone was moving in slow motion around her the next day. She mentally groaned as she realized that by not sleeping, she'd possibly made a truly horrible day almost impossible to take. *I should have tried to get at least a few hours of sleep.*

But it was too late now. The flight was over. They'd flown from Denver to San Francisco and then taken a late flight off the mainland. It was now almost 10 a.m. on Saturday morning in Hawaii, but with the time difference, that meant Becca had been awake for almost thirty-two hours.

She looked back out the window, and called up the image of Kaillar she'd created in the wee hours of the morning. Yawning, she closed her eyes, and envisioned a beach with waves crashing off the shore as men and women tested their abilities against Mother Nature. It wasn't hard to imagine her companion in that setting. Coming across the sand in knee-length board shorts, his shoulders tan from many hours in the sun, the muscles rippling as he carried a surfboard on his shoulder. He'd use his free hand to sluice his too-long hair back and then stand the board up in the sand before walking towards her...

She'd participated in just such a scene many times, just with a different lead actor. The last time, the actor had been her beloved brother. She remembered the smile on his face dying as he got his first glimpse of her, and the angry way he'd grabbed his board and headed back to the ocean. It would be his last ride, and for that, she would never forgive herself.

The plane stopped moving as it docked at the terminal gate and Becca sighed. Most people came to Hawaii to vacation. But she and Kaillar weren't in Hawaii to play on the beach. In fact, she wasn't sure she wanted to play with the handsome man his friends referred to as Kai at all.

She'd first met him when she and her two friends had tried to climb Maroon Peak on the cusp of a major winter storm. Becca hadn't known the danger they were in, but she'd soon found out. The wind and snow had come upon them so quickly even now she found it miraculous that Gracie had been the only one hurt on their descent.

Kaillar and his brother Mason had come up the mountain to rescue them. Mason had gone after Gracie, and Kaillar had escorted her and Melanie to the small town of Silver Springs. Everything had been going fine until she'd slipped and Kaillar had reacted and caught her.

Even now, she felt horrible for how she had reacted. Gracie seemed to think she needed counseling to get past the attack that had happened not so long ago, but Becca felt sure she could conquer her own demons – she'd done so once before.

She'd never been one to confide in others, and most especially not matters of a personal nature. *Is that why you never sought any help with reconciling with your dad? It's too late now. Just like it was too late to save Kevin...*

Becca forced her thoughts away from that dark abyss, not willing to allow the past to torture her at this moment in time. The present was doing enough of that all on its own!

"Hey! We're here." Kaillar leaned towards her, craning his head to get a glimpse out the plane's small window.

"Very observant," came her flippant reply before she could stop it. She blushed and covered her mouth before sighing, "Sorry. Coming home..."

Kaillar sat back, pulled her hand away, and folded his long fingers around it, ignoring her small tug of protest. "I know this must be really hard for you. Gracie mentioned you hadn't been home in over four years?"

Becca looked at him, seeing the questions in his eyes, and then turned her head towards the window. "Yeah. Four years." She thought about leaving it there, but then she didn't want him assuming that she and her family were all nice and cozy. Once upon a time...

"Look, you should probably know that I've not even spoken to my family since I left Hawaii. Things were...difficult...when I left. My father...well, let's just say that not having to see me each day as a reminder of what he'd lost was a blessing."

"To him?"

She nodded, "Yeah. To him."

"And what about you? Was it a blessing being separated from your family for so many years?"

Becca looked at him and then shook her head once, "Yes, and no. But I'm not going to discuss that right now. I can't. I just wanted you to know that things may be a little tense when we reach my home."

He nodded once, and then pushed his arms forward as he stretched; an action that drew her eyes to the tight t-shirt he wore and how well it molded to his muscles. Realizing her brain was once again heading down a path that was only vaguely familiar to her, she forced herself to look away as she slowly gathered up her belongings from the seat in front of her.

"So, how far from the airport..."

"We have to grab a charter flight to the Big Island. This is only Honolulu." At his blank look, she smiled tightly, "Oahu. Where Pearl Harbor is?" When he nodded, she continued, "My family lives on the Big Island – Hawai'i."

"Okay. So, I didn't have Jessica grab us a charter flight..."

"Don't worry about it. Unless things have really changed around here, we shouldn't have any problem catching a flight."

"Does anyone know you're coming besides your mother?" Kai asked, the look on his face warning Becca that he would only take half answers for so long.

Becca gave him a rueful glance, "I'm not even sure I agreed to come home before passing out. I should probably call her, but I know she's got a lot on her plate right now." *And I don't know if I could handle it if she'd changed her mind and didn't really want me here. Better to just show up, and then deal with whatever outcome there was.*

The pilot turned off the fasten seatbelt sign and Becca felt her anxiety go up another notch. *Breathe in, Becca. You can do this. One. Two. Three. Breathe out. Good girl.* She could almost envision Gracie standing over her and counting as she went through the breathing exercises that had seen her through more than one panic attack. She opened her eyes, and tried to see the island as any other tourist would.

Hawaii was a place that people came to make beautiful memories. Until that fateful day four and a half years ago, she'd thought it was an idyllic place to grow up. Her parents owned a small upscale beach resort in Opihikao. It was more like an over-achieving bed and breakfast, and as far as she knew, her parents had still been running it upon her father's death.

Becca scooted to the aisle when it was her row's turn to disembark, and felt a small measure of thankfulness when Kaillar stepped back and waited for her to precede him from the plane. She nodded her thanks to the stewardess, and then stepped off the plane, immediately feeling a wave of homesickness as she breathed in the humid air that was like no other.

Fragrant flowers coated the air in a way only found on the islands, and the Hawaiian shirt clad greeter smiled broadly as she lifted a flower lei over Becca's head. "Aloha!"

"Mahalo," Becca offered softly in return, the syllables rolling off her tongue as if she'd not kept them locked away for years.

With her strawberry blonde hair and pale green eyes, she looked like any other tourist come to the islands for a bit of culture, some sand, and the chance to see a live volcano erupting. But Becca considered herself as much of a Hawaiian as the dark-skinned, dark-haired young men and women who could trace their Hawaiian heritage back for generations.

Becca's mother had come to the islands as a young adult, fresh out of high school. She'd fallen in love with a surfer, skipped returning home for the fall school semester to watch him train, and then compete during the winter months on the islands. An orphan, she didn't have any family to answer to, only herself.

When spring had arrived, the surfers had headed south and she'd been left behind. Four months pregnant with a baby on the way. A baby the father adamantly denied was his.

Her mother, Stacie, had refused to chase after him and had refused to name him on Becca's birth certificate. To this day, she didn't know who her biological father was, and had accepted that the secret would go to the grave with her mother. According to her, the man was already dead, and naming him now would serve no good purpose.

Becca had accepted that, and until tragedy had struck their family four years earlier, she'd never wanted to call anyone but the man who'd raised her – dad. She still didn't now, but words spoken from the midst of a broken and hurting heart couldn't be taken back, and she'd allowed them to fester now for four years.

She stepped further into the airport terminal, her mind continuing to think too hard about things she couldn't change. About the man she had lovingly called father all of her life. *Makoa Kahoalani.*

Three months after Becca was born, her mother had met the man when she took a job as a housekeeper at his family's resort. The two had fallen in love and when Becca was only six months old, they had been married in a traditional Hawaiian ceremony out behind the resort on the green grasses overlooking the ocean.

Her parents had been so happy, and she'd grown up knowing that she was loved. She and her brother...

Becca took a short breath, the pain of remembering making it almost impossible to face what she knew was going to be the hardest time in her life. She'd tried to mend her broken heart while living in

Colorado, and it seemed that every time she thought she could see the light at the end of the tunnel, a new tragedy appeared in her life.

She'd been well on her way to healing before the attack in Colorado. Now, here she was, heading home to the place where all of her troubles had begun, to face yet another tragedy. And she was scared. Scared she wouldn't be able to handle the memories. Scared she'd run again. Scared she wouldn't recover this time.

Hearing Kaillar speaking to the greeter behind her, she turned and pasted a smile on her face that didn't even come close to reaching her eyes. She was in Oahu, and now she needed to face her past and find them a transport to the Big Island. So far, things had gone smoothly, but Becca was too pessimistic to imagine they would continue to be so.

This trip could very well destroy me. Again!

Chapter 4

Kaillar watched as Becca looked back at him, seeing the strain around her mouth, even though she was trying to smile for his benefit. He wanted to pull her into his arms and tell her that everything was going to be all right, but he didn't even know what everything was.

He'd tried to get her talking about her childhood, and she'd given him some facts, but nothing that would help him understood why she'd fled to the mainland to begin with.

Every time he even got close to asking a personal question, she'd changed the subject. He'd finally given up, and allowed himself to close his eyes and sleep. He'd hoped that she would do the same, but looking at the bruising beneath her eyes, he would guess that she hadn't slept for more than an hour since leaving Colorado the morning before.

"So, do we need to grab our luggage?" Kaillar asked, joining her, the flower lei around his neck almost overpowering, the fragrance was so strong.

"Luggage is downstairs. And yes, we do need to grab it." They hadn't brought much with them, this trip coming up suddenly and without notice. Becca had been able to pack hurriedly, but Kaillar only had a few changes of clothes with him, and his travelling toiletry bag. He'd assured her that he could purchase anything he needed once they reached their destination, and she hadn't argued with him. Because he was right.

The islands offered a plethora of shopping venues, and the Big Island was no different. Home to Kilauea, it was a popular destination for tourists wanting the complete Hawaiian experience. The volcano had been erupting in one form or another ever since Becca could remember.

When it wasn't spewing forth molten lava and steam, slow moving lava tubes were creeping across the surface of the island, consuming anything in their path. A recent event had a small tube gradually moving towards Opihikao. So far, no homes had been destroyed, but Mother Nature and the volcano herself wouldn't be stopped before they were ready. If things continued to move in the same direction, her family's resort would barely make it to ring in the New Year before becoming yet another victim of the volcano.

She led him towards the escalators that would take them to the ground level and baggage claim areas. It would also give her an opportunity to see who had a charter flight heading back to the Big Island.

"Becca?" an incredulous voice grabbed her attention, making her swing her head around to confront a very rotund face from her past.

"Kalino?" Of all the people she'd expected to see at the airport, her brother's best friend wasn't even on the long list.

"Aloha! What are you doing here? The last time I spoke to your father…" The man broke off seeing the sadness on her face. "Oh no! What happened?"

Becca swallowed painfully, and then whispered, "He's dead."

Kalino watched her for a moment, glancing at her companion, before turning to her with a raised brow, "Did you speak to him before…"

She shook her head, wanting him to let the matter go. "My mother called…"

"When is the funeral? I would like to attend."

Becca's head was reeling, but Kalino's words registered, and she nodded. "He would have liked that. I believe it's tomorrow. We just arrived from the mainland, and I need to find us a ride."

"Done! I don't have any other fares scheduled for today or tomorrow. I was going to head to Maui, and get some practice rides in before the competition starts next weekend."

"Competition?" Kaillar asked, stepping in behind Becca and wondering who this man talking with them was.

"Surfing. Kalino is one of the best." Becca looked between the two men, wondering what was going through Kaillar's head. She was hoping she wouldn't have to explain her comment or how she knew it to be true. She might have left Hawaii, but she'd secretly followed Kalino's career as a world class surfer, and she only hoped he turned out better than Dagan had. Fame and popularity could be anyone's downfall, and having scores of scantily clad women throwing themselves at you all the time, telling you how wonderful they think you are, was enough to make even the strongest man of integrity think with his ego instead of his mind and heart.

She would be heartsick if that ever happened to Kalino, and part of her was silently rejoicing at the evidence in front of her to the contrary. Kalino was barely nineteen, and other than growing in stature and the deepening of his voice, he seemed much the same as before. Before he'd lost his best friend and her world had come crashing down about her ears. *Kevin would have been the same. If only...*

It was as if Kalino had picked up her train of thought. He searched her eyes for a moment before turning to Kaillar and shaking his head. "No. A close second. Kevin was the best," he murmured to her softly.

Becca looked at him sadly and shook her head, "Please. Don't go there. This is hard enough."

Kalino sighed in frustration, "You leaving was hard." Becca merely shrugged, as if her agreement mattered not. "Look, why don't you all grab your luggage and meet me at the charter desk in half an hour? I'll go file a new flight plan, and we'll head out right after that."

"Thank you."

"Don't mention it." He looked at her companion, and Becca realized she'd yet to make any introductions.

"Sorry," she mumbled to both men. "Kalino, this is Kaillar Donnelly. Kai, this is Kalino. He was a friend of my brother's."

Kalino gave her a strange look, which she ignored. He'd been more like a brother to her growing up, and something told her he could be again, if she could just get past her own guilt.

"Nice to meet you." Kaillar shook his hand, and then placed a gentle hand on her lower back, "We really appreciate your offer of a ride. This has been hard on her, and anything you can do to make things easier is welcome and appreciated."

"*A 'ole pilikia*. See you both soon." Kalino strode off, and Becca released a breath she hadn't even known she was holding. She'd known that she would see people from her past, but seeing he brother's best friend right off the bat had been more than merely hard. *Guess you no longer have to wonder if seeing people you once knew was going to send you running off.*

Becca glanced at Kaillar, and then interpreted for him, "He just told us not to worry, and that's all."

Kaillar nodded his head, and then directed her with light pressure on her back towards the sign indicating the baggage claim was still ahead of them. They had to navigate several large groups of people who seemed to be enthralled with the airport, wanting to document their arrival in Hawaii with photos from every angle.

Becca wished that she could tell them they needed to step outside if they truly wanted to experience their first moment in Hawaii, but then again, that would require interacting with strangers. Something she rarely did unless forced to.

"So, I didn't know you have a brother," Kaillar offered once they were moving toward the baggage claim again.

Becca nodded once, "Yeah. I did have a brother."

"Had? What happened?" he wondered aloud.

"He died. Can we change the subject?" she asked through tightly clenched lips.

"Sure." Kaillar watched her for a moment, knowing that whatever she was hiding more than likely wasn't going to stay hidden while she was here. How could it? The past always had a way of catching up with you and forcing you to deal with it. The only question that remained was whether you would choose the how and when, or find yourself being thrown into the chaos, struggling to find an anchor to hold on to.

Kaillar hoped for Becca's sake that she took control of the situation and dealt with her past on her terms when she was ready and strong enough to deal with them. When she was strong enough to handle whatever the past might entail. Whatever the case may be, Kaillar mentally promised her to stay by her side and provide whatever support she needed in the coming days. It was what he wanted to do. Help her.

Chapter 5

He was prevented from thinking more about the subject as the baggage carousel starting moving and their bags appeared a few moments later. "Now where do we go?"

Becca relaxed a bit, acknowledging that he was willing to stop his questioning for the moment. "This way."

"So, how long of a flight is it over to the Big Island?"

"Not long. Kalino and his family operate a charter service, so their planes aren't commercial grade nor do they carry many passengers. When I left, their largest plane could only carry up to ten passengers."

"Must have been nice to know someone growing up who could shuttle you around to the various islands. Did you do that often?"

Becca nodded her head, "All the time. Kalino's dad was always offering to let us kids tag along."

"So which of the islands is your favorite?" Kaillar asked.

Becca smiled, "That's easy. Molokai." She smiled as she remembered the island's many valleys and waterfalls. It was a beautiful island, the hillsides brilliant green as they rose up from the ocean's floor.

"Maybe we'll have time for you to show it to me before we go home?" Kai suggested, liking the smile that had flitted over her face for just a moment.

Becca nodded her head, "Maybe. That might be fun." Molokai only held good memories for her, so a trip there would be most welcome.

They took the escalator back up, and she led them through the various shops hawking their souvenirs to the unsuspecting tourists who had waited too long to pick up that last memento of their time on the islands. They would pay almost double the cost for t-shirts, sweatshirts, and postcards, but they would smile while doing it, and everyone would be happy.

"Tourism is big here," Kaillar commented, having noticed the plethora of shops himself.

Becca nodded, "Yeah, it doesn't seem to have improved any while I was away. The Big Island is slightly better, unless you are in the larger areas of the city or the commercial beaches."

"Commercial beaches?" Kaillar asked. He'd been to California a time or two, but the beaches there mostly belonged to the State of California and were managed like State Parks.

"There are quite a number of private beaches in Hawaii. It's possible to not only purchase the dry land, but a large portion of the ocean front. In addition, you have different types of beaches here. There are the traditional white sand beaches, but also some gorgeous black sand ones as well."

"Black sand beaches? Never heard of such a thing." He directed them towards a small coffee shop, continuing their conversation while they waited in line. "What makes the sand black?"

Becca smiled, "It's not really sand, not like you would typically define it. Rather, its cooled lava that has been weathered by the waves until it has been broken down into small particles that cover up the beach. There are good things and bad things about those beaches."

"What's the good?"

"The black sand particles are larger, and don't tend to stick to everything quite as readily."

"That sounds like a good thing, although I don't imagine building sand castles works well."

Becca laughed softly, "Not at all, as a matter of fact."

"What's the bad?"

"The bad comes when you go into the water. The icy cold water. It tends to numb one's feet up, so they don't immediately realize their treading upon very sharp, very ragged cooled lava. The farther out one goes, the less weathered the ocean floor becomes. It's like walking around on shards of broken glass.

"Most people don't realize what's happening to their bare feet until they return to the beach and as their body temperature returns to normal, so does their blood flow. They find themselves on the beach with stinging, hurting feet that are bloody and covered in small cuts and punctures."

"Ouch! Why don't they warn people?"

"Oh, they do. Most of those beaches have signs advising people to not enter the water without water shoes on their feet or dive socks in place. But tourists tend to think they know best and many of them don't come prepared. The worst part is after they go back home to wherever they're from."

"How's that?" Kaillar asked, giving the barista their orders and then paying for them before Becca could protest.

"The cooled lava provides a great breeding ground for coral and other microorganisms to hang out. If they don't properly clean their cuts, they get back to the mainland with injuries that continue to get infected and won't heal. Most of the bigger resorts and hotels have onsite medical stations to help educate and treat people who have injured themselves by not reading the warning signs."

"Sounds like it would behoove people to have someone knowledgeable about the island with them."

"It does help. Hawaii is a beautiful place, but also very dangerous. Even deadly."

Kaillar handed her the cup of coffee, and then led her over to a railing that looked down upon the terminal below. "You know firsthand about that." It was a statement, not a question.

Becca sipped her coffee and nodded sadly, "Yeah. I do."

"Will you tell me about it? Not right this minute," he told her when she started to deny him with a shake of her head. "Just...sometime while we're here, will you talk to me about what happened? Something tells me you haven't done that with many people."

Becca looked down and murmured, "No one actually." She looked up at him, her eyes growing slightly watery and she cleared her throat, "People think they know what happened that day, but no one truly does. Not that's still alive to talk about it. They all just assumed...," she cleared her throat again. "I haven't talked to anyone about that day."

"Why not?" Kaillar asked softly, amazement in his voice.

"What difference would it have truly made? The only people that mattered thought I was guilty, and I am. Just not for the reasons they believe. But the reasons don't change the fact that because of me, and my actions, my brother is dead."

"You might be surprised at how ...."

"No. Nothing will ever make this better." She glanced up, and saw Kalino standing by the charter desk, waving to them. "Looks like he's ready to go."

Kai watched her carefully for a moment and then nodded, as if he'd agreed to her silent request to change the subject. He stepped up close to her, searching her eyes for some hidden answer, "You don't sound all that thrilled about going home."

"No."

When she didn't elaborate, he touched her shoulder, "Becca, if there's anything I can do..."

"There's not. I mean, having you here is helping already." When he continued to look at her in grave concern, she attempted a smile, "I'm fine. Tired. Hungry. And in need of a shower, but I'll be fine. Stop looking so worried."

"I wish there was something I could do to make this easier for you," he murmured. "Gracie would probably..."

"Gracie would be too emotional and trust me, that's not what I need right now." *I thought I wanted Gracie with me, but she would force me to deal with the emotions, and I'd be a bawling mess by now, and probably for the rest of my stay. I need to be strong, get through the funeral, and then get back to Colorado where I can bury all of these useless emotions once again.*

Chapter 6

She finished walking across the tiled terminal floor to meet Kalino, offering him up a forced smile. She could see the worry and questions in his eyes, but after dealing with Kaillar's questions, she didn't have anything left in her defenses. She sent a silent plea up that he would leave things alone.

"You all ready to fly?" Kalino asked with a big smile, seeing the worry on Becca's face, and knowing she was afraid he was going to force her to talk about the past. He wasn't sure what she'd been doing for the last four years, but dealing with the past didn't seem to be one of them.

He owed it to Kevin to help his sister while she was here, but not right now. She looked exhausted and he could see she was teetering on the edge of losing control. He'd be patient and when the time was right, he'd do what he could to help her heal. But he couldn't let her think that he didn't care. That he hadn't thought about her and wondered how she was doing. He had to at least let her know that much before they flew home.

Becca nodded her head, "Ready as I've ever been."

Kalino's eyes clouded at the trepidation he heard in her voice. He met her just before she went through the doorway, lowering his voice, "Becca, I never got a chance to say how sorry I was about Kevin. Things were so crazy, and I..."

Becca shook her head at him, "You were in a coma. I waited to leave until I knew you were going to be all right, but I couldn't stay any longer. It was just too hard."

Kalino nodded, "It took me a long time before I could go back out on a board. I still think about him every time I do."

Becca felt tears sting her eyes, and she wiped them away with a hand, "Thanks for being his friend. He was happiest when he was with you out on the water." She took a deep breath, and then stood up a little taller, "I'm ready to go home."

"Then let's do this thing." Kalino gave Kaillar a nod of his head, and then he led the way out to his twin engine, fixed prop, Cessna plane with the bright hibiscus flower painted on the side.

"Nice ride," Kaillar commented, ducking his head as he climbed into the seating area behind Becca. With her diminutive figure, she'd had no trouble entering the small aircraft, but his height wasn't nearly as kind. At 6'6" tall, he was always having to watch bumping his head in places others didn't. The plane presented a new problem, in that he couldn't stand up completely even once he cleared the doors.

He quickly chose a seat directly across from Becca, glad for the opportunity to sit, rather than stoop.

"Not much head room back there, sorry," Kalino called from where he sat in the pilot's seat.

"No worries," Kaillar assured him. His phone buzzed, and he quickly turned it off.

"One of your brothers?" Becca asked.

"Yeah. Justin's called twice now, wanting to make sure we arrived safely and to see how you're doing." He looked at her, and then lowered his voice, "What do I answer?"

"About how I'm doing?" she asked, waiting for his nod before she thought for a moment. "Well, I'm sure he's only asking because the girls are. Tell him I'm fine and that we should be back in a couple of days."

A couple of days? "Really? You don't want to stick around and help your mom?"

Becca turned her head to the window and shrugged, "I doubt she would want my help. Things between us weren't good when I left."

Kaillar was quiet for a moment and then asked, "Is this about your brother?"

"Partially. So many things happened at the same time, and my mother was grieving. We all were, but I think my brother's death hit her harder than the rest of us." She shook her head, "I'd rather not dredge all that up again."

Kaillar nodded his head, "I'm here if you need to talk. Why don't you tell me about this resort you grew up on?"

Becca nodded; taking the opportunity he was giving her to change the subject. "Well, it started out as a large beach house and over the years, my grandparents built additional bungalow style living units on the property. At one point in time, it was a pineapple farm, but they discovered there was much more money to be made catering to tourists than there was in growing pineapples."

"Are your grandparents still alive?"

"No. They both died when I was little. My grandmother passed first, when I was in the fifth grade. It was the first funeral I'd ever gone to, and I was a little mystified that everyone seemed so happy. I remember sitting up in the trees watching everyone eat and laugh, wondering why no one was crying. I felt like crying."

"Funerals are tough on kids," Kaillar commented.

"Yeah. Anyway, my mom found me and explained to me that sadness served no purpose. It wouldn't bring them back, and it only made getting on with living harder. I believed her, and when my grandfather passed away a few years later, I joined in the festivities and tried not to feel sad."

"But you were?"

"I was. My dad was too. He hid it well, but I would find him sometimes late at night, standing in the backyard with tears streaming down his face. He never knew I saw him, and he always composed himself before he came back inside."

"Crying wasn't acceptable to your father?" Kaillar asked, wondering if she'd learned to hide her emotions from him.

"Not to a man. I think that's why my brother and he fought so often. My father spent his entire adult life hiding his emotions away from the world, while my brother wore his heart on his sleeve for all to see."

Kalino had been listening to the conversation and interjected, "Kevin was the coolest kid in school. Smart. Athletic. Good looking. All of the guys were jealous of him."

Kaillar asked, "He was younger than you?" When she nodded, he asked, "By how much?"

"Five years. Mom had a couple of miscarriages, and she always said Kevin was her miracle baby."

"What did she say about you?" Kaillar wanted to know.

Becca looked at him and then away, mumbling, "I'm the one who broke her heart."

Kalino heard her, turned his head, and shook it, "You know that's not entirely true. Your mom doted on you. Whatever you think you know, remember you left before anyone had time to heal. Your mom was grieving and continued to do so, not only for Kevin, but because you'd left."

Becca stared at him, "That's not true. They were glad when I left. They didn't have the constant reminder of how much I'd cost them."

Kalino made an angry sound, and then faced front again, "If I weren't flying this plane, I'd shake you for saying something so stupid. Your parents loved you, and Kevin, so much."

Becca fell silent, Kalino's threat sliding off her shoulders as if it had never been uttered. She wasn't afraid of him, but he seemed very angry over her perception of things.

Kaillar wasn't quite so ready to let the subject drop. He felt the conversation needed to continue, so he pressed, "What's he talking about?"

"Remember that whole, I don't want to talk about this right now, conversation we had just a few short minutes ago?" When he nodded, she continued, "That's what he's talking about."

"The conversation you never had with anyone." He stated it as fact, not a question.

Becca sighed, "Yeah. That one."

Kaillar looked at her, and then spoke to Kalino, "Do you know what happened?" He tried not to notice the look of defeat on Becca's face. He needed to know what he was walking into, and since she wouldn't tell him, he'd ask someone else. Someone who seemed to be intimately acquainted with the entire situation. Whatever the situation was.

Chapter 7

Kalino looked at him and asked, "The day her brother died?" Kaillar nodded, "I think that's the day I'm talking about. The day that she isn't."

Kalino gave Becca a sad look. An apologetic look that said he was sorry, "You let them all believe the worst, didn't you?" He was remembering the bruising on her cheek and around her throat. No doubt, she had allowed them to assume the worst. "Tell me you didn't protect him," he demanded, even this many years later, he was not willing to give Dagan a pass on his deplorable behavior.

"I didn't have to, no one asked. They automatically assumed." She answered him woodenly, her gaze fixed out the small window.

"What, that you'd let him have his way with you? How did you explain the bruises around your throat?" Kalino demanded, trying to calm down so he didn't crash them into the ocean below. The emotions of that day were bubbling up, and he strove to keep them in perspective. Something Becca obviously hadn't done.

"My mom was the only one who seemed to notice them, and her looks said it all. Whatever had happened was entirely my fault, and mine alone. She'd warned me about Dagan..."

"Wait a minute!" Kaillar interjected, his mind scrambling to keep up with the conversation. He turned to Becca and demanded with his eyes and his voice, "Bruises around your throat?"

"It's not what you think...," she tried to calm him down, looking at him with a haunted look in her eyes that was a knife to his heart.

"That's good, because I'm thinking this Dagan character deserved to be beaten to a pulp."

"The ocean did that for you. Thanks," Becca told him sarcastically before turning her head away once again. She was tired of this conversation, because it was getting nowhere. The facts didn't change the outcome. Her brother had blamed Dagan for her condition, and gone after him. She'd not been able to stop him, and both of them had lost their lives.

Kaillar watched her shields come up, and mentally kicked himself. Kalino met his eyes briefly, and then began to tell him about that day's tragic events. By the time he was finished telling the story, Becca had tears running down her face, and Kalino was speaking to the tower at the Hilo airport in preparation for landing.

Kaillar reached over and grabbed her hand, holding on tight when she tried to tug it away. "Shush. Becca, I don't know what's been going through your head, but as soon as we can, you need to call Gracie and talk with her about this. You've been hiding for four years from something that should have been dealt with immediately. I'm sorry that the people in your life let you down."

Becca took a shuddery breath as she struggled for control, "No, you have it all wrong." She looked at him, and the sadness in her eyes broke his heart. "I let them down. I was older, and should have taken steps to protect Kevin. I should have never gone down to the beach. He was only fourteen and..."

"It doesn't matter. You should have had someone in your life you could talk to about what Dagan did. He hurt you, and if you never say what happened, he gets away with it."

"He's dead! He's not getting away with anything!" she insisted.

Kaillar shook his head, "That's where you're wrong. If you don't explain what happened, at least to one person, he does get away with it. In your own mind, he gets away with it because it's a secret you have to keep locked away; along with all of the bitterness and pain it brought to your life."

Becca shook her head, "I tried that. The counselor was kind enough to affirm that my guilt was right where it belonged. I'd acted without a care for my own well-being, leading Dagan on, and the aftermath of that decision cost my brother his life."

Kalino was furious that anyone would dare to let her believe that the events of four years ago were her fault. She was the victim! But he couldn't have this conversation with her, because the tower was responding and they were getting ready to land.

He clenched his jaw for a moment, and then let out a breath, "We're landing. Hang on," Kalino called from the cockpit.

Becca was grateful for the interruption, but as they landed and retrieved their luggage, Kaillar's words kept replaying in her mind. *Had she really let Dagan off the hook by not telling anyone what had really happened? In effect, she'd protected his memory from being tainted by his horrible actions. She'd saved others from having to face the reality that their friend and family member wasn't honorable or the cool guy they'd idolized. He was an abuser, and she had no doubt in her mind that if the park ranger hadn't arrived when he did, he would have been able to add rapist to his list of crimes.*

Kaillar watched her, as did Kalino, but neither of them said anything more on the subject. She was left to muddle through her own thoughts; trying to make sense of what was real and what was the result of hiding the truth for so long. *Would speaking the truth to someone about that day be what she needed to finally heal? Someone who wasn't there to judge her, but just listen and possibly, maybe...agree that she'd been the victim? Kaillar and Kalino thought that way. Well, they sounded as if they thought that way, but then again, they didn't know all the facts. They didn't know that she'd willingly gone with Dagan. That would change everything.*

She had no doubt in her mind that Gracie would feel the same way. Gracie had told her time and again that the attack in the parking

garage wasn't her fault. That she was the victim. But the counselor...
Who was right?

She wanted to move on with her life so badly, but she'd only ever made it so far. *Maybe Kaillar was right, and she needed to call Gracie and confide in her.* She couldn't confide in either Kalino or Kaillar. It wasn't because she didn't think they would understand, it was simply her own fear of judgment from that quarter. She didn't think it would make things any worse, but she was beginning to really like Kaillar, and didn't want to jeopardize that by showing him how stupid she'd been.

If she was going to put herself back out there and risk judgment again, she'd choose the source she was almost positive would be supportive. She couldn't trust a stranger to do that. Not again.

No, she'd talk to Gracie, and that would be the end of it. She wasn't sure when that would happen, but if today was any indication, she needed to make the call sooner than later.

"So, you two want a ride to Opihikao?" Kalino asked after following them into the terminal.

Becca shook her head, "No. We'll take a taxi out. Thanks for the lift." Kalino had told her that he lived on the opposite side of Hilo, and she didn't want to take him any further out of his way.

"You don't have to thank me," Kalino told her, pulling her close for a hug before releasing her. "*E komo mai.* Welcome home, sister. Welcome home."

"Thanks. Come by later. I'm sure mom will be happy to see you."

"I will. Kaillar, it was good to meet you. Take care of her, and don't let her take too much on those tiny shoulders. Guilt is a horrible thing to wrap around one's neck. Just remember that, Becca."

She walked away, stepping out of the terminal to hail the first cab she could find. She was done discussing the past, and trying to focus on the difficult task that lie before her. Hopefully, the community had gathered around her mother to make the funeral preparations easier. There would be a burial ceremony, but the feast and party afterwards would be the hardest for both of them to bear. Becca didn't want to hear the drums beating happily along or hear the people laughing as they danced and ate the food so soon after her father's body had been placed in the ground. She understood about celebrating a person's life, but somehow she would much prefer a more quiet remembrance than a party type of atmosphere.

She knew without asking that his body would not be cremated. He came from a very staunch Hawaiian ancestry that believed the bones of a human carried with them divine power. To cremate them would be to disrespect that power and intolerable. His body would be carefully preserved, and placed in a casket before being buried in a traditional gravesite.

While some Hawaiians would have a burial at sea, she knew her mother would never allow that. The sea had already claimed her son; she wouldn't willingly give it her husband as well.

Becca might have been gone for four years, but she still knew her mother. And that was part of the problem. Her mother had always been opinionated, and the last few weeks before the tragedy, she'd been short tempered with Becca's insistence on following Dagan around. She'd warned her daughter that the man was nothing but trouble, and she'd been right. Becca should have listened to her.

Chapter 8

"Becca?" Kaillar touched her on the shoulder, bringing her back to the present.

She blinked, and then realized a taxi was parked directly in front of her, the back passenger door open and awaiting her arrival. "Sorry. I guess I got sidetracked."

She slipped into the taxi, and gave the driver the address to the resort. She watched out the window as the vehicle made its way out of the airport and began the drive along the coastal road. When she began seeing the warning signs about the slow moving lava tubes, she couldn't resist asking, "How close are they to the location I gave you?"

"About two miles, miss. They have everyone on standby alert, but I wouldn't worry while you're here. The tube hasn't really moved much in the last month or so."

"Really? That's good news." Becca breathed a sigh of relief. She'd seen the coverage on the national news, and she'd been relieved when they'd put up the map and she'd realized her childhood home wasn't in the direct path of destruction.

"It is," the driver agreed. "My family's home is in the evacuation zone, and we've already moved my grandmother to another place, and removed the furniture and keepsakes."

"I'm sorry," Becca told him.

"No, do not be sorry. It is as my grandmother say. This land was birthed from the volcanoes, and eventually everything circles back to its origin."

"Dust to dust," Becca nodded her head.

"Yes."

"Lava tubes? Are we talking about molten rock here?" Kaillar asked.

Becca smiled at him, glad for something to talk about that didn't include her family or the past. "There are three main volcanoes on the island. Kilauea is the smallest of the three now..."

"Now?" Kaillar asked.

"Yes. She blew her top back in the 80's, and is only about four thousand feet above sea level right now. The other two mountains you saw as we flew around the island were Mauna loa and Mauna kea. They are both just short of fourteen thousand feet, but neither of them are really active. Mauna loa erupted back in the 80's as well but doesn't seem to have much activity since then. Kilauea is a different story. She hasn't ever stopped erupting, and the crater rises and falls over time."

"When you say erupting, you mean like explosions and such?" Kaillar asked.

"Sometimes," Becca offered him a small smile, and then she looked out the window and her smile broadened. "We're here."

Kaillar looked out the window, and saw what looked like a little piece of paradise. A large two story building with wrap around porches on both levels stood behind a large expanse of green foliage and grass. Palm trees, flowering hedges, and a plethora of large leafed plants bordered the property.

To the side of the main house, small bungalows were connected by a covered walkway, painted white and enclosed here and there with lattice boards.

"You grew up here?" Kaillar asked, thinking that it looked like something one would see on a postcard.

"I did," she told him, watching him and liking the joy she saw on his face. That was something she'd noticed about Kaillar, his ability to take joy in his surroundings. If was infectious, and more than once since meeting him, she'd been jealous of his ability to enjoy his life. That was what she wanted most – to just enjoy being alive and not feel as if she didn't have the right to do so.

"It's absolutely gorgeous."

Becca nodded, but before she could reply, her attention became focused on the small woman with the graying hair who had come out of the house to greet her visitors. Becca knew the exact moment her mother recognized her. She tossed down the dishtowel in her hands, and started crying even as she ran towards Becca.

Becca felt tears start, and was helpless to stop them as she met her mother in the middle of the yard and felt those slim arms surround her for the first time in over four years.

"Becca! My sweet girl! Welcome home!"

Becca held her mom close, the feeling of being held in her mother's arms one that completely broke down the rest of her defenses. She held on, sobs coming from a place deep within her. Her mother simply held her and cried with her.

Becca had no idea how long they stood there on the grass, but she sensed Kaillar behind her, and slowly pulled away from her mother. Not sure what to say regarding what had just taken place, she opted for making her introductions.

She wiped her cheeks, and then stepped back so that her mother could see Kaillar, "Mom, this is Kaillar Donnelly. Kai, my mother, Stacie Kahoalani."

Kai stepped forward and shook her mother's hand, "Ma'am. Your place here is amazing!"

Stacie offered him a soft smile, "This is your first trip to the islands?"

"Yes, ma'am." Kaillar's smile was easy, and compassion shown in his eyes when he took her mother's hand in his own and softly told her, "I'm very sorry about your husband."

"Thank you." Stacie looked between the handsome man and her daughter, and then she stepped back, "Come inside."

Becca had seen the speculative look in her mother's eyes, and knew that at some point her mother was going to want answers about...everything. After her crying jag, her eyes felt puffy, and her throat was clogged with unshed tears. But she felt better. Almost as if the load she carried was lighter.

Stacie led them into the main house, leading them directly to the large sitting room at the rear of the property. It overlooked a private salt water pool and a large patio where guests were welcome to barbecue and enjoy the sunshine away from the crowded beaches.

"I'm so glad you came. When I didn't hear back from you, I got worried," her mother told her.

Becca started to answer, but Kaillar came to her rescue. "I'm afraid that's my fault. Your news was so shocking to Becca she fainted. Once her friends and I figured out what had happened, it was only a matter of a few hours before we were boarding a plane in Denver..."

"Denver?" Stacie asked, turning to look at her daughter. "Is that where you've been these many years? I saw the postmark on your yearly cards, but the town never made much sense to me." Seeing Kaillar's confusion, she explained, "Becca has sent a post card every year just before Christmas, but it was always postmarked North Pole. Her father and I were afraid she'd moved to the top of the world."

Kaillar smiled and then asked Becca, "You drove to the North Pole to mail your cards?"

Becca nodded her head, "It wasn't much of a drive, and I actually enjoyed being there every year during the holidays."

Becca turned to her mother, "Yes. I've been living in Colorado. North Pole is a small town about an hour's drive from Denver." She paused and then added, "I just finished college."

Stacie smiled at her daughter, "Your father would have been so happy to hear that. He..." She paused, glancing at Kaillar, uncomfortable with discussing family issues without knowing his connection to her daughter.

"It's okay mom. Kaillar knows what happened."

"Does he?" her mother asked with a raised brow. "Then maybe you could fill me in as well."

Becca shook her head, "You know what happened. You were there..."

Her mother was quiet for a moment and then sighed, "I saw what you wanted me to see."

Becca hadn't a response, and finally she changed the subject. "What do you need me to do for tomorrow?"

"Nothing. Everything's already been taken care of. Your presence is all that is required."

"Fine. Dress?"

"Traditional white. Did you..."

"I brought something appropriate with me. I'm going to go get Kai and myself settled. Any guests?"

"No. Julia cancelled everyone's reservations for me," she offered, referring to the older woman who helped her mother manage the cooking and cleaning tasks for the guest rooms. Julia was about the same age as her mother, and had been a figure in Becca's life for as long as she could remember.

"I'm glad Julia's still helping you out." She didn't wait for her mother to say anything else; she stood up and headed for where Kaillar had stacked their bags by the door. "Ready?"

Kai nodded his head, giving her mother a brief smile, and then followed her from the house, both bags in his hands. "You doing okay?"

"No. I just needed...I need to talk to Gracie." Becca sniffed as she led him down the covered walkway towards the standalone bungalows.

"Where are we going?" Kai asked as she passed several without stopping.

"The end. I just need some distance..."

"Becca?" When she turned and looked at him over her shoulder, he shook his head at her, "Stop!"

She did, and then crossed her arms protectively over her chest, "What?"

"Are there no guest rooms in the main house?"

She nodded once, "Yes."

"Then why aren't we staying there? Close to your mom?"

She watched him for a moment and then looked up, blinking her eyes furiously as she tried not to cry. "I just need some space."

"Fine. Then let's drop these bags off and take a drive. But you came home to say farewell to your father and if I'm not mistaken, reconcile things with your mother before you no longer could. Am I right?"

She nodded once, and then wiped a tear away with her fingertips.

"Then it's my job as your escort to see that you do that. To save you from making a mistake that you will most certainly regret. Let's go back to the main house, and then you can show me your island. Yes?"

She took a steadying breath, and then reversed course. She entered the main house from a side door this time, and led him up a flight of stairs. She stopped at the top, and pushed open the first door they came to. "You can use this room. It has its own bathroom through that door."

"This will be fine. Where are you going to stay?"

"My old room. The only other room was my brother's, and I just..."

"Don't say any more. Go make your call to Gracie, and then come find me. I'm going to call Justin, and make sure he doesn't call out the cavalry."

Becca found that mildly funny, "No cavalry here. Fly boys, yes. Sea dogs, most certainly. But no cavalry. You're in Hawaii now."

Kaillar gave her a small smile, and then nodded towards the door, "Go take care of things." He waited until she left before blowing out a breath. Since arriving at her childhood home, things had been a rollercoaster of emotion, and he was afraid that there was much more to come. He only hoped she could handle it, and that he'd have big enough shoulders to help.

He placed his call to Justin and at the end of the call, he asked his brother to call Pastor Jeremy and get the prayer chain going. Becca needed help, and after speaking with Justin for a few minutes, he realized that while he could offer her his support and be there to listen, ultimately she was going to have to deal with the emotional trauma that had been festering for way too long. He only knew one person who could help her through that, he only hoped when the time came, she was open to seeking help from a higher power.

Chapter 9

Becca entered her childhood bedroom, shocked to see that it was just as she'd left it. She walked around the room, looking at the pictures and posters hung on the walls as memories assailed her of happier times. When she reached the window, she pulled the blinds open, and was saddened to see that her view of the ocean was no longer there. The palm trees planted at the edge of the yard had grown up and now blocked her view.

She turned away from the window, and approached her desk and the small hutch that stood atop it. There were pictures of her and Kevin there. A picture of Kevin holding his trophy after winning a surf competition. Kalino and he had tied for the win, and another picture stood on the opposite side of the hutch of Kalino in a similar pose, holding an identical trophy.

She reached for the picture, and that's when she realized there was no dust. None. She looked around the room, and could tell that someone had been cleaning the room on a regular basis. She walked to the closet, finding the clothing she'd left behind hanging neatly from the rod.

The bureau, likewise, was just as she'd left it. Her clothing from four years earlier still neatly folded and awaiting her return. It was as if the room had been suspended in time!

Before she could dwell on that too much, her cell phone rang, and she pulled it from her pocket. One glance at the screen told her Gracie had gotten tired of waiting for her call.

She sank down onto the edge of the bed, and swiped the screen, "Gracie?"

"Yeah, sweetie. I just heard Justin talking to Kaillar, so I figured I'd try to call you now. How are you holding up?"

Becca felt the tears she'd been holding back fall from her eyes, "This is so hard."

"I know. But you're strong enough to get through this. How's your mom handling your dad's death?"

"I guess okay. She ...when I arrived, she met me on the lawn and hugged me. She cried."

"And you?" Gracie asked softly.

"Like a baby. But I don't know that it solves anything. Gracie, there are things that happened...she believes one thing, but..." She couldn't finish talking, the tears were coming so fast that she could barely take a breath.

"Take a breath, Becca. Why don't you tell me what really happened, and then we'll deal with what your mom thinks happened?"

"I don't know that I can. I've never..."

There was a pause and then Gracie softly asked, "Sweetie, have you never talked to anyone about what happened?"

"No. Not really. I mean, I went to see a mental health guy a few times, but that was an utter disaster and I felt even worse afterwards. God, this is so hard."

There was a pause, and then Gracie asked, "Do you believe in God, Becca? I know you used to go to church with Melanie and me from time to time, but I never asked. I didn't want to pry."

"I guess I believe there is a God, but I wasn't raised in church or anything. What about you?"

"Yeah, I believe in God, and I believe that He watches over us and is ready and waiting to help us if we just ask Him for help."

"If that's true, He must not care too much for me."

"Why do you say that?" Gracie asked, wishing she wasn't thousands of miles away.

"You don't know...if God was watching over me four years ago, He must have blinked."

Gracie assured her, "God was watching, but He never promised that we wouldn't go through tough times. Why don't you tell me what really happened four years ago?"

Becca took a small breath, and then began to tell her about Dagan and how she'd fallen head over heels for him. "I really liked him, but it turned out that he wasn't the person I thought he was."

"What happened?"

"He was training on a neighboring island at one of the most dangerous surfing points in the world. My brother and his friend were not quite fifteen, and were the junior champions. They weren't anywhere near ready to take on Pe'ahi size waves, but surfers constantly challenge themselves, and Kevin convinced my parents that he and Kalino would only ride the secondary waves."

"So, you went to this island, and then what happened?"

"Dagan was already there, and he'd told me to find him when we got there because he wanted to talk to me about something. He and his buddies were renting rooms at my parents' resort, but we didn't have a lot of privacy. I was excited, and hopeful that maybe he was going to ask me to go with him when they moved to their summer training grounds."

"That's not what he wanted to talk about?" Gracie asked, trying to keep the conversation moving.

"He didn't actually want to talk. He wanted sex. It sounds horrible, but what he did was horrible. He took me up the beach a ways, and told me we were going to walk, but once we reached the sand, he attacked me. When I fought back, he slapped me, and then tried to choke me as he tried to tear my clothes off."

"Becca? Sweetie, I have to ask, but did he rape you?"

"No. A park ranger heard me cry out and came to investigate. Dagan made up a story about things getting a little out of control, and I was so embarrassed, I didn't say anything. I kept my head down, trying to cope with the fact that my supposed boyfriend had just assaulted me."

"I'm glad his actions were interrupted. Then what happened?"

"He drove us back to the beach, and told me to clean my face up before I joined his friends on the beach. The rental Jeep didn't have any mirrors inside the vehicle, and I didn't think to look in one of the side mirrors. I sat there for a long time, and then went to find my brother and his friend.

"I had decided we were going straight back to the airport and then home. I had every intention of telling my parents some of what had happened, and having them kick Dagan and his buddies off the property."

"Did your parents believe you?"

"I never got the chance to find out. Kevin saw the red mark on my face and the bruising around my throat and took off after Dagan. He'd already started paddling out, and Kevin grabbed his board and gave chase. Kalino heard me yelling at him to stop, and he too headed out after Kevin."

Becca grew silent for a moment, closing her eyes as the events of the next few moments replayed themselves in her mind. "Dagan went out to where the big waves came in, and Kevin followed him. He'd never been in such big water before, but he didn't even pause. This giant wave formed, and Dagan went for it. Kevin tried, but he'd barely gotten to his feet on his board when the wave broke. Right on top of him."

She was crying now, tears streaming down her face. Kalino was too far away to stop him, but also too close to escape the wave's massive power. Dagan wasn't even a match for the wave. He rode it for several seconds before it crashed over him as well. He and Kevin were killed, and Kalino spent three weeks in the hospital in a coma."

"Oh, sweetie! How horrible! Did your parents come..."

"No. Kalino's dad showed up, having heard the call for a medivac over his radio. He found me sitting in the sand, almost catatonic and freezing. He flew me to the hospital where they took Kalino, and my parents were called from there. They drove up to get me, and that's where they learned about Kevin's death.

"My dad was more upset than I'd ever seen him. My mother took one look at me, and immediately assumed the wrong thing. I know she thinks I was off playing games while Kevin was killing himself. The press was horrible. Dagan had been the country's best chance for winning the world title, and now he was dead.

"They had this massive, televised funeral for him. Reporters from around the world showed up. How was I supposed to tell anyone what had happened? Everyone idolized him, and was mourning the loss of one of the best surfers the world had ever known. If I had even breathed a hint of what he'd tried to do, no one would have believed me."

"Your parents..."

"No. They were grieving the loss of their son. My father made sure to let me know that Kevin was his only real child, and that because of me, he no longer had any children."

"But he was your father..."

"Not really. He raised me, but my mom and he never got around to changing my last name. It was and still is Edwards. The way he looked at me was horrible. And my mother, she'd been warning me away from Dagan and his friends. She had firsthand knowledge of the damage the surfer mentality could do to my future. My biological father was a surfer who abandoned her when he found out she was pregnant. In her opinion, I'd ignored her advice, and my brother had paid for my mistake with his life."

A noise from her bedroom door had Becca glancing up to see her mother standing in the partially opened doorway.

Chapter 10

S he had a stricken look on her face, and a hand clutching her chest. "Mom?"

Becca dropped the phone when her mother's color drained away, and she collapsed to the floor. "Mom!"

She rushed to her mom, and quickly checked for a pulse. She could hear Gracie yelling at her through the phone, and she quickly crawled back to it before returning to her mom. "Gracie! She collapsed."

"Who?"

"My mom. She was standing in the doorway listening to us talk. She clutched her chest and collapsed. Oh, what do I do?"

"Check for a pulse. Where's Kai?"

Becca glanced down the hallway, and yelled out for him. He stuck his head out of the door a moment later, and rushed to her side. "I can't find a pulse! Oh God, I can't lose her too. Gracie, help me!"

"Whoa! Calm down and check again."

Kaillar took the phone from her hands, and put it on speakerphone, "Hey Gracie! What do I need to do?"

"See if she has a pulse, and get some medical help on the way."

Becca was crying, "Mom! You can't do this. Not now."

"She has a pulse."

"Good. Is it strong and steady?"

"It seems to be. Wait! She's coming around."

"Mom! Can you hear me?" Becca asked, clasping her mom's hand as her eyelids fluttered opened. "Don't move. You passed out. Where do you hurt? Is it your heart?"

Stacie opened her eyes, and then looked at Kaillar before returning her gaze to her daughter. She lifted a hand to Becca's check, "Becca, what you told your friend on the phone...it's just not true. Your father...he never meant for you to take his comments the way you did. It nearly broke him when you left. And I never assumed you were at fault for Kevin's rash actions."

"Dad said..."

"I know what you heard, but he only meant that Kevin was his only biological child. He always loved you as if you were his own flesh and blood. We never had your last name changed because of the difficulty it would have posed with the courts. I would have had to name your biological father, and I wasn't willing to do that. I'm sorry if that choice made you feel less loved."

"I always felt loved. Until Kevin died. It was my fault. If I hadn't gone off with Dagan, he wouldn't have attacked me, and Kevin wouldn't have gone after him."

"Kevin went out there trying to defend your honor?" her mother asked, her eyes clouding with the memory of his loss. "Somehow, that makes his death better. Knowing that he wasn't just being a cocky teenager, taking on too much and trying to grow up too fast."

"No! Kevin would have never attempted those big waves, but he was intent on making Dagan pay for hurting me. I didn't realize that he'd be able to tell anything had happened. It wasn't until I got the hospital and saw my reflection in the bathroom mirror that I saw the bruising he must have seen."

Kaillar picked up Becca's phone and moved back a few feet, taking it off speakerphone. "Gracie, I'll have her call you back later. I think her mother just fainted." Kaillar listened for a moment and then he said, "I'll tell her."

"What?" Becca asked, helping her mom to a sitting position.

"Gracie tells you to remember to only own what's truly yours."

"Good advice. I look forward to meeting this friend of yours one day," her mother commented, using Becca's arm as she got back to her feet.

Stacie looked at her daughter, and then at Kaillar, "We'll talk more about this, but I'm glad to finally know the truth. Now, I think we all need a break from these emotions and memories. Why don't you take one of the Scouts up to the volcano, and show this mainlander the lava flows?"

Becca was amazed that her mother could so easily turn off her emotions. She envied her the ability, but was also grateful to be given a chance to collect herself. She turned to Kai and asked, "Does that sound good?"

Kai nodded, "Yes. Who knows when I'll get another chance to see lava flows."

Stacie gave him a small smile, "Stick around Hawaii too long and you'll see more than lava flows. In the last few weeks, the volcano has been acting up. That usually means an eruption is imminent."

"Why don't you sound more concerned?" he asked, wondering how safe they truly were.

"Kilauea erupts constantly. She can't blow her top, because she already did that. Unless she would really get going, we're in no immediate danger here. Take him up, and show him what I'm talking about."

"Is the crater safe to drive around?" Becca wondered.

"Check at the ranger station. Last report I heard, the crater was still down thirty meters or more."

"We'll do that. Come on. Let's go expand your education about volcanoes and Hawaii." Becca didn't wait to see if he was following her. She darted into the closest bathroom, and grabbed a handful of tissues. She'd already cried off whatever makeup she'd still been wearing when they landed in Honolulu, so she dried her eyes as she headed for the parking area.

A trip up the mountain was just what she needed to remind her that life went on. No matter how bad the circumstances became. It was impossible to view the damage a volcano could cause and not realize that truth.

Chapter 11

Three hours later at the Hawaii Volcanoes National Park Visitor Center...

"This place is amazing," Kaillar told her as they drove along the crater rim. Tendrils of steam and gases rose from the crater in the distance, the landscape looking as if they had been transported to another planet.

The black swirls and folds of cooled lava obliterated the landscape beneath. As far as he could see, the ground was blackened. The remains of trees that had been caught in the fiery flow stood as ghostly reminders that at one point in time, green grass and tall trees had occupied this same location.

"It's a weird feeling, isn't it?" Becca asked, doing her best to put the events of earlier behind her.

"Weird doesn't even come close," Kaillar told her with a look.

"There are some benches up there where we could get out and sit. It might smell a bit if the wind is blowing just right, but if you listen closely, you can hear the sounds from the crater echo across the landscape."

"I'm game." By mutual consent, Kaillar was driving, and he located a vacant parking spot and pulled the vehicle over. As they headed for the benches, it seemed like the most natural thing in the world to reach over and take her hand in his own.

He felt her start, but when she didn't try to reclaim her hand, he silently patted himself on the back. He was making progress, or rather, she was making progress. *Maybe she's beginning to trust me a little.*

They sat in silent contemplation for many minutes. Kaillar was astonished at the young woman sitting next to him. At the age of twenty-three, she'd dealt with more tragedy in her life, and yet she was still trying to move ahead with the act of living. After hearing her story, meeting her mother, and having spoken to Kalino, he realized that while not ideal, her leaving when she did might have been the best thing in some respects.

"So, I know you were feeling very apprehensive about coming home. How are you feeling now?"

Becca gave him a look, and then shook her head, "You sound like Gracie."

"Thank you?" he questioned, trying to keep the mood light.

"It's different than I imagined. I knew that my parents had the wrong idea about what had happened, but things were so tense back then. They were grieving my brother's passing, and it just didn't seem to be getting any better three weeks later.

"When Kalino woke up from his coma, and the doctors said that he would make a full recovery, I realized that I needed to do something different if I ever wanted to be able to say that about my own life. I think my leaving hurt my parents."

"I think that's probably a fair statement. But as you discovered earlier, your mother didn't understand that you had suffered an additional trauma no one knew about. I don't think anyone could have expected you to stay here without some way of dealing with those feelings."

Becca gave him a rueful smile, "But I didn't deal with them. I just locked them away. I thought I was doing a pretty good job of it too, until that attack a few months back. It brought everything back and I realized I'd not gotten rid of any of the guilt."

"Guilt that isn't even yours," he reminded her.

"It's much easier to say that than to believe it's true," she replied with a face.

"I get that. Why don't you let someone else carry the burden for a while?" he suggested, hoping he wasn't stepping over the line with her.

"What? Why would anyone else want to carry around my burden? One you seem convinced isn't even mine to own."

"Because God loves you, and He's the only one that can take the guilt you're feeling and turn it around."

"God again, huh? Gracie went there as well. You really believe in prayer and all that stuff?"

"I do. I've seen it work in my life and in others. Look at it this way; you don't have anything to lose. You did say you believed in God."

"I do, but I don't know that I believe He's the kind of God that takes a personal interest in the lives of his subjects."

"Not subjects. Children." Kaillar thought for a moment, and then explained, "God called us His children. Think of him like a Father. One that only wants good things for His children."

Becca looked at him, and then spoke so softly he could barely hear her, "I've never thought of Him that way. I always envisioned God as this powerful being that watched us like we might watch the nightly news."

Kai smiled at her, "You couldn't be more far from the truth. He wants to be part of your daily life."

"Is He part of yours?" she asked.

"Not in the same way He is with Pastor Jeremy, but – Yes. God is a part of my daily life."

Becca was quiet for a few moments, and then she nodded, "I'll think about it. For now, the wind is shifting, and the smell of rotten eggs doesn't do anything for me."

"I noticed that the odor seems to have gotten stronger. Shall we head back?"

"Yeah. I know my mom said there wasn't anything she needed help with, but I don't believe her. I don't even know what time the service is tomorrow."

"Let's go," Kaillar led her back to the vehicle, and then drove them back down the mountain. He actually felt a sense of relief when green foliage and trees reappeared along the roadway. The devastation done by the volcano was tremendous and yet, as they got closer to the unaffected ground, small plants had begun to push their way up through the charred, hardened lava. The contrast between the black ground and the bright green plants was a great reminder that even though the volcano had destroyed everything in its path, the destruction was only for a time. Life went on, and could flourish even in the midst of such devastation.

He wasn't aware that Becca's thoughts were travelling along that same path. Or that she was doing some serious thinking about this God that both he and Gracie seemed to put so much faith in.

Chapter 12

Sunday, early afternoon...

Kalino and Kaillar stood a short distance away from the closed casket containing the remains of Makoa Kahoalani. The funeral service had been brief, and now all that was left was for Becca and her mother to say their final farewells.

"She's handling this pretty well," Kalino commented to Kai.

"Yesterday was pretty hard on both of them."

"I know. Her mom called me after you both left, and wanted to know why I'd never said anything about Dagan attacking Becca that day. I guess I always assumed that they'd figured it out. By the time I woke up, everything had started to settle down with the media, and Becca was gone. I not only lost my best friend, but Becca had been like an older sister to me. Her leaving felt a lot like I'd been abandoned."

"Didn't you ever think to contact her?" Kai asked, remembering how she'd explained that she'd left her phone number the same and no one had ever called her.

"Her dad told me to leave things alone. That she needed time to deal with everything that had happened, and I assumed he knew her best. I never dreamed that she would stay away for so long."

"Well, I know from talking with her two roommates these last four years that she never even mentioned having a brother. I think she thought if she stayed away, she would never have to deal with the pain."

"That's not how life works. I remember the first time I surfed Pe'ahi after the accident. I stayed away for almost three years. And then one day about a year ago, I realized that if I wanted a shot at winning the Island championship, I'd have to eventually learn how to handle the big waves."

"Isn't that where her brother was killed?" Kai asked.

"Yeah. I watched the forecast, and chose a day where the chances of the waves increasing was minimal. I flew over by myself. I didn't want anyone to see me fail if I chickened out."

"What happened?" Kaillar asked.

"I swam out, and then sat on my board for almost an hour before I got the nerve to make a run for the next wave. I watched surfer after surfer get overtaken in that time. Guys I'd gone to school with, and had competed against for years. Not a one of them was successful in riding the entire wave out."

"Let me guess, that made you more determined than ever to prove that you could do what they couldn't?" Kai asked with a grin.

"Don't you know it," Kalino grinned back at him.

"I'm the same way with downhill racing. Nothing fuels my determination more than watching the skier right before the wipe out."

"There is definitely something wrong with us," Kalino suggested with a broad smile.

"No. We're just competitive. My brother tells me all the time it's going to be my downfall, but I'm also cautious. I assume you are as well?"

"I'm probably the safest surfer I know who still takes on the big ones. If the waves looks too iffy, I'll gladly pass and let someone else take it. The object is to score points. Some of these guys would rather ride for six or seven seconds on a high scoring wave. Not me. I want to go for the thirty second or more ride, on a slightly lower scoring wave. In the end, I score more points, and my parents can sleep at night."

"What are you two up to?" Stacie asked as she and Becca joined them.

"Not much," Kai told her, sobering and watching Becca carefully for signs that she wasn't doing well. Her father had been an island figure, and his funeral had drawn the attention of several reporters from the mainland and Oahu. One of them had recognized Becca, and had been brazen enough to ask her where she'd been hiding. They'd gone on to mention her absence at Dagan's funeral, wondering if she would mind sitting down with them and talking about that tragic time in her life.

Kaillar had instantly become furious, and had stepped between her and the reporters. His sheer size alone had sent them backing up, and the look on his face had warned them not to press their luck. "Miss Edwards will not be giving any interviews. Now or in the future. Please respect her and her family's privacy today."

Becca had given him a grateful look, and then been hustled away by both her mother and Julia.

Kaillar sighed, wishing this ordeal was over for her. "We were just chatting."

Becca nodded, "We're ready to go. Mom's friends should have everything set up back at the house."

"I'm going to ride back with Kalino," Stacie told her daughter. She'd seen the careful way Kaillar kept watch over Becca, and was hoping to give them a few moments alone before they were bombarded by friends of her father's wanting to talk about the man they both respected and loved. It would be a trying afternoon, but also a time to heal and remember the good times.

Kaillar walked her to the car, and then opened the passenger door, squatting down to look into her eyes after she was seated. "How are you really doing, sugar?"

"What is it with you people from Colorado? Gracie calls me sweetie, and you call me sugar. Like I'm a piece of candy or something."

Kai looked hurt, "You don't like it?"

"No, that's not what I meant. I just...sorry, I don't know what I meant."

Kai smirked, "So you do like it when I call you sugar?"

Becca blushed, "Maybe too much. Kai...I don't do relationships...I mean, I haven't in the past four years..."

"Becca, I'm not pushing here. But I think you can tell I really like you. I know you're leery of men in general because of everything that's happened, but I won't ever hurt you like that."

Becca's eyes softened, "I know you won't. I know I kind of scared you the first time we met, but the situation was scary, and when you grabbed me, I didn't know you and it was so much like the parking garage, and..."

"Becca, stop. You don't have to explain anything to me. I am amazed at your strength, and I would understand if you never wanted to trust another man, but I'm hoping that's not the case."

She studied him for a minute, and then she blushed and dropped her eyes.

"What was that thought?" he asked, watching her cheeks turn pink.

"Nothing..."

"Hey! You can tell me to mind my own business, but don't lie to me or to yourself. If you don't want to tell me, I'm okay with that."

She looked up at him, and then bit her bottom lip, looking uncertain before saying, "I was just wondering how you kissed."

Kaillar let out a small laugh, and reached out a hand to cup her jaw, "Sugar, how about you stop wondering?" He gave her plenty of time to pull away, but when she only continued to watch him, he dropped his eyes to her mouth and tenderly kissed her soft lips.

He didn't prolong their first kiss, but backed away so he could see her eyes. "How was that?"

"Better than I remembered," she said before she could think about it. When she realized what she'd said, she blushed again and told him, "Sorry. I wasn't meaning to compare you to..."

Kaillar chuckled, "I'm not worried. I know it was good."

Becca laughed in pretend shock, "Conceited much?"

"No. Just honest." He stood up, walked around the vehicle, and got in. Once he had the vehicle running, he turned to her, "Your mom's going to wonder what happened to us."

"Probably, but I also think she designed it this way. She likes you."

"How can you tell?" Kai asked as he pulled out onto the main road.

"I can tell. I may have been gone for four years, but I lived here for nineteen before that. She definitely likes you." *So do I. Maybe too much.*

Chapter 13

T*wo days later...*
"Becca?" Kaillar called out into the backyard. She and her mother had been getting reacquainted for the last two days, and Kalino had been coming around to keep him company. He really liked the young man, and the pair were already making plans for Kalino to travel to Colorado after the holidays to try his hand at skiing.

With his keen sense of balance, Kaillar was sure he'd be a natural. "Becca?"

"Over here," Becca called to him. "What's up?"

"Kalino just called and said there was an outbreak, and you and your mom needed to turn the news on."

Becca nodded her head, and then she and her mom hurried towards the house. They found the local news station, and watched in growing understanding that Kilauea was on the move again and this time, she wasn't going to stop before she did considerable damage.

Reports coming in a few minutes ago show that the outbreak is moving considerably faster than in the past few months. Moving at speeds close to six feet per hour, the lava is going to reach Highway 130 by nightfall. Emergency Response Teams are already in the area, and are urging residents to be on alert for possible evacuation.

"What does all that mean?" Kaillar asked, seeing the worry on the two women's faces.

"It means that if the lava flows comes this direction, all we can do is pack up and leave."

"Six feet per hour seems kind of slow, doesn't it?"

Becca walked over to the refrigerator, and pulled a map of the island off the front. "Kai, this is where the lava flow has currently been held up. It's been building upon itself for the last several months, never making forward progress. This outbreak is off to the side, and moving directly towards Opihikao. Once it crosses the highway, we will only be ten miles or so from its current location."

"Ten miles seems like a lot..."

"Maybe, but the danger that once it starts moving is that it will gain speed as it finds new land to consume. There is also a slight decrease in elevation, which will aid the movement."

"Isn't there anything that can be done?"

Stacie nodded her head, seeming to be unconcerned about the news, "They will install large concrete barriers on the opposite side of the highway to help direct it away from populated areas and residential buildings. It will work in the short term, but if the volcanic activity doesn't slow down, it will only delay the inevitable."

"So, is the resort in danger?"

"At the moment, not really. But in three or four months, maybe. Only God knows the answer to that."

At the mention of God, Kaillar looked at Becca's mom, "You believe in God?"

Stacie smiled, "I was raised in a very nice Catholic orphanage. When I came to Hawaii, I figured God hadn't seen fit to keep me with my birth parents, and I could handle things on my own." She gave Becca a soft smile, "It wasn't until Kevin's death that I realized I hadn't done such a good job. Your father wasn't raised in a church environment like I was, but he still believed in an Eternal Creator.

"After you left, we both had to do some soul searching. Mine led me back to a little non-denominational church in Hilo. I realized that while I'd left God, he'd never left me."

"Mom, I never knew you even thought about God," Becca told her mother.

"I regret that. I do."

Kaillar smiled at Stacie, "Becca and I have been talking about her giving her guilt and feelings of sadness for what happened four years ago over to Him."

Stacie smiled at her daughter, "You won't regret it if you do."

Becca sighed, "I'm still thinking about it."

"Good. Now, I think maybe I need to go have a talk with Julia. We always knew the day might come when the volcano would take back what was hers. We have boxes already in storage, and between the two of us, we've got an evacuation plan all worked out."

"Mom, there's no need to evacuate right now."

"I think maybe there is. Without your father, I don't want to run a resort. A developer gave your father and me a standing offer to purchase the property three months ago. He called me yesterday upon hearing of your father's death, and told me his offer still stands. I'm thinking I will take him up on it."

"But what will you do?" Becca asked, confused at how fast things could change.

"Well, now. I haven't gotten that worked out quite yet, but I will. Now, would you and Kai mind running a few errands for me?"

Kaillar looked at Becca and then answered, "We wouldn't mind at all."

Ten minutes later, he and Becca were headed back into the more populated area of the island surrounding Hilo, "So, she really means to sell?"

"It sounds like it."

"You don't sound very happy."

"I guess I don't like knowing that the resort won't be there the next time I come home."

"Are you planning on coming home more frequently?" Kaillar asked with a smile.

Becca nodded her head, "I think I'd like to see my mom more often. With my dad gone, she only has me now. Julia has plenty of family on the island, but my mom doesn't have anyone."

Kaillar was quiet for a moment and then asked, "Have you considered asking her to come live in Colorado with you?"

Chapter 14

"Colorado? I don't know if she'd even consider it," Becca told him. *Why didn't I think of that? There's nothing really left for her here. If she's going to sell the resort, that might be the perfect time for her to move back to the mainland.*

"Well, maybe you should mention it to her. Justin told me last night that Gracie had been talking to Mason who had been talking to Sarah."

"Sarah with the motel and boarding house?" Becca inquired.

"That's the one. Anyway, the doctor who performed Gracie's knee surgery and Sarah are in love, but Sarah won't even consider moving to Vail until she's found someone to manage the boarding house. Something about leaving the town without adequate accommodations for guests and visiting family members."

"That sounds like Sarah." Becca had stayed with the woman while Gracie was having her surgery, and she'd discovered that the woman had a compulsion to make sure that her guests were completely taken care of. Having been raised around a tourist resort, Becca had seen several things the woman was doing that could be done differently.

"It really does. Anyway, Gracie thought maybe you would be interested in taking over the boarding house for Sarah when you got back. She was going to talk to you the day you got the phone call about your dad."

"Me? But that would mean I'd have to move to Silver Springs..." Becca started laughing, "Gracie thinks she's so smart. She's trying to get me to move up into the mountains!"

"Is that a bad thing?" Kai questioned.

"Not really. I still want to take photos for the Division of Wildlife, but the position isn't full-time, so I'd have to have a second job." *Live in Silver Springs? Where Kaillar lives? Yes, please.*

"Why don't you call Gracie and get the details? Maybe if you had something like that all set up, your mom would feel more comfortable coming to live with you."

"Maybe. She's run that resort for most of my life. A small boarding house like Sarah's would be no problem at all."

Before he could answer, her phone rang and she answered it, "Hello?"

"Hey Becca! It's Kalino. Did you see the news?"

"I did. Thanks for the heads up."

"Yeah. Hey, I'm going to Maui tomorrow, and was wondering if you and Kai wanted to tag along and go sightseeing?"

"Are you surfing?" Becca asked, trepidation in her voice. She wasn't sure if she could watch Kalino surf the same waters that had taken her brother's life or not.

"I am, and while I'd love for you to come watch for a bit, I'll understand if you can't."

Becca looked out the window, and made a snap decision. "We'd love to come, and I'll let you know about the surfing. Kai mentioned to me he wanted to give it a try before we went back to the mainland, but Pe'ahi is no place for beginners."

"Uhm...he didn't tell you?" Kalino asked hesitantly.

"Tell me what?" Becca asked, looking to Kai for answers.

"I'm taking him surfing this afternoon."

Becca smiled and watched Kaillar as she replied, "Really? Now that I will come and see."

"You going to join us?" Kalino asked. "If I remember correctly, you didn't do too badly on a longboard yourself."

"No, I think I'll stay on the beach and take pictures. I'm sure his brothers will pay good money for some good blackmail shots." She could already hear the three brothers bantering back and forth and realized in that moment that she missed that. She also missed her friends and the camaraderie she'd come to love. Moving to Silver Springs wouldn't be any hardship at all.

Kaillar shook his head at her and then whispered, "I'm taking you skiing when we get back to Colorado. Be careful how much retribution you want."

Becca laughed, and agreed to meet Kalino back at the resort after running her mother's errands. It was the first time since arriving on the islands when she actually felt happy and carefree. Whether it was the company, or just the passage of time, she wasn't questioning it. She was just going to enjoy herself.

· · ❧ · ·

LATER THAT EVENING, she watched as Kalino and Kaillar exited the ocean, carrying their boards and with happy grins upon their faces. Kaillar had been a natural, and if she hadn't known better, she would have said he'd been surfing most of his life.

Kalino had been thrilled with how quickly he caught on, and they had taken wave after wave until they were both joyously exhausted.

"That was so awesome! My brothers have got to come over here and try this!"

"Hey, bring them out whenever."

"I will. But before I bring them here, you need to come skiing. Or maybe even snowboarding. Now that would be much easier since you surf. It's a lot like surfing, come to think of it. Both feet on a single board."

Kalino smiled, "Having two different boards to control sounds a little difficult. But snowboarding, yeah – I could get into that."

"Great! Vail Mountain has this awesome half-pipe!"

"If you two are done salivating over your next adrenaline rush, maybe we could go get some food?" Becca told them when there was a break in the conversation.

Kalino and Kaillar shared a look and then they descended upon her, abandoning their towels as they came after her with water still dripping from their heads. When they were close enough, they shook their heads, spreading droplets of water in her direction and causing her to shriek and back up.

She was giggling by the time Kaillar finally caught up with her, Kalino standing off to the side watching her and Kai with a smile upon his face. When she raised an eyebrow at him, he simply stated, "It's nice seeing you smile again, *hoapili*."

Becca's heart melted at the term, and she translated for Kai, "It means close friend."

Kai stepped closer to her and asked, "So is that the term you would use to describe me?"

Becca felt the atmosphere change, and she noticed Kalino stepped away to give them a bit of privacy. She shook her head at him, "No."

Kai lifted a hand to her face, moving a loose tendril of hair behind her ear, "So, how do you say sweetheart in your Hawai'ian?"

Becca fought the urge to close her eyes and tip her head into his caress. "Sweetheart is *ku'uipo*."

Kai repeated the terminology, and then lowered his head, "I want to kiss you again."

Becca gave into the desire to close her eyes and nodded shortly, "Yes."

Chapter 15

Kaillar kissed her softly and then wrapped his arms around her, smiling when she flinched as her body made contact with his cold wet one. When she didn't pull away, but snuggled closer, he thanked God and kissed her again.

He was falling fast and hard for the woman in his arms. He kissed her once more and then let her go, "So, what kind of food do you want to eat?"

Becca was blushing but she met his eyes anyway, "How about traditional Hawai'ian barbeque?"

Kaillar grinned, "Sounds good to me." He turned and waved Kalino over, "Barbeque?"

"You bet. Annie's?" Kalino asked Becca with a grin.

"Is there any other place?" Becca wanted to know. When Kalino shook his head and laughed, she joined in, grabbing Kai and his hands as they headed for the truck. The guys tossed their boards into the bed and then dusted the sand off their feet.

The drive to Annie's only took about ten minutes, and then they were stepping into a small building, the fragrant smells coming from the kitchen had Kai's mouth watering before they were even seated.

The waitress took their drink orders, and then invited them to the food bar. Annie's was an all-you-can-eat food bar with different stations that catered to different types of cuisine. There was a sushi bar, as well as a carving station where the barbeque meat was freshly shaved or cut from the bone.

Kaillar followed Becca and Kalino around the different food stations, taking what looked good, and laughing when Becca occasionally added a spoonful of something to his plate. When she picked up a bowl of what looked like purplish-grey pudding, he made a face and quietly suggested she put it back.

"This is a Hawai'ian tradition and a must try. At least once."

"What is it?" he asked, lifting it to his nose and sniffing it.

"Poi."

"Poi? Dare I ask what it's made from?"

"Taro root. They cook it and then mash it."

Kai looked at the bowl again and then whispered, "What's it taste like?"

Kalino heard his question and stopped, putting his head between the two of them, "Imagine eating warm wall paper paste."

Kaillar looked at him in mock horror. "Really?"

Becca laughed, "Really."

"Why on earth would anyone want to eat wall paper paste?" This time his horror wasn't all for show. There were trays of the stuff, and he couldn't imagine why anyone would willingly eat something so unappetizing when there were all these other choices before them.

Kalino walked by him with a plate laden high with food a moment later, and patted him on the back, "Don't waste too many brain cells trying to figure it out. I've lived here all my life and I still don't understand why anyone without a gun being held to their head would eat that stuff."

"My father's parents ate it with every evening meal. After they passed away, I remember overhearing my mother telling my father she wasn't ever making poi again, and if he had to have it with his evening meal, he could take his evening meals someplace else."

Kalino laughed, "I can see your mom saying that." Becca's mom had a refreshing sense of humor, and Kalino had thoroughly enjoyed hearing her retell exploits from Becca and her brother's youth.

They sat back down, and Kaillar pushed the bowl of poi to the center of the table, "I'm sharing it with everyone. I would hate to deprive either of you of this traditional food."

Becca giggled, "You have to at least taste it once. Just one spoonful. In fact, we'll all take a spoonful together. Deal?"

"I can live with that," Kaillar agreed. The all picked up a spoon and took a small amount on the utensil and then lifted them towards their mouths. "One."

"Two," Kalino said.

"Three," Becca added with a grin. She lifted her spoon up, opened her mouth, and watched as both guys took their bite. Instead of eating her spoonful, she carefully set it aside, watching the faces both guys made as they struggled to get the sticky substance down.

After drinking an entire glass of water, Kaillar looked at her and then shook his head, "No fair."

"Totally fair. Tell me you would willingly take another bite of that stuff."

Kaillar shook his head and whispered, "I wouldn't even let that stuff in my house." He thought for a moment, and then he amended his statement, "Although, I have to admit it would definitely be worth watching Justin and Mason try it."

"We'll get some to take home with us."

Kaillar searched her eyes, "Did you mean Colorado home, or Silver Springs?"

Becca licked her bottom lip and softly answered, "Silver Springs? I spoke with Gracie while you boys were playing in the ocean. She's going to talk to Sarah and work out the details on my behalf. She's also going to contact my landlord and give my notice."

"So now all you need to do is talk to your mom. If nothing else, maybe she would come to Colorado for the holidays."

"Maybe she will." Changing the subject, she asked Kalino, "What time are you wanting to leave tomorrow?"

"Is 8 o'clock too early?"

"Not at all. We'll be at the airport."

"Great." It grew quiet as everyone dug into their food. Light conversation between Kaillar and Kalino about surfing and other mundane things kept the conversation going, giving Becca a chance to just sit back and listen.

She loved how easily Kaillar had fit into her life here. But she wondered if she would find it as easy to fit into his life. She'd seen the girls on the beach staring at him today, and that little devil – jealousy, had risen up inside of her.

She'd hated that they only saw him for a great body, and cared nothing for what lie between his ears. Or about his character. They liked his looks, and that was as deep as they let their relationships get.

That had been Dagan's problem. He'd believed the propaganda that said it was all about looks. He'd believed himself to live by a different set of rules than the rest of the world. Rules that allowed him to act with impunity and without feeling any guilt.

"Are you finished?" Kai asked her a few minutes later.

"Yes. We should probably get back. I'd like to speak with my mom before I go to bed tonight."

"Then that's what we'll do."

"You should keep your eyes open on the drive back. You'll be able to see the glow from the moving lava the darker it gets. That will give us a good idea of how close it really is." Kalino offered the word of caution, knowing that the worry was there in the back of Becca's mind.

Becca nodded her head, "Thanks. We'll do that." She didn't add that she was anxious to get her mom off the island before tragedy could strike the resort. It might not happen this month, and maybe not the next, but at some point in the future, Kilauea would be knocking at the back door of the resort. Becca would prefer that her mother not be there to greet her.

Chapter 16

The next day on Maui...

"So, you two head on up to 'Iao Valley. The Needle is about a two hour hike, but well worth it." Kalino pulled a map of the island from his pack, and tossed it to Becca. "Just in case you've forgotten which trail goes which way."

Becca nodded her head, hoping she wasn't going to embarrass herself by suggesting she and Kaillar go hiking today. She'd given a lot of thought to watching Kalino surf Pe'ahi, and come to the conclusion that she couldn't do it.

He understood completely. He'd suggested she and Kaillar do some hiking, and Kaillar had jumped at the chance to see more of the Hawaiian landscape up close and personal.

"So, there's a small shop just before you enter the park that can rent you packs and anything else you need."

"Great!" Kaillar was a like a kid in a candy store at the mention of packs, climbing ropes, and mountain trails.

Becca nodded again, hoping she hadn't bitten off more than she could chew. She'd been up late last night talking with her mom about the future. Stacie wasn't opposed to moving back to the mainland, and she'd been very interested in the motel and boarding house combination in Silver Springs. But, she was afraid of encroaching on Becca's life. Becca had assured her that she wouldn't have even mentioned it to her if she wasn't onboard with her moving to Colorado.

Stacie had promised to pray about the decision, and let her daughter know before she and Kaillar flew home in two days. Becca had asked Kaillar to schedule their return home, knowing that the longer she stayed, the harder it would be to leave. Her future was in Colorado, not Hawaii, and the sooner she got back on the mainland, the better.

"Ready to go?" Kaillar asked.

"Sure thing." Becca watched the scenery pass by as they headed for the inland road that would take them to the green landscape of the majestic island. She was reminded of those past times when she, Kevin, and Kalino had gone on similar excursions. She loved nature, but she'd allowed the events of four years ago to steal that enjoyment. *No more! I'm taking back my life, starting right now!*

"So, are you really wanting to go hiking?" Becca asked, an alternate plan forming in her mind.

She'd overheard Kaillar talking to Justin and Mason on the phone the night before. He'd had his cell phone on speakerphone and she knew he'd thought he was alone in the house. She'd come inside to grab a light sweater, and when she'd heard her name mentioned, she'd been unable to walk away.

Kaillar had been discussing where he wanted his relationship with her to go. Justin and Mason were both getting married; the final details had all been worked out. Justin and Jessica were getting married in a week and a half in a small ceremony at the Silver Springs church.

Not wanting to steal any thunder from his brother, Mason and Gracie were going to wait until the weekend before Christmas to tie the knot, allowing Justin and Jessica a chance to go on their honeymoon and return.

Both women expected Becca to be in their wedding, and they'd already found and ordered her bridesmaid dress. A single dress for both occasions. Becca had thought the idea brilliant.

The upcoming weddings had evidently started Kaillar thinking about his own future and she'd heard him tell his brothers that he intended to marry her. Their relationship was so new, but because of the circumstances, it had moved very quickly, and Becca knew she'd never find another man like Kaillar. He made her happy, and there wasn't anything about him she didn't like.

The only thing standing in the way was her lack of a relationship with God. Kaillar had been very upset about that. *I can't marry someone who doesn't share my faith. It would be a failure from the start.*

Becca felt badly that she hadn't taken time to tell him about her early mornings with her mother. She'd found her mother a few mornings earlier, sitting on the porch with a cup of hot tea in one hand, and her Bible open in the other.

Her mother hadn't been reading the book, but staring off into space. Becca had joined her, and soon they had begun talking about God, and how her mother had come back to a relationship with Him after her brother's funeral and after Becca had left the Islands.

Becca had always thought her mom a strong individual, and she was shocked to hear her mother admit to being weak and wanting to give up. Stacie shared with her daughter, after the initial shock of Becca leaving had worn off, how self-doubt and self-incrimination had overtaken her thinking. She'd been ready to give up, feeling like a failure.

Becca's dad hadn't fared much better, and it had been Julia who had invited them to the little church she attended faithfully. Becca's mom had recommitted her life to God, and her dad had started his own journey of faith. Together, they had prayed that God would one day bring their daughter back to them and restore their relationship.

Becca had cried, knowing that she'd waited too long to have that with her father. Her mother had held her close, and told her that she knew her father was waiting for her in heaven. She could see him again one day, but the choice was hers.

Becca had pondered those things all day long. That night, as she lay in bed, she'd talked to God for the first time ever. She'd expected to feel silly doing so, but something had happened in her small little bedroom. She hadn't felt silly, and she'd had the strangest feeling that someone was actually listening to her ramblings.

She'd felt comforted, and as she'd drifted off to sleep, she'd felt peace. She couldn't explain it, but she hadn't known whom to ask so she'd called Gracie. Her friend had been thrilled to see her walking down this particular road. She'd made Gracie promise not to say anything, not even to Mason, and Gracie had promised, but refused to let her hang up until she'd prayed for her.

Heavenly Father, you know the hurts Becca has suffered. I ask that right now you would let her feel Your presence in her life. Let her know that You do care and are ready to carry her burdens for her. Let her feel Your love and I ask that You would continue to heal her from the inside out. Show her how much You want to be a part of her life. I ask that You would place people in her path to help show her the way to You.

In Your Holy Name we ask all these things.

Amen

Gracie's prayer continued to roll around in Becca's head, and then she'd heard Justin pray with Kaillar on the phone, using some of the same words with one exception. Justin had prayed that God would give Kaillar the right words, at the right time, to help her find her way. *Instead of praying that God would send someone to help her, Justin was assuming Kaillar was that someone...*

Becca blinked her eyes, suddenly realizing that the vehicle was no longer moving. She glanced around, and then turned to find Kaillar watching her. "Why are we stopped?"

He smirked and then quickly hid it, "So glad you noticed. We've been parked here for almost five minutes."

"What?" Becca glanced around. Here was the side of the road. Here was actually nowhere. "Why did you pull over?"

Kaillar smiled, "Because you were completely zoned out on me. One minute you're asking me if I really want to go hiking, and then you were off on some mental excursion that didn't include me."

"Sorry," she dropped her eyes and sighed. *Way to go there, Becca.*

"So, I'm getting that you'd rather do something other than hike?" Kaillar asked with a smile.

Gathering her courage, she nodded, "Yes. If that's okay with you."

Kaillar smiled at her and nodded, "I don't care what we do. I just want to spend some time alone with you." He leaned across the console and kissed her lightly.

Becca bit her own lip when he drew away. "That's what I want as well. I..." Words failed her as she struggled to tell him what was going on in her brain.

"Hold that thought. Why don't I find us a spot to pull over by the beach, and we can get out and take a walk?" He lifted a hand to her cheek and searched her eyes, picking up on the nervous energy that was swirling around her.

Becca released the breath she'd been holding and nodded. "That sounds really good."

"Great." He started the car moving again, turning off at the first public beach sign they came to. Once parked, he slipped from the vehicle and then assisted her out.

They headed towards the sand, and Becca was relieved to see that this particular beach was almost deserted. Large rocks precluded it from being a safe surfing area, and the beach offered no amenities at all. She slipped her tennis shoes off, and tossed them near a piece of driftwood.

"Aren't you afraid they won't be there when you come back?" Kaillar asked, doing the same with his own shoes.

"There's kind of an unspoken rule about the beaches in Hawaii. We don't mess with other people's things. That includes beach towels, surf boards, and shoes."

Kaillar grinned at her, "Good to know."

Chapter 17

Shoes taken care of, Kaillar grabbed her hand and they started walking, just shy of the water's edge. "So, what's going on in that beautiful mind of yours?"

Becca blushed, "That's a loaded question."

Kaillar grinned down at her, "Give it to me. I can handle it, I promise you."

Becca glanced at him and then took a deep breath, "I heard you last night." She hadn't meant to say it quite like that, but...there it was.

Kaillar didn't say anything for a while and then he asked, "You were eavesdropping on me?"

Becca shook her head, afraid he was upset with her. "No! I came inside to grab a sweater and I heard my name. Then I just couldn't walk away. I heard you and your brother praying for me."

Kaillar looked down at her and asked, "How did that make you feel?"

Becca looked at him and quit walking, "Really? You sound like Dr. Phil."

Kaillar reviewed what he'd said and then chuckled, "Guess I did. But really, were you okay with what you heard?"

Becca nodded and started walking again, "Gracie kind of prayed the same type of thing with me a few mornings ago."

"You called Gracie?" Kaillar asked, curiosity in his voice.

"My mom and I have been talking in the early mornings. About God and stuff. I tried it, and I felt...well, it was strange so I called Gracie. She told me I should talk to either you or my mom, but after last night..." She stopped walking again and looked up at him, "Did you mean what you said?'

Kaillar turned to face her, pulling her close enough that he could put his hands on her shoulders. He moved her hair back off her shoulders, and then nodded, watching her face carefully. "I did. I know that you have lots of concerns, and questions, but I've prayed about it and I think we belong together."

Becca bit her bottom lip and then hazarded a look up at him, "What about the God thing?"

Kaillar pursed his lips for a minute and then sighed, "Yeah. God is a really important part of my life. If He wasn't going to be part of yours as well, we would only have problems down the road."

"I think...," she broke off. Taking a breath, she tried again, "I think I'd like to learn more about Him, but quite frankly, I'm not sure I know how. Gracie would help me, but she's not here."

Kaillar smiled at her, "I'd be more than happy to help you. Let's walk some more." As they walked, Kaillar asked her questions about what she knew and didn't know.

Becca's version of God was as a gamekeeper. He put all the pieces on the board and then just sat back to watch and see what would happen. The God that Kaillar knew was so foreign to her. And yet sounded so perfect. She couldn't imagine anyone having unconditional love. The concept boggled her mind.

"That's where faith comes in. Take for instance surfing. Every surfer has faith when they go out on the water. The same holds true for skiers. We have faith that our equipment is going to work properly. We have faith that the laws of physics aren't going to change. We have faith that we've properly trained and that we have prepared ourselves for the challenge ahead."

"So, believing in God is having faith."

Kaillar smiled at her, "Yes! Faith that He's there and cares for us. Faith that no matter what, He will never leave us. Faith that He never gives us a challenge too big to handle."

"But if that's true, that God loves everyone, why does he allow all of these horrible things to happen. And I'm not just talking about Kevin. What about the starving children around the world? Or natural disasters? If He loved us, wouldn't He stop those things from happening?"

Kaillar pulled her into his arms, resting his head on the top of her own, "Those questions have plagued man since the beginning of time. God never promised we'd have an easy life. There are challenges, but overcoming them makes us stronger people. Gives us insight into what others are facing. Helps prepare us for the next challenge we'll face."

Becca listened to his deep baritone voice, loving the image of a loving God he was creating in her mind. When he stopped talking, she pushed away from him and smiled, "I can't promise anything, but I'll try. Gracie said there's a class that meets at the church every week. She thought I might get some answers there."

Kaillar smiled, "You will. Pastor Jeremy and his wife teach the class. It's designed for people who are searching, just like you. Would you like me to call and let him know you'd like to attend?"

Becca nodded her head, "Yes. Uhm...well, uh...would you consider coming with me?"

Kaillar tapped her nose, "Wild horses couldn't keep me away. I'd be honored to come with you. And when you're ready, it will be my honor to pray with you."

Becca snuggled back into his arms and sighed, "Thanks for agreeing to do that with me. And thanks for coming with me here. I know you didn't have to..."

Kaillar nudged her head up again, "That's where you're wrong. I did have to come here with you, like I needed my next breath of air.

You stole my heart up on that mountain." He dipped his head and kissed her, drawing the moment out as long as possible.

"So, what shall we do now?" he asked, turning them back to where they'd left their shoes.

"I think maybe I'd like to go watch Kalino surf."

Kaillar looked at her, "You know you don't have to do that. Kalino and I discussed it, and he doesn't want you to do anything that makes things worse."

Becca nodded her head, "I know. But I think I need to do this." She glanced up at him, and then wrapped her arm around his, "Besides, I'll have you there with me."

Kaillar nodded his head after searching her eyes for a long moment, "I will always be there for you, Becca. I want you to know."

Becca laid her head against his shoulder, "I know."

Chapter 18

Two days later, back in Colorado ...

"I'm so tired of sitting," Becca complained as they exited the terminal at the Denver International Airport. They had just flown back from Hawaii and she was more than ready to get home. She took a breath and then shook her head, "It's cold here."

"There's Mason and Gracie," Kaillar told her, waving to his brother and fiancé as they crossed the lanes of traffic.

Gracie was out of the car and hugging Becca before he knew it, and he watched in amusement as the two women hugged and cried on each other's shoulders.

Mason rounded the vehicle and opened the trunk, "Is it always going to be like that with them?"

Kaillar nodded his head, "Yep. I think so. We'd better invest in boxes of tissues."

Mason grinned, and tossed their suitcases into the trunk. "Ladies, I'm glad you all are happy to see one another, but you need to take this little bonding experience into the vehicle."

The two girls broke apart and slipped into the backseat, talking a mile a minute as they tried to catch up on everything. Mason grinned at Kaillar as he pulled away from the terminal, "I now know why those fancy limos have a sliding glass partition in them."

Kaillar looked over his shoulder at Becca, and grinned at the happy look on her face. Her mascara was smeared, and Gracie was handing her a mirror so she could try to repair the damage her tears had done. Again.

"I'm just glad we're home. That's a long flight."

"Well, I hate to be the bearer of bad news, but it's snowing really hard at the tunnel. I don't know that we're getting back to Silver Springs tonight. They've already got the chain law in effect for big trucks, and are advising all non-essential traffic to make other travel plans."

Becca slid forward, "We can stay at my place for one night. Gracie can sleep with me, and you and Mason can take the couch and the second bedroom." She turned back and asked Gracie, "When are the movers coming?"

"Two days from now. They already dropped off some boxes. If we spent the rest of the afternoon, we could probably get most of your stuff packed up."

Becca turned back to the front with a questioning look directed towards Kaillar. "Will that work?"

Kaillar smiled at her, "That will work just fine. Why don't we stop and grab some lunch, and then we can get started?"

Mason nodded and headed towards the foothills. Becca lived in a small suburb on the outskirts of Denver, in a two bedroom apartment. She'd been planning to turn the second bedroom into an office and workroom, but now she wasn't even planning on staying in Denver.

"So, Sarah's okay with everything?" Becca asked.

Gracie nodded, "She's so excited that you and your mom are going to take over her place. When is your mom coming?"

Becca smiled at her, "Well, she closes on the resort Friday. Julia, my mom's longtime friend is going to come with her. I want to be able to focus on my photography and this way, mom won't have to manage the guests by herself."

"That's a great idea. Sarah already has her stuff packed for her move to Vail. She and Stan are flying to Las Vegas next week to get married."

"That's quick," Becca commented, causing both Mason and Kaillar to laugh. "Why is that so funny?"

"Stan and Sarah have been dating, long distance, for almost seven months. With his schedule at the hospital in Vail, and her commitment to the motel and boarding house, they've only been able to see each other a few times each month."

"That's hard. How do you keep a relationship going long distance like that?" Becca asked.

"You have to truly love the other person. But I agree," Gracie told her, "That would be the hard way to have a relationship."

Becca thought for a moment, and then she brightened, "What if we put together a small celebration for when they return from Vegas? We could use the common room at the motel and invite some of Dr. Geske's friends from Vail."

"Becca, that's a great idea," Mason told her, directing the vehicle into the drive-thru of a popular burger joint.

"I'm sure both Stan and Sarah would appreciate that," Kaillar told her with a proud smile on his face.

Mason pulled up to the order spot and then asked, "What does everyone want?"

After receiving their food, Mason drove them straight to Becca's apartment. They ate amidst talk about Hawai'i, and Kaillar spent most of his time talking about surfing. "Becca's friend is really good and I think I've convinced him to fly out here after the holidays and try his hand at snowboarding."

"Kalino is looking forward to it," Becca told him. "He texted me to find out what kind of arrangements he needs to make for lodging. I told him I'd talk with you and not to worry about it."

Kaillar nodded, "Yeah. He can room at the lodge, or even down at the motel. Next time you talk to him, remind him that we'll need his flight schedule so that someone can meet him at the airport."

"Why don't I just give you his cell phone number and you and he can work out the details?" Becca asked.

Kaillar chuckled and handed her his phone. "That sounds fine."

They split up after that, the girls taking the kitchen, and the boys heading towards the hall closet and living room. Their focus was to deconstruct the electronics and pack them correctly into the moving boxes.

Gracie and Becca made short work of the kitchen cabinets, and then they headed for the bathroom and linen closet. As they were working, Gracie asked questions about Becca's time on the Island, and Becca found herself completely opening up. About everything.

"Kaillar was really supportive through everything."

"Meaning what?" Gracie asked.

Becca put the towels she was holding in her hands into a box, and then she told Gracie about their walk along the beach. "He spoke to Pastor Jeremy. There's a class meeting Sunday afternoon he thought might be a good fit for me."

"Are you nervous?" Gracie asked, remembering how nervous and unsure of herself Gracie had been.

"A bit, but not about meeting new people. I just don't want to let Kaillar down. Or myself."

Gracie stopped what she was doing and asked, "How do you think you're going to let anyone down?"

Becca shrugged, "I don't really know. But if this doesn't work..."

"This? You mean a relationship with God? That's what you think might not work?"

Becca nodded, "Why are you looking at me like that?"

Gracie burst out laughing, "Oh Becca. You don't have to worry about it not working out when it comes to God. He wants to have a relationship with you so badly. Did you and Kaillar talk about how it all works?"

Becca shook her head, and Gracie repeated the gesture. "Men. Leave them to do one thing right. Come with me and let's take a small break." She pulled her back out to the living room, and sat them both down on the couch.

Gracie began to tell her about the price that had already been paid for her. At one point, Mason and Kaillar started to come into the living room, but after seeing the two women sitting on the couch, their heads bent close together, and an open Bible sitting on Gracie's equipment, they had retreated to the bedrooms to begin packing up the contents of the closets.

"She's going to be fine," Mason told his brother. "You know that, right?"

Kaillar nodded his head, "I hope so. I really do."

Chapter 19

O ne week later, back in Silver Springs...
Pastor Jeremy walked Becca out of the church, "Becca, I can't tell you how happy I am that you've chosen to stay in Silver Springs with us. I'm really looking forward to meeting your mother and her friend as well."

"Thanks Pastor. And thanks for that in there. I was so nervous, and now I don't even remember why." Becca had a broad smile upon her face, and she couldn't wait to see Kaillar. She looked around and then frowned, "I wonder where my ride is?"

Before Pastor Jeremy could answer her, a truck pulled up and Justin climbed out, "Becca, are you ready to go?"

She nodded, "Where's Kaillar?"

"He and Mason are on their way down the mountain. Pastor, tomorrow's the big day."

"Yes. Are you and your bride ready to get married?"

"Jessica is stressed out. She keeps telling me there is so much to do, but really, all she needs to do is show up. Nothing else matters."

Becca shook her head at him, "That's why guys are never put in charge of things like this. Left up to you, she'd probably be getting married in a pair of sweats and a T-shirt."

Justin shook his head, "No. I amend my statement. I'm dying to see this dress she found."

Becca sighed, "Me too. Gracie's dress is pretty cool as well."

Justin grinned, "So when are you going to be heading into Denver to find the perfect dress?"

Becca blushed, "I don't know. Your brother and I are taking things slow."

"What's to take slow? You love each other, get on with your lives."

Pastor Jeremy laughed at that, "Justin, you're not helping our cause at all. I'm sure Kaillar and Becca will move their relationship forward when the time is right."

. . ◦§◦ . .

THAT TIME CAME THE next afternoon. Justin and Jessica's wedding had been amazing. This close to the holidays, Jessica had gone with pine boughs, holly berries, and poinsettias instead of flowers. All except for her bridal bouquet.

That had been a mixture of pine fronds, little sprigs of red berries, and white calla lilies brought in from a greenhouse in Denver. They had draped beautifully from her hands, and Becca thought she was the most beautiful bride ever.

Her mother and Julia had called an hour earlier to say that they had landed safely in Denver. Her mother had sold everything before leaving Hawaii, and was now going to take a few days to find a new vehicle.

Her father had maintained a substantial life insurance policy, and with the sale of the resort, her mother could well afford to buy herself a new car. The Donnelly Brothers had insisted that she purchase an SUV with four wheel drive. The chances that her mother would ever use that feature seemed unlikely, but then again...this was Colorado, and they did live in the mountains.

Kaillar came up behind her and wrapped an arm around her waist, nuzzling her ear, "You look beautiful this afternoon."

Becca glanced up at him and smiled, "Thank you kind sir. This dress is amazing."

Kaillar spun her around and perused her from the top of her strawberry blonde hair that had been expertly braided and wound around her head to the tips of her ivory boots. Becca was wearing the bridal dress the girls had picked out for her, and they couldn't have done a better job. It was a deep emerald green, almost matching her own pale eyes, and causing them to shine brightly. A soft velvet fabric that clung to her curves, and yet was loose enough to be comfortable.

They'd chosen a long gown, with a high low hemline, letting her ivory boots peek out from the front, and the material of the skirt slightly dragging behind when she stood still. "Beautiful," Kaillar told her once more before taking her hand and leading her out the back door of the church.

"Where are we going?"

"I want to show you something." He pulled her behind him, snagging two jackets off the rack on his way.

"Kaillar! Those aren't ours."

"Doesn't matter. It's too cold to stay outside for long, and we'll put them back. Slip this on." He handed her the smaller of the two jackets, and she dutifully slipped her arms into it.

He took her hand again, and pushed through the glass doors. It was dark outside, the back of the church having outdoors lights, but they had not been turned on. He continued pulling her along the shoveled sidewalk, almost two feet of snow rising on either side.

Becca shivered a bit, but the stillness of the night begged her not to utter a word of protest. She followed along, feeling a sense of excitement in the air, but not knowing why.

Kaillar finally stopped in the middle of a small courtyard and turned to face her. "Look up," he encouraged her.

Becca slowly tipped her head back and then gasped in awe. The sky was alight with stars! She let her eyes track the night sky, the absence of artificial light and clouds letting the entire Milky Way appear for her to appreciate.

"Wow!" she whispered reverently. "That's the most beautiful thing..."

"No. You are the most beautiful thing. Becca?"

She took one more look, and then tipped her head down to see Kaillar down on one knee with a small velvet box held out to her. She covered her mouth with her hands, searching his eyes for answers.

Kaillar watched her eyes fill with what he hoped were happy tears, and hurried to get his words out before she started crying. That was something he was slowly getting used to, but barely. He hated seeing her cry, and it didn't matter if they were happy tears or not.

"Becca Edwards, those stars above don't hold a candle to how you light up my life. I know we need time to grow as a couple, but I can't go another minute without knowing that you're going to be mine. One day."

"Would you do me the extraordinary honor of agreeing to be my bride? To live here in this mountain town with me? To support me as I support you? To raise a family with me here?"

The tears won out and spilled from her eyes even as she nodded her head and whispered, "Yes. I love you too."

Kaillar surged to his feet and swept her up in his arms, kissing her to celebrate their newfound commitment. "Thank you. My number one goal in life is going to make you so happy, you run out of tears." He removed the ring from the box, and slipped it on her finger.

Becca smiled at him and then kissed him again, "Kai, you are the most amazing man I've ever met. I thank God every day for bringing you into my life."

Kaillar hugged her close, "As do I." He closed his eyes and then softly started to pray. For the healing that Becca was experiencing. For restoring her relationship with her mother, and for coming home to God. For bringing the perfect woman into his life, and providing him with just the right answers at the right time.

Becca started shivering, and he hustled them both back inside, returning the borrowed jackets, and then taking her hand and leading her back inside the reception. She was glowing with happiness, and he wasn't surprised at all when both Gracie and Jessica crossed the room and wrapped her in a hug.

He took the box of tissues Mason produced, and handed them to the women. The tears were already flowing. "I'm telling you, we need to invest in a company that makes tissues. Can you imagine what they're going to be like when kids start arriving?"

Mason grinned, "Beautiful. And crying."

Kaillar chuckled, and then retrieved his new fiancé from the small circle of women, "Sorry girls, but she's mine. Jessica, go cry on your husband. Mason, you and Gracie will be getting married in another week and a half."

Mason smiled, watching as Justin joined them. "Lose something, brother?"

Justin smiled and pulled Jessica into his arms, "No. I knew she was just over here getting rid of any extra tears she might have stored up. You girls need to figure out another way to express your emotions. Every time we see tears falling from your beautiful eyes, it breaks our heart."

"These were happy tears," Becca told him softly, liking the feel of having Kaillar's arms wrapped around her waist.

He bent his head to whisper next to her ear, "Doesn't matter, sugar. It still breaks our hearts."

Becca glanced up at him and promised, "I'll try not to cry as much."

He smiled, "Go ahead and cry. Then I have an excuse to offer you the comfort of my arms."

Becca grinned and realized his brothers were taking advantage of the situation as well. She looked at the other two couples, and couldn't believe how much her life had changed in such a short amount of time. Three weeks earlier, she'd been looking at living alone in Denver, no firm job prospect in mind, and both of her friends moving to other cities.

Now she was getting married, going to be running a motel and boarding house with her mother and family friend Julia, and living in a town that was so special to her. Silver Springs might be a small town, but the miracles that had been wrought in her life because of this small town were anything but small.

Epilogue

*F**ive months later, Saturday morning in early May at the Three*
Brother's Lodge...

"I'm sad the school year is almost over," Jessica said to the room in general as she helped bring food to the table. She and Justin had been married in the first part of December, with Gracie and Mason following a week and a half later.

Mason had moved to town with Gracie, taking over the second master suite in the William's house. As the town doctor, she felt that it was important for her to be close to her office, and Mason had readily agreed. The school board had leased the property for their new school teacher, Jessica, and there were still times when she and Justin stayed in town, especially on nights when the weather turned foul, and driving up and down the mountain to get her to school was dangerous.

Kaillar and Becca had gotten married the second Saturday in March. It had been a cold and blustery day outside, with snow falling, and grey clouds blotting out the sunshine. But inside the small church, flowers had been blooming, and love had flowed around them as they celebrated the beginning of their married life.

That had been two months ago, and as had become custom, all three couples were at the lodge for the weekend. While the girls made brunch, the guys had gone out to take care of the chores. Everyone was working well together, and these times were always the highlight of not just Becca's week, but everyone seemed to look forward to them.

"That just about does it," Becca told the other two women. Before anyone could reply, the front doors opened, and the three men came walking in.

"Breakfast smells amazing," Kaillar told her as he joined her and kissed her on the cheek.

Justin kissed Jessica and took a seat at the table, pulling her down to sit beside him. Mason and Gracie took seats on the opposite side of the table, and soon everyone was enjoying good food and good company.

"I was thinking that we could saddle up the horses and go for a ride after we eat," Justin suggested.

Mason and Kaillar both nodded their heads before Mason turned to Gracie, Sounds good, huh?"

"Sounds fun, but I think I'll stick around here this morning. I've got just a few work things I need to clear up so I can enjoy the rest of the weekend."

Mason looked disappointed, "Are you sure?"

Gracie smiled at him and nodded, "I'm sure."

Justin took Jessica's hand, "You up for a ride?"

Jessica shook her head, "I think I might stay here as well. You guys go and take Becca with you. I'll even start lunch while you're all out."

"Mac and cheese?" he asked with a grin.

"Sure. Mac and cheese it is."

"Uhm...I think I'll stick around as well. But you guys go and have fun," Becca said in a too bright voice.

"Becca, you like to ride. Now anyways. Come with us..."

Becca shook her head, "I really shouldn't....I mean, I can't..." She was stammering all over herself trying to come up with a reason to not go riding. She didn't do a good enough job, and Kaillar narrowed his eyes at her.

"What's going on?"

"Yeah, I think I might like to ask the same question," Mason replied, watching his wife carefully.

Becca blushed and then shook her head, "Nothing is going on."

"You're hiding something."

Her blush intensified, and she closed her eyes and wished she'd practiced being a better liar. "I just don't want to go riding. Not today."

Kaillar watched her, suspicion lurking in his eyes before he asked, "And when might you feel like going riding."

Becca smiled up at him, realizing he was putting two and two together, and coming up with five. "Maybe another six months, give or take a few weeks."

"You're pregnant?" Gracie asked, joy lighting up her features.

Becca nodded, "I think so."

Gracie beamed at her, and then whispered to the room in general, her eyes firmly fixed on her husband, "We can raise our children together then. I'm two months pregnant as well."

Mason looked at Kaillar, who was still watching his wife with a mixture of shock and approval. "Well, here I thought we might be to a point where I didn't have to pack a box of tissues around with me. Guess I was wrong."

Kaillar shook his head, and looked at Jessica. "Don't tell me you're pregnant as well?"

Jessica stuck her tongue out at him and tossed her hair, "Fine I won't. Justin dear, I'm pregnant."

Becca, Gracie, and Jessica were all crying by this time and chattering away about how close their children were going to be. "This is so cool!"

The three men finished their brunch, and then headed out for a ride. When they were standing on the top of the ridge, overlooking the mountains and valleys below and in the distance, Justin finally spoke up.

"What are the odds that we would all find the loves of our lives within a few weeks of one another? And now, we're all going to have children."

Mason grinned, "What do you think Uncle Jed would say if he could be here right now?"

The three men were quiet for several long moments. Finally, Justin spoke up. "I think he'd remind us of all the life lessons we learned. How to be a good steward of the land and resources. How to love the Lord and our family."

"But most of all, I think he'd remind us that children need to be nurtured and led in the right direction. He'd remind us to always be good role models. And I think he'd tell us how proud he is of the men we've become."

Justin looked at his brothers, one on either side of him and laughed, "The Donnelly Brothers are going to be daddies!"

Mason whooped and laughed. Kaillar tipped his head back and howled. "God has been very good to us."

Justin and Mason agreed. "He sure has been. Now, I say we go back to the lodge and spend some time with our women. Hopefully by now they've stopped crying."

"Don't bank on it. They're probably already planning nurseries and playdates."

Mason frowned, "You think so? That means they'll expect us to put together cribs and changing tables, and whatever else they can find."

"Welcome to fatherhood, boys!" Justin told them, turning his horse around and heading back to the lodge. He'd take whatever blessings God sent him and Jessica's way.

Once they had taken care of their horses, he stopped and waited for Mason and Kaillar to join him. "Boys, we're going to be much better parents to our kids than our mom even tried to be. Uncle Jed was only one man, and he taught us well. Our children are going to be the most loved kids in the county."

Becca, Gracie and Jessica were standing on the front porch and overheard his comment. "We already feel like the most loved women in the county," Gracie called out.

"Good." Each man collected his wife, and soon they were sitting around the living room, making plans for workdays and deciding where they were going to put a nursery. When Stacie and Julia walked in several hours later, the boys accepted their congratulations, and then each man handed their wife their own box of tissues.

Life was good, and they were living proof that God could take any situation and turn it around for good. The Three Brothers Lodge was intact and would be for generations to come. Filled with love and the promise of God's blessing over their lives.

.....

Did you love *Second Chance Romance Series*? Then you should read *No Place Like Home*, Home to You Series Book 1 by Morris Fenris.

Grab your copy here: https://books2read.com/u/bOJPDo

Chapter 1

Wednesday, December 12th
Central Mountains of Wyoming

Jerricha Ballard, known to her adoring fans as the lead singer for the pop band, *Jericho*, yawned and struggled to see the road sign up ahead. She'd been driving for what felt like two years, but in reality, it had only been for the last two days. She and her traveling partner had spent last night in a small motel, in an even smaller town, paid for in cash. She smiled as she recalled feeling like a criminal on the run as she'd paid for the room and accepted the well-worn key.

She turned the windshield wipers up a notch, trying to clear the rapidly falling snow, but it didn't really seem to help. It was

December in Wyoming and she'd been driving in this storm for the last six hours. It was taking a toll on her concentration.

"Does it snow here all winter long?" a voice whined from the passenger seat. "*Brr.* I've never been so cold in my life."

"What did you expect, Cass? Palm trees and sand? This is Wyoming, after all." Jerricha risked a glance at her best friend, Cassidy Peters.

The tires hit a patch of ice and their massive truck slid. Jerricha gripped the steering wheel and corrected its course, peering into the storm.

"Whoa! Take it easy," Cassidy warned her, grabbing the bar above the passenger door. "We've made it this far, don't land us in a ditch now."

Jerricha grimaced, "I've been driving in snow like this since I was sixteen. I can handle it."

"I didn't say you couldn't, but if you wreck Ben's truck, he's going to be doubly ticked off."

Ben Morgan was Jerricha's manager and producer all wrapped into one package. He abhorred traveling on the tour bus and instead chose to drive himself from venue to venue. Jerricha's last three albums had gone platinum, and with the percentage she paid Ben, he'd more than been able to afford the fifty-thousand-dollar truck she'd *borrowed* two nights ago.

"Ben will be fine," Jerricha stated, a note of wishful thinking making its way into her voice. *He's going to be furious with me! Maybe so mad he'll actually make good on his threat to not represent me anymore. That would be such a shame.* She shook her head at the sarcastic thoughts running through her mind and returned her attention to the rapidly deteriorating road conditions.

Cass released a rueful laugh. "That's why he's called over a hundred times in the last two days. Because he knows you're taking such good care of his baby." His baby being the cherry red, double cab, Ford F-350 truck with the lift kit, chrome everything, leather seats, and more amenities than any one person really needs in a vehicle.

"We haven't hurt his precious truck and I even texted him a picture of it at breakfast this morning to prove it."

"Did you tell him where we were?"

"I'm not stupid. Of course not. If I had, he'd have made up some story to get the State Police involved and we would not be almost there now."

Cass looked out the window at the snow-covered landscape and frowned. "Where exactly is it we're going? All I see are mountains and more mountains, and snow. Lots and lots of snow."

"We're headed to Warm Springs, Wyoming," Jerricha replied, relieved when she saw a new road sign up ahead, indicating they were only thirty miles from their destination.

"Warm Springs? What's there?" Cass asked. She'd become best friends with Jerricha several years ago and now went practically everywhere with her. She handled her phone calls, managed the adoring fans always wanting a meet and greet with their favorite pop singer, and, when things got overwhelming, she was the last line of defense between Jerricha and everyone else. Even Ben. Cassidy was the sister Jerricha had never had.

Jerricha nodded, replying softly, "It's where I spent my teenage years. I haven't been here in almost a year. The last time... well, suffice it to say, I could have done without coming back to bury my aunt. Remember last year when I disappeared for two days and everyone was speculating that I'd checked myself into a rehab facility?" When Cassidy nodded, Jerricha grinned. "I came here."

She and Ben had created an elaborate diversion for the press, which had allowed her to travel to Warm Springs for the funeral and fly right back out when it was over. She'd not even been in the town forty-eight hours, something she still regretted. The media had taken the opportunity to speculate, just as she assumed they were doing now. She and Cassidy had made an agreement not to turn on the news or check their social media until they'd reached their destination. Jerricha was taking this time for herself and she wouldn't let anything interfere with her enjoyment of it. She'd missed this place. It was the closest thing she had to a home.

In reality, she'd not been home more often because she refused to subject the town of Warm Springs and her family to the madness her popularity brought. Instead, she and her family kept in touch via video chatting and once in a while she had flown her aunt, uncle, and cousins to a remote vacation destination where photographers and the press were not allowed. But that was before her aunt had suffered a massive stroke that had taken her life a week later. There would be no more family trips. Not for a while. Maybe not ever.

So instead, Jerricha was coming to them this year. The only reason why there wasn't a line of reporters following them now was because she and Cass had skipped out of her Kansas City concert while fans had been screaming for an encore performance.

The band had expected Jerricha to come back onstage, as well, but instead, Cass had snatched Ben's truck keys, packed some of their clothing up during the first half of the concert and tucked their luggage away inside the truck. She'd been waiting for Jerricha at the delivery entrance of the stadium. They were on the highway headed West before anyone had caught on.

They'd stopped at an all-night truck stop on the outskirts of Kansas City and Jerricha had removed the purple streaks from her hair, pulled out the hair extensions, and changed into a pair of well-worn jeans, a flannel shirt over a tank top that she'd had since high school, and a pair of snow boots.

She glanced over at her friend and once again could only shake her head in disbelief. She'd told Cassidy they were heading into the mountains in the middle of the winter, but that evidently hadn't meant much to the city-bred girl from Miami. Cassidy had abandoned her torn leggings, mini skirt and halter top, but her choice of alternate attire wasn't quite what Jerricha had in mind. Cassidy currently wore leather pants, and a bulky sweater with a bright red bra showing through the wide weave pattern. Her hair still sported multi-colored stripes, and her ears and neck were still adorned with lots of jewelry. She would stick out like a sore thumb in Warm Springs. *I'll have to get her some proper clothing as soon as we get there. She's liable to scare half the town dressed this way.*

"So, is all of your family still in Warm Springs?" Cass asked, oblivious to Jerricha's thoughts on her behalf.

Jerricha shook her head. "Not all of them. My parents still live there, and I have an aunt and uncle there in the summer months. They spend the rest of the year in Florida, playing golf."

"Florida. Now that's where we should have gone. Plenty of palm trees, ocean, and tanned guys."

Jerricha chuckled and shook her head. "It's almost Christmas. I haven't been able to spend Christmas in Warm Springs since I was nineteen. That changes this year."

"You must really love this place. But I don't get it. You've never really talked about your childhood. In fact, I don't even know if you have siblings. Why is that?"

Jerricha gave her an incredulous look. "You've fought off the cameras and microphones right alongside me and you can ask that? I don't talk about my hometown because this is mine. I don't want it destroyed by the media and their constant lies."

"I can understand that, but you know it's only a matter of time before someone finds out and comes here looking for you. You can't just disappear without a trace and expect people to let it go."

"I don't have another concert scheduled until after the first of next year. No one will be looking for me. And I hardly look like the lead singer from *Jericho*. Even if they come looking, they won't be looking for a mountain girl with normal hair, no tattoos, and no makeup on." *I hope. Maybe I should call Ben and make sure he's running interference for me.*

"You're thinking of calling Ben," Cass said, watching her carefully.

Jerricha nodded. "I probably need to, but..."

"But..."

"He does know where I'm from and if he thinks this is where I've gone, he won't hesitate to come here and that would be a disaster. I'll call him when we get there."

"What are you going to say?" Cassidy asked with wide eyes.

Jerricha shrugged. "I have no idea. Maybe I'll just tell him I quit." At the look of horror on Cassidy's face, Jerricha sighed and then told her, "I'll figure something out. Don't worry. As for siblings, I have two brothers. Kaedon is four years older than me and runs a construction company that specializes in restoring old homes and such. He travels quite a bit, but he still has a home in Warm Springs. Rylor is a social worker in Cheyenne."

"Wow. Two brothers. I never knew that. Like I said, you rarely talk about your family."

Jerricha smiled, deciding to keep the fact that Rylor was also her twin a secret for now. Instead, she replied, "I've gotten so used to keeping my personal life a secret, not even the band members know about my personal life."

"Afraid they'll talk to the wrong person?"

Jerricha nodded. "You know it. The band was put together by the record label when I was nineteen. We seemed to all work together really well in the early days and before we knew it, the band was a success."

"Yeah, but don't you think your fans will get tired of you all refusing to give interviews and do the award shows?"

"Maybe, but given that our last record went platinum in the first week, I'm not really buying into the panic that Ben likes to peddle. A little mystery surrounding myself and the band members keeps people interested."

"Yeah, well, one of these days your little secret is going to get out. What then?"

"I'll cross that bridge when I come to it. Besides, who knows how much longer the band will be together? In case you haven't noticed, some of the band members don't exactly exude high morals."

Cassidy grimaced. "I've noticed. So has the rest of the world."

"Yeah, I'm getting tired of hearing Ben yell about legal fees and such. I wish they'd all just settle down and stop acting out."

"Maybe this is just a phase they're going through," Cassidy offered.

"Maybe." Jerricha turned her attention back to the road. The snowdrifts on the road's sides were a testament to how much snow had fallen in recent days. It was still coming down strong and she was anxious to get to town and off the roads before the storm got any worse. She was anxious to see her parents and start relaxing. It had been way too many months since she'd even thought about doing nothing and the idea was really appealing. *Almost home. Just a few more miles.*

Chapter 2

"So...," Cassidy drew the word out and then changed the subject. "Don't the townsfolk know who you are and why haven't they told anyone?"

Jerricha smiled at Cass. "You've never met the people of Warm Springs. They protect their own and they hate reporters. Years ago, a man from Warm Springs, Godfrey Merkel, decided he could do a better job as governor than the current man sitting in Cheyenne and he ran for office. The reporters descended on the town with their news trucks and lights... It quickly turned into a circus."

"I can see why that might have been annoying to the townsfolk, but hate? That seems a little strong."

"It's not. The reporters were so intent on digging up dirt on the man, nothing was off limits. They completely took over the town. They parked their trucks wherever, were constantly asking everyone questions, and left a trail of destruction behind them. The final straw was when one of the news trucks' drivers, arriving late at night, thought he'd found a nice vacant patch of grass to park his truck on for the night."

"What he'd do, wind up in the city park?" Cass asked.

Jerricha shook her head. "Much worse. He was parked in the cemetery, right on top of the would-be governor's late wife's grave. The press had been in town for a week, and everyone was sick and tired of the hoopla they created. Desecrating the cemetery was the final straw.

"The sheriff, along with half a dozen men from town, had had enough and ran every last media person and photographer out of town."

"Didn't they just come right back?" Cass had witnessed firsthand how tenacious the press could be.

"They tried, but there's only one road into and out of Warm Springs. The sheriff and men from town set up a blockade and then manned it, armed with rifles. He even deputized them to make it all legal and such. After a few days, everyone gave up and they never came back."

"What happened to the man who wanted to be governor?"

"Godfrey? Well, he decided that level of politics wasn't for him and when the position of mayor became available, he ran and won. He's been mayor ever since."

"But how does that keep you protected?" Cassidy wanted to know.

"It just does. Not everyone knows who I am and those that do... they guard my secret very closely. You said it yourself. No one would recognize me if I'm dressed like this."

"But the minute you open your mouth and sing anything, everyone will know exactly who you are," Cassidy argued.

Jerricha's throaty, raspy voice was her trademark sound and easily recognizable by anyone who listened to popular music. "I'll just have to keep my singing relegated to the showers then, won't I?"

Cassidy chuckled and shook her head. "I'll believe that when I see it." Jerricha's life was one big song. She ate, slept, and breathed music of one sort or another. "I bet I catch you singing in the first twenty-hours we're here."

"Maybe, but I'm certain my secret is safe here. You'll understand that once you meet some of the townsfolk. Nicer people don't exist on the planet."

Jerricha put on her blinker and slowly navigated the turn onto the road leading to her hometown. The place where she could be herself. Her sanctuary. The one place in the world where she could count on being accepted for who she was as a person, not as a celebrity.

"Cass, I hate to ask this, but it's kind of necessary. We need to turn our cell phones completely off. You can turn it back on whenever you need to make a call, but I wouldn't put it past Ben to try and track our phones and I just want to be alone for a while."

"Hey, you don't have to justify things to me. Truthfully, I don't know how you put up with the constant attention and having your privacy invaded all of the time. It's no wonder you're close to a breakdown."

Jerricha sighed in agreement. Five nights ago, she'd collapsed while taking a break halfway through her St. Louis show and she'd barely been able to go back out on stage and finish, albeit, sitting on a hastily procured stool. She'd been on tour for the last ten months, and in between concerts and traveling around the world, she'd also found time to record a new album of Christmas songs that would be released on December twenty-first. Nine days from now.

Ben had wanted to add a whirlwind promotional Christmas tour to her already full schedule, but she'd put her foot down and refused. Kansas City had been her last scheduled performance on this tour, and she'd already announced she would take a sabbatical for the entire next year.

Ben had been furious with that decision, sure that she would become a has-been if she didn't keep producing new songs for her adoring and fickle fans. Jerricha didn't agree and she was willing to take that risk. She was tired, mentally, emotionally, and physically. Taking a year off had been her choice and since she could very well afford to do so, she wasn't seeking anyone's advice. She just wanted to be left alone and have time to find herself once again.

As for the band, well, they were all fine with having some time to party wherever the wind took them, and she knew that several of them were headed across the pond to hang out around Europe for a while. Part of her hoped they would all find other things to do during the next twelve months. If that happened, Ben would have no choice but to give her a shot at a solo career.

As far as the media was concerned, she was supposed to be flying to Tahiti to meet up with Bryce Lansing, a solo male pop singer who had shown an interest in her at a celebrity fundraiser she'd attended six months earlier. Since he was represented by the same record label, they'd been thrown together and rumors had been leaked that she and Bryce were having a secret relationship and would be making it public right after the first of the year.

The record label had been trying to boost Bryce's popularity and connecting him to Jerricha had been just the thing. His latest album had risen sharply in the polls, reaching the Top 10 within just a few weeks of his name being tied to hers. It hadn't really done a thing for

Jerricha's career. Her fan base was one she'd been building since she'd first broken onto the music scene at nineteen.

The record label wanted to continue the façade, even hinting that they'd love to see a fake engagement sometime during January. Jerricha was adamantly against that idea, but Ben hadn't listened to her protests. She'd decided to take matters into her own hands.

She'd advanced her holiday plans a few weeks, and she wouldn't apologize for that to anyone. Warm Springs was her refuge and she was going to hibernate here for the winter, reconnect with her family and friends, and hopefully find the motivation to pick her life back up once again when the year was up. In a week or so, she'd send a message to one of the social media sites that usually made her life so miserable. She'd tell them of her terrible breakup with Bryce and then disappear for the next year. By the time she reappeared, her supposed breakup with Bryce would be old news and she could get back to her normal life.

Or not. She'd had fame and fortune and it wasn't all it was purported to be. She could easily go the rest of her life without signing another autograph or smiling for the camera alongside another celebrity looking to boost their popularity by being seen with her. In short, she was tired of being used.

As the small town came into view half an hour later, Jerricha felt a peace settle over her soul she'd not been able to find anywhere else in the world. "Welcome to Warm Springs."

She slowed the truck at the top of the small hill, bringing the vehicle to a stop on the snow-covered road, so that she could take in the familiar sight of mountains surrounding the small community. Snow covered the rooftops and lights already burned brightly in most of the homes, even though there were still several hours before the sun would disappear behind the mountains. Smoke rose in wisps from fireplaces and Jerricha couldn't stop the feeling of peace that settled over her soul. *Home. This is home.*

"It's like something out of a magazine," Cass whispered, the sight before them awe-inspiring to a city girl like her.

Jerricha nodded and then told her, "This place is sacred to me. No one knows about it except Ben and now you."

"The band members haven't been here before?"

Jerricha frowned and shook her head sharply. "No. I can't stand to be around those guys when we're not on stage. There was a time when we could laugh and joke with one another, but lately, they seem to be more into drugs and alcohol and women. I don't want any part of that lifestyle. Besides, can you imagine them in a place like this? No adoring groupies clamoring for their autograph or a quick tour of the bus. No photographers shoving cameras in their faces anytime they went out in public. They would be bored out of their minds within an hour, and they'd never appreciate the town for the gem it is."

"I've noticed there seems to be more and more partying happening. Is that why you stopped spending the night on the tour bus and started getting hotel rooms?"

Jerricha nodded. "Exactly. I explained it all to Ben and told him about my concerns. He assured me it's just a phase the guys are going through. Once they get used to how popular we are, they'll settle down and things will be back to normal."

"You don't believe him," Cass stated.

"No, I don't. I think Ben's assuming the guys will wake up one morning and realize how they're screwing up their lives, but they won't. They enjoy all the negative attention. I'm the one who's holding them back from even greater fame and fortune because I'm being the goody two shoes. They're afraid I'm going to try to go out on my own. My contract is up at the end of December and I haven't signed the renewal yet. I'm not sure I want to. I've kind of thought about going out on my own and doing my own thing for a while. No more tours. I can write and record..."

"That's not the worst idea I've ever heard. I mean, you write most of the songs now and sing them. You could become a solo act rather easy."

"Ben says the record label doesn't want a solo act. He doesn't, either. He wants to fill the stage with lights and videos, guitar licks, drum solos... the entire band experience."

Cass shook her head and made a sound of disapproval. "What do you want? I mean, without your voice, there is no *Jericho*. So, from where I sit, you hold all the cards."

Jerricha started up the truck again and headed down into the town. She couldn't stop thinking about Cass's question. *What do I want? What will make me truly happy?*

She'd kept herself from going down that mind path in the past, but now she had a little over two weeks in which to explore her feelings. Two weeks to take stock of her dreams and aspirations and measure them against the life she was currently living. Two weeks to measure them against the life she wanted to live. Two weeks to find the answer to Cass's question and set a course for her future happiness.

Chapter 3

Warm Springs, Wyoming

"See you, Mr. James," a group of teenagers called to him as they rushed out of the school building, grabbing handfuls of freshly fallen snow and throwing it at one another.

"Bye, kids. Drive safe."

"Always do, Mr. James. See you Monday."

"Bye, Coach."

Logan waved and stepped back inside the building, shaking the snow from his hair as he headed for the school offices. He walked to the large windows behind his desk and watched as the last of the students left the parking lot. *Drive safe kids. I don't want to hear of any accidents because of this snow.*

"Do you care if I head on home now?" Stella Ziegs asked.

Logan James turned and smiled at the school secretary. "Not at all." Stella was a well-known icon at the local high school, having been there since before Logan had been a student there a dozen years earlier. Her hair was grayer and her step a little slower these days, but without her organizational prowess, Logan knew his job would be much harder.

"The last bus left a few minutes ago and based on the vehicles still in the parking lot, I think most of the teachers have left, as well. Go home and enjoy a good book." Stella always complained how she didn't have time to read for the fun of it. Well, Mother Nature had just provided her an extra day and a half to do just that. A roaring fire. A good book. Hot Chocolate. Logan could even see himself spending the rest of the day in such a fashion.

It was barely one o'clock in the afternoon, but the winter storm that had been forecasted to arrive the next day had arrived early. The school day had already been in session when the first flakes started to fall, and within the first hour, over four inches of new snow had blanketed the valley with no signs of slowing down or stopping in the near future. It had fallen to Logan as the principal to notify everyone that the school day would be cut short. As he'd walked around to the various classes, he could only smile at the students' responses. Cheering. Slapping of hands above their heads. Teachers closing textbooks and announcing there would be no homework for this first major storm of the year. More cheers and smiles.

As students and teachers filed out of the building, there had been an air of excitement that had become infectious. There was only one more week of school before Christmas break would begin, and this unexpected vacation time had everyone, young and old alike, looking forward to building snowmen, skiing, and the Christmas holiday.

Logan had stationed himself at the exit doors, cautioning young drivers to go slowly and arrive home safely. He had only been back in Warm Springs since the beginning of the school year, but he took his responsibilities to the students very serious. It was his intention to make sure all the students got safely home before the temperatures dropped and the snow-covered roads became impassable.

Stella slipped her coat on with a smile. "I love snow days."

Logan nodded. "Me too. Get out of here and I'll see you Monday, weather permitting."

Snow days were one of the benefits of coaching and working for the Fremont County School District. Warm Springs was located in the mountains, nestled in a small valley with only one road leading into and out of the town. To the east of the small town was a popular ski resort that brought many tourists and sports enthusiasts to the area. While the town only boasted a population of around fifteen hundred people, the surrounding mountain communities brought the student population of his secondary school to well over five hundred. Warm Springs held the secondary school, with a dual campus consisting of a middle school and a high school. The elementary school was located about ten miles outside of the town, halfway between Warm Springs and the next closest mountain town of Drummond. The two campuses also served the surrounding communities, some close to thirty miles away. A bus system transported the students to and from the neighboring towns, with some students riding nearly an hour each way, making it even more critical that the school day ended with plenty of time for everyone to arrive home while there was still some daylight left.

"Mr. James, are you heading out soon?" Bill, the janitor, called to him from the end of the hallway.

"Just as soon as I clear some papers off my desk. How about you?"

Bill nodded and leaned on the broom he held in his hands. "I told the wife I'd be home before it got dark and started to freeze. She worries about my driving these days."

Logan smiled easily. He'd known Bill and Tammy for as long as he could remember, and he wasn't sure of his exact age, but he knew Bill was at least seventy, maybe even a few years older. According to the information Logan received when he moved back to Warm Springs and took over the job of running the secondary school, the previous principal had tried to get Bill to retire, but he'd adamantly refused. He enjoyed being around the kids and taking care of the school had been his job for his entire adult life. He had no intention of stopping until he simply couldn't do the job any longer.

Logan waved at the man and headed back to his office. Clearing off his desk didn't take all that long, and within an hour, he shoved his arms into his winter jacket and headed for the parking lot. He climbed into his truck after dusting off the accumulated snow on the windows and headed for the only grocery store in town.

Since moving back to Warm Springs, he'd taken up residence in his childhood home, left vacant when his parents had retired to Arizona, where the weather was much warmer and kinder to his mother's arthritis. He'd traveled to Arizona for the Thanksgiving holiday, and they would be coming to Wyoming for Christmas. That gave him just over a week to unpack the rest of his boxes and put the house back into some sort of order.

Life had been hectic since his arrival in Warm Springs, with the beginning of the school year, and the sudden vacancy of a football coach. The Warm Springs Wildcats football team had taken second in the state the year before and had been projected as a serious contender for the state title this school year. But their longtime coach had been diagnosed with Stage 3 Leukemia during summer break and was currently seeking treatment somewhere in California.

Logan had not only been the captain of the football team and quarterback in high school, but he'd played college ball, and, at one point in time, he'd been a second-string quarterback on a professional team. That was until he'd torn his rotator cuff. Surgery had repaired the torn ligaments, but the team doctors had refused to clear him to return to the field for fear another injury would be irreparable. His football career had been finished. During his months of rehabilitation, he'd gone back to school and started his Master's program, taking his parents' advice and turning his love for kids and sports into a career. Teaching.

The fact that he'd coached the team to the State Championship just last weekend didn't matter as much as seeing the excitement on the kids' faces when they had been awarded the trophy. The entire town was still celebrating their victory. Logan refused to take any credit for their winning streak, believing that their past training had been far more instrumental than his one season of guidance. Several of the boys were being considered for college scholarships and he only prayed they would have better luck in pursuing their dreams than he'd had.

He parked in the lot, admiring a bright red oversized truck as he did so. The vehicle wasn't from Warm Springs and he briefly wondered whose relatives were visiting this early before the holidays. It was a little too soon for tourists to start descending upon the town. They usually didn't arrive until the week before Christmas and would then stay until after ringing in the New Year.

The doors of the store were decorated with festive bows, garland, and multi-colored lights. A large Christmas tree sat just to the inside of them, reminding Logan that he still needed to get his own tree up and decorated. Hopefully before his parents arrived, or he'd never hear the end of it. His mother was a hopeless romantic and Christmas was her favorite time of year. As such, it was also one of his favorite holidays. *I've just been so busy with the State Championship and school board meetings... Well, Mother Nature has seen fit to give me a nice five-day holiday and I should take advantage of it.*

He made a mental note to head out the next day and locate the perfect tree. He could go find one up in the mountains, but Warm

Springs boasted an easier solution. On the outskirts of town, the Millers had a tree farm, and whilst most of their Christmas trees were shipped out of state each year, they always kept plenty of trees for the locals who wanted to cut down their own. That was where his parents had always obtained their tree, and he would do the same this year. *I'll just be doing it alone. I'm getting kind of tired of doing things all alone. I'm thirty. I should be married and have a couple of kids by now.*

But circumstances hadn't worked out that way, and even though Logan had come close, even being engaged for all of three weeks' time, he was still very single. And looking. *Might have thought about that before moving to a town where everyone is already spoken for or can't wait to get out of town.*

The town of Warm Springs didn't actually have any single, unattached females of marrying age at the moment. There were several single bachelors still living in the town, but most of them worked in other places and only used Warm Springs as a stopping place between jobs. They weren't ready to settle down and start a family. Logan didn't consider himself and them in the same category at all. *Maybe I should add a bride to my Christmas list. Maybe there really is a Santa Claus.*

.. ⁂ ..

Here is a list of Boxsets published by Morris Fenris. You can grab these by clicking the relevant links below:

.. ⁂ ..

CATHEDRAL HILLS SERIES
Grab your copy here: https://books2read.com/u/me9rnR

.. ⁂ ..

PARADISE MOUNTAIN RANCH Series

Grab your copy here: https://books2read.com/u/4Nx8a6

. . ⚜ . .

HEALED BY LOVE COMPLETE Series
Grab your copy here: **https://books2read.com/u/3GwzxQ**

. . ⚜ . .

THREE BROTHERS LODGE Series
Grab your copy here: https://books2read.com/u/bPQDwR

. . ⚜ . .

THREE CHRISTMAS ANGELS Series
Grab your copy here: https://books2read.com/u/baGl2Q

. . ⚜ . .

THREE SISTERS RESORT Series
Grab your copy here: https://books2read.com/u/mvoMWq

. . ⚜ . .

TAKING THE HIGH ROAD Series Books 1-4
Grab your copy here: https://books2read.com/u/mKwAEZ

. . ⚜ . .

TAKING THE HIGH ROAD Series Books 5-7
Grab your copy here: https://books2read.com/u/b6vaj6

. . ⚜ . .

TAKING THE HIGH ROAD Series Books 8-10
Grab your copy here: https://books2read.com/u/mlEMAA

. . ⚜ . .

IF YOU ENJOY MY BOOK(s), kindly help me by writing book review(s) on your favorite retailer – thank you!

. . ⤗ . .

Thank You

Dear Reader,

Thank you for choosing to read my books out of the thousands that merit reading. I recognize that reading takes time and quietness, so I am grateful that you have designed your lives to allow for this enriching endeavor, whatever the book's title and subject.

Now more than ever before, reader reviews and social media play vital roles in helping individuals make their reading choices. If any of my books have moved you, inspired you, or educated you, please share your reactions with others by posting a review as well as via email, Facebook, Twitter, Goodreads,—or even old-fashioned face-to-face conversation! And when you receive my announcement of my new book, please pass it along. Thank you.

For updates about New Releases, as well as exclusive promotions, visit my website and sign up for the VIP mailing list. Click here to get started: www.morrisfenrisbooks.com[1]

I invite you to visit my Facebook page often facebook.com/AuthorMorrisFenris[2] where I post not only my news, but announcements of other authors' work.

For my portfolio of books on your favorite platform, please search for and visit my Author Page:

You can also contact me by email: authormorrisfenris@gmail.com

With profound gratitude, and with hope for your continued reading pleasure,

---

1. http://www.morrisfenrisbooks.com

2. https://www.facebook.com/AuthorMorrisFenris/

Morris Fenris
Self-Published Author

Did you love *Three Brothers Lodge Series*? Then you should read *Sara in Montana*[3] by Morris Fenris!

What happens when a California girl in the middle of a crisis meets a Montana guy?

Sara wished for a husband for Christmas this year and then married her boss. Now she is running for her life from him, with a warrant out for her arrest, and really needs a miracle to save her. To top off her week, she finds herself in the middle of a Montana snowstorm and sicker than she's ever been.

Trent quit the FBI to return home and became a sheriff. As the most eligible bachelor in Castle Peaks, he's had his share of women chase him but has been disinterested; until now. He has a sworn duty to protect the town's citizens and assist other agencies in doing the

3. https://books2read.com/u/mYGzgw

4. https://books2read.com/u/mYGzgw

same. When faced with a suspect in a criminal case, will he make the arrest or lead with his heart?

Join Sara Brownell as she runs for her life, straight into the waiting arms of local sheriff Trent Harding. Throw in a life-size nativity and plenty of snow, and watch the magic of Christmas come to life.

See how Sara forever changes the lives of Trent, as well as those around him.

Read more at https://www.facebook.com/AuthorMorrisFenris/.

Morris Fenris
Author

About the Author

With a lifelong love of reading and writing, Morris Fenris loves to let his imagination paint pictures in a wide variety of genres. His current book list includes everything from Christian romance, to an action-packed Western romance series, to inspirational and Christmas holiday romance.

His novels are filled with emotion, and while there is both heartbreak and humor, the stories are always uplifting.

Read more at https://www.facebook.com/AuthorMorrisFenris/.

Lightning Source UK Ltd.
Milton Keynes UK
UKHW010730300921
391439UK00001B/181